I Nearly Died

CHARLES SPENCER

I Nearly Died

VICTOR GOLLANCZ

LONDON

First published in Great Britain 1994
by Victor Gollancz
A Division of the Cassell group
Villiers House, 41/47 Strand, London WC2N 5JE

A catalogue record for this book is
available from the British Library.

ISBN 0 575 05851 X

Typeset by CentraCet Limited, Cambridge
Printed by St Edmundsbury Press Ltd, Bury St Edmunds, Suffolk

For Nicki and Edward

Wednesday

It was chucking it down outside Tower Hill Underground and I wasn't feeling at all well. In fact as the rain lashed my face and trickled down inside my collar, I realized I was feeling sick. Just the thought of throwing up, here, now, amid the pressing throng of anoraked tourists, turned the possibility of being sick into a certainty. There was no help for it. I rushed down the steps to the public lavs, stormed into a cubicle, and threw up, none too accurately, the patent Benson hangover cure.

I decided the Tizer on top of aspirins, Rennies and vitamin C had been a mistake. There had been a heart-stopping moment when I feared I was suffering a massive internal haemorrhage. Visions of ambulances, stretchers, the dimly lit calm of the intensive care unit flashed through my mind before I noticed that the bright red contents of the lavatory bowl were still fizzing. Tizer the scarifier. I pulled the chain, stumbled over to the wash-basins and splashed water on my face. A tiny old man, apparently in charge of this subterranean hell-hole and wielding a mop taller than himself, eyed me with a mixture of suspicion and concern.

'You all right?' he croaked.

'Yes, thank you very much,' I said, trying to sound respectable, trying, with a forlorn attempt at airy insouciance, to persuade him that it was the most natural thing in the world to dive into a public lavatory at 11 in the morning and heave your guts out.

'Bit of a gyppy tummy, that's all. Must have been the curry last night. Sorry.' Never apologize, never explain. That was always going to be my motto but I never managed it when it came to the crunch. 'I'm afraid I've made a bit of a mess in there. Can I clean it up?' I made a half-hearted movement towards the man and his mop.

'Nah, s'all part of the job.'

'Well thanks very much. I really am terribly sorry.'

The mouth twitched on his wrinkled walnut face and I realized he was grinning.

'Late night last night, sir?'

This was turning into something out of *Brideshead*, the dissolute undergraduate and the tolerant old scout.

'Something like that. Late night at work, few drinks afterwards . . .'

Any moment now I'd be having a cup of tea in his cubby hole and telling him the story of my life. I patted him on the shoulder, mumbled more incoherent thanks and apologies, and walked unsteadily out into the rain.

One of the worst things about working in Docklands, apart from the sheer gall of living in central London and having to commute to what feels like the outer fringes of Essex, is that people with nice offices in St Martin's Lane or Kensington High Street think it's all terribly glamorous and exciting. What they particularly like the idea of, especially the chaps, is the Docklands Light Railway, which looks like the sort of futuristic vision *The Eagle* went in for in the early sixties. It's an elevated railway that starts out from both Bank and the Tower of London, runs through such notable areas of inner-city decay as Shadwell and Limehouse before turning right into the Isle of Dogs, the gleaming new enterprise zone and home of Canary Wharf, Europe's largest, emptiest office development with its massive but uninspiring skyscraper.

Going up the escalator to the DLR, my path was blocked by a party of Scandinavian schoolgirls, cosily clad in their cagoules, chewing gum and giggling. I could hear the tannoy announcing that the train on platform two was about to leave for Island Gardens but the tourists were too busy jabbering on to let me pass. Fuming, I rose slowly to the top and fought my way through the toothbraces and frizzy hair on the concourse, managing, quite by chance but with a tremendous feeling of satisfaction, to catch one of them a vicious blow in the lumbar region with my briefcase, and ran, in really horrible pain now, on to the platform. The doors shut in my face and I caught the eye of the absurdly titled Train Captain – in reality little more than a ticket collector – shaking his head in mock sorrow. I hammered desperately on the door but the train glided smugly away. All this exertion hadn't done me any good at all. I flicked a limp V-sign at the rear of the train and turned round, heart pounding, to see the Scandinavian girls grinning with delight at the plight of the fat Englishman. I scowled at them and stamped back to the concourse and one of the metal benches which have been cleverly designed to ensure that you can never get comfortable on them no matter how hard you try.

Sitting there, his cheeks the colour of shiny red apples, his moustache insufferably jaunty, was Victor, self-proclaimed doyen of the gossip columnists and longest-serving member of staff on *Theatre World* (incorporating *Show Business Today*), from which I, too, draw a meagre salary. Victor had joined soon after the Second World War, a war, he let it be understood, in which he had done the State some service and they knew it. We were never actually given any precise details of this service and I always suspected that he had worked for ENSA, entertaining the troops. He still got the odd booking for children's parties – Uncle Victor, Magician and Ventriloquist – and on Saturday afternoons he would trudge out to the leafier suburbs with his battered dummy, Lord Marmaduke, who betrayed a worrying addiction to dirty jokes on the rare occasions when Victor got him out of his suitcase at office leaving dos. Whether he toned down the libidinous old toff for little Hannah's seventh birthday we never knew, but knowing Victor, a bloody-minded old goat, I somehow doubted it.

Victor didn't do that much in the office these days and I sometimes wondered whether our proprietor, who Victor still called 'young Mr Torrington' even though 'young' Mr Torrington was now approaching retirement age himself, still paid him

9

a full salary or whether Victor just turned up because he couldn't keep away. His main contribution was a diary, archly signed, Thespis, called 'The View from the Stalls', a curious amalgam of rewritten press releases no one else in the office was interested in and hoary, occasionally scandalous anecdotes about the great stars of the past. I'm convinced he made some of these up, exacting revenge on personalities who had patronized him in the distant past. Since almost all his subjects were safely dead the libel laws didn't bother old Victor, and his memories of 'dear' Jessie Mathews and 'darling' Anna Neagle and just what each had said to the other at the first-night party of some long-forgotten Cochran revue were written with a mixture of honey and bile.

'You're looking a bit rough, boy,' he cackled as I tottered into view. He was one of the few people I've ever met who really did cackle. 'Fancy the hair of the dog that bit you?'

There was an Edwardian raffishness, a stage-door Johnniness about Victor. He flamboyantly unscrewed the silver top of his malacca cane and withdrew a small glass beaker with a cork stopper. I knew from past experience that he kept sweet Cyprus sherry in it and declined with a shudder. Victor took a swig himself, aaahhed with great satisfaction and dabbed at his moustache with an enormous white handkerchief. There were no flies on our Victor. I liked the daft old buffer very much.

'Paper go all right yesterday?' he asked. On Tuesdays *Theatre World* goes to press at a small computer setter's in Clerkenwell, and it was the regular celebratory drinks after this weekly, more or less successfully accomplished mission that had left me so pathetically enfeebled.

'OK. We're leading with the RSC – they're closing all their theatres for a night in protest against the cuts.'

'Wankers,' said Victor.

'And Colin had an exclusive on ballot rigging in the Equity election.'

'Boring,' said Victor.

Say what you like about the old boy, his news judgement was sound. I hated Colin, a thrusting little shit of twenty-three, six years younger and a great deal thinner than me, whose name was usually plastered all over the front page.

Eventually another train arrived and Victor and I climbed on board. I might complain, but Victor had to make the trek from his flat in Golders Green every day and he'd lived through the halcyon days when *Theatre World* (Estab: 1889, Circ: 38,000) was based in Dickensian offices in Covent Garden. The lease had expired, the new rent was exorbitant and a year or so ago, shortly before I joined the staff, young Mr Torrington had moved into a supposedly high-tech but in fact jerry-built new office on the Isle of Dogs, rubbing his hands over the tax breaks.

Not for us the gleaming marble and pretentious malls of Canary Wharf across the dark waters of the dock. Our base is little more than a prefabricated hut, a two-storey shell of aluminium, plastic and glass in unpleasant shades of cream, red and green with a couple of stick-on columns and a broken pediment over the entrance to show how post-modern it is.

The train drew up at South Quay at last, and not a moment too soon as far as I was concerned. It was always unwise to dismiss Victor as entirely gaga but he did sometimes display alarming signs of dottiness. After delighting the Scandinavians by ostentatiously unscrewing his stick and taking another sip of sherry, complete with the smacking of the lips and the hankie routine, he'd launched into one of the more regrettable sections of his ventriloquist's act, undeterred that Lord Marmaduke was safely at home in his case in Golders Green.

'What have you been up to recently, Lord Marmaduke?' This was Victor in his normal voice.

'I've been to the chemist's,' replied Victor in the strangulated, squeaky voice of the appalling aristo, his lips not moving all that much. 'I said to the assistant, "Have you got cotton wool balls?" and he gave me a dirty look. "What do you think I am," he says, "a fucking teddy bear?"'

'I don't think the boys and girls want to hear about that,' said Victor.

'Well they can piss off then,' replied the invisible Lord

Marmaduke before launching into his theme song: 'Tits and bums, tits and bums, I like them whatever size they come.'

I hauled Victor to the automatic doors and as they opened behind him he took a slow, dignified bow to each side of the carriage.

'What did you go and do that for?' I said, once we'd reached the safety of the platform and the doors had closed behind us.

'Fucking foreigners, can't stand 'em,' he said, and as he hobbled down the stairs his face lit up with a smile of pure mischief.

It was still pissing down, and the wind was even stronger now, whipping the rain into our faces in great malevolent gusts. Neither of us had an umbrella, not that it would have been any use in these conditions, and as we stumbled over the broken paving stones my head started a steady throb, throb, throb, like one of those huge diesel engines that power the rides at funfairs. 'Lovely weather for ducks,' giggled Victor. I could have killed him.

Theatre World occupies the upper storey of Unit Three, East Wharf Service Road, though we share a reception area and switchboard operator with the computer magazine on the ground floor. This common territory is patrolled by a sour woman called Martha who puts on a voice as sweet and artificial as saccharine when she is answering the phones. Coming back from the pub one lunchtime I'd heard her telling a caller that Mr Benson had gone to lunch 'two – or was it three? – hours earlier' and that it might be wiser to phone again the following morning, the clear implication being that Mr Benson would be far too pissed to take any calls that afternoon. As she uttered this calumny she caught my eye and, without a flicker of embarrassment, held it, challenging me to rise to the bait. Since I was sober, after a late, hurried lunch consisting of a couple of modest units and a tinned salmon and cucumber sandwich, I lacked the courage, and floundered silently up the stairs with that feeling of raging impotence you get when, despite having every last vestige of moral right on your side, you still end up the loser. Martha had retained the advantage ever since.

Theatre World is more like a cottage industry than a full-scale newspaper. There are seven people in advertising, five in accounts and nine in editorial, including the editor, JB. The proprietor, Mr Torrington, has assigned himself a characteristically humble little office that the 'architect' probably intended as a broom cupboard and from which he rarely ventures. Apart from a sulky, seventeen-year-old odd-job boy, whose violently dyed orange hair clashes alarmingly with the painful eruptions of his skin, that's the full complement. Advertising and accounts think editorial are noisy, pushy and far too pleased with themselves. Those in editorial think advertising and accounts are full of old deadbeats who deserve to be patronized. Peace only breaks out at the Christmas party, which, under Mr Torrington's benign eye, is usually a landmark of drunken high spirits even by the exacting standards of *Theatre World*'s journalistic staff.

It was almost noon. The official starting time was 10 a.m. but Victor always comes and goes as he pleases and no one worries what time you turn up on Wednesdays, the slow, hung-over first day of the following week's paper. Up in the newsroom, with its dying rubber plants, cigarette-scarred desks and dusty piles of ancient press releases, whiz-kid Colin was already giving it plenty of mouth on what he tediously referred to as the 'old dog and bone'. He was indeed barking with pleasure as he took down the details of some tale of woe.

'What? The whole company hasn't been paid, you're joking? . . . Threatening not to go on? And of course you feel you have a duty to your fans . . . Excellent, no sorry, not excellent for you of course, no I quite see that, it must be most embarrassing, I mean an actor of your calibre.' He pronounced calibre to rhyme with fibre.

'And no one's answering the phone. Well thank you very much indeed, Mr Maxwell. Keep in touch and I'll see if yours truly can track him down. Yeah, thanks. Cheers. Take it nice and easy. God bless. Cheers, yeah, cheers.'

Finally even Colin tired of these obnoxious effusions and put down the phone with a smug little smile.

'Unless I'm much mistaken that's next week's splash we're looking at here: Jason Maxwell, mightily pissed off. He's starring in that tour of *And Then There Were None*. They've not been paid this week, nor last week either, they're stuck in Leamington, the bookings are dreadful and they're threatening not to perform unless our old friend Mr Regis stumps up the cash. The only problem is that Regis appears to have gone AWOL.'

Stephen Regis was a terrible old medallion man of a producer who put on tatty shows and shuttled them round the less than grateful provinces. His posters usually featured cut-out photographs of the heads of his cast attached to tiny cartoon bodies. Almost all these 'stars' were minor TV personalities whose success was on the wane and who now talked grandly, if anyone could be bothered to interview them, about how they had long felt the need to return to 'their first love', the theatre, which was, of course, 'so much more of a challenge than the box'. Jason Maxwell had played the 'much-loved' police constable Henry Herbert in the twice-weekly soap *Any Old Road* until the producer had written him out six months ago in a nasty car accident on the M6. Maxwell hadn't worked since his battered body, giving a forlorn final thumbs-up sign (his 'much-loved' trademark) was seen being lifted out of a crumpled police car and into the ambulance. Like many a soap-star before him, he'd finally taken Stephen Regis's shilling, though now it seemed he wasn't even getting that.

Colin's subordinate reporters, Barbara, a slightly dim and engagingly giggly girl from Preston, and Mirza, a handsome, normally charming Indian who was occasionally driven into week-long murderous silences by the insufferable Colin, tried and failed to muster the required enthusiasm for this scoop. *Theatre World* had always been an agreeably unhierarchical organization until a couple of months before my arrival when Colin had somehow persuaded JB to give him the title chief reporter and an extra couple of grand a year. He now disdained the bread-and-butter stories and frequently tried to hijack or downplay Barbara's and Mirza's contributions.

Colin was already back on the dog and bone. 'Old Jason was right,' he said, replacing the receiver, on easy first name terms now he wasn't actually speaking to the actor. 'No answer *chez* Regis. I think I'll go round and ring his bell.'

Another morsel of good news. Colin out of the office, doorstepping in the rain. No one else would have dreamt of doing this so early in the week.

'Where's JB?' I asked the editor's secretary, Julie, a mousy woman in her mid-thirties whom we suspected of a grand, unreciprocated passion for the boss.

'He's gone to Basingstoke to do a piece on the new civic centre. He won't be in today,' she said mournfully, and went back to the tattered paperback of *War and Peace* that she had been reading, without any signs of substantial progress, for the past six months.

I went to my desk, sat down, and rested my head on my arms. There was no sign of Kim, kind, cuddly, comforting Kim, and I felt cheated and bereft. Kim's the chief sub-editor, in charge of production. She and her gay and melancholy number two, Kevin, are the unsung hero and heroine who ensure that the paper actually comes out every week. *Theatre World*, not forgetting *Show Business Today*, is, as the editor never tires of pointing out to Colin, who pompously describes it as Britain's National Arts Weekly, a trade paper. With splendid impartiality and a complete lack of elitism it covers anything that moves in showbiz, from talent contests in working-men's clubs to the Royal Opera. Quite a few stage-besotted members of the general public read it, but most of all it is read by those in the business themselves – theatre administrators, directors, agents, bookers, producers, exquisitely insolent box-office staff, hairy, beer-gutted stage hands and the great, largely unemployed armies of actors and light entertainers. The one thing a raddled old exotic dancer and an intense young actress straight out of RADA probably have in common is a regular order for *Theatre World* at their newsagent's.

It would be nice to think that they and everyone else buy it for our news stories, reviews and features. But the blunt truth is that most people buy it first and foremost for the job advertisements at the back. One of life's more consoling comforts is that when Colin is smirking about a particularly juicy front-page lead, most of our readers will have postponed looking at it until they've checked to see if there are open auditions for the latest Lloyd Webber musical in the jobs section. But they read the editorial copy in the end, or at least a good many of them do to judge by the angry letters we receive whenever a fact is wrong or a show has received a particularly unfavourable review. It's the house journal of the bitchiest, most insecure and self-regarding profession in the world. The howls when egos are bruised or stories distorted in what the readers regard as 'their' newspaper are frequent, voluble and high-pitched. But then for everyone who gets cross, there are probably another ten delighting in a colleague's discomfort. And since there's no other publication covering the same field and carrying the same ads, they have to like it or lump it. There are many threats of cancelled subscriptions, but few of them are carried out. The circulation climbs slowly but steadily each year as more and more saps with stars in their eyes join a ludicrously overcrowded profession.

I came to *Theatre World* after seven happy, unambitious years on a rural weekly where I'd landed a job straight after university and finally risen to the dizzy heights of news editor with a salary of £12,000 a year. To be frank, there wasn't that much news to edit in Bridport and I'd supplemented my income by stringing for *Theatre World*. With so small a staff, the paper relied on its provincial correspondents to review the theatres in their area and supply any titbits of theatrical or entertainment news that might come their way. Like me, most of the stringers were journalists on local papers, and after several years my beat extended from Plymouth across to Bournemouth, and up to Bristol and Bath. One day the year before, the editor had rung out of the blue and asked if I'd like a staff job, suggesting, with cumbersome irony, that it would probably be cheaper to have me on the staff in London rather than gallivanting all over the South West at the company's expense. The money wasn't all that much better than I'd been getting in Bridport, but I needed a change. I'd never hungered after Fleet Street but nor did I want to turn into a vegetable. The affairs of Bridport Town Council had lost what little charm they once possessed and the idea of spending yet another bank holiday weekend in a leaking tent, typing up the results of the guinea pig competition at the Dorset County Show, was intolerable. What's more, it seemed like the last opportunity I'd get for a civilized bust-up with Cathy, but on a dreary Wednesday morning in Docklands I was trying not to think about Cathy. I sold my ludicrously picturesque thatched cottage in Powerstock and bought a two-bedroom flat in a Victorian terrace in Vauxhall for a good few thousand more than I'd got for the cottage. I was thrilled to bits.

JB did me proud when it came to the job. He could have bunged me on the reporters' desk under Col the Obnoxious but, perhaps because he was as paranoid about Colin's empire-building as everyone else, he gave me what he rather portentously described as a 'floating brief'. This involves helping Kim and Kevin with the paper's production on the busiest days, Monday and Tuesday, and doing features, interviews, reviews and the odd dull news story no one else has time for in the rest of the week. As a result, the crafty bugger gets several jobs done for the price of one, not to mention a more or less willing volunteer for the tedious, duty-calls sort of tasks he used to get lumbered with himself. But I'm not grumbling. Anything's better than guinea pigs and bewildered menopausal women up before the magistrates on shoplifting charges.

I was just drifting off into a blessed slumber when a hand patted me soothingly on the head. It was Kim, and not just Kim but Kim with a sugar-charged cappuccino from the Leopard sandwich bar across the road.

'I thought you might need this,' she said as I painfully raised my head. 'Christ, you look terrible,' she added when she'd had the benefit of a full view.

'I was sick on the way to work. In the public lavatories at Tower Hill.'

'You certainly do some living, Will. What did Cathy say when you got home last night?'

I wrapped the tattered remnants of my dignity around me.

'I'm not even thinking about Cathy this morning, still less talking about her.'

'Fair enough. Have some coffee.'

One of the nice things about Kim is she never pushes it. Nor is she shocked by the more squalid displays of drunken excess, perhaps because she's not entirely immune from them herself. I was half in love with Kim but she treated me with a matey affection from which any hint of a sexual spark was entirely absent. She lived with a man much older than she was, the boss of a West End ticket agency whom we only half-jokingly referred to as the Godfather. He might have been honest but then again he might not. Anyone who worked quite so indefatigably on behalf of the Variety Club of Great Britain, who had indeed been known to drive a Sunshine coach full of crippled children down to Brighton for the day, struck me as a man with something to hide. Kim had once come to work with a black eye and insisted she'd had an accident with a Welsh dresser. None of us made any cracks about the Godfather belting her one because we all secretly thought he might have done just that. Like a rebellious schoolgirl, she always called him the Godfather herself in the office and one of my fondest memories of her was the day she carefully selected for publication the most unflattering photograph she could find of him, presenting one of those outsize cheques to the Variety Club's Chief Barker after a 'kiddies' showbiz fun day' in Hyde Park. The camera had caught him with eyes squinting against the sun, his beer-gut oozing out over the waistband of his trousers, the long, lank strands of hair he normally arranged so artfully over his bald spot flapping in a brisk breeze. His clenched smile looked like a threat with menaces.

'Won't he be furious?' I'd asked.

'Fuck him,' she'd replied with a hint of hysteria.

The trouble, as far as I was concerned, was that Kim did just that.

With the editor off all day and Colin getting wet somewhere, an early lunch seemed called for. Victor always has nightmarish fish-paste sandwiches at his desk and the editor's secretary never seems to eat anything at all. But the rest of us ventured out. The wind had died down and the rain was now little more than a steady drizzle. We made for the Perseverance.

The Perseverance is such a ratty pub, presided over by such a ratty landlord, that it has acquired a kind of glamour for us. Little posters in the windows advertise such delicacies as 'Scampi and Chips', 'Chicken and Chips' and 'Full English Breakfast', the quotation marks seeming to suggest that these dishes aren't really served at all, that the words are mere euphemisms for horrific ersatz ingredients that dare not speak their true name. But best of all at the Perseverance is the jukebox.

I'm convinced that Larry, our less than genial host, was required by the brewery to have a jukebox against his will and that he had therefore stocked it with records no one could possibly want to play. No one usually did apart from us. The temptation to select half an hour of the crappiest hits ever to pollute the singles' chart and then watch the expressions of pain and disgust creep over the faces of the other customers and the ever mournful Larry was irresistible.

I felt nauseous again as I entered the pub and took in a lungful of the familiar smell of stale beer, chip fat and last night's tobacco. Beyond all this, the Perseverance always had a strange, malodorous dampness in the air, as though the carpet had once been flooded by Thames water and was now quietly rotting in dark corners.

I bought the first round. Mirza had a pint and Barbara, displaying her proletarian origins, had a lager-blackcurrant. Kim and Kevin had gin and tonics, a large one for Kim. That girl's drinking too much, I thought hypocritically. The hair of the dog would have been too little, too late for me, so I had a double Coke. Kim and Kevin were giggling over by the jukebox and came back looking smug after playing a blinder. It all started innocuously enough, with Marie Osmond's 'Paper

Roses' and 'Little Arrows' by Leapy Lee. The first signs of serious irritation among the lads playing pool came with the St Winifred's School Choir and 'There's No One Quite Like Grandma'. Then Kim and Kevin hit them with the old left, right, left, Clive Dunn's 'Grandad', Rolf Harris's 'Two Little Boys' and Benny Hill's 'Ernie', the fastest milkman in the west. We were on to our second drinks by then, and a degree of tired, hung-over hilarity was setting in.

'"He said Do you want pasteurized? 'Cos pasteurized is best,"' intoned Kevin in his campest voice.

'"She said, Ernie, I'll be happy if it comes up to my chest,"' we roared back at him.

'Lunch' arrived. I toyed delicately with a ham and tomato sandwich while the others, with every appearance of pleasure, munched their way through egg, sausage and chips and home-made chilli con carne, which came in its own 'microwave compatible, rustic plastic casserole pot'. The contents looked like something the dog had sicked up.

After the orgy of Rolf and Benny and Clive, conversation was desultory. More idle speculation about whether JB had ever succumbed to his secretary's importunate glances and given her one, pleasant musings about how wet Colin might be getting, a debate on the relative merits of Bob Dylan and Van Morrison.

The others went off to claim the pool table but I still felt too weak to stand up when it wasn't absolutely essential and picked up the paper which had arrived from the printer's just before we went out. The official publication day is Thursday but you can buy it in some London shops on Wednesday, much to the annoyance of provincial readers who think this gives Londoners an unfair advantage in responding to job adverts.

Colin appeared three times on the front page, but Kim, Kevin and I had decided that he would be unbearably bumptious with three page one by-lines above the story and had reduced him to a 'writes Colin Sneath' on two of them, tacked on to the end of the first paragraph in 8pt italic. He wouldn't be pleased about that, which was something else to be pleased about.

I turned to the review pages, with a familiar and rather ignoble feeling of excitement, to read what I considered to be my best piece of the week, a demolition job on a production of *Romeo and Juliet* at the Camden Basement Theatre. Even by the almost heroically low standards of the Camden Basement, this one had been a stinker. To ensure maximum discomfort it had been a promenade show, with the audience obliged either to stand or sit on the concrete floor. The warring Capulets and Montagues had been presented as rival gangs of football hooligans, chanting "Ere we go, 'ere we go, 'ere we go', swigging lager from cans and sporting National Front T-shirts, and Romeo made his first entrance on an enormous motorbike, revving it so violently that the airless theatre was at once filled with choking exhaust fumes. It was a genuinely novel touch to cast an actor with a speech impediment as Romeo – he couldn't pronounce the letter r – though in these circumstances he wasn't too conspicuous since most of the rest of the cast delivered the verse as if it were a particularly difficult foreign language which they'd just started learning at evening class. There was, however, a wonderful Juliet, Harriet Smythe. Although the programme informed us that she had left drama school a year earlier with the Donald Sinden Gold Medal, she really did look fourteen, a girl just awaking to her own sexuality and capacity for love. She had a beguilingly husky voice, delivered the verse beautifully and, bless her, had consented to the director's inevitable request that she remove all her clothes in the wedding night scene. Romeo, cravenly, retained a pair of greyish Y-fronts.

It says a good deal for Harriet Smythe's skills as an actress that after getting a quick eyeful of her tiny breasts, hard nipples and the wisps of pubic hair that proved she was a natural blonde, I spent more time watching her face than her body in that great scene of dawn parting. Only when Romeo started chomping up the lines was the spell broken, leaving the mind free to turn to more carnal thoughts that were given an added *frisson* by the fact that the actress looked so young, so pubescent. This Juliet was jailbait.

Kim had come up with the cruel headline WHEREFORE ART THOU WOMEO? and I felt a pang of pity for him. It had seemed funny during a fraught press day. Now it seemed merely spiteful. So, to be frank, did the rest of the review. Written in rage, but read in tranquillity, it was bad tempered rather than amusing, patronizing rather than wittily detached. Still, at least I'd given Juliet a rave, a rave in which I'd done my best to keep my lust in check. Or rather, I thought I'd given Juliet a rave. I read through to the end of the longish review. No Juliet. The actors playing Romeo, Friar Laurence, the Nurse, Tybalt, Mercutio and Mr and Mrs Capulet all received their less than favourable mention. But of Miss Smythe there was no trace.

I knew what had happened and it was entirely my fault. I'd saved Juliet for the last paragraph. After all the other dross, the account of her performance was meant to shine more brightly. But the piece had been three centimetres too long and when Kim had asked me to suggest a cut, I'd airily told her to lose the last paragraph, forgetting that I'd saved her for the end.

Kim wandered over from the pool table. 'What's up? You're looking even worse.'

'I've just made a prick of myself. Again,' I said in maximum *mea culpa* mode.

'Well, if that's all it is . . .'

'No, a real prick. You know the *Romeo and Juliet* review. Well, it must be the only review ever written of the play in which the actress playing Juliet doesn't even get a mention.'

'But you were having orgasms about her in the office.'

Even in my mortified state, I fancied I could detect the faintest trace of jealousy in this, or if not jealousy, then at least irritation, and it cheered me up a bit. 'Yeah, but I saved her up for the end and I told you to cut from the bottom.'

'Jesus. I should have read it,' she said magnanimously. 'I got Roy to slice off the last par on the stone and it fitted perfectly so I didn't even look at it.'

'No, it's my fault. I should have remembered. The trouble is, the rest of the review is so negative it looks as though I've deliberately left her out so as not to spoil a good piece of knocking-copy. It's a horrible piece. I don't like the bloke that wrote it.'

'Poor Will.' She gave me a mock mournful look. 'You can always write a piece for Victor's diary, you know all the usual stuff about printer's gremlins, particularly unfortunate since little Miss so-and-so was so good . . .'

We tended to use Victor's 'View from the Stalls' to correct the more monumental cock-ups without making them look too much like crawling apologies. I cheered up considerably.

'I could give her a ring, flesh it out a bit, find out what she's doing next.'

'And suggest a drink as well, I expect, you disgusting old goat.'

'You know my heart belongs to you.' It sounded much more facetious than I'd meant it to.

'Oh fuck off,' said Kim with unusual asperity. 'Why don't you have a proper drink?'

'Are you getting them in?' I asked, puzzled. Was I flattering myself, or was Kim annoyed because I'd seemed to be taking the piss out of the idea that I might have a soft spot for her? And might that indicate that she had a soft spot for me?

'I'll have a Bloody Mary,' I said. 'A large one.'

'Thank Christ for that.'

I watched her walk over to the bar. She was a short girl, and far from glamorous, yet she combined a reassuring wholesomeness with the promise of an enthusiastic sexuality. Her cropped hair was dark, her face, with its button nose and oddly lopsided smile, almost comical. As usual, she was wearing jeans and a huge, faded rugby shirt that almost came down to her knees. Even that baggy, friendly number didn't entirely conceal the size of her splendid tits. As she stood at the bar, Kim turned round and grinned, as if to apologize for her earlier snappishness. I felt a sudden, aching wave of tenderness for her, washing over me, submerging me. Sex was there, or rather the imagined aftermath of sex. But it was more than that. I didn't just fancy Kim, I realized, I wasn't just half in love with her. I was fathom deep.

She came back with the drinks.

'Get that down the old red lane,' she said. I took a sip and knew the Bloody Mary had been another dreadful mistake.

'Sorry, Kim, I think I'm going to be sick again.' By the time I'd reached the door to the Gents, I was running.

I spent the afternoon dozing on the floor of the boardroom where the ancient directors of the family firm occasionally meet under Mr Torrington's hesitant chairmanship, and which we use the rest of the time for interviews, private phone calls and, as now, a bit of peace and quiet. About four o'clock Kim came in with a cup of tea. 'How's the patient?' she asked.

'Terrible. I think this is the worst I've ever known it.'

'You didn't have that much last night. No more than usual. Not a throwing-up amount.'

'I carried on with the Scotch when I got home. Cathy and I had a full and frank exchange of views. The trouble is, I can't remember what the full and frank exchange consisted of. God knows what she'll say tonight. I think I might as well go home now. I'm not going to get anything done here.'

Kim was sitting on a chair, looking down at me with wry amusement. 'I'll give you a lift if you like. There's nothing much to do and JB's not coming back. Try and pick yourself up and walk all the way to the car without throwing up.'

I caught hold of her hand and she pulled me up on to my feet with surprising strength. When I was standing I found I didn't want to let her go, but it seemed a bit silly just standing there in the boardroom holding her hand so I kissed her on the lips.

'No, Will,' she said. 'Things are bad enough for you as they are and your breath smells disgusting.'

Written down like that, it sounds like a terrific put-down but Kim somehow contrived to make it sound kindly. I hugged her and the feeling of her breasts against my chest brought on a surge of the randiness that seems to underlie even the most terminal hangovers.

'Come on then, Florence Nightingale. Lead me to the ambulance. Sorry about the kiss . . . and the sick . . .'

'Save it for Cathy,' she said.

Kim drove a filthy, clapped-out Mini and although she'd passed her test years ago she still seemed fazed at finding herself behind a steering wheel. Kim was enviably cool and competent in the office, and I'd always found her hesitant, granny-like driving, hands gripping the wheel as if it were a deadly enemy's throat, one of her more endearing qualities. There wasn't much traffic on the roads at ten past four so I risked a bit of chat.

'How's the Godfather?' I asked.

'Still Godfathering along,' she said enigmatically, stuck now behind a milk float with an articulated lorry overtaking her on the right.

'How's Cathy?' she said a few minutes later, when the milk float had turned left and she had an open road before her.

'Still Cathy,' I said.

Kim grinned. 'Touché.'

I could have sat in that car with her for hours, companionable, quiet, close, but all too soon we were turning into Rita Road. Kim quite often took me home, since she lived just a bit further south in a large, early Victorian house in Stockwell. The Godfather's, of course, not hers, though she still kept the studio flat in Brixton she'd bought when she first came to London. I think, or rather I liked to think, that she kept it as a bolt-hole, an acknowledgement that she wasn't stuck with the Godfather for ever.

She pulled up outside my place. 'Here we are then. Good luck with Cathy.'

'She won't be in for ages. You could come in for a cup of tea if you like.'

'No thanks. I'm going home to curl up with Tom Jones.'

Kim had a terrific inferiority complex about never having been to university. She'd joined a local weekly paper near her home in Newcastle straight after her A levels, got her proficiency certificate there and had come to *Theatre World* three years ago as chief sub. Whenever Kevin, Colin or I talked about what we'd done at university, she'd go all quiet and moody, as if we were deliberately teasing her. Very often we were. At the start of the year she'd embarked on the Open University's Arts Foundation Course and had, only last week, sat the exam. She took it extremely seriously, and though it was only October now and her new course on the Enlightenment didn't start until the following February, she kept saying how determined she was to get ahead with her reading. During her course, she'd occasionally asked me if I had any views on free will and determinism, or the Victorian crisis of faith or the Pre-Raphaelite Brotherhood. I didn't really, but usually managed to bluff my way through a few glib sentences. 'That's just it,' she'd say exasperatedly. 'You know bugger all about it but because you've been to a public school and Oxford, you've got this gift of the gab and give the impression that you know it all even when you don't. You're a fraud, Will, and one day I'll be a better fraud than you are.'

The rain had begun to ease off as I climbed out of the car. 'I don't suppose there's any chance of a fuck, is there?' I said through the open door, the old public school charm still functioning despite the hangover.

'With an old sick-bag like you?' said Kim. 'You're joking.'

She stuck her tongue out, then smiled. 'See you tomorrow. If Cathy doesn't kill you that is.'

I let myself into our ground-floor flat rather gingerly, just in case Cathy was back, but she wasn't. I couldn't decide whether to dredge my memory and try to bring to the surface all the awful things I knew had happened the night before or keep them safely submerged. There was no blood on the carpet, for which relief, some thanks, nor could I see any smashed crockery. There was, however, a pile of crumpled and still slightly damp tissues by the sofa from which I deduced, with Holmes-like acumen, that either Cathy or I had been crying a good deal.

Otherwise the flat was, as always, impeccably clean and tidy, for Cathy was becoming increasingly obsessive about the housework, never happier, it seemed, than when she had a bottle of Jif or a can of Pledge in her hand. Even the bed was made. I'd spent the night on the sofa, fully clothed, and when I'd woken at five the needle was still going round and round the end of a Grateful Dead record. The hum from the speakers, the scrape, scrape, scrape of the needle, had alerted me even then that I'd been playing it unacceptably loudly, and I hadn't dared to creep into bed with Cathy. I'd taken the first dose of the hangover remedy and gone back to sleep on the sofa. Cathy had woken me as she clattered round the flat before going to work but I'd pretended to be asleep and she'd left me in peace.

I sat down and found the whisky bottle, lying on its side between the sofa and the wall. By some miracle the cap was on. It was just over half full. It had been completely full the night before and Cathy never touched Scotch. Almost half a bottle, on top of the six pints of Holsten in the pub after the printer's. No wonder the hangover wasn't shifting.

I'd met Cathy almost eight years earlier, right at the start of my time on the *Bridport Chronicle*. She was the winner of the Miss Bridport Carnival Queen contest (it hadn't exactly been a vintage year) and I'd interviewed her in her hour of glory. She was eighteen then and had just started work in the Midland Bank, the same branch as my own. After we'd run her picture in the paper, wearing a rather unflattering swimming costume on the beach at West Bay, I'd asked her out the next time I'd gone to pay in a cheque, the first from *Theatre World* as it happened, a princely £12.50.

It had been great at first. After a long and entirely unwelcome period of celibacy at Oxford, I thought of Cathy as the first in a long line of conquests by the new Casanova Benson. She'd surprised me by agreeing to go to bed after our first date (*The French Lieutenant's Woman* at the local cinema), and I'd mistaken her for a right little raver. But what I thought of as a brief fling, she saw as The Relationship. She became so alarmingly hysterical when, after a couple of months, I'd gently suggested that it might be time to call it a day that in the end I lacked the courage to go through with it. When I climbed down and said no, of course I was quite wrong, of course we should carry on going out, she'd clumsily unzipped my flies, knelt down, and with tears still streaming down her face, given me a blow job for the first time, a victory of mind over matter achieved only by an all-too-evident effort of will.

Ever since that joyless bout of fellatio, in which Cathy had seemed to abase herself with such despairing humility, it was I who had been emasculated. Cathy had stooped and sucked to conquer. After that, I'd never had the heart to cause a fuss. Most of the time I did more or less what I was told, and when I didn't I was told off like some grubby schoolboy. Even worse was the knowledge that I actually liked this subservience, that I had come to need her nagging care and control. She loved me, or thought she did. I quite liked her when she wasn't too clingy. Passion subsided and we became more or less contented companions who occasionally had a fuck. Oral sex was right out, of course.

Then came the offer of the job on *Theatre World*. I told her I was going to take it, that it would mean moving to London and selling the cottage but that naturally we'd still see each other at weekends. I'd expected sobs and shrieks but Cathy stayed calm, even saying it was time I moved on, that I'd been stuck in rusticity for too long. I couldn't believe my luck. No need to break up all at once, just a gentle, civilized parting of the ways, regular visits that would become less regular, and the resumption of my long-interrupted, indeed never started, career as promiscuous chap about town. About a week later she came home late looking smug.

'I've got a new job, too, Will.'

I only had to look at her face to know where that job was.

'I saw the boss and said you were going to London and asked if he could find me anything there.'

The bastard had of course. Assistant manager with responsibility for loans to small businesses at the Sloane Square branch. Unknown to me, she'd been up to the Smoke for her interview that morning and been offered the post there and then. With London weighting and another step up the promotion ladder she would be making an extra five grand a year as well.

I'd sort of known Cathy wasn't just a humble clerk behind

the counter any more but I found her monologues about the bank so dull that I switched off whenever she started them, offering vague ums and aahs when the tone of her unlistened to voice seemed to call for it. This was a new Cathy, Cathy the assistant manager at twenty-six, working in a swanky branch, and earning, I'd quickly calculated, quite a lot more than I would be when we moved to London. When *we* moved to London. Shit and derision. Twenty-five years of mortgage repayments and togetherness stretched drearily ahead.

I heard Cathy's key in the door. It was only five o'clock and she wasn't normally back until seven at the earliest, much later on badminton nights. My old friend Mr Panic started doing strenuous physical exercises in my stomach. Something irrevocable had happened last night and I still couldn't put my finger on what it was. Not knowing was going to create a whole heap of fresh trouble. I took the coward's way out, lay back on the sofa and pretended to be asleep.

'You drunken slug,' she began charitably. 'Haven't you moved off that sofa all day?'

I felt an immense weariness and couldn't summon up the effort to say no, I'd gone to work actually, been sick a couple of times, come home again.

'Er . . .' I said with a flash of Wilde-like wit.

'I was hoping to be out of here before you got back but now you can damn well help me pack.'

'What's that, Cathy? Where are you going?' I mumbled, really worried now.

'I thought you'd have forgotten. How much *do* you remember about last night?'

It hadn't gone down a storm last time, but why not try it again?

'Er,' I said.

She sat down in the armchair opposite the sofa. She looked tired, pale, feverishly excited and there was a coldness in her manner I'd not come across before.

'You came home pissed at eleven-thirty, you found the bottle of Scotch I'd hidden in the back of the bedroom cupboard and you drank half a big tumblerful in about ten minutes. I tried to take the bottle away and you said I was a fucking cunt, that you'd wasted eight years of your life on me, that I was no good in bed and bossy out of it.'

I couldn't look her in the face and rolled over to stare at the back of the sofa, dying, for the first time all day, for a cigarette. Oh dear, oh dear, oh dear.

'Then we had a lot of stuff, though you weren't all that coherent by now, about how you'd never wanted me to come to London, that I'd sucked all the spirit out of you and that you hated my guts. Then you started crying.'

The tissues had been mine then, not Cathy's. Knowing Cathy she'd probably brought them from the bedroom for me.

'You got through about twenty Kleenex, snivelling away, knocking back the Scotch, and then you started on about how you were in love with Kim, that at least she'd got a sense of humour and a decent set of tits and I didn't have either, that I was a boring wanker-banker. You seemed to like that, and muttered "wanker-banker" over and over again, then you started screaming it, then you put on the Grateful Dead at a ridiculous volume and told me to fuck off. Before I did, I told you I'd be moving out this afternoon and that you weren't to come home till eight o'clock. You must have passed out soon afterwards. You certainly didn't put any more records on.'

Oh Christ in heaven. Who would have thought the young man had so much bile in him? Unscrew that bottle and hark what discord follows.

'God, I'm sorry, I truly am sorry, Cathy.'

'I've always distrusted people who say "truly" and "honestly" to emphasize their sincerity. It suggests that when they're not saying them they must be lying and when they are, that they're still lying but have an even bigger lie they want to get away with.'

'Honestly, I'm sorry,' I said, hating myself and realizing that I too was lying.

I was truly and honestly sorry that I'd behaved so loutishly, truly and honestly sorry that I'd caused Cathy pain, truly and honestly sorry that I hadn't even had the grace or the brain cells to remember it afterwards. But I wasn't sorry I'd said it. It needed saying, or something like it, and it should have been said years ago, in calmer, kinder words. But honestly, truly, it was the truth.

'You seem so calm, Cathy. I'm really ashamed of myself.'

'It's too late now,' she said. 'I was upset last night of course, but lying in bed, trying to ignore that racket on the record player, I realized I was glad. You're a feckless idiot. I used to care so much about you but I don't any more. You haven't really given a toss about me for years, you hardly listen to a word I say, you do nothing around the house and get all resentful when I do. We've just drifted along, you getting more and more bored, me getting more and more bitter, but lacking the courage to admit it. Who wants to be on their own? I used to ask myself. It's better than nothing. But it's not, Will, and now I'm looking forward to being on my own.'

I was expecting a lecture about 'personal space' but it didn't come. Cathy was still putting the boot in.

'But you'll hate being on your own, Will. You'll miss the ironed shirts, the clean house, you'll miss someone nagging at you because you drink too much and you'll miss instantly available sex when you're sober enough to get it up. I can't wait to go.'

As you might imagine, all this was doing me the world of good. And she was right. I'd been a shit, and I would miss her, miss the security of having a girlfriend, the comfort blanket of being nagged. What was the fun of getting pissed, of lusting after other girls, when there wasn't a feeling of rebellion and guilt to go with it? Like an old lag, with his cushy job in the prison library and a nice little snout racket going, I didn't want to be thrown out of my cosy cell, out into the cold.

'But Cathy, it's been so long. We can't just throw it all away. It's not as if either of us have got anyone else. Why not give it one last try?'

I was whimpering. It's terrible. When the gloves are off and irony has long since flown out of the window, you end up talking like Rita Fairclough.

'Don't be pathetic. You meant what you said last night, it's just you haven't got the drink to prop you up any more.'

How right she was. I eyed the whisky bottle then pushed it right out of my mind.

'And anyway, what about Kim and her lovely tits?' For the first time there was real venom rather than an infuriating weary reasonableness in her voice and I liked her for it.

'Come off it, Cathy. I've never laid a finger on Kim,' (well, not with any encouragement from her, I added to myself). 'She's happily ensconced with some old fart from the Variety Club.'

'Well, you'll just have to try and unensconce her then.' She sounded almost encouraging.

'Where are you going to stay?'

'I'm staying with a friend from the bank and I'm not saying where she lives in case you turn up drunk on the doorstep demanding your non-marital rights,' she said.

I was ignobly relieved she'd said 'she' rather than 'he'. 'But the mortgage, Cathy?' I bleated. 'I can't meet the repayments on my own.'

'Well, you'll have to find a lodger then, won't you.'

'This is all very grown up, isn't it?'

'Yeah,' said Cathy.

She stood up and went into the bedroom, got her suitcase from the top of the wardrobe and began to pack with her usual neatness. 'I'll leave the furniture and the curtains and so on. But I want my desk and my bookshelf. You can give me a thousand for the rest of the stuff we bought together, and I think you're getting a bargain.'

I probably was.

'I'll come round on Saturday for the desk and the bookshelf and the rest of my nicknacks. I've arranged to borrow a van. And I'll take some of the kitchen stuff too if that's all right.'

'Have the lot. You chose it, just leave me a mug and a plate and a knife and fork.'

'Don't sound so feeble, Will,' she said in the brisk tone that had become so familiar over the years.

'No Cathy, sorry Cathy,' I said, and meant it, despite the automatic sneer in my voice. 'The less crockery I have, the less the washing-up will pile up.'

'And try to be out on Saturday. We don't want another farewell scene.'

'I'm sorry it's all turned out like this,' I said, thinking I meant it.

'No you're not, Will, not really, not if you think about it and don't go all maudlin on me. And try and cut back on the drinking. You've got a bit of talent there. It would be a shame to piss it all away.'

I picked up her suitcase and we walked out of the flat and along to the corner where you could usually pick up a cab. As always when you really needed one there was a complete dearth of the buggers, and it wasn't even raining now. We stood side by side, everything worth saying already said or too late to say.

'I don't suppose there's any chance of a blow job, is there?' I asked. Cathy, as so often, looked shocked and cross, then picked up on the reference.

'You're a bastard, Will Benson,' she said, and laughed, not bitterly but with the battered remains of affection. It was better than nothing.

A cab cruised past and I flagged it down, loaded the case in the front and opened the door for Cathy at the back. She kissed me lightly on the cheek.

'See you, Will.'

'Off on your holidays?' the taxi driver yelled back at her. I hesitated on the pavement before closing the door behind her.

'You could say that,' said Cathy. 'Could you start the cab before I tell you where I'm going.'

'All right, Cathy. Point taken,' I said, and shut the door. The taxi chugged down the road and turned right at the lights, towards Vauxhall Bridge. I went back to the flat and picked up the bottle of Scotch.

'Just you and me now then, mate,' I told the Famous Grouse sternly, then walked to the kitchen and poured what was left

33

down the sink. 'Just me now, then,' I said, putting the bottle in the waste bin.

I went and lay on the bed, and buried my head in Cathy's pillow, which still smelled of her but wouldn't for much longer; a comforting, clean smell. Then I cried a bit. Self-pitying, hung-over tears at first, then tears of real regret, of love for Cathy and all the nice things about her that I'd taken for granted, wasted and spoilt. After about an hour I got up and washed my face, made a pot of tea and switched on the telly. Anneka Rice was on. It really was my lucky day.

Thursday

The hotel was smaller and far classier than I'd expected, hidden away in a cul-de-sac near Victoria station. Even after a night of broken sleep and with the stubborn, day-two remains of the hangover still giving me spiteful little nudges, I found myself smiling at the sight of it. It was late Victorian or early Edwardian, gabled and turreted in red brick Gothic, and extravagantly adorned with a host of terracotta bas-reliefs depicting writhing vegetation, abundant fruit and exotic animals. The whole façade, from the ground floor to the attics seven storeys up, was hung with scores of hanging baskets filled with red and white geraniums. Joe 'The Big Cunt' Johnson appeared to be a man of some discernment.

Not that you'd have guessed it from his act. On his occasional appearances on mindless quiz shows, Joe came over as yet another rent-a-celeb. Bluffly northern and hideously over-weight, his trademark was an extraordinary chuckle, half rumble, half asthmatic wheeze, which appeared to have been developed with the help of sixty Senior Service a day. On telly, Joe Johson (no 'Big Cunt' on such occasions) seemed like just another ageing, over-the-hill comic, picking up what crumbs he could.

But there was nothing over-the-hill about Johnson on stage, where he made his real money. He never appeared live in the south, his territory stretching from Blackpool and Newcastle down as far as Birmingham. Here he could sell out a big theatre or civic centre in a matter of hours, thanks to his word-of-mouth reputation and the tapes and videos of his act that circulated round the northern pubs and working-men's clubs. The Big Cunt, as he was affectionately known to his fans, or The Big C*** as he appeared on posters, was the filthiest comedian in the business. I'd seen him the year before, at the Scarborough Futurist, soon after joining *Theatre World*, and had been amazed and appalled in roughly equal measure.

Dressed in baggy khaki shorts, a scarlet Hawaiian shirt crawling with green parrots and with a plastic policeman's helmet perched on his head, he seemed a benign, quaintly absurd figure as he sauntered on to the stage. Then he opened his mouth. His sex jokes were almost unimaginably foul, ramming home the proximity of the organs of generation and excretion. He hated all foreigners, not just the blacks and the Pakistanis, but the Chinese, the Japanese, even the Dutch. Homosexuals came in for particular abuse, with the Big Cunt delightedly speculating on who, in British show business, was going to die next from Aids. 'This is a fuckin' masterpiece, this one,' he'd begin, before launching into a gag about nuns and vaginal discharges or sex after a vindaloo or the benefit of Winnie Mandela to the South African tyre industry. As he swore and coughed his heart out, the sweat ran down his face like a lump of lard melting in the sun. Occasionally he'd dry himself off with a towel sporting the Tampax logo in foot-high letters. 'This is as near as I get to sucking fanny,' he'd leer.

There was a terrible exhilaration in seeing so much bile erupt, in witnessing a vision of human life that didn't even admit to the possibility of kindness, tolerance or love. 'You've got to laff, you've just got to fucking laff,' Johnson would yell, and the whole house was indeed helpless with laughter. But it was a laughter of hate and ugliness and fear. We were afloat in a sea of shit and if we didn't laff we'd want to top ourselves. The Big Cunt was a troubadour of disgust and despair, conducting guided tours of a moral wasteland.

Or so at least I'd felt after his show, weak with lager and mindless laughter. We'd headlined the piece THE FRANCIS BACON OF STAND-UP COMEDY, which I'd thought was frightfully good at the time though I now blushed to think of it. The Big

Cunt's personal manager, Harry Meadows, had phoned up furious. 'What are you trying to do, get Joe a bloody Arts Council grant or what? He's never heard of Francis Bacon and nor's anyone else in his audience. He's just a comic and he doesn't need intellectual wankers like you coming along and queering his pitch.'

I'd feebly remonstrated that it was just my view, that I thought Joe Johnson was some kind of perverted genius and then he'd calmed down a bit. 'P'raps you've got a point, he's certainly a fucking headcase and that is *not* for quotation.' The other week Meadows had phoned again suggesting an interview when Johnson came to London for a televized children's charity bash. Children in need needed the Big Cunt like a hole in the head.

'I thought he hated the review,' I said.

'Nah, I just thought he'd hate it. I hadn't spoken to him when I rang you. Turned out the silly bugger was dead chuffed. He even bought a book on what's he called, that terrible artist?'

'Francis Bacon,' I said. 'Blimey, he's not going up-market is he?'

'What, and kill his following,' said Meadows sharply. 'He's not completely daft. He knows the value of a wallet.'

We'd arranged to meet at the hotel and here I was, feeling apprehensive. Just what kind of a headcase was Joe Johnson?

It was cool and sepulchral in the lobby and even the air – cut flowers and furniture polish – smelt expensive. I went up to the desk and a snooty, Sloaney woman looked down her nose at my shabby sports jacket and the Tesco's carrier bag that held my notebook and expensive tape recorder I'd borrowed from Colin.

'Can I help you . . .' Did I imagine it, or was there a just perceptible pause before the 'sir?'

'I have an appointment with Joe "The Big Cunt" Johnson,' I said. 'Could you let him know I'm here?'

If I'd thought this would faze her – and naturally I'd hoped it would – I was wrong.

'Oh yes, the Big Cunt,' she said in a tone of nostalgic reminiscence. 'I saw him a couple of years ago at the Birmingham Hippodrome. A remarkable man.'

She rang the number and I stood there with my carrier bag, feeling like the wally she'd intended me to.

'Third floor, the Laurence Olivier suite, turn left out of the lift. Tell him from me he's a sexist shithead.' I looked shocked. I felt shocked. 'He'll never believe I said it even if you've got the balls to tell him.' She carefully studied my flies as if actually checking on their presence and their size, then looked up with a bright professional smile. 'No, I don't think you'll tell him,' she said smoothly. 'Have a good meeting.'

I beat a hasty retreat to the lift. They breed their receptionists tough at the Pimlico Court Hotel.

Joe Johnson's door was opened by a man in his forties wearing one of the comic's more disgracefully explicit T-shirts. He had dead, disconcerting eyes, like cold chips of grey slate.

'Are you Will Benson?'

I assured him I was.

'Harry Meadows.' No shake of the hand. No invitation to come in.

'I've been on to your office since nine this morning to tell you the interview's off. Joe's not well.'

'I came straight from home. Did you speak to anyone in the office?'

'Just some obstructive cow on the switchboard. She said it was impossible to get a message to you as your present whereabouts were unknown.'

I recognized dear Martha, who had all our home numbers.

'What's up with Joe, then?'

Meadows looked at me and his eyes were blanker than ever.

'Badly upset stomach. ITV food I expect. Bloody disgrace, it was.'

'I know how he feels,' I said with a sneaking feeling of relief. I wasn't looking forward to talking to the Big Cunt. I could think of damn all to ask him anyway.

'I'm afraid you've had a wasted trip.'

As Meadows was in mid-sentence there was a crash and Johnson staggered into view, his shirt unbuttoned to reveal the inevitable gold medallion, his hair matted with sweat, his face

an alarming shade of puce. He was carrying an empty whisky
bottle.

'I've finished this one, Harry. And I've just smashed the glass
in the basin.' He wheezed horribly and I realized it was his
famous laugh. 'Give us another bottle or I'll smash every
window in the fucking room before starting on the furniture.'

While Johnson was talking, I'd squeezed past Meadows and
into the luxury suite. The manager stared at me and there was
a hint of alarm even in those dead eyes.

'You're not going to stitch me up on this one, are you? Not
Theatre World?'

'I shouldn't think so, Harry,' I said.

'Where's that sodding drink?' asked Johnson in an aggrieved
voice as he slumped on to one of the sofas.

'Coming up,' said Harry and went over to a cupboard in the
corner. It contained a fridge, glasses and lots of bottles.

'I expect you'll want to be on your way now,' he hissed at me
over his shoulder. 'I'll speak to you later in the office.'

While he was busying himself with Joe's drink I switched on
the tape recorder without taking it out of the carrier bag, finding
the record button through the plastic. For the first time, Johnson
seemed to notice there was someone else in the room.

'Who's this cunt, then?' he inquired thickly, his eyes focusing
with difficulty.

'It's the reporter, Joe. Remember, you were going to do an
interview this morning. But Mr Benson's on his way now.'

'You mean the Bacon bloke, the clever-dick wanker?'

'That's right, Joe, but he's on his way now.' Meadows was
making desperate gestures towards the door.

'Nah, I'll do the interview, I've nothing else on,' said Joe, like
royalty now, graciously granting an audience. Harry looked
haunted as he came over with half a tumbler of Scotch that
jingled merrily with ice cubes.

'But you're not well, Joe, not well at all. It's been a long
night.'

'What'dya mean not well?' said Johnson, energetically

39

scratching his crotch. 'I've just had a few drinks that's all. I'm fit as a flea. I'll do the fucking interview. Give the man a drink.'

I glanced at my watch. It was five past ten.

'Just an orange juice, please.'

Johnson looked as though I'd insulted his dead mother. 'No one's drinking orange juice in my company. Give him a Scotch, Harry, a large one, and have one yourself.' It wasn't an invitation.

Harry went back to the drink's cupboard.

'It doesn't look as though you've been to bed, Mr Johnson,' I said pleasantly.

'That's right lad, I have not been to bed. I've been drinking, on me own because bloody Harry over there wouldn't keep me company, and I've been wanking over the memory of the lovely Anneka Rice with whom I had the pleasure of working last night.'

'Somehow one doesn't associate you with charity work.'

'I've given thousands to charity, thousands and thousands.' His voice was suddenly slurrier and he seemed unbearably tired and defeated. He gazed out of the window, took another huge pull on his drink and lapsed into a brooding silence that seemed impertinent to intrude upon. Harry came over with my drink. I took a sip and felt grateful to him. It looked a huge and wicked brew but as far as I could tell it was all ginger ale.

'That's a strong one, Harry. Cheers,' I said.

I got my notebook out of the carrier bag.

'Well, shall we make a start then, Mr Johnson?' I sounded like a briskly efficient doctor at a BUPA health check. There was no response from the Big Cunt, but I pressed on regardless.

'How do you feel about all the complaints about your act? People say it's sexist and racist and you've been banned by several local authorities. Are you actually doing anything more than pandering to the lowest common denominator of public taste?'

It was far too long a question, of course, it's the short, simple ones that get the best results, but I'd kept wittering on because the comic appeared to be asleep.

He was asleep. He looked peaceful, sprawled out on the sofa, but it didn't last. He snored, and the snore woke him with a start.

'You what? I'm sorry, I didn't quite catch your question.'

This was pathetic. I thought of Cathy and all the times she'd seen me in a similar state, and didn't blame her a bit for going.

'I was just asking if there was any justification for the material you use in your act, Mr Johnson.'

He began to laugh and very horrible it was too. It began with the allegedly endearing wheeze-rumble but then laughter seemed to take possession of his whole body, like a fit.

'Eugghh, eugghh, eugghh, eugghh, eugghh.' It went on and on. He was in the grip of some hellish hysteria and it looked as if it could kill him. His eyes bulged, tears streamed down his face, the whole massive bulk of his body writhed and twitched on the sofa.

Meadows, much too late, strode over and shook him by the shoulder. 'Eugghh, eugghh, eugghh, eugghh.' Johnson was fighting for breath, exhaling in great gasps with the next spasm coming before he had a chance to get enough air back into his lungs. I went into the bedroom, where Johnson had indeed smashed his glass in the sink, emptied my ginger ale, filled the tumbler with cold water and threw it in his face. He spluttered and coughed, but the laughter died at last. He'd burst a couple more buttons on his shirt, allowing a full frontal view of the Johnson paunch, like a small, but not that small, barrage balloon, white, hairless and bedewed with sweat.

'Christ,' he croaked. 'I couldn't fucking stop. I feel all done in.' The words came in short, incoherent bursts and he looked dreadful. But his right hand, surprisingly steady, reached with eerie accuracy for the glass by his feet, which had somehow survived the cataclysm. He drained it in one.

'Get us another, Harry, and one for thing here. Waddya say your name was?'

'Will,' I said, 'Will Benson.'

'Well come and sit beside me here on the sofa, Will. I'm a bit deaf if the truth be told. Over sixty now, you know.'

It was like a different man talking. Johnson suddenly seemed amicable, almost charming. He must have drunk himself sober, I thought, something I'd been trying to do on and off for years, with disastrous results. Sober or not, however, I didn't fancy sharing a small sofa with the Big Cunt.

'Come on, over here, Will,' he said, and pulled a crumpled packet of Seniors out of his pocket.

'Do you want a smoke?'

I went over, taking my plastic bag with me, and put it on the floor between my feet. He gave me a cigarette and lit it with a flashy lighter that produced a ludicrously fierce flame. He had three gold rings on his right hand, each set with a large solitaire diamond.

'Yeah, they're real all right. Hundred grand's worth there.' Johnson took a drag on his fag and Meadows came over with the drinks.

'Forget the interview, Joe. You and Will sup up, then call it a day. You need to sleep, you've got a show tomorrow. Couple of sleepers, twelve hours in the sack, you'll be right as rain.'

'No, I wanna talk,' said Johnson, the spoilt, petulant child now. 'Where's your reporter's notebook, Will?'

It was on my lap and I waved it wanly at him.

'Well, get this down, then. They're always trying to ban and censor me. They're always saying I'm sick and disgusting. But I'm the only comedian who dares to speak the truth. The truth,' he added after another of his alarmingly long silences. 'The truth, the whole truth and nothing but the fucking truth.' There was another pause that Pinter might have envied.

'It's a horrible world, Will,' he said at last. 'A truly horrible, horrible world. I was abused as a kid, you know, me father, he was always at me, coming into the bedroom, fiddling about, getting me to jerk him off. There was no fucking Esther bloody Rantzen then, you know.'

Meadows looked appalled. I kept scribbling it all down in my shaky shorthand. I didn't want Meadows to know I had a tape recorder.

'And in this strinking, horrible arsehole of a world, I make people laugh, I make 'em feel better for an hour or two.'

He was in full sentimental flow now, and there was no point in arguing with him, no point in suggesting that the best comedians unite people rather than erect barriers of hate and bigotry. In any case it was an argument I wasn't sure I believed myself. Almost all comedy is about fear, sitting round the fire in the dark and laughing at the frightening shadows on the wall. It was just that Joe's act was all shadows and no warmth.

'Yeah, I make people feel better, I let them get it off their chests. My people hate Pakis, hate poofs, hate the fucking lousy jobs that grind them down. I'm a force for good, I really am, I should get a knighthood like Jimmy Savile, I brighten up the dim and dismal lives of the fucking dim and dismal proletariat.'

There was no sentimentality now. Johnson's tone was witheringly sarcastic. He hated his audience just as he hated everything else, just as he hated himself. I'd half guessed as much at Scarborough, though there had been a kind of tenderness in his final words to the audience. 'God bless, enjoy your holidays, now fuck off back to the pub.'

He was slurring again as he repeated his catchphrase. 'You've jush gotta laff, you jush gotta fuckin' cuntin' soddin' laff.' I was having a bit of trouble with my shorthand. What was the outline for "cuntin'"? My shorthand instructor had been strangely silent on the point. I wrote it out in full and looked up expectantly at Joe, waiting for more words of wisdom. Far from laffin', the Big Cunt was cryin'.

'Cheer up, Joe, you've gotta laff,' I said in a desperate, doomed attempt at jollity. It came out high pitched and panicky. There was something frightening about the big comic crying. He was rocking himself now, holding his knees, back and forth, back and forth, sobbing quietly, the tears streaming down his face and joining the sweat on his chest.

'Of course, you know I'm queer,' he said between sobs. 'Joe Johnson, mincing poof and pissing pervert.'

Harry Meadows was rigid in his chair. He'd got the bottle of

Scotch by his side and he poured a hefty shot into the remains of his ginger ale.

'For Christ's sake, Joe, what are you trying to do, do you even know what you're fucking doing? This is a reporter, Joe, a REPORTER, he writes things for the newspapers. Do you want this crap all over the front page? It will kill you, Joe, it will kill you stone dead.'

The Big Cunt was not to be stopped.

'I was wed of course, thirty years, and I was faithful, absolutely faithful, looked after her when she got the rheumatoid arthritis, had a wank when I was feeling randy. And then she dies and I realized I didn't fancy another woman. I'd been getting the gay magazines already by then of course, masturbating over the pretty, well-hung boys, wondering what it would be like. Straight after the funeral I got the train to London, went to Piccadilly, picked up a rent boy. Bloody marvellous it was. I keep going back. I've got my little auburn wig and my stick-on moustache and no one knows who the fuck I am. Couple of hours in the hotel – not this one of course – then back home again. Just the job. Right as rain. Lovely grub.'

I kept scribbling, Harry kept drinking, Joe kept talking. The tears had stopped now and he was delivering his confession in a calm, rapt monotone.

'What about Aids, Joe?' I said gently, just to keep him going really.

'I've always used rubbers. Even before Aids. There was always a risk of a dose with lads like that. I've been tested, couple of months ago. I'm in the clear.'

'But why are you telling me all this?'

I didn't like the reply. I didn't like it at all. I should never have asked.

'Why do you think? Because I'm pissed and I'm after your body. Why else? I'll pay you for your trouble.'

I tried clinging to the hope that this was another of the Big Cunt's sick jokes, but not for long. He leaned over and planted a wet kiss on my mouth and I could feel his tongue trying to force its way past my clenched teeth. The smell of booze and bad breath was overpowering.

I pulled myself violently away from him, leapt off the sofa like a jack in the box, and sought sanctuary round the back of Meadows' chair. Joe had lost his balance as I made my escape, and his head was now resting where I'd been sitting, his legs waving in the air. He seemed to be finding it difficult to get himself upright again.

'I see what you mean about a headcase,' I gasped at Meadows.

'He's done it now,' said the manager expressionlessly.

Johnson was lumbering to his feet and he'd found the empty Scotch bottle by the side of the sofa. Half a ton of armed, drunk and rapacious homosexual was heading towards me.

'Come on, just a quick blow, there's a hundred quid in it for you,' he yelled. 'Otherwise I'll smash your fuckin' head in.'

Harry was on his feet as well now, and I cowered behind him. Joe gave him a vicious kick and Harry started hopping round the room, clutching his knee in agony. My first and only line of defence was gone.

'Come on, Will, it won't take long. I'll suck you off first if you like, it'll be a pleasure.'

I felt like the heroine in some Victorian melodrama, menaced by the vile Sir Jasper.

'Fuck off, Joe, I'm not interested, I'm not bloody gay,' I shouted.

'Just makes it more of a challenge, Will. Pretty lad like you, you'll love it.'

There was method in the Big Cunt's madness. Instead of coming straight at me, he'd slowly worked his way round the room to the door, cutting off the only exit apart from the door that led into the bedroom, and I didn't want to think about that. I backed up by the window, the other side of the room from him. If he wanted me, he'd have to come and get me. And when he approached my side of the room I'd make a run for it. There was of course the tape recorder to consider, still whirring round inside its Tesco's bag. I moved slowly to the front of the sofa, picked it up, rescued my notebook from the floor and stuffed it in my pocket. I was holding my Bic biro like a dagger.

Meadows had finally stopped hopping and was slumped back in his chair, rubbing his knee and drinking whisky straight from the bottle.

'OK, Joe, party's over,' he said.

Johnson evidently took a different view. He stared at me, screwing up his eyes to get me in focus, and then he pounced. I stood my ground for as long as I dared. 'Wait until you can see the whites of his eyes,' I told myself. They weren't white actually. They were a murky yellow, or at least the bits that weren't bloodshot were. I skipped to my right with balletic grace and Joe cannoned into the sofa, which overturned with him on top of it. Right, speedy exit, I thought, but he was like one of those psychopaths in a horror film who keep coming back no matter what you do to them. He was on his feet again, far quicker than seemed humanly possible, making his way back to sentry duty by the door at the double.

'For God's sake, Harry, don't just sit there,' I cried in desperation.

You had to hand it to Meadows, he was a cool operator when it came to the crunch. As Joe headed for the door, Harry got his weight behind a glass and metal coffee table and heaved it across Joe's path with just a fraction of a second to spare. It was too late for Joe to stop, too late to swerve, and he was far too heavy to jump. The metallic edge of the table hit him an audible crack on the knee and Joe dived gracefully over the top, coming down with an almighty thump on the other side. He tried to break his fall with his hands but his stomach bore the brunt and his feet turned the table over in mid-flight. There was a satisfying crash of breaking glass. From Joe there was no sound at all.

'Jesus wept,' said Harry. He took another swig from his bottle and went to look at what was left of his client.

'He's breathing, the fat slob, but he's out cold,' was Dr Meadows' diagnosis. With some difficulty we rolled him on to his back. There was a rip in his trousers and a nasty cut in his fleshy skin. It had already bled quite a lot on to the carpet. Harry went into the bedroom and brought back a shirt, ripped it up with some difficulty and contrived a rough bandage. I picked up a cushion and placed it under Joe's head. His breathing was reassuringly regular, if you could call an asthmatic wheeze reassuring.

'Well, well, well,' I said. 'Life's full of little surprises.' Meadows gave me a wintry smile. 'Do you want a drink?' he asked.

I certainly did. I had one, straight from the bottle, just like Harry.

'You print a word of this and I'll murder you,' he said. His mouth was still smiling but those grey eyes were unreadable. He sounded as if he meant it.

'You can't prove a thing and if you print a line I'll have a writ on you as quick as you can say "shit". Then I'll kill you after we've collected the libel damages.'

In comparison with Meadows, Johnson seemed soft and cuddly. Harry noticed the notebook sticking out of my pocket. 'And I'll have that, please.'

I handed it over. 'Did you know he was gay?' I asked.

'Of course, he tells me everything. A good deal more than I want to know. But I'm the only one who does apart from you and a gross of rent boys.'

'Haven't any of them tried to blackmail him?'

'No one's tried so far, so QED no one's recognized him. Scum like that wouldn't waste much time if they did. You should see him in his red wig and little 'tache. His old mum wouldn't know him.'

He gazed at the comatose lump on the carpet with something approaching affection.

'He's just lonely, lonely and oversexed, though how he manages that with all the booze he takes on board I'll never know. He really did care for that wife of his. Couldn't stand watching her suffer but stayed with her right to the end and never touched a boy till she'd gone. What harm's the poor old bugger doing anyway? He pays them well enough.'

47

I had the distinct feeling I was being got at. I was also pretty sure Meadows was right. The rent boys weren't going to pack it in just because Joe Johnson stopped using them.

'So you'll keep quiet about this, then? And I mean quiet, not just not printing it in the paper. You start talking to people and they'll start talking to people and the news will spread and it'll be even worse than if it's appeared in black and white because I won't be able to sue and clear Joe's name.'

He was loyal, Harry Meadows, or at least loyal to his 20 per cent. The dance Joe must lead him, I reckoned Harry earned every penny.

'If I hear a whisper from anyone that people are saying Joe's a fag and goes with rent boys, I'll have you fixed. Properly and permanently fixed.' Harry was giving me another of his chilly grins. He only seemed to smile when he was making threats. If you didn't look into his eyes, you'd have thought he was enjoying a joke.

I picked up my carrier bag, shook Meadows by the hand, looked into those dead eyes and wished I hadn't.

'I'll not say anything,' I said. Naturally the tape recorder chose that moment to switch itself off with a decisive clunk.

For a moment we both stood rooted to the spot. Then Meadows made a lunge for the bag. 'You've been taping this, you bastard,' he screamed. I ran. Out through the door that he'd obligingly opened for me a couple of seconds earlier, down the passage to the top of the stairs. Harry came after me, shouting 'Stop him, stop, thief!' at the top of his voice. Even in my panic the thought flashed through my mind that he was quite right, that I was indeed a thief, stealing Joe Johnson's life and livelihood, what few scraps of comfort his disgusted existence offered him, carrying it all away in a Tesco's plastic bag.

I took the steps two at a time, but Meadows was more circumspect. Perhaps his knee was still giving him gyp. I knew I'd never make it through the front hall, with the Sloane at reception, the bell captain, the doorman and God knows who else, so at the first floor I turned off the steps and down a corridor, hoping to find the service stairs. I couldn't believe my luck. Glancing over my shoulder as I ran, I saw Harry limping on down the steps to the ground floor. The cries of 'Stop, thief' became more distant. There was a door at the end of the passage and I pushed it open. A different world. No carpets, no hessian-covered walls, no fox-hunting prints. Just strip lights, concrete steps and peeling paint. I went down slowly. At the bottom there was another passage, leading, I guessed, to the kitchens or the laundry room. There would be people there. I could try to bluff it out, pretend I was a guest who had got lost, but it would mean time and talk. By now Harry might have persuaded the management that there really was a thief on the loose. Then I saw the window. Four feet up but big enough to crawl through if it opened. I lifted the latch and pushed and it swung easily outwards. With some difficulty I pulled myself up so I was lying half in, half out, balanced on the sill. There was a pile of black plastic bin bags beneath me and I hoped they weren't full of empty bottles. The idea of jagged glass ripping into my hands and wrists made me weak. I dropped the carrier with the tape recorder in it and there was no clink of metal against glass. I shifted my centre of gravity, put my hands in front of me like a diver and landed in a heap on the bags.

Smelly but soft. I was in a yard at the back of the hotel. There was a high wall all round, topped with barbed wire, and a door in one of the corners. I ran over, turned the knob, pushed desperately, then pulled. The door opened. I was in a quiet residential street of handsome, stucco-fronted houses. I closed the door behind me and walked down the road, panting for breath and trying to look calm and inconspicuous. I looked at my watch. It wasn't even eleven yet. There was a busy T-junction ahead with cars going past. I made it to the corner with no one shouting at me to stop, and wondered whether to keep going or wait for a cab. I looked up the road and there was a black taxi with its yellow light on. Astonishingly it stopped as I stuck my hand up.

'Where to, mate?' asked the driver. I told him the Isle of Dogs. He closed the glass partition. A cab in the rain. A driver who didn't want to talk. I lounged back in my seat, reached for my cigarettes and matches, lit up, and thanked God with real sincerity. There was an angry tap on the window as I got the benefit of my first lungful. Grateful for the absence of one of those infuriating notices thanking passengers for not smoking, I'd somehow failed to spot the little round badge dangling from his rear view mirror with the even more tiresome legend 'YOU SMOKE. I CHOKE'. I threw the fag out of the window. 'Thanks a lot, God,' I said, and I meant it to sting.

The Embankment was traffic-jam free for once and I was back at the office by 11.30. Martha was in her lair, clicking knitting needles. 'Thanks for letting me know the interview was off,' I said calmly, trying to keep the snide out of my voice. She was gratifyingly disconcerted. 'I'm sure the editor will be interested to know why I've wasted half my morning.' Nasty, eh? I was feeling nasty.

'Sneak,' was all she said, not interrupting her knitting.

'That's right,' I said, and went up the stairs. Thanks to Martha I'd come close to being homosexually assaulted. Thanks to Martha I'd just been handed the most sensational story of my career on a plate. I stopped and turned round half-way up the staircase. 'It's all right, Martha,' I said emolliently, 'it can be our little secret.' She didn't even have the grace to look up, just shrugged to show she'd heard and couldn't give a toss.

The hacks were all hard at it when I went into the newsroom and JB was almost hidden behind an enormous pile of proofs. *Theatre World* hasn't caught up with new technology yet. The copy is all marked up and subbed by hand, and only then sent off to Clerkenwell for computer setting. On Tuesdays, Kim, Kevin, JB and I decamp for Clerkenwell ourselves, working in a cubby-hole office and on the floor with the lay-out people, subbing and designing the front four news pages, making final corrections and signing off the rest of the paper. It's a cumbersome process, quaintly antique in these days of on-screen page make-up, but it works and our hectic day at the printer's gives us the spurious feeling that we are somehow 'real' journalists rather than technology bores.

'How was the Big Cunt?' JB asked with a grin.

'The interview was cancelled. I got to the hotel at ten and his manager said he'd got food poisoning.'

'Couldn't face you asking him about Francis Bacon, I expect, and who can blame him, you old poser. Have we got anything to fill the gap?'

Kim looked up. 'There's that interview with Jeremy Isaacs we've been holding for a couple of weeks because it's so dull.'

'If only he knew,' said JB. 'The director of the Royal Opera House only makes it into *Theatre World* because Britain's filthiest comedian has gone down with a stomach bug. I like it.'

JB liked a bit of mischief. He was over fifty but wore his editorship lightly and without a trace of pomposity. His greying hair came down to his shoulders, though there wasn't much left up top any more, and he had a grizzled beard to match. His office uniform consisted of jeans and sweatshirts. If he was going out he'd nip into the Gents and change into a brown double-breasted suit with flared trousers or, if it was a posh evening do, an ancient dinner jacket that had an alarming greenish tinge to it. This was worn with an absurdly ruffled dress shirt, a huge purple velvet bow tie and a synthetic silk cummerbund. Whatever the outfit, he always looked like some ageing sixties rock star, too set in his ways to bow to the vagaries of changing fashion, still too much the old hippy to start shopping in Marks and Spencer like everyone else.

He had begun his career as *Theatre World*'s pop correspondent in the early sixties when Mr Torrington, newly installed as managing director following the death of his father, had decided that there might be something in all this pop music nonsense after all. Beatlemania was sweeping the country, the Rolling Stones were scandalizing middle-class parents by peeing against garage walls and refusing to climb on to the revolve at the end of *Sunday Night at the London Palladium* and JB was *Theatre World*'s freelance likely lad about town with his own weekly column, 'Fab Sounds Around'.

He'd joined the staff at the end of the sixties, worked as a reporter and sub for a few years and taken over the editorship in 1975. Like all the sixties pop stars he'd interviewed who'd talked about their ambition of becoming 'all-round entertainers', JB was an all-round entertainment journalist. There was nothing he liked more than some lefty new play at the RSC followed by a session at Ronnie Scott's, or a trip to the ballet before seeing some unknown band at the Marquee. Talent contests, West End premières, opera and ice shows; JB covered them all, in short reviews that managed to be both discriminating and benign. He was unmarried – it was hard to imagine any partner putting up with such a chronic addiction to showbiz – but he appeared to lead a vigorous sex life. Working late in the office one night before press day, I'd run out of cigarettes. A search of the desk drawers of the office's sadly dwindling band of smokers failed to produce the goods. 'Try JB's dinner jacket,' Kim had suggested. 'He brought it in this morning for that Covent Garden gala, then changed his mind and went to see Chuck Berry instead.' I opened the metal cupboard and felt in the pockets. Ah, just the job. But what I'd hoped was a packet of his favoured Embassy turned out to be a 12-pack of Durex with three left inside. Who was he planning to pull at the Garden?

As Kim got on to the Royal Opera's press office, I sat at my desk and thought for a bit, then eavesdropped on Colin as he picked up the phone. He was still working on the dodgy impresario story, indeed he appeared to have got a reply a côté de chez Regis. The whole newsroom stopped work. Even Victor came over from his desk in the corner and stood with a delighted smile on his face. Colin was talking in French, fractured, schoolboy French with an irredeemably English accent.

'Monsieur Regis, est il là maintenant?'

'Qu'est-ce que vous disez Madameoiselle? Monsieur Regis a retourné à son maison hier soir à huit, pardonnez moi, a vingt heures mais il et son femme ont quitté a neuf heures ce matin? Quand expecté vous qu'ils rentrerons?.

'Merde. Vous ne pouvez pas être sérieux. Pourquoi avez vous ne pas téléphoner comme je vous dites.'

There was a lot of indignant squawking at the other end. We couldn't hear it properly and I'm damn sure Colin couldn't understand it properly. Huffy Gallic pride in full flow. Eventually Colin got a word in edgeways.

'Merci beaucoup pour absolument rien,' he concluded with a fine flourish of colloquialism, then slammed down the phone. The newsroom gave him a spontaneous round of applause.

'Hidden talents, Colin,' said JB. 'Who'd have guessed we had such a cunning linguist in our midst.'

'It was the bloody nanny,' said Colin, oblivious as always to mockery. 'I got on to her yesterday afternoon when I'd checked on Regis's office. I managed to find his home number.' He tapped the side of his nose significantly, as if this coup had required particularly devious cunning. 'I made her promise she'd phone me either here or at home whatever time our friend finally got in. I spent all night waiting in for her to call.'

'But why did you think she'd bother?' asked JB.

'I promised her a tenner,' said the ace reporter.

'I see, I get the picture. Chequebook journalism, eh?' Unable to keep a straight face any longer, JB returned to his desk.

Colin looked sulky. 'It's a bloody good story,' he said to no one in particular. 'Bloody French bitch.'

I went over to JB's desk and asked if I could have a word with him in the boardroom. Everyone tried to look as though they weren't listening but I knew they were. Little chats with JB in the boardroom were usually only requested for two reasons – when people were trying to screw a rise out of him or else handing in their notice.

'All right, Will,' he said wearily.

We sat down at one end of the long table. He pulled a packet of Embassy out of his pocket, offered me one and lit us both up.

'You're not leaving us so soon? You seem happy here.'

'No, it's not that at all. I love it apart from the bloody Isle of Dogs.'

'Good,' said JB. He looked relieved and I was glad he was.

'It's this interview with Joe Johnson. I wasn't telling the truth a moment ago. I wanted your opinion in private.'

I told him about my visit to the Pimlico Court Hotel, not omitting the receptionist's crack about my balls.

The recording was amazingly clear, every profanity, every crash, every pounding foot on the carpet easily distinguishable. JB left his fags on the table and indicated that I should help myself as required. I found I was chain-smoking. Listening to it was almost as bad as going through it all over again, except at this remove the Big Cunt seemed less threatening and a great deal sadder. At times, I explained what was going on and at first JB chuckled a bit, though not for long. Joe Johnson's booze-fuelled despair chilled the heart.

'And then what happened?' JB asked when the tape ran out. I told him about Meadows' fury when he realized everything had been recorded, our chase down the stairs and my escape through the hotel yard.

'I'll tell you something, Will. That receptionist was wrong.'

I flushed with pleasure and was alarmed to find tears pricking my eyes. I greatly valued JB's good opinion.

'So what now?' he asked.

'Well, as I see it, there are three options. *Theatre World* could run the story.' I paused and JB shook his head.

'I'd much rather not. It's a good yarn, no doubt about that, but not our kind of thing at all.'

'Secondly, I could flog it to one of the tabloids. Joe Johnson's a bit of a folk hero at the *Sun*, they phone him up for right-wing quotes sometimes. But they wouldn't think twice about stitching him up. They'd love this, rent boys, child abuse, the fact he's just been on the children's charity show. And with the tape there's no worries about libel. He may be pissed but it couldn't be anyone else. I've got to be looking at a few hundred.'

'You'd be better off with the *News of the World*,' said JB. 'They might well splash it on the front with the full works on a double spread inside. It's only Thursday. They'd have time to confront Johnson with the tape, talk to some of the rent boys. If you played your cards right you could be looking at a lot more than a grand. I wouldn't stand in your way.'

It was all good, solid, even-handed advice. JB looked thoroughly depressed while delivering it.

'There's a third option,' I said.

JB looked a bit sick. 'You're not thinking of a spot of blackmail, are you?'

'Don't be daft. I mean we could do just what Harry Meadows said. Keep quiet. Forget the whole thing.'

'It's not because you're worried about the threats is it? A good personal manager like Meadows was bound to try that on.'

'Well, I can't say I'm over the moon about them. There's a certain authority about Meadows. But it's not that. Or I hope it's not. I was scared and trembly in the taxi but above all I was excited. It's a terrific story. Then I started thinking. Johnson may be an odious man but he's pathetic too and whatever you think, he's got talent. I was killing myself up in Scarborough.'

'I know, I've seen him myself. All very regrettable and all that, but like the man says, you gotta laff.'

'Why should I wreck his life? Half his act's based on slagging off gays. His audience would turn on him. They'd eat him alive.'

'Might serve him right, the hypocrite,' said JB.

'Come on JB. We all have little areas of our life we're ashamed of,' I said, thinking of the tear-drenched blow job. 'And we all say things when we're pissed that we'd rather die than admit when sober. Never mind seeing it all in print.'

JB didn't drink much these days but rumour had it that he'd hit the sauce pretty hard until a few years ago when his doctor had showed him the yellow card.

'You're right of course.' He looked uncomfortable, and took such a long last drag on his cig that it burnt the end of the filter tip. 'So you're just going to drop it, then?'

'Yes. It's not very professional I suppose, but sod it.'

JB looked relieved.

'I'm very worried about Colin, though,' I added. 'He's not going to let it drop if he hears about it. We'll get all the usual platitudes about never letting anything stand in the way of a good story.'

'Yeah, he can be a right pillock, and you can forget I said that. The trouble is there's no doubt he gets us a lot of good stuff. The nationals are lifting a couple of stories a week off us now, and more often than not they give us a mention. Doesn't do us any harm at all. But we'll keep quiet on this. If Colin gets wind of it, I wouldn't be at all surprised if he started doing a bit of digging himself. Or passed it on to one of the nationals as a tip.'

We agreed on a conspiracy of silence. Back in the newsroom, I made a big production number of suddenly remembering the tape recorder and getting it out of the bag as though it had never left it. I hit the eject button, removed the tape, and handed Colin his two hundred quids' worth of bugging equipment, putting the cassette in my top drawer. Colin was so mean that he'd insisted on me buying my own tape rather than using one of his. Otherwise he'd have wanted that as well. And I wouldn't have had time to wipe it.

'Thanks a lot, Col,' I said. 'Just as well I didn't need it. I'd probably have got it all wrong anyway.' Never apologize, never explain. Oh well.

'What was all that about with JB?' he said, trying and failing to keep the paranoid curiosity out of his voice. 'You were in there for ages.'

'Oh this and that, future strategy, forward planning, you know the kind of thing.'

He didn't, of course, because such meetings never occurred, not in the privacy of the boardroom anyway, but I knew the suggestion he'd been left out of something important would wind him up nicely.

I went over to the office edition of *Spotlight*, an invaluable directory – in five thick volumes – of virtually every actor and actress in the profession, and looked up Harriet Smythe. She had chosen a demure photo which made her look more like a deb announcing her engagement in *Country Life* than an actress slumming it in a profit-share on the fringe. A child bride. Harriet Smythe. Eyes blue, height 5ft 6ins read the accompanying text. Not much there.

I phoned her agent. 'Could I speak to Mr Simon, please?' I said, trying to sound like Peter Hall.

'Who's it in connection with?'

'Smythe, Harriet Smythe. I've just seen her giving a stunning Juliet at the Camden Basement.' There was more chance of getting through if it sounded like an offer of work.

There was a click on the line, and a longish pause before Simon came on, sounding eager but not too eager.

I found I was sweating. 'Hello. It's Will Benson of *Theatre World* here.'

There was a silence. Mr Simon clearly didn't believe in making things easy for wayward journos. I floundered on.

'I don't know if you've read my review of *Romeo and Juliet* at the Camden Basement?'

'I've read it,' he said. I waited for him to continue but he didn't. The ball was back in my court.

'Well, it's the most frightful cock-up,' I said.

'You're telling me,' he replied, with the faintest suggestion of humour.

'I wrote about a hundred words at the end, saying how good your client, Miss Smythe, had been.'

'I can't say I noticed them,' said Simon dryly.

'That's the point. They were cut. In error. The idea was to make the praise seem all the greater after the vitriol that had gone before. I mean, did you see the show?'

'At the Camden Basement?' He pronounced the words as if he'd just stepped in some dog shit. 'Life's too short, Mr Benson.' I found myself warming to him.

'I was wondering if it would be possible to have a word with Miss Smythe, so we could put a little piece in next week, saying how good she was as Juliet, how sorry we were that she'd been cut out of the review, what she's hoping to do next. You know the score.'

'I do, as you say, know the score. I also know that Miss Smythe is distraught. She phoned me this morning and told me to sue the paper. She is, as you know, very young. As indeed you've seen. I explained to her as patiently as I could that it would be fruitless to sue a paper that hadn't even mentioned her. Then the tears started. Part of the trouble is that no one else seems to have reviewed the production yet and Miss Smythe is convinced that it's a masterpiece. Well, the mainstream critics wouldn't go, would they, not another *Romeo and Juliet*, not at the Camden Basement. Your hatchet job is all they've had.'

'Shall I give her a ring then? Or you can get her to phone me here if you don't want to dish out her home number.'

Mr Simon had a better idea. Harriet Smythe had been cast in a big West End musical that was being produced at the Alhambra by Raymond Hawkes, one of my least favourite impresarios. There was going to be a big press conference to announce it tomorrow afternoon. Harriet would be there. I could meet her then and Simon would warn her I was coming.

'Who are the stars?'

'Sir Ian McKellen, for one,' said Simon.

'What, in a musical?'

'You've not heard the half of it yet. Anyway, she'll be there and I'll tell her to be polite.'

'Thanks a lot. I'm sorry to have caused so much grief.'

'She's got to learn to take the knocks. She's only twenty-two and she already thinks she's the best thing since Judi Dench.'

With an agent like Simon, who needed enemies? Still, presumably he'd got her into this new musical. We rang off cordially.

At one o'clock we set off for lunch at the Perseverance. Colin was in peculiarly odious form, bragging about how wonderful the Stephen Regis story was going to be. I also noticed that he seemed to be touching Kim a lot, tapping her on the back of the hand when he made a point, punching her roguishly on the shoulder when he told a joke. Kim didn't seem to mind nearly as much as she should have done, which made it worse. Unbearable, in fact.

'How was Cathy?' she asked quietly while Colin was breaking the habit of a lifetime and getting a round in at the bar and the others were playing pool.

58

'Too awful to tell you about now.'

'Fancy a quiet drink somewhere after work, then?'

'I've got to go to Romford. Talent contest. I don't suppose you'd like to come?'

She made a face. 'Talent show in Essex, chicken in a basket, as much cheap wine as you can drink and five different versions of "Memory"?'

'That's about the size of it,' I agreed.

'Yes, all right. You certainly know how to give a girl a good time, Will.'

I felt more pleased than I could say. Colin came over with the drinks. He'd brought me a half of bottled Guinness rather than the pint of draught I'd requested but I was feeling so bucked I didn't bother to complain.

'Will's taking me to a talent contest in darkest Romford tonight,' Kim told him.

'Well, if you want to be bored rigid, that's your business,' he said sullenly.

'Yes it is, isn't it?' said Kim sweetly. A nice vote of confidence in us both, I thought.

'What happened with Cathy, then?' Kim asked as we walked to the car park that evening.

I told her the grisly details of my drunkenness, sparing myself little. The only bit I censored was my lachrymose ramblings about Kim and her tits, confining myself to 'And then I started going on about how much I liked you.' Kim, however, seemed embarrassed even by this edited version.

'God, thanks for bringing me into it. Bloody cheek,' she said, very frostily for her.

'Sorry, Kim. It's true though.'

She went quiet, and gripped the steering wheel tighter than ever. I pressed on.

'So then I watched Cathy pack and we went and got a cab for her. I don't even know where she's staying.'

'I'm sorry, Will. Mind you, even by your own account, I can't say I blame her.'

'Nor me. It was time for it to end. I just wished I'd managed it with a little more grace and then remembered that I'd done it.'

She gave me a sisterly squeeze on the knee and I longed to stick my hand up her skirt. When she'd decided to come to the talent show, Kim had realized she could hardly attend in jeans and rugby shirt, so she and Barbara, who dressed like a high-class tart, had amiably swapped clothes for the night. She looked terrific. I could hardly take my eyes off her leather mini-skirt, I had a hard on and I didn't know what to say next. I tried to look busy with the road map.

'The club's coming up soon, I think, just off the A12. Yes that's it, we turn off at the next roundabout.'

Kim slammed on the brakes as a kid on a bike wobbled across the road and the large *A to Z* fell off my lap. Kim glanced down, then back at the road.

'What was it Mae West said?' she asked, as if apropos of nothing in particular. '"Is that a pistol in your pocket or are you just glad to see me?"'

'I'm delighted to see you,' I said, blushing furiously.

'Good,' said Kim, her face a picture of innocence.

The Essex Showbar was an old thirties roadhouse, a rambling mock-Tudor establishment that appeared to have known better times. Huge posters in dayglo green and orange adorned the brickwork, advertising the weekly attractions.

Monday: Heavy Metal Nite with DJ Trev Brooklyn
Tuesday: Hen Night featuring Toni, the Italian Stallion
Wednesday: Miss Wet T-Shirt Contest
Thursday: Search for a Star. Grand Final. Fabulous Prizes
Friday: Strolling Back to the Sixties with Radio Basildon's 'Diddy' Dudley Ferguson
Saturday: The Best Disco in Romford. Ladies Free Admission before 9pm. Happy Hour 7–9.30
Sunday Lunchtime: Strip Tease. Local Lovelies Welcome

'We've got the wrong day,' I said, pointing at the sign. 'I'll bring you along Sunday lunchtime.' Kim stuck her tongue out.

It was dark inside, and the smell of the afternoon's disinfectant operation in the Gents lingered unappealingly. The DJ was playing Take That and the audience, many of them looking like loyal mums and dads, sat grimly at their tables, munching their way through pallid piles of chips in plastic wicker baskets. A few hard lads were putting away large quantities of lager at the bar and laughing without a trace of good humour; the competitive, derisive laughter of blokes tanking up before trying to pull a bit of stray.

The manager, a youngish man sporting a dinner jacket and an incongruous crucifix earring, was among them. One of those landlords who spent more time on the customers' side of the bar than helping his staff behind it. It was 7.30 and he seemed half pissed.

'I've come for the talent contest – one of the judges,' I told him.

'Right.' He gestured towards a woman sitting alone at a table on a raised platform.

'Over there. I've nothing to do with it except to see you get enough to eat and drink.' He turned back to his unlikable mates.

Kim and I wandered over to the platform. The woman was blonde and encumbered with large quantities of gold jewellery which hung heavily from her neck and wrists. I introduced myself and Kim.

'How honoured we are, two correspondents from *Theatre World* to grace our humble little competition,' she gushed unpleasantly. 'I'm Susie Smiles. Used to be on the stage myself. Legit of course. But in recent years I've concentrated more on personal management. But I like to keep busy and when we saw this place I said to my dear husband Bernard, "What about running a little talent contest here, dear, to make a change from all that dreadful music and those naughty, naughty ladies."'

Susie's attempt at spraying girlish innocence and excitement all over us was somewhat spoilt by the rigidity of her smile and her neurotic fiddling with a cigarette with a white filter and a showy gold band. The much-lifted face was virtually unlined but her hands were those of a woman emerging from the wrong side of middle age.

'Would you like Kim to be a judge as well?' I asked.

'But of course she must join our happy band,' said Susie. She had made her first mistake of the evening and looked as if she instantly regretted it. She carried on gamely nevertheless. 'Darling Gerald Harper was due to come but he had to cancel yesterday.'

I bet he had, I thought. Though come to think of it, I bet he hadn't. Darling Gerald wouldn't be seen dead in a place like this.

'I played with him, you know,' she said dreamily. 'I gave my Beatrice to his Benedick. One of my finest performances and Gerald, well, as you can imagine, he was superb. And such a generous co-star—'

I didn't think I could stand much more of this treacle. 'Who else is on the judging panel?' I put in quickly before she started reprising some of her favourite speeches.

She looked miffed at being stopped in mid-flow. I could imagine her delivering a chilling 'Kill Claudio'.

'Well, there's me of course, as chairperson. You two and dear Billy Walter. Books a lot of the holiday camps, or holiday centres as I suppose we must learn to call them. And finally we have last night's lovely winner of the Miss Wet T-Shirt competition.'

Hardly a panel of Bookerish distinction, I thought.

'There's a wonderful first prize of three thousand pounds plus a week-long residency at the Talk of Catford for the lucky winner,' breathed Susie as if it was a pools jackpot, birthday and holiday all rolled into one. 'Supporting', she added, as if this really put the tin lid on her munificence, 'the fabulous Freddie Starr.'

By now we were sitting at the table, making inroads into a warm bottle of Essex Showbar House White (Medium). The other judges drifted in. Billy Walter was reassuringly fatter than me and not much older. He had the unhealthy pallor of a man who spent his life in dives like this, feasting on things in baskets.

He exuded large quantities of sweat and a faintly absurd *joie de vivre* that nevertheless seemed genuine. Miss Wet T-Shirt, whose real name was Maureen, wasn't wearing the garment that had brought her to this acme of showbiz glitz. She was crammed into a demure floral frock that was doing an all too efficient job at concealing her winning features.

'I'm never wearing a bleedin' T-shirt again,' she squawked indignantly when Billy joshed her about the missing garment. 'It's no bloody fun having buckets of water sloshed all over you and a load of morons gawping at your tits.'

Neither Billy, Kim nor I had the courage to ask why she'd gone into the competition if she felt so strongly about it, but after a pause for breath, Maureen volunteered the information herself.

'Still, seven hundred and fifty smackers. I'm not grumbling. Well, not that much anyway. I'm gonna take my old mum on holiday in January. Tenerife, somewhere hot like that, while you're all freezing your balls off here.' She was all right was Miss Wet T-Shirt.

We ate our scampi and chips and drank too much. As we were tucking into our orange sorbets in a scooped-out orange, bullet hard and with a chemical taste that seemed to take a layer of skin off the roof of your mouth, Susie gave a little speech.

'I know it's normal on these occasions to issue everyone with voting forms, and have specific marks for content and star quality and so on, but that would be so dreary for you, much too much like hard work, and this is meant to be a FUN evening after all. So what we'll do is go into a little huddle after the show, and everyone can award marks out of ten to each act, a total of fifty from the five of us, and we'll decide the winner like that.'

'Oh good,' said Miss Wet T-Shirt. 'I'm terrible with figures.'

'With a figure like yours,' put in Billy with elephantine gallantry, 'you add up a treat, sweetheart.'

'Oh piss off, you old scumbag,' said Miss Wet T-Shirt with a giggle.

This was all the encouragement Billy needed. He clamped

his hand on her knee. Amazingly Miss Wet T-Shirt didn't seem to mind a bit.

Susie had exhausted her stock of bright and vacuous chit-chat, and was betraying signs of real nerves as the coffee came round, chain-smoking her St Moritz and knocking back the Château Essex Showbar as if it were lemonade. At last her husband, Bernard Williams ('Smiles is a stage name, darling'), who had introduced himself to us briefly before busying himself backstage, walked up to the microphone, an emaciated figure with a gaunt face and a bald head. His bright red cummberbund and mauve dress shirt did little to relieve the chilling impression that one was gazing at the skull beneath the skin.

'Welcome to Essex's glittering heart of show business,' announced the walking *memento mori* without a trace of irony. 'We've got a wonderful bill for you tonight, ladies and gentlemen, and all the acts have already fought their way through the punishing rounds of preliminary heats. If you like them, please give them a warm round of applause. And if you don't, you can still give them the clap.' This last dreadful jest provoked a couple of mild titters from the sycophants in the audience and a bell-like peal of laughter from his wife. Bernard introduced 'our distinguished panel of judges' and got Kim's name wrong. Then, 'without further ado', it was on with the show.

As talent contests go, it wasn't much, and as talent contests go, it went. A fat ugly girl sang 'Memory' very well, and a thin and pretty one sang it very badly. By way of variety, a mediocre-looking girl sung it competently. The 'saucy dance troupe' Felicity's Follies minced and ground their way through a selection of pre-recorded dance music in leather bondage gear and were, Bernard assured us, available for 'stag functions' when their act was 'even hotter, you know what I mean, fellahs'. A likable, and for the most part rather good young magician looked close to tears when the deck of cards he was shuffling fell all over the stage, and a cockney comic came on and told a few blue jokes with an obnoxious exuberance that made one think kindly of Jim Davidson. He was followed by a pop group called Kinda Kinky who performed a set of Kinks' cover versions with real panache and enjoyment, the lead singer getting Ray Davies's nasal drawl off to a tee. Any group that performed 'Waterloo Sunset' as well as they did were going to get my vote and I nodded at Kim at the other end of the table, who nodded back and winked. Susie was busy whispering into Miss Wet T-Shirt's ear and Billy, who was sitting on the other side of her, had by now moved his hand several inches up her thigh.

The final act was an Elvis Presley impersonator, 'the other EP, Mr Eric Preston' announced Bernard Williams. There's always an Elvis impersonator, the Las Vegas Elvis, all rhinestones, bared chest and sobbing false emotion. This one was a particularly embarrassing example of the benighted species since Mr Preston experienced considerable difficulty in singing in tune and forgot the words of 'Love Me Tender'. Bernard had given him a far more enthusiastic build-up than any of the other acts, had indeed gone as far as suggesting that Eric Preston was a rather more impressive performer than Elvis himself. 'What a star, ladies and gentlemen, what a star,' he cried as Preston lurched off stage.

I made my excuses and went for a slash before adjourning to the manager's office for the voting. Billy, his questing hand temporarily untethered from Miss Wet T-Shirt, joined me at the adjoining urinal.

'You realize this is all a fix, of course,' said Billy, shaking his willy.

'You what?' I said, zipping up my flies.

'The competition's bent. Old Ma Smiles and her corpse of a husband have been running this scam for six months now. They go all over the country, finding run-down clubs like this one and offer to organize a talent contest, for a fee of course, and the club puts up the prize money as well. Well, all the local deadbeats enter but darling Susie always puts in one of her own acts – they manage half a dozen, including our friend EP who, by the look of him tonight, has been putting too much sherbet dab up his nose. Then they pack the jury. There's always someone above board like you, editor of the local paper or something, to make it look respectable. But then there's someone like me, more often than not it is me, though I expect she's got her hooks into a few others, and some little innocent like the lovely Maureen who can be persuaded to play the game. You probably missed it because you were on the other end of the table, but Susie's been softening her up all evening. You know: "I'm sure I can get you some modelling work, dear, you'd be a natural, and oh, by the way, do look out for Eric Preston, he's terribly, terribly good and I'm sure you'll want to give him a good mark."'

'Why are you telling me all this? You don't exactly come out of it smelling of roses.'

'Sad story. The thing you've got to know about Susie is that underneath all those false smiles and the sentimental swill about her great career as an actress, she's as thoroughgoing a bitch as you're ever likely to come across. And devious with it. She'd got a young singer on her books, a very young singer as it turned out, I met her at a show like this in Yarmouth. I was the innocent member of the panel then, being bought with a bribe. Susie told me how much I'd like this girl and how she knew she'd already taken a fancy to me. I took her back to the hotel after the contest, which naturally I'd helped ensure she'd won, though she wasn't that bad actually, certainly not as bad as Preston. The following morning Susie rang and said she was sure my employers and the police would be interested to know I'd been screwing an underage girl. She said that as we spoke my little friend was making an affidavit and if I wanted it kept locked up in her safe, all I had to do was act as a judge at a few more talent contests.'

'Nice,' I said. 'And neat. Does the T-shirt girl come as part of the Susie Smiles service?'

Billy looked embarrassed but not embarrassed enough to stop him putting a quid into the condom machine and purchasing three mint-flavoured Mates.

'Yeah, I s'pose so. She sometimes arranges these little extras to keep me sweet. She's told Maureen I've got a lot of contacts

66

in the modelling business. In fact I think I heard her telling the poor bitch I was David Bailey's brother-in-law.'

'I still don't see why you're telling all this to me. It's too good a story not to print.'

'I want you to print it, matey, provided you keep me out of it. I met that scrubber of a singer the other day in a pub. She said no hard feelings and she was sorry she'd caused me so much aggro, but Susie had been putting the pressure on her too. Apparently she'd never made an affidavit and had no intention of doing so. What's more, she'd just had her sixteenth birthday. Susie's got nothing on me and I want to see the cow's udders well and truly wrung. Anyway, that Kinks band were good. It would be nice to see a decent act win one of Susie's contests for once.'

'Is there any way we can make sure they do win though?'

'There's two of you. Susie hadn't reckoned on that and I can see she's worried about it. If you both give Eric Preston nil punt the maths has got to be working against her.'

'What about you?'

'I want the story in *Theatre World* to be a nice little surprise for Susie but I'll give him a low score if it looks as if there's any danger of him winning.'

'Well, thanks a lot, Billy. I suppose we'd better get back to the voting. Won't Susie or her husband suspect you've been dishing up the dirt if we go back together?'

'It's OK. I said I'd got to make a call and I'd do it from my car since it was quieter.' Billy looked distinctly sheepish. 'I said I was going to ring my photographic brother-in-law as a matter of fact. You go up now and try and put that sexy little girlfriend of yours quietly in the picture and I'll follow you up in a few minutes.'

Billy went out to the car park and I scribbled a few words in my notebook and went up to the office. Old skull-face was there, together with Kim, Miss Wet T-Shirt and Susie. None of them seemed to be enjoying themselves though Susie was doing her best to reconnect the supply of gush. 'Oh, Mr

Benson,' she trilled when I came in. 'You've been such a long time we thought you'd got lost.'

'Bit of a dicky tummy,' I said. 'I don't think that scampi agreed with me.'

'I'm not feeling so good myself,' said Miss Wet T-Shirt, coming to the aid of the party.

Skull-face looked suitably apologetic. 'Is there anything I can get you?'

'A brandy normally does the trick,' said Maureen sweetly. 'A large one.'

She was nobody's fool. I wondered what Billy's chances were.

'I'd like one too,' said Kim.

'Me, too,' I said.

Williams went out with the order and I went over to Kim and sat down next to her on the sofa.

'Kim, you remember that interview I did with Joe Johnson this morning?' I said, digging her gently in the ribs so she didn't say, Whatdya mean, it was cancelled. 'I'm having trouble reading back a bit of my shorthand and I wondered if you could have a look. You're better at T-line than I am.'

I opened my notebook on a page containing an old interview. At the bottom, written in much neater shorthand, I'd put a few extra outlines.

'Look, it's this bit,' I said, pointing at them.

$$7 \; \hbar \, \smile \, \cdot \, \gamma \, o \, \jmath \, \imath \, \vec{o} \, \vec{}^{\jmath} \, \vec{\zeta} \, \vec{\mathcal{K}} \, \omega \, o$$

For a horrible moment I thought she was going to read it out loud. Susie, her suspicions raised, or perhaps it was just habitual paranoia, came over to have a good look at my notebook too.

'My goodness, it looks like Arabic,' she said. 'How clever of you to write like that.'

'It's reading it back that's the problem,' I said.

'Oh, I don't know, Will,' said Kim. 'I don't think that bit's too hard. It says: "I've always hated that fat bastard Elvis Presley. Fucking useless twat." Typical Joe Johnson I'd say.'

It didn't actually say that at all. What I'd scribbled in the Gents was: 'The talent contest is a fix. Give no marks to the

Elvis Presley impersonator.' Kim was simply letting me know she'd got the message.

'So it does. Thanks a lot, Kim.'

Billy came back, swiftly followed by Williams with the drinks. He'd brought one for everyone. The one he handed to Susie, who hadn't even asked for one, looked like a quadruple. Before the voting got under way, Miss Wet T-Shirt endearingly announced that she was tone deaf so her marks might be a bit unpredictable.

'Don't worry, gorgeous,' said Susie, 'it's star quality we're really looking for and I don't think there's much doubt about who was the real star tonight.'

We went round in turns, with Bernard totting up the marks on a pocket calculator. He was acting as a judge himself, though Susie hadn't previously announced him as a member of our 'happy band' and it seemed a strange task for the MC.

Kim and I gave high marks to the Memory girl who could sing and low marks to the one who looked good but couldn't. The magician got fives and sixes from everyone apart from Maureen who gave him nine. 'I thought he was reely sweet,' she explained.

There was no doubt however that the big battle was going to be between Kinda Kinky and Eric 'You'll Believe You're Seeing Elvis Live' Preston.

Susie and her husband had cleverly arranged matters so they gave their votes last. Since Preston was also the last act on the bill this meant that with a fair wind they ought to be able to ensure his victory while keeping the result unsuspiciously close.

'And now to Kinda Kinky, yet another of those sixties revival bands,' said Susie with a sneer in her voice and a significant look at Maureen. We went round yet again.

'Billy?'

'Eight.'

'Maureen?'

'Six.'

'Will?'

'Ten,' I said, and got a nasty look.

'Kim?'

'Ten,' she echoed, and got an even nastier one.

'Bernard?'

'Four.'

'I'm afraid I'm only giving them two,' said Susie. 'So unimaginative.' This was pretty rich coming from a woman whose favoured candidate was one of a veritable army of clones, and a defective clone at that.

'That makes forty,' said Bernard. It was easily the highest score so far.

'And last but by no means least, Eric Preston, the fabulous Presley impersonator,' said Susie. 'Billy?'

'Six'.

Susie looked at him narrowly. 'Are you sure, dear? Are you sure you feel absolutely safe with that mark?'

Billy smiled charmingly. 'Absolutely safe, thank you, Susie.'

'Maureen?'

'Ten, well I did say I was tone deaf, didn't I,' said the T-shirt girl, knowing which way her bread was buttered but registering a token protest nonetheless.

I'd been doing my sums and hoped Kim had too.

'One,' I said when Susie asked me for my score. Susie looked daggers but kept quiet.

'And Kim, dear?'

'Two,' said Kim, whose mental arithmetic was spot-on after years of casting off copy for length.

We were home and dry. If we'd had to write down our marks confidentially, as at any properly organized talent contest, it would have been far more difficult. Susie and her hubby could simply have doctored the score and no one would have been any the wiser. They'd been screwed by their own bent system.

Bernard was sweating a lot and Susie was lighting another cigarette with her dinky little lighter.

'Darlings,' she said. 'I cannot imagine that your editor would be delighted to learn that you'd given a class act such low marks.'

Kim's dander was up. It happened rarely, but when it did, it was impressive.

'What do you mean a class act? He couldn't sing in tune and he forgot the words, for Christ's sake. I'd make a better Elvis than he does and I don't believe that yarn you were spinning me before he came on about his mother dying of cancer last week. He looked quite cheerful over at the bar earlier on. If you can call a drunk yob cheerful.'

I silently prayed that Kim's righteous indignation wouldn't extend to declaring that the contest had been rigged. Like Billy, I wanted to surprise Susie with the story. I also wanted to get out of the Essex Showbar in one piece.

'Yeah, I suppose he was a bit wonky,' said Miss Wet T-Shirt. 'Do you know, on second thoughts, I'd like to change my mark.'

'Quite impossible,' snapped Susie. She turned to Kim and me. 'Are you certain you won't change your marks?'

Maureen gasped loudly at this brazen inconsistency and Billy whispered in her ear. Susie was too occupied with us to notice while Maureen looked first shocked, then amused.

'So you're not going to think again?' said Susie.

'No,' said Kim and I as one.

'Well in that case we'd better get on with the presentations.'

Bernard gave a discreet, Jeeves-like cough. 'I think we ought to vote, Susie, just for the form of the thing. I give Eric ten.'

'Ten,' snapped Susie.

Bernard tapped away at his calculator. 'That makes thirty-nine,' he said, as if anyone needed telling by now. 'Kinda Kinky are the winners, Eric Preston the unlucky runner-up by one point.'

'An exciting contest, wasn't it?' said Maureen mischievously.

Susie, looking as if she'd just swallowed something nasty, icily suggested that we might as well go downstairs to bring 'this disgraceful fiasco' to a conclusion.

She and Bernard took to the stage together and the rest of us stood at the bar. Bernard spouted all the usual guff about what a close and thrilling contest it had been and how much trouble the judges had had in reaching their decision.

'I should coco,' Maureen yelled rebelliously. I looked around and noticed with pleasure that three of the lads were making their respective advances on the three Memory girls. I suspected that the one chatting up the prettiest had drawn the short straw, however much he might be congratulating himself on his good taste. She looked bored stiff, and frigid and petulant with it. The ugly one giggled as her swain smacked her cheerfully on the bum and bought her a large gin and sweet Martini. She'd got a nice smile and would probably go like the clappers. I was glad Kim and I had given her a good score. Bernard had finished now and Susie had taken over.

'And the third prize goes to an extremely talented young magician, he's come all the way down from Hull to take part. Ladies and gentlemen, a big hand please for Mr Philip Larkins.' Young Phil collected his cheque for a hundred quid with every appearance of pleasure and then pretended to drop it. I had high hopes of Mr Larkins. I hoped he had a girlfriend who was taking pills or wearing a diaphragm.

'And the second prize of two hundred and fifty pounds goes to Eric Preston, the brilliant Elvis Presley impersonator.' Susie was doing her best to keep the anger out of her voice, but it wasn't quite enough. There was a hint of broken glass in the honey.

Eric, I noticed, was at the end of the bar furthest from the stage, in the middle of getting his round in. He'd changed out of his Elvis costume but as he turned round on hearing his name, his lip curled in disgust and he looked like Elvis for the first time all night, the young, dangerous Elvis.

'Someone's cocked up,' he said, quite audibly, to his attendant crowd of admirers. It took him ages to reach the stage as he forced his way sullenly through the throng at the bar. When Susie gave him his cheque, he didn't even have the grace to say thank you but turned on his heel and headed straight back to the bar.

'And finally, tonight's very lucky winners, who receive three thousand pounds and a week's residency at the Talk of Catford – Kinda Kinky.' Susie put the emphasis on 'very lucky' and pronounced the band's name as if handling verminous sheets with tongs. Her smile was a silent shriek.

The band shambled on, still in their sixties collarless suits. Susie gave the cheque to the Ray Davies soundalike and when he smiled I was pleased to see his gappy grin bore a remarkable similarity to that of the Bard of Muswell Hill.

'Thank you, Romford. Thank you, Romford!' he yelled in a passable imitation of a stadium superstar. Susie was giving him little prods in the small of the back, desperate to get him and the rest of the band off and bring the débâcle to as swift a conclusion as possible. I looked round and saw that Eric Preston's friends were buying him snakebites now. Susie probably wanted a word before he passed out.

'Well, that brings the contest to a close, ladies and gentlemen,' said Williams. 'But the bar stays open until 1 a.m. and Trev Brooklyn will be along soon to play all the platters that matter.'

'One more drink?' I asked Kim.

'Why not, I'm way over the limit already.'

I got her a large gin and tonic and a Scotch for myself.

'So what's going on?' she said.

I began to tell her, then saw Susie making a beeline for us after her little chat with Eric Preston. 'You two are looking very pleased with yourselves to say you can't tell class from crap,' she said, and it was hard to reconcile this bitter old crone with the ghastly girlishness she'd been exhibiting earlier. I marginally preferred this real Susie to the fake version.

'I'll be in touch with your editor tomorrow morning to tell him about your deliberate attempt to sabotage the contest.'

'Rather more than an attempt,' said Kim. 'As you may have noticed, we got a result.' She smiled enigmatically into her gin and tonic. 'And, funnily enough, our editor was only telling me the other day how much he rated the Kinks.'

Billy Walter came over with a bottle of champagne and Maureen in tow. I was glad of their company. Susie didn't look capable of containing her rage for much longer.

'Well, thanks for a most interesting evening, Susie,' he said.

73

'I've just been talking to Kinda Kinky. I'm booking them for a tour of the holiday centres. Let's have a drink on the strength of it.'

Susie looked as if she was about to vomit. 'I'd sooner drink piss than drink with you,' she said, very Beatrice and Benedick. She started to leave on this exit line, which suited me fine, but then she turned back for a parting shot with her smile more or less back in place.

'Do take care on your way home, Will and Kim. You've both had a great deal to drink and I should hate to think of you running into any trouble.'

It was time to go. We drank the champagne in less than ten minutes. Billy, like the gent he was, offered to drive Maureen home.

'No, let's go back to your place. Mine's a tip.'

Billy looked uneasy. 'You don't want to believe all that rubbish about my brother-in-law, you know. I haven't got a fucking brother-in-law. I know sod all about modelling.'

'I never thought you did,' said Maureen. 'It's your body I'm after, not your contacts.'

'My lucky night, then,' said Billy with a smirk.

We made for the exit and Billy's Granada. On the way he gave me his card.

'Can I ring you tomorrow?' I asked as he opened the door for Maureen.

'Sure,' he said. 'Not too early if you can help it.'

He winked at Maureen who told him to get a bloody shift on.

'About eleven suit?' I asked.

'Fine.'

They drove off and we lurched towards Kim's Mini.

'Are you all right to drive?'

'Never better than when pissed,' she said.

'I don't think it's wise. I wouldn't put it past old Ma Smiles to take your number as we leave and phone the filth. I didn't like that last crack of hers.'

'Shit. What shall we do?'

'Phone for a minicab. You can leave the Mini in the car park and get another to bring you here tomorrow.'

'It'll cost.'

'I think JB will sign the exes when he's heard this story.'

'How did you know it was fixed?'

'Let's get the cab first.'

We didn't. We were in a dark section of the car park, about five yards from Kim's car. A battered Escort stopped near us and three men climbed out and surrounded us. I wasn't at all pleased to recognize Mr Preston and a couple of the blokes who'd been buying him snakebites.

'Beat it, bitch,' said Eric. Kim looked indecisive.

'Better do as the man says,' I croaked.

She ran to the Mini, climbed in, turned it round so it was pointing straight at us and turned the headlights on full beam. Nice work. If the boys wanted to do any beating up, they would have to give a public performance. People were drifting out of the Showbar fairly regularly now. Inside, Trev Brooklyn was playing 'Lola'.

Preston and friends looked bemused. They were well pissed but hadn't entirely thrown caution to the wind.

'I hear you've been a naughty boy, Mr Benson,' said EP at last. The *Minder*ish cliché and the fact that he pronounced Benson 'Benshon' cheered me up a little. Our Eric had been watching too much telly. He was fake hard, not real hard.

'What do you mean?' I asked.

'Susie's told me the full SP and you're well in the frame,' he said.

Jesus wept.

'Well it's a fair cop, guv, I gotta put my hand up to this one, I done the blag.' It was the booze doing the talking.

Eric grabbed me by the shoulder and pushed me against the side of the Escort.

'You taking the piss or what?' he slurred.

I resisted the temptation of telling him that with an act like his he was more than capable of doing that himself. It was only a matter of time before the boots started going in.

'There's not much we can do here now that tart's turned the lights on,' said one of Eric's mates.

'Round the back,' said Eric.

I'd been wondering when they'd think of that. Rather cleverly Eric and a friend put their arms round my shoulders as though assisting a drunk. To help the pantomime, the third gave me a crafty punch in the stomach so that I doubled up and staggered. No fun at all.

It was then that Kim went into action. With the recklessness of 16 units of alcohol sloshing around inside her, she put her car into first and screeched towards us with her hand on the horn. The people walking back to their cars all looked our way. For a moment I feared she'd blown it and wouldn't be able to stop in time. Preston and co. certainly thought so. They jumped to one side. In my winded state I moved rather less swiftly to the other. Kim jammed on her brakes and stopped a foot or so from where we'd been standing and threw open the passenger door. Eric and the lads were on the other side. They tried her door, but Kim had locked it.

'In you get, Will. Quick as you like.'

I half fell, half jumped in, slammed the door and locked it. Kim revved up, just missed another couple who were strolling back to their motor and made it to the car park exit. I looked back. Eric and his friends were in hot pursuit, though surely they couldn't catch us now.

Kim turned right and, back in nervous granny mode, drove at a stately 25 m.p.h. towards the A12. My breath was coming back but I'd started to shake.

'Bloody hell, how many James Bond films have you been watching recently?'

'All part of the service,' she said smoothly.

I was still concerned that Susie or the boys would phone the police. Getting someone done for drink-driving would be right up their street. It was well past midnight and on the almost empty A12 we were much too conspicuous for comfort.

'Look, there's a sign for Barkingside. Let's turn off and see if we can find a minicab office open,' I suggested.

Kim was actually driving pretty well, all things considered, though she clipped the kerb as we cornered. She cruised down a shopping parade and we spotted a cab firm on the right-hand side. We drove past, turned into a side street and parked the car. It was uncomfortably hot inside the office, and the strip lights glared down unkindly on the battered furniture and the cigarette-scarred carpet. A large middle-aged woman sat behind a desk with a microphone.

'Where to?' she asked.

'Vauxhall, please,' I said, and Kim gave me a look. 'Then on to Stockwell.'

After a couple of minutes, a driver turned up, a Rastafarian in an ancient Ford Cortina. Sober, he drove far more heart-stoppingly than Kim when pissed.

'You don't mind the music, man?' he said above the blare of lovers' rock.

'Not a bit,' said Kim.

'All right to smoke?' I asked, grasping for my Camels.

'Any shit you like, man,' said the Rasta, and laughed immoderately. I lit up and Kim asked for one too. I'd never seen her with a cigarette before.

'I used to smoke a lot when I was doing my proficiency course, up to five a day at one time.'

I watched her fondly as she coughed on her first drag, but she persevered, holding her fag in that endearingly amateurish way of the irregular smoker.

'Stop gawping at me and tell us the tale, for heaven's sake.'

I described my conversation with Billy in the Gents in as much detail as I could. Kim was a good listener and I warmed to my theme.

'What a story,' she said when I'd finished. 'Particularly if you describe the judging session and the heavy stuff in the car park afterwards.'

'I'll have to be a bit careful. Billy doesn't want his name in the paper and I can't say I blame him. I'll talk to him tomorrow and find out how far he's prepared to go and whether he can put us in touch with anyone else to stand the story up.'

Without really thinking about it, I put my arm companionably round Kim's shoulder and she didn't seem to mind at all.

'Thanks for saving me from a bashing up.'

She kissed me chastely on the cheek.

'You've got a funny enough face without a cauliflower ear and a black eye to go with it.'

The driver lit up a five-skin joint which he'd rolled, with amazing dexterity, at a red light.

'You don't mind?' he inquired above the strains of Bob Marley.

'Not if we can have a hit ourselves,' said Kim.

'That's cool,' he said. He took a couple of deep lungfuls, then passed the joint back.

This time Kim dragged away like an expert, holding her breath to get the full benefit.

'Don't tell me. You took a lot of drugs on the local paper as well.'

'That's right,' Kim giggled inanely.

We were in the City now, driving through deserted streets. I took a couple of puffs myself, felt a bit sick and passed it back to the driver.

Swearing Kim to secrecy, I told her about the Big Cunt and my chat with JB. It already seemed a very long time ago. She laughed a lot and it sounded funnier in the telling than it had seemed at the time.

'You really must promise not to tell our Col. I don't trust him an inch.'

Kim looked hurt. 'You know I wouldn't,' she said. 'His nose is going to be badly out of joint over this talent contest story anyway.'

We cruised along the Embankment, the lights shining on the Thames at full tide. Even the National Theatre looked quite attractive against the dark sky with its science-fiction glow of reflected sodium street lights.

'Do you want to come in for coffee or a drink?' I asked.

Kim knew I meant, do you want to spend the night, and answered as if I'd said just that.

'I'd love to, Will, but I can't. Everything's all fucked up at the moment.'

I looked at her and she was crying, quietly, the tears flowing easily down her cheeks. I got out my handkerchief and wiped them away and she sniffed a 'thanks' and snuggled her head into my shoulder.

'Don't say anything, Will, don't ask any questions. Just hold me tight till we get to your place.' It was no trouble at all.

We crossed Vauxhall Bridge and I gave the driver directions to Rita Road.

'Do you want me to come with you tomorrow to pick up the car?' I asked.

'No, I'll get a cab, pick it up and drive straight to work. I don't want a lot of gossip about us arriving together. Can we have lunch tomorrow? Just the two of us?' she added.

'Natch. Sure you won't come in?'

She looked me in the eye. 'Believe me, Will. I really want to. But I can't.' She spoke in a husky voice with a residual trace of a Newcastle accent, which I was beginning to love so much.

'The Godfather?'

'I'll tell you tomorrow.'

We were parked outside my flat now. I kissed Kim and she responded with astonishing fervour, as if in agony, the tears running down her cheeks again. You could taste the salt. I wanted to stay in the aching whirlpool of her mouth for ever.

'Come on, man, you wanna fuck you get out the cab and pay the fare just like everyone else,' said the driver cheerfully.

'No, I want to go on,' said Kim, disentangling herself. 'Brixton, please.'

'Not Stockwell?' I said, then realized that wherever Kim was calling home now, I ought to see her to it. I offered but she refused, insistently. She put a finger to my lips.

'We'll talk tomorrow. Lunch.'

I climbed out of the cab, waved her off and hoped our amiable driver wasn't a rapist in disguise. Once inside the flat I had a spasm of self-fury that I'd poured the rest of the Famous Grouse down the sink, then remembered that a couple of months earlier I'd hidden a quarter bottle of Bells behind the Dick Francis paperbacks on the bookshelf. I'd never sleep tonight, I was too tired, too excited. I poured a treble into my favourite tumbler, put the Grateful Dead's *Skullfucker* on to the record player and lay on the sofa and thought about Kim, and fat comics and Gerald Harper's Beatrice. I finished my drink, toyed with the idea of having another and decided not to, washed, brushed my teeth and managed to take all my clothes off before getting into bed. Cathy would be proud of me, I thought, then remembered that Cathy wasn't around to be proud of me any more. I felt bereaved. Was it possible to be in love with two people at the same time, I wondered. The easiest thing in the world, I answered myself, and turned off the light.

Friday

The Weekend Starts Here

It was the sort of autumn morning old men write about in their memoirs, bright sun, blue skies, every object crisply defined by a wonderful clarity of light. I'd slept well and felt unusually crisply defined myself.

Going up the steps at the office after giving Martha the curtest of nods, I almost collided with Colin who was coming down two at a time.

'The nanny's just phoned. He's back and he's having a lunch party at his house in Barnet. I should catch him just as he's putting the champagne on ice.' In Colin's hack's-eye view of the world, impresarios never drank anything but champagne. He looked as though he'd had a couple of glasses himself, positively euphoric.

'Has the cab come?' he yelled as he bounced through reception.

'It's just arrived,' said Martha with unprecedented solicitude. 'Good luck with the story.' Colin, never high on my Christmas card list, dropped right off it. Someone who had wormed his way into Martha's barren affections must be an even bigger creep than I'd previously suspected.

Upstairs, JB was looking insufferably pleased with himself. 'Just had that nasty piece of work Susie Smiles on the line. She says you and Kim were disgustingly drunk last night, gave top marks to a duff act and deliberately voted down by far the best performer in the show.' He rubbed his hands together gleefully. There wasn't a hint of reproach in his voice.

'You haven't heard the half of it,' I said, and filled him in with the gory details, as well as explaining why Kim would be a bit late for work that morning. JB knew Billy Walter and looked sorry when he heard the hold Smiles had had over him.

'We must respect his wishes and keep him out of it,' he said when I'd finished. 'But we can hardly have an anonymous source blowing the whistle without anything to back it up.'

'I've been thinking about the best way to go about it,' I said. 'I'll get Billy to give me the details of all the contests he's been on that have been fixed. For a start we can check if all the winners are on Susie's books. That's bad enough – the organizer of a talent contest entering acts she manages and then sitting in judgement on them. Then if we go through the cuttings we should be able to find reports of a few more contests she's been in charge of. If we look at them together you might spot the odd act you think should have won. Some of them may have done a bit of digging themselves and they might talk, or their agents might. If Eric Preston's won any others, they'll almost certainly have an idea of what's been going on. Preston appears to be permanently out of his head and he's a right old blabbermouth.'

It doesn't often happen, but when it does it's marvellous. The story just fell into place. For once, almost everyone I phoned wasn't only in but ready to talk as well. After looking through the cuttings, JB kindly asked if I'd mind if he did a bit of sleuthing himself. 'It's your story, Will, your by-line, but I'd like to lend a hand. I've had my doubts about Susie Smiles for some time and some of these results are astonishing.'

I said I'd be delighted to have his help and then phoned Billy, who sounded tired but cheerful after his night with Maureen. 'Absolutely fucking knackered' was how he put it. I reluctantly interrupted his rhapsody on pneumatic bliss and got him to fill me in on the other contests he'd helped fix. I told him, too, about the other Susie Smiles events we'd found in the cuttings. Three had been won by the great Eric Preston, and another three by a magic act called the Mighty Vizier and his Eastern Promises. The other contests had been won by odds and sods, but a glance at the *Show Business Directory* revealed that all of them had one thing in common. They were all represented by Smiles Better Personal Management.

'Who was judging the contests I wasn't on?' asked Billy.

One name appeared in all the reports, Freddie Stanbrook, manager of the Tottenham Cabaret Club.

'Well devious, our Freddie,' said Billy. 'But not a goer. Entirely asexual as far as I can make out. And clever. I can't think what kind of hold Susie could have had on him. He was probably on a cut of the prize money, unlike poor muggins here.'

Billy gave me the names and numbers of a couple of acts who'd failed to win thanks to his and Susie's efforts. One of them was a girl Billy felt particularly guilty about, a gifted singer pipped at the post by Eric Preston. When I got through she revealed that EP had told her exactly how he'd won while charmingly trying to persuade her of the merits of a quick knee-trembler round the back of the club.

'I told him to get stuffed. I don't think his heart was in it really. He was practically incoherent by then.'

JB came over, looking like an excited 52-year-old schoolboy. 'I've just been talking to one of Susie's winners,' he said. 'Nice lad, young cockney comic called Tony Brown, doing a season at the Blackpool Big Nite Out. I've seen him a couple of times. He's good.'

'If he's good, why does he need an agent like Susie?'

'That's just the question I put to him. He said he'd no idea the contest was bent when Susie suggested he went in for it and he was mighty surprised when he saw she was on the panel of judges. He demanded an explanation at the end and Susie calmly asked for half the prize money. "You don't honestly think you'd have won without my help," she told him.

'Tony was sure he'd have won anyway and was furious she'd fixed it. He resigned from Smiles Better on the spot, gave half his winnings to the girl who came second just in case she might have won and signed on with someone else. He says he's been doing far better since. Apparently a lot of bookers won't touch any of Susie's acts because they know most of them are rubbish and have a pretty shrewd idea of what's been going on at the talent contests. I'm enjoying this. Haven't used the old shorthand for ages.'

JB returned to his desk and I rang the lead singer of Kinda Kinky, whose number Billy had given me. He called himself Roy Davis. Without the 'e'.

Apparently things had got even rougher at the Essex Showbar after Kim and I had made our speedy departure. After failing to stop us, EP and his thugs had staggered back to the celebrating members of Kinda Kinky and told them they'd fucked up a nice little earner (the Arthur Daley touch again) and they weren't going to get away with it. A fight had broken out.

'Great it was. Me and the rest of the band were sober, more or less, but Preston and his lot could scarcely stand before they started and they certainly couldn't by the time we'd finished with them. We got out just before that lousy drunk of a manager woke up enough to call the cops.'

'Quite a night then?'

'Yeah. You heard we'd got the HoliDaze tour?'

'Yes, congratulations.'

'Just as well, really. Susie Smiles has already found something in the small print that means she can cancel our week at the Talk of Catford.'

'Who needs it. Stick with Billy Walter.'

'We intend to. Nice guy. So we'll be reading all about it then? In your Autumn Almanack?'

He really was obsessed with his master's voice.

'That's right. Next Thursday.'

'Great,' he said. 'I'll order a few copies.'

My next call was to the Mighty Vizier. I told him about what had happened in Romford and the story we were working on.

'Oh Christ,' he said, 'Eric bloody Preston. You'd better phone Miss Smiles.'

'We'll be doing just that, Mr Vizier,' I told him. He slammed the phone down.

'Do you think you could bear to phone Susie?' I asked JB after telling him the latest. 'It'll sound much better coming from the editor. She might even do something really silly like offering you a lot of money to keep it out of the paper.'

'Nothing I'd like better.'

While he was dialling, Kim came in looking a bit strained. I asked her if she'd picked up the car all right.

'Fine. No heavies. You still on for lunch?'

I certainly was. She sounded depressed but I was more concerned about listening to JB who had Smiles at the other end. He was doing a good impression of the prosecuting counsel in an old courtroom drama.

'I put it to you, Miss Smiles, that you have been consistently rigging the talent contests you organize: entering your own acts, packing the jury and then taking a cut of the winnings. Let's not be mealy-mouthed about this – organized fraud.'

There was a lot of squawking at the other end and JB moved the receiver a couple of inches from his ear for quite a while before speaking again.

'Very well, Miss Smiles. Thank you, Miss Smiles.'

He put the phone down and grinned at Kim and I.

'She's rattled. She said if we printed one word of the "disgraceful allegations" I had made, she'd sue.'

'No bribes then?'

'No, just a lot of sound and fury. Mind you, when she's had a little think about it, as she will, she may have second thoughts.'

Victor wandered in, wearing his favourite outfit; a beautifully cut dark grey pinstripe suit, bright red silk waistcoat and the salmon pink and cucumber green Garrick Club bow-tie that clashed with it so horribly. A hint of Poirot-like wax gave his moustache an even jauntier air than usual.

'Going anywhere special?' asked JB.

'They're announcing that new musical at the Alhambra this afternoon. Thought I might totter along and pick up a story for the diary.'

I asked Victor if I could tag along too and explained about Miss Smythe.

'Delighted to have your company, boy,' he beamed.

I went to my desk and searched in the top drawer for the spare packet of fags I usually kept there. A nice unopened packet of plain Camel. I try to smoke tipped most of the time but you can't beat the burn of the old *sans filtre*. Then I realized something wasn't there that ought to be. The Joe Johnson tape. I rifled through the other drawers but knew I'd left it in the top one, just under the press release for the Alhambra launch. The editor's secretary usually came in at nine, an hour earlier than the rest of us. How could I put this tactfully?

'Julie, was Colin in when you arrived this morning?'

'Yes, he was in the conference room. I didn't realize he was there until just before ten when he came out. He went straight off to see that producer Stephen Regis.'

Or straight to the *News of the World*, I thought gloomily. But perhaps I was doing him an injustice. Surely even Colin couldn't flog someone else's story. Yes he could. But it seemed a shame to spoil the good humour in the newsroom. Colin might have pinched the tape, might have listened to it, but he might not be going to do anything about it except gloat and call me an idiot for sitting on so good a story.

'I was going to take Kim for lunch if that's OK,' I said to JB. 'A longish lunch, actually.'

He got out his wallet and handed me a note. Fifty quid.

'Have a drink on me.'

'That's an awful lot of drinks, even by my standards.'

'Go to the Pagoda,' he said. 'You'll not get any change out of that. You've earned it, both of you. Get the taste of Susie Smiles and Eric Preston out of your mouths. There's no point in trying to write the story until Monday and you've broken the back of it now.'

It was 12.30.

Kim and I walked round South Quay to the Pagoda. With the sun shining, the Isle of Dogs looked almost beguiling. The restaurant was way out of our usual class, a stylish brick tower surrounded by water on three sides and trying, quite success-fully, to look like a legacy of the old docklands while actually having been built in 1989. Inside, the waiters were smarmily attentive, and there was a different kind of orchid in the middle of each gleaming white tablecloth.

'Well, it makes a change from the Perseverance,' said Kim. She was trying to sound jolly, and failing.

We consulted the menu. Fish soup and turbot for Kim. A dozen oysters and the lobster for me. It was kindly meant but JB's fifty quid wasn't going to come close to covering it.

'Screw the cost, let's have champagne,' I said. 'I've got my Access card and it should just about be able to stand the strain.'

'I'll pay my shout,' said Kim.

'No, just for once forget fair play and being one of the lads and let me treat you.'

'Oh, all right.'

She looked and sounded horribly depressed. The cork popped, the waiter poured and Kim drained most of her glass in one greedy swallow. 'Come on Kim, what's the matter?' I asked.

˙ She covered a piece of toast with *rouille*, put a lot of cheese on it and sank it to the bottom of her soup.

'Well, it's none of your business really.'

'It's up to you of course,' I replied, hurt. 'But last night you seemed sorry not to come back to the flat and you certainly hinted that all would be revealed today.'

'True enough,' said Kim. 'I've changed my mind, that's all'.

I sucked at an oyster and crushed it against the roof of my mouth with my tongue. It reminded me of spending a day by the seaside and was almost as good as sex.

'I don't know how you can eat those foul things, it's like swallowing a great lump of salty snot,' said Kim.

'Let's talk about something apart from your private life and my lunch,' I suggested stiffly.

'All right. Sorry.'

It wasn't too bad after that, though apart from the quality of the food we might just as well have been in the Perseverance with all the others. The warmth and intimacy of the previous night had gone. Kim was at her most determinedly chappish. I told her I was going to the Alhambra that afternoon with Victor and that Harriet Smythe would be there.

'You'd better have some more oysters, Will. Put some lead in your pencil.'

'Oh, cut the crap, Kim,' I said wearily.

'I'll cut the crap if you get another bottle.'

'Champagne?'

'No, it's a grossly overrated, overpriced drink and it always gives me an acid tummy. How about a Pouilly Fumé?'

She could be a pain in the arse sometimes, but she'd got taste. Then she snapped her fingers at the waiter. You couldn't take her anywhere.

'Bottle of Pouilly Fumé as soon as possible,' she commanded.

The waiter looked down his nose at her and repeated the order as if she'd just requested a couple of bottles of methylated spirits.

The lobster and the turbot came and went, and so did the Pouilly Fumé. We ordered half a bottle of Côtes de Rhone to go with the cheese.

'Such a sexy, dirty taste, cheese and red wine,' said Kim with a sexy, dirty laugh. She was well lit-up now.

'You know the Godfather and I have gone our separate ways?' she added with studied casualness.

I repressed a surge of excitement.

'He's quite a nice bloke, actually.' It was the warmest tribute I'd ever heard her pay him.

'What's he really called? I've completely forgotten.'

'Oh, so've I,' she giggled. 'Marmaduke Clarence, actually'.

'Blimey, what did you call him at home? Not the Godfather, surely?'

'No, Dukie. All his friends call him Dukie.'

'Sweet,' I said and didn't mean it.

'He is quite sweet. Most of the time.'

'That black eye—'

'No, you can forget that. I'm not a victim of domestic violence. Demestica violence more like. He's got some Greek friends he met on holiday years ago and they came round one night with a lot of Greek wine and retsina. It got quite riotous. We started smashing plates on the kitchen floor and dancing. I was going to the fridge to get some mineral water, skidded on a bit of broken plate and bashed my head on the dresser. I was out cold for a couple of minutes apparently, and woke up in Dukie's arms. He looked scared to death.'

I found I wasn't much enjoying this heart-warming account of life with Kim and Dukie.

'So why the separation?' I asked.

'Well, he can be dreadfully moody, really foul sometimes. But then so can I. The real problem was he wanted to have kids and I didn't feel ready for them. Not his kids anyway. He flushed all my pills down the lavatory one night and I had to go over to Barbara's at midnight to get some more. When I got back we had a huge row about it and because I was so furious I told him I was having an affair with someone else. Just to hurt him. And then I got into my little Mini and drove to Brixton.'

I ought to have been feeling sympathetic about this sad story. I really knew I should be, and I made sympathetic little aah-ing sounds as Kim related it. But by far my strongest feeling was exhilaration. Cathy gone, the Godfather gone. What could be more natural than we poor orphans of the emotional storm clinging together for comfort?

'When did all this happen, Kim?'

She held my gaze. 'About two months ago. We don't all have to wear our hearts on our sleeve like you do.'

Well, that put me in my place. I suggested a brandy.

'Calvados,' said Kim. 'Large ones.'

The waiter gave a contemptuous Gallic shrug as we ordered and I asked for coffee as well. It was 2.30 and I was feeling pretty pissed. I'd better try to sober up for Miss Smythe. Calvados fumes on top of that review were going to create a wonderful impression on that highly strung talent.

'There's more to come, Will,' said Kim.

I should have felt a sense of impending doom, but I didn't. Not then.

'I told you last night that things were all fucked-up.' She toyed with her drink, took a sip, put it down again.

'I feel a real cow, Will. When I told Dukie I was having an affair, I said it was with you. So it was pretty hypocritical of me to get ratty when you said you'd been babbling on about me to Cathy.'

Well, it was but I didn't mind a bit. Kim saying she was having an affair with me seemed almost as good as actually having one. What could be easier than turning her fiction into the truth? I could hardly wait to suggest doing just that but Kim was still in full flow.

'Dukie was furious. Called you a fat bastard.'

I had met the Godfather only once, at a one-off *Theatre World* cricket match against a bunch of actors in which he'd saved the honour of our side with an impressive 84 not out. I'd been out third ball for a duck. I thought we'd got on pretty well in the pub afterwards. Fat bastard, indeed.

'He said he'd kill you,' said Kim. 'I don't expect he will.'

The Bensons are a brave breed. 'Just let him try,' I said. I ask you, cool or what?

'How about taking the afternoon off and going back for a place?' I slurred. The booze was really kicking in now.

Kim looked genuinely puzzled. 'I think I've had enough fish, thanks,' she said.

I stumbled on, conscious that the Calvados had suddenly tipped the balance and that I was now scarcely capable of getting a coherent word out.

'What I meant,' I said slowly, negotiating the words with extreme caution, 'was how about taking the afternoon off and going back to bed at my place.'

It was, of course, at this moment that the waiter chose to come over to see if the alcoholics on table eight wanted another drink.

'Oh hello,' I said as he swam into view. 'It's you again.'

Kim ordered two more Calvadoses and refills of coffee. I was in no mood to stop her. I looked at my watch. Ten to three. We'd have to be quick if I was to get back to Victor and tell him

I wouldn't be joining him after all. Or I could give him a ring. That was the best idea. All the time in the world, then.

Kim was looking at me with almost maternal concern.

'I still haven't finished, Will. Things are more complicated than you think. I'm seeing Colin.'

The booze was acting like an anaesthetic, the message wasn't getting through to my alcohol-sodden brain.

'What's so complicated about that? We're all seeing Colin, more's the pity, every day of the working week.'

'Don't be thick,' said Kim. '"Seeing" him, you know what I mean, I don't need to spell it out for you.'

Oh, so that was it, was it, of course I knew just what she meant now. So naturally I pretended I didn't.

'Seeing?' I said, screwing up my face into what I imagined to be an expression of bewildered but patient inquiry. It probably looked more like a sneer.

'Oh, for Christ's sake,' said Kim. 'Sleeping with him, fucking him.'

I looked around wildly but the waiter appeared to have missed his cue for once, missed the best line of the lunch. It wasn't entirely wasted, though. One of the shiny suits at the adjoining table was looking our way, indeed he'd half turned his chair round to get a better view. He'd heard all this coming long before I had. His eye caught mine but he didn't seem remotely embarrassed, just nodded affably, cheerily raised his glass and returned to his raspberries and cream.

My stomach was lurching while my hands trembled uncontrollably. I tried to pick up the glass of water which I hadn't touched throughout the meal and slopped half of it on the tablecloth. I put it down again with a bang and shoved my hands in my pockets.

'Are you all right, Will?' said Kim.

'Never better,' I said. 'I hope you'll both be very happy together.' It came out sounding far nastier than I'd meant it to. Kim looked distressed.

'How long has this been going on?' I asked.

'A couple of weeks, ten days.'

'Are you sure you weren't telling the truth when you told the Godfather you were having an affair, you know, and just changed the names out of an entirely understandable sense of embarrassment?'

Kim's eyes filled with tears. My whole body was trembling now and I was curiously breathless. I couldn't seem to get nearly enough air into my lungs. I wanted to hit Kim, hit her hard, hurt her, bruise her. Then part of my mind seemed to float up into a corner of the restaurant, up among the fancy cornice coving near the ceiling, quite detached, looking down at the quivering wreck below. So this was what sexual jealousy was like, I observed, this was the emotion that betrayed Othello into strangling Desdemona. For the first time it all seemed quite logical. My separate self calmly noted that the rest of me was in the grip of the strongest emotion I had ever experienced. It was overpowering and entirely negative. Goats and monkeys, indeed.

'Goats and monkeys,' I hissed out loud.

I was seeing double, two of Kim's face, both of them looking worried.

I found I couldn't speak, but knew I had to stand up, get out. I nearly knocked my chair over as I staggered to my feet but caught it with a dexterity that astonished me just before it fell. Now everything seemed to be happening terribly slowly. I began to cross the miles of carpet to the lobby. After what felt like hours, I made it into the cool marble spaces of the Gents and suddenly felt better. I looked at myself inquisitively in the mirror. No sign of any horns. Quite normal, in fact. Cheerful almost. I grinned, embarrassed by my own reflection and the madness that had touched me.

'You're all right, Will,' I said, reassuring as an elderly country doctor. I splashed water on to my face, remembered that I'd been wanting a pee for ages, had one, and washed my hands carefully. I looked at my watch. Unbelievably it was still only five to three. Victor hated being kept waiting so I went to the phone in the lobby, dialled *Theatre World* and told him there had been a change of plan and I'd join him at the Alhambra.

'Good lunch, eh?' he cackled.

'Out of this world, Victor,' I said.

I walked back to the restaurant. Kim was looking sad and solemn and, suddenly to me, almost unbearably lovely.

'Sorry about that,' I said. 'One of the oysters must have disagreed with me.'

'Are you all right? At least you've stopped shaking now.'

'I'm OK,' I said and then it all came flooding back.

'Why Colin, Kim?,' I said. Whimpered really. 'No wonder he was pawing you in the Perseverance and looking so fucking smug. Christ, I'm not sure I can bear to hear about it.'

Kim talked quietly, calmly, her voice almost expressionless. 'I was in the office the other Monday, working late. You'd gone to that wretched *Romeo and Juliet*. Colin was working on a story. There were just the two of us. He went to the toilet and I suddenly felt so lonely and miserable I burst into tears. You know I do that sometimes.'

I nodded. 'Usually when you've had a skinful,' I said.

'I was sober this time. Colin came back, saw I was crying and it all came flooding out about Dukie.'

Dukie. For Christ's sake, I thought, Dukie.

'Colin was sweet, he really was.'

I bet he was.

'We went down to the Perseverance and had a couple of drinks. He's not nearly as bad as you think, Will, he's very insecure—'

'Spare me the do-it-yourself psychology,' I cut in and she bridled.

'How do you think he feels? He's a good reporter but you're JB's little favourite. Barbara and Mirza hate his guts. You despise him quite openly.'

Like a man picking painfully at a scab, I found I'd got to have all the gory details.

'So how did he get you into bed?' I asked, my voice not quavering all that much.

Kim had clearly had enough and looked at me with undisguised hostility.

93

'He didn't. I got him into bed. When the pub shut I suggested having another drink in Brixton and we took it from there. He's surprisingly good, you know. In bed. Very imaginative. Very virile. Very considerate.'

She'd meant it to hurt, and it hurt like hell. I went on burning my few remaining bridges with exhilarating recklessness. I picked up my half-drunk glass of Calvados and swigged it back. I felt quite sober now. Calm and capable.

'And last night? After the talent contest? When you seemed so fond and upset. Was dear little Col waiting up for you with a mug of cocoa?'

'He was very upset that I went at all. We'd half planned to go and see a film. I gave him a key. I didn't know if he'd be there or not when I got in last night. He was. He's very keen. I think he's in love with me, or thinks he's in love with me. He certainly says he's in love with me. I don't want to hurt him. As I said, he's very vulnerable. And sweet.'

But we still hadn't got right down to the nitty gritty.

'We still haven't got right down to the nitty gritty,' I said.

'For God's sake, Will, what more do you want, the size of his cock, the number of times he came last night?'

It was like a bucket of water in the face.

'I couldn't give a toss about you and Colin. You can go to bed with Victor for all I care. You'd probably like that. To judge by the Godfather you like older men. Colin's just a boy. No, what I want to know is whether you told Colin about the Joe Johnson interview while you were enjoying your post-coital cuddle? He's nicked the fucking tape.'

She looked stunned, though whether by my spite or Colin's felony or the idea of screwing Victor, I couldn't guess.

'Of course I didn't tell Colin,' she said quietly. 'I promised.'

I believed her. No doubt at all. Kim was a girl of honour. It was one of the reasons I loved her.

'I don't believe you,' I said. Well, why not? What's the point of trying to save the sinking ship when you can kick an even bigger hole into it?

'There's no way Colin could have had any idea about what's

on that tape unless you told him. You felt guilty when you got back to Brixton and found him there, guilty about all the cuddles and the kisses and standing him up, so you gave him this nice little bit of information to make amends. And Colin got up bright and early this morning, went to the office, listened to it on his dinky little tape recorder and is probably even now playing it to a delighted assembly of tabloid hacks, naming his price.'

'I didn't,' she said, and the tears were rolling down her cheeks and dropping on to the tablecloth.

'Why should I believe a word you say?'

Kim dabbed her eyes with the edge of the tablecloth. 'Oh, Will' was all she said.

We sat in silence for a couple of minutes and I watched her grave face staring at the table. I thought about her and Colin, then tried not to think about her and Colin but couldn't stop, and kept imagining them, in bed together, him sucking her tits, her sucking his cock, him coming into her from behind. It was like some hideous pornographic film, with me trapped in the middle of a row of men in dirty raincoats, unable to get out into the fresh air, unable to turn it off.

'Why don't you piss off,' I said savagely. 'I can't bear to sit here with you any longer. I'll pay the bill.'

She got up at once. Came round and kissed me on the forehead. I'm sorry, Will,' she whispered. 'I really didn't tell him.'

I wanted to touch her, hold her, tell her how sorry, how ashamed I was. No words came. I stared straight ahead and watched her go. At the door she turned, smiled, the bravest smile I ever saw, and blew me a kiss. I looked right through her. She was full of grace and I was full of shit.

The waiter came over and asked if I wanted anything else. I looked at my watch again. It was ten past three. Twenty minutes since I'd suggested taking the afternoon off and going back to my place.

'Just one more large Calvados and the bill, please,' I said.

95

'And could you order me a cab for as soon as possible, going to the London Alhambra?'

It was amazing how sober I sounded and felt. I seemed to be getting drunk every couple of minutes and then instantly sobering up again. I lit a plain Camel and counted the butts in the ashtray. Nine of them. Not bad going, Benson, I congratulated myself. The waiter brought the Calvados and the bill, £168, excluding service. Worth every penny, I thought. The lunch of a lifetime. I gave him my credit card, and sipped my drink. By the time he'd brought the docket for signing I was drunk again, scarcely able to hold the pen to write. With the magnanimity of the seriously inebriated, I rounded the bill up to £200. It saved on the mental arithmetic. Ten per cent of £168 was £16.80. But what was £168 plus £16.80? That was a tough one, Magnus. When he saw the size of the tip the waiter smiled for the first time.

'Thank you, sir. Your taxi's waiting outside. Hope you enjoyed your meal.'

I couldn't be nice to Kim but it was the easiest thing in the world to be nice to him.

'Absolutely delicious. Thanks a million,' I said.

As I got out of the cab at the Alhambra, Victor was emerging from the Tube. He looked absolutely bushed.

'You rotter,' he said with a heroic attempt at good cheer. 'You might have told me you were getting a cab. We could have shared.' I mumbled apologies and, slapped him on his frail shoulder.

The press conference was in the Alhambra's Cinderella Bar, all pink lights, huge mirrors and posters of ancient variety bills. The PR man, Danny Timson, was at the door with a visitor's book. He was a cynical old hand, much given to maligning the shows he was meant to be promoting.

'You're not going to believe this one,' he said out of the corner of his mouth. 'Oh, I see you've brought your granddad along, that's nice.' Victor had gone off into one of his little trances, giggling madly to himself as he looked at the posters. 'Sign the senile old fucker in,' said Danny. 'He's not going to wet himself, is he?' Timson sounded genuinely concerned, always a sure sign that he wasn't. When he had a decent story to give you, or was complaining about *Theatre World*'s coverage of something or other, he adopted a tone of such elaborate irony that it sounded as if he was having you on.

I picked up the pen, signed in Victor and myself. I was writing better now than when I'd dealt with the credit card but I was making silly mistakes. Name and publication were OK, but I found I'd put my home address rather than *Theatre World*'s. It looked as though Victor and I were co-habiting but I couldn't be bothered to put it right.

'Have you got a press pack, Danny?' I asked.

'After the announcements,' he said. 'That fuckwit of a producer Raymond Hawkes wants it all to be a big secret to whip up a bit of suspense. He's like a bloody kid with a new toy.'

I went over to Victor. 'You see this poster, boy,' he said. 'Marie Lloyd in pantomime here. I saw that show myself. Remember it as if it were yesterday. Wonderful talent, Marie Lloyd. They don't make stars like that any more.'

I looked at the poster more closely. It was for the Christmas season of 1890–91.

'Are you sure you mean this particular pantomime, Victor?'

'Course I am, boy.'

Even Victor wasn't over a hundred, though in my alcohol-fuddled state I suddenly had a nightmarish conviction that perhaps he might be. No, of course he wasn't. I didn't have the heart to point out his mistake and steered him away from the poster before he saw the date himself and started worrying about whether I'd seen it too.

'The bar's open, Victor,' I said with what little gaiety I could muster. There were about thirty journalists lounging round it, making the most of Mr Hawkes's hospitality. All the serving staff, men and women, were wearing kilts, and looking thoroughly embarrassed. Something Scottish, then. *Brigadoon*? Surely not. I asked Victor what he fancied. He consulted his watch.

'Mmm, five to four. What's the best drink for this time of day, I wonder?'

If anyone knew it would be Victor. He did.

'Crème de menthe, boy. On the rocks. With a dash of Worcester sauce. A double, naturally.'

I shuddered and went to the bar. 'A large crème de menthe on the rocks with Worcester sauce, please,' I said, embarrassed to be giving so bizarre an order. 'And a double Scotch,' I added. 'No, make that a double Glenfiddich.' The drinks were free, after all. I knew that I needed a large malt like I needed a week's camping holiday with Colin, but it was too late to stop now. I couldn't face the horrors of sobriety. I handed Victor his ghastly concoction and he ambled off to talk to a female journalist who was almost as old as he was. 'A beautiful woman in her day,' he leered as he left me. 'Many's the lunchtime legover I've had with her.' As so often with Victor, I didn't know whether to believe him or not.

I stood at the bar, tried not to drink too fast, tried not to think about the last few awful hours. There were a couple of showbiz reporters on the other side of the room whom I vaguely knew but I couldn't face talking to anyone. Suddenly my back was violently slapped and I choked on my whisky. A rheumy-eyed cove in a battered leather jacket and a mustard-coloured kipper tie, circa 1971, was beaming at me with his hand outstretched.

'Bill Benson, isn't it, *Theatre World*?'

I recognized him and didn't bother to put him right about my first name. We'd met at the previous year's *Royal Variety Show*, that annual trial by light entertainment, and had a few drinks together at the press reception afterwards. He worked on the *Sun*, I thought. I couldn't remember his name.

'Johnny Jewel,' he said.

'Great to see you, Johnny,' I gushed as if greeting a long lost friend. Why on earth was I doing that, I wondered. It was coming back to me now. He'd become thoroughly maudlin at the end of that long, long evening, and confessed that his biggest ambition in life was to go to bed with Sarah Brightman.

'Why that bastard Lloyd Webber threw her over I'll never know.'

'How's life on the trade press?' he asked patronizingly after ordering a gin and tonic and sinking his face into it.

'Oh, not bad. And how's Wapping?'

'Bloody as usual.'

Definitely the *Sun* then.

'Any joy with Sarah Brightman?'

He looked pained. 'A word to the wise – don't intrude on a private grief, old son.'

'Do you know anything about this show? I suppose there must be a lot of tits in it, if you're interested?'

He looked distinctly miffed. 'What do you mean?' he said, instantly shedding all trace of his irksome jocularity.

'Well, it's what your lot are interested in, isn't it? Tits, sex scandals, confessions of the soap stars.'

'Have you gone out of your mind?' said Johnny Jewel, suddenly sounding very cross indeed. My stomach gave another of the sickening lurches that were proving such a feature of the afternoon. Johnny Jewel. If it hadn't been for the Calvados I'd have recognized the name, which was presumably why he'd taken such pleasure in announcing it. A senior correspondent of *The Times*. Only a part-time piss artist and now standing very much on his dignity. Oh, shit. Get out of this one, Benson.

'I've just made a frightful mistake,' I said. 'I'd somehow got it into my head that you worked for the *Sun*.'

I didn't add that his kipper tie, saloon bar matiness and lurid fantasies about Sarah Brightman had reinforced that impression.

'I think it would behove', he began. Oh Christ. 'A reporter on a trade rag like yours to know something of the correspondents on our great national newspapers who labour in the same vineyard,' he said. I suddenly felt terribly tired. How much worse could today get?

'I think it would behove you to stop talking like a pompous prat and piss off,' I said. Not Oscar Wilde standard, certainly, but it made me feel a lot better. I warmed to my theme. 'I think it would behove you to take off that ridiculous tie and take it down to the Oxfam shop where it belongs. I think it would behove you to stop using ludicrous phrases like "I think it would behove". I think it would behove . . .'

I suddenly found myself at a loss for words. A quiet cry in the Gents seemed called for. 'Can I get you another drink?' I asked politely.

Jewel said nothing.

'Sorry,' I said. 'I'm a bit pissed.'

'So much is evident,' said the man from *The Times*, before turning smartly on his heel and hailing a couple more congenial labourers in the vineyard. No doubt he would tell them about the dreadful young man from the dreadful trade rag and they could trample all over me in my absence. I realized I didn't give a toss, really didn't give a toss for once, and was about to order another drink when the air was rent by an appalling shrieking, the kind of noise feral cats make when they're killing something in the middle of the night. Bagpipes. Six pipers paraded into the room, then all the lights went out except a single spotlight illuminating a small stage at the end of the room furthest from the bar. A curtain parted, and Raymond Hawkes stepped up to the microphone stand, the most oleaginous impresario in the business, the man who had once solemnly declared that musicals were his whole life and there was no greater privilege than playing a part in the industry of human happiness.

'Ladies and gentlemen,' he said in his curiously high-pitched voice, running his hands through oiled silver hair with a thoroughness that made one dread the possibility of having to shake hands with him. 'It gives me the greatest pleasure to announce my next show, which will open in this theatre next spring: *Macbeth, the Musical.*'

Then the spotlight went off and we were left in complete darkness. A tune was played over a powerful public address system. It sounded oddly familiar. A bit like 'Memory', a bit like 'Don't Cry for Me, Argentina', a bit like Paganini, a bit like Verdi, a bit like almost everyone you could think of really. There was no doubt about it. Sir Andrew Lloyd Webber was going to do for Shakespeare what he'd already done for T. S. Eliot. By now there was a chorus of female voices.

'Fair is foul, and foul is fair:
Hover through the fog and filthy air,'

they carolled. After some time the singing stopped and the light went back on stage to reveal the smirking Hawkes. 'That, ladies and gentlemen, was the show's opening number, a classic in the making I hope you will agree. I would now like to introduce our creative team. Sir Andrew Lloyd Webber, Mr Trevor Nunn, and our stars Sir Ian McKellen and Miss Cilla Black.'

It was even more ghastly than anyone had any right to expect. Sir Andrew came out looking even more boyishly bashful than usual. 'It's great to have a new lyricist. I've tried the rest, now I've got the best,' he jested. 'William Shakespeare.' I regret to report that some of my fellow hacks laughed at this as if it was the best gag they'd heard for weeks.

Trev, looking trendy in a black suit, whispered that he saw this as a real, a very real opportunity to bring Shakespeare to the widest possible audience. With a budget of £5 million it would be the most expensive Shakespearian production ever mounted, anywhere. I could see no sign of Miss Smythe but Hawkes was back at the mike.

'Before I throw the proceedings open to questions, let's have another song from the show.' A dozen girls crowded on to the tiny stage, all wearing T-shirts bearing the logo: MACBETH, THE MUSICAL: YOU'LL BELIEVE A WOOD CAN WALK. Miss Smythe was second from the right. They mimed their way through a bouncy little ditty called 'Eye of Newt' that sounded like Neil Sedaka on one of his off days.

'Meet our beautiful witches, ladies and gentlemen,' gushed Hawkes when they'd finished. 'We believe even a musical as revolutionary as *Macbeth* needs a beautiful chorus line and I think you'll agree we've found some of the loveliest young ladies ever to grace the West End stage.' Hawkes lubriciously licked his lips like the cat who'd got the cream.

The girls filed off and Sir Andrew, wearing his 'I've just won the prep school scripture prize' expression, took the mike. 'If there are any questions, my colleagues and I will do our best to answer them,' he said humbly. Johnny Jewel got in first. 'Sir Andrew, will your former wife, Miss Sarah Brightman, be appearing in the show?' he asked coldly. Andrew assumed a sombre expression.

'There are no plans for Miss Brightman to appear in the show,' he said primly. A few hacks shouted shame.

A man in an expensive suit, blue striped shirt and Old Carthusian tie was next. 'Gervase Mortimer, the *Sun*,' he announced in a languid public-school drawl. Of course. How could I have been so stupid?

'Mr Hawkes, a rumour has reached our office that the witches will be appearing nude in this show. Could you confirm or deny this please.'

There were a few sniggers. 'The artistic content of the show is entirely in the hands of Trevor Nunn,' said Hawkes. 'Trevor, have you any comment?'

'I believe *Macbeth* is one of the most erotic plays ever written,' said Nunn in his quietest, most intensely sincere voice. He moved back from the mike. Mortimer wasn't letting him off the hook that easily.

'Never mind the art, Trev,' he said, somehow sounding even plummier as he put the knife in. 'Will the girls be getting them off? And come to think of it, will Cilla be getting them off?'

Cilla snorted as if she had just heard a particularly racy joke on *Blind Date*. Mortimer ploughed on, 'I must press you on this, Mr Nunn, I think our readers have the right to know. Will the witches be appearing nude?' He still sounded like a Sotheby's auctioneer.

Nunn returned to the mike. 'Yes they will,' he snapped. 'It will all be done with the greatest possible taste when Shakespeare's great text seems to demand it.'

The chief theatre critic of one of the snootier Sundays began to huff and puff about the show being a gratuitous insult to Britain's greatest writer and suggested that all those involved should feel thoroughly ashamed of themselves for embarking on such a project at Shakespeare's expense. He was quite right of course, but his sanctimony immediately made one side with Nunn and the rest of the gang.

'Wait until you see the show,' said the director, all emollient now naked girls were off the agenda. 'I believe we are remaining absolutely faithful to the spirit of the original work.'

Hawkes was looking less than pleased at the way the conference was progressing. 'One last question and then we can all have a drink,' he said with an edge of desperation.

A notoriously sycophantic hack pitched in. 'Five million pounds is a huge budget, can you give us any indication of where all the money will be going?'

'Into Lloyd Webber's pocket,' called a rebellious voice from the back. It was Victor. Hawkes ignored the interruption.

'I'm glad you asked that question. Over half the budget is being spent on the most advanced, state-of-the-art technology ever seen on any stage. In the scene when Macbeth sees the dagger, for instance, a twenty-foot dagger will fly at an estimated thirty-five miles per hour around the auditorium, within inches of the audience's heads. But the biggest *coup de théâtre* will be the Birnam Wood scene. Using the latest in mobile holograms, giant oak trees will appear to move down the aisles of the theatre and climb on to the stage. You really will believe a wood can walk. It will be the most amazing spectacle the West End has ever seen, I am quite confident of that.'

There was a brief silence. Lloyd Webber went to the mike and thanked us for coming. 'I think I can honestly say this is the most exciting project I've ever worked on. And I believe that with *Macbeth* I've really written my masterpiece.'

'About time too,' called Victor from the back.

Hawkes led his creative team down the steps at the front of the stage and a few conscientious hacks and radio reporters collared them for further questioning. The shutters had come down on the bar, and the kilted bar staff were now passing among us bearing trays.

'A *Macbeth* cocktail, sir?' said one as she passed. It was a

Bloody Mary to you or me, but a good strong nutritious one. Wine, Calvados, malt whisky and now vodka and it was still only half past four. I took a deep swig. I was going to have to crash soon, but not yet, I needed just a few more anaesthetized hours. Victor came over, looking pleased with himself. I congratulated him on his brilliant cabaret. Then I noticed that Raymond Hawkes was bearing down on us. He and Victor were old mates. Hawkes was the one man I particularly wanted to avoid. A few months previously he had made one of his rare forays into straight theatre with a singularly mawkish drama about incest in a working-class family. I'd given it a hostile though far from intemperate review but Kim hadn't been able to resist the headline AND DADDY CAME TOO despite my best endeavours to talk her out of it. Hawkes shook Victor greasily by the hand. With the spotlight in his eyes, he couldn't have guessed that the old buffer was the person who'd come closest to sabotaging his carefully stage-managed press conference. 'Sounds a fascinating show,' said the hypocritical bugger.

'I think it's going to be something really rather special,' said Hawkes smugly. 'I mean, Andrew's a genius and with Trevor, Ian and Cilla, how can we fail?'

Victor introduced me to his friend. He never knew when to keep his mouth shut.

'Ah yes,' said Hawkes, 'the young man who is trying so hard to make a reputation for himself.' He sounded as smarmy as ever. 'You know, of course, that the play you so spectacularly panned was based on the author's own harrowing personal experience? Or didn't you bother to read that most moving interview in *Time Out?*'

Of course I hadn't seen the bloody interview.

'And that disgraceful headline . . .' Mr Hawkes still sounded delightfully jocular, as if announcing the winners in a charity raffle. 'A little more compassion, Mr Benson, a little more compassion, if you please.'

All this and I'd still got Harriet Smythe to deal with. I supped up the remains of my *Macbeth* cocktail.

'I'm afraid I had no idea the play was based on personal

experience,' I stammered. 'There was nothing in the programme to say so, and I was judging it simply as a play. But
you're quite right, the headline was a bad lapse of taste.' I
almost added that I didn't write it myself and then felt a vestigial
tug of loyalty to Kim.

'Which headline was that?' piped up Victor, helpful to the
last.

'And Daddy Came Too,' Hawkes obliged. 'A searing, real
life account of the most grotesque child abuse and our friend
here has to make a cheap joke about it.'

'Tut, tut,' said Victor and I gave him a filthy look. It was
wasted on him of course. He beamed back affably.

Raymond Hawkes went off to pour some of his copious
supplies of oil on to the troubled waters that were developing
between Andrew Lloyd Webber and Johnny Jewel. Victor
announced that he was toddling along too and I suddenly
realized I didn't want him to go. Apart from his mischievous
mug there didn't seem to be a single friendly face in the room.
Harriet Smythe was over at the bar, chatting earnestly to a hack
I didn't recognize and taking tiny sips at her Bloody Mary like a
teenager having her first Babycham. 'Chin up,' I told myself
firmly. I could hardly ask a pensioner to be my minder. 'Thanks
for your company, Victor. Have a good weekend.' He gave a
theatrical wink and left.

I went and hovered by La Smythe and the reporter. 'I simply
can't wait to work with Trevor,' she was saying. 'I just know this
is going to be the greatest production of *Macbeth* ever.'

'Well, the greatest musical version, perhaps,' said the reporter
gamely. 'If you discount the Verdi opera.'

Miss Smythe was clearly annoyed by this doubting Thomas
but tried hard to look winning.

'Oh, you haven't heard the score yet. Andrew's is much
better than Verdi's. It's now music, music for the 1990s.'

How could such a beautiful girl talk such crap, I wondered.
She seemed a little older than she had in *Romeo and Juliet*
and looked astonishingly elegant in her absurd T-shirt. Her
long blonde hair was sexily tousled, but her clear eyes gleamed

with the fanaticism of raw ambition. She looked at me inquiringly.

I didn't want to go through the rigmarole of apology with another reporter as a witness, but he seemed to have finished. 'Do you think we could have a word in private, Miss Smythe?' I asked.

'Oh, how wonderfully mysterious,' she said, with all the artful bogusness of her craft. We found a quiet corner of the bar. 'I owe you an apology,' I said. 'I'm Will Benson from *Theatre World*. I hope your agent Mr Simon has been in touch about the unfort—'

I didn't get any further. Her face went into an involuntary spasm of fury and she threw her *Macbeth* cocktail straight into my face. She'd hardly touched it. My eyes stung like hell, and the cold tomato juice sliding down my face felt just like, well, cold tomato juice sliding down my face. I wasn't sure what to do next. There seemed to be no easy answer to a Bloody Mary in the kisser. I tried anyway. 'Didn't your agent Mr Simon explain . . .' I began but it was no good. I was talking to myself. Miss Smythe was making her flamboyant exit, was indeed leaving the Cinderella Bar as though the last stroke of midnight was chiming. A group of journos gathered round. 'What was all that about, then?' drawled the man from the *Sun*. 'Well, whatever it was, she's clearly a young lady of rare discrimination,' said Johnny Jewel. 'Damn good aim, too.'

Nothing much seemed to happen for a very long time. I just stood there, dripping and humiliated, while the others looked on. Eventually a barman handed me a cloth. I rubbed my face, and gazed down at what had once been a clean white shirt. Hawkes hurried over. 'Well, Mr Benson, you certainly take the prize when it comes to upsetting people. What did you say to so annoy a member of my cast?'

'About a dozen words, all of them polite. She didn't like a review I wrote.'

'And who can blame her?' said Hawkes, rubbing his hands together with glee.

The urge to cry that had been with me ever since lunch with Kim was almost overpowering.

'I think I'll just go to the Gents, try and clean up a bit,' I mumbled, striding off with what little dignity I could muster. None at all, really. In the Gents, all I succeeded in doing was smearing the tomato juice over a larger area of my clothing and making myself even wetter. The juice was all over the shoulders of my jacket as well, I noticed miserably. How was I going to get home looking like this? But there was one thing the vodka facial did seem to have achieved. I felt more or less sober. Nor, I realized with some surprise, did I feel like another drink. Well only a cup of tea anyway.

Almost everyone had gone by the time I got back, though a smear of diarists lingered in the hope of getting a paragraph out of my misfortune. Raymond Hawkes had told them who the striking chorus girl was and they wanted to know what I had written that had so offended her. Frankness was the best policy, I thought.

'I didn't write a word about her, or rather I did, but it didn't get into the paper.' I told the tale. I was getting tired of it.

'And how do you feel about Miss Smythe now?' asked one of the hacks.

'I still think she's a wonderful actress. Those that dish it out must learn to take it.' Rather good, I thought. I'd have cheerfully strangled the little bitch.

I turned to Hawkes and asked if there was an old coat or something I could borrow to go home in and he went off in search of the house manager. Danny Timson came over with press releases.

'You look perfectly sweet, dear,' he told me. 'She's going to be trouble, that one.' I manfully resisted the temptation of telling him that trouble was my business. I was experiencing a strange attack of cheerfulness. The house manager came over with a filthy beige mac with what looked like a duvet sewn into the lining.

'It was in the lost property room,' he said. 'No one's claimed it for the past six months, so you can have it with the compliments of the London Alhambra.' He made the offer sound as generous as an all expenses paid trip to Disneyland.

The last of us went upstairs and out into the sunlit street. It was surprisingly hot for October, without a cloud in the sky. I felt a wally in my mac. 'You look a wally in that mac,' the friendliest of the diarists told me. The four of them shared a cab up to Camden with the idea of doorstepping Harriet Smythe at the theatre, and I found another after walking a sweaty quarter of a mile down Oxford Street. The driver eyed my disgusting garment suspiciously.

'Blimey, don't you dirty old men even take time off in weather like this?' he leered happily.

'It's a vocation, flashing,' I told him. 'Can't let a spot of sunshine spoil the fun.'

Back in Vauxhall, the flat seemed sad and dusty. The idea of a weekend in London, brooding about Cathy and Kim, was unbearable, and Cathy had said she wanted me out of the way anyway. I made a cup of tea, stuffed the mac into a black bin bag and my tomato-flavoured clothes into the laundry basket, and had a cool bath. I toyed with the idea of making the bed and doing the washing up, then thought fuck it. An answering machine was all I got when I phoned the treacherous Mr Simon. I left a message asking him to ring me at *Theatre World* on Monday to discuss dry-cleaning charges, then wrote a note to Cathy saying how sorry I was, how I hoped we'd keep in touch, that I missed her. I put fondest love and lots of kisses on the bottom. I was getting soft. I raided the bookshelves for all the Noel Streatfeilds in the house, always a present help in time of trouble, packed a small suitcase and took the Tube to Victoria as a penance. My head was beginning to throb unendurably and the train was packed with commuters. 'Never mind,' I told myself, 'you're off on your hols.'

At Victoria I scanned the destination boards. Brighton was more fun than I felt I deserved and the temptation to carry on drinking would be compounded in that splendidly raffish resort. Eastbourne. That was the place for broken-down old men like me. I bought a ticket and a big plastic beaker of weak tea, and resisted the temptation of a Casey Jones Quarter-pounder with less difficulty than usual. Two days of sea and Miss Streatfeild. Just the idea of it cheered me up.

I crashed out on the train as soon as I'd finished my tea and was woken by the guard at Eastbourne. My mouth tasted foul and my head was still throbbing. I found a bed and breakfast place on the front, checked in, drank four glasses of water, took a sleeping pill, a couple of Disprin and an effervescent Vitamin C tablet and went to bed. It was nine o'clock. Half a dozen pages of *Ballet Shoes* and I was out like a light.

There's one thing to be said for getting drunk at lunchtime. If you abstain in the evening, you get the worst of your hangover later the same day and sleep off the rest. I felt pretty good when I woke at seven after ten hours of the dreamless. The landlady was plumply maternal, thought I looked peaky and gave me an extra slice of black pudding with her prodigious fried breakfast.

I sauntered on the front, spent a lot of time reading *Ballet Shoes* and *Apple Bough* in a deckchair, played a couple of games of clock golf and drank only modest halves of Carlsberg with my large lunch and supper. I felt solitary, but it was a pleasantly melancholic feeling, not a great ache of loneliness, and Noel Streatfeild kept the horrors at bay. I went to bed at ten, and after fifty pages of *Gemma and Sisters* felt brave enough to turn off the light. This was the life, I thought, as I waited for sleep to wash companionably over me.

On Sunday I had to decide whether to buy the tabloids and discover whether Colin had done his worst. I'd bought all the papers on Saturday and there hadn't been a line, but as JB had said, the Joe Johnson story was a natural for Sunday. I decided not to spoil the day. In the event I had it spoiled for me. After assiduously averting my eyes at every newsagent's I passed, I ended my stroll round town in a cheerful pub near the front. 'A lime and lemonade, please,' I asked the barman. Eastbourne was doing me the world of good. I looked round the pub as he poured my drink. There on the counter, face up, was his copy of the *News of the World*. TOP COMIC IN GAY VICE BOY SHAME screamed the 144pt headline alongside a picture of the Big Cunt. The barman gave me my soft drink. 'And a double Scotch, please,' I added.

I borrowed his paper. The *News of the Screws* had gone for broke. All the quotes about rent boys and the death of Johnson's wife had been lifted straight from my tape in what was billed as an 'amazingly frank interview with a *News of the World* reporter' who rejoiced in the improbable name of Herbert Fitzpatrick.

Johnson was described as being 'tired and emotional' after appearing on the Children in Need Telethon and, in time-honoured tradition, the 'reporter' had 'made his excuses and left' after the comedian had indecently propositioned him. Johnson's confessions continued on a spread inside, with pictures of him and his former wife, a shot of his 'luxurious detached £400,000 mansion in up-market Cheadle Hulme' and an artist's impression of what he might have looked like in his red wig and little moustache. A rent boy called Julian had either been found or invented who said he'd always had his suspicions about Mr Jones, as he'd called himself, and that he had appeared nervous on the occasions when they'd been together. 'He was often so drunk he couldn't get it up,' Julian confided charitably. There was a sanctimonious comment column describing Johnson as a hypocritical sicko who should seek urgent medical advice, and the feature was broken up with little black boxes containing some of Johnson's more regrettable pooftah jokes with the swear words asterisked out.

I read it through a couple of times. It was as efficient and nasty a demolition job as I'd ever come across. I felt a stab of compassion for the sad, fat comedian whose life I'd played a part in wrecking, and a surge of cold fury for Colin. I'd managed to avoid thinking about him and Kim for most of Saturday. The vision of them reading the *News of the World* together at breakfast was hateful. After another Scotch, I realized this was unfair. Kim, I was sure, would be appalled by Colin's behaviour and was now quite certain to give him his marching orders. That was a scrap of comfort. I thought about phoning her, but after our dreadful lunch I needed to see her face to face, preferably grovelling on my knees. There was nothing to be done till Monday. I decided to stick to my original plan of taking an early train on Monday morning and going straight to work. Noel Streatfeild continued to prove her sterling worth. I spent the rest of the day with *Gemma*, then with *White Boots* and *The Painted Garden*, folding myself into the cosy security blanket of her world in which everyone was kind and decent at heart and the worst crime was selfishness, closely followed by bumptiousness.

There was a James Bond film on the telly that night and I watched it in the residents' lounge with a couple of pleasant middle-aged men who'd ducked out of seeing Val Doonican in the Winter Gardens with their wives. Very companionable it was. But as I turned out the light that night the thought I'd been resisting all day leapt out of the shadows and bit me. When Harry Meadows had said he'd kill me if a word got out about his client's secret, he'd sounded as though he meant it. I remembered those slate grey eyes. I was scared.

Monday

I got up at six after a troubled night, in which sweaty waking anxieties merged imperceptibly with sleeping nightmares. The landlady had left me a Thermos of coffee and I drank it and smoked a couple of cigarettes before walking through the empty early-morning streets to the station. I'd acquired a taste for cooked breakfasts in the last couple of days and was looking forward to the consolation of a British Rail Super Sizzler, even if it did cost me fifteen quid. I bought all the papers and read them on the platform. Most of the tabloids had attempted a follow-up though none of them had managed to find much that was new.

The train rolled in and I climbed aboard. 'No restaurant car,' the steward told me with great good cheer. 'We've got some sandwiches, though.' I make a point of never buying British Rail sandwiches because there's a terrible risk they might be signed by Clement Freud.

I settled for a couple of rounds of biscuits. And a cup of fresh leaf tea. Which means a tea-bag and that revolting milk substitute whose ingredients read like a fairly advanced experiment in post-graduate chemistry. As I forced it down, I noticed that the *Mail* Diary had a brief account of my encounter with Miss Smythe under the headline BLOODY MARY? BLOODY HECK! Miss Smythe was described as the highly promising young actress with a leading role in the £10 million (had the budget doubled over the weekend?) musical by Andrew Lloyd Webber, MackBeth. I was described as 'trainee trade journalist' Phil Henson who had 'got right up attractive Harriet's nose'.

'Quizzed about the incident afterwards, Miss Smythe said: "He's an obnoxious little squirt and he got what he deserved. It is time this great profession of ours hit back at the mockers and the scoffers."' So that's what a bad review feels like, I thought. I could take it. Just. At least they'd got my name wrong.

The train reached Victoria at 8.45, only fifteen minutes late. I dumped all the papers in a bin, bought thirty quid's worth of flowers at a stall and made it to work by 9.30.

The newsroom was deserted apart from JB, who looked embarrassed when I came in with my suitcase and the huge bunch of flowers.

'Been spending the wages of sin?' he asked, quite spitefully for him. 'You changed your mind about Joe Johnson then?'

'You saw the papers?'

'I bought the *Screws* yesterday. Very unpleasant reading it made too. I was thinking some nasty thoughts about you yesterday.'

If this were some wholesome school story, if indeed this were a Noel Streatfeild story, I'd have taken all this from JB like a man and kept quiet about Colin. But it isn't and I didn't. I felt absolutely no desire to cover up for him. He'd stolen my tape and Johnson's life, and Kim. I couldn't wait to sink him in the shit.

'The tape was nicked from my drawer last Friday,' I said. 'Draw your own conclusions.'

'Blimey, the little bastard,' said JB. 'I'm sorry, Will, I've done you an injustice.' He looked suddenly old again and coughed as he took a deep drag on his Embassy.

'I'd better go and see old Torrington about this. Meadows may phone him personally and he ought to be in the picture.'

I went over to Kim's desk, laid the flowers on it and wrote a note. 'So sorry about my disgraceful behaviour at lunch. Will you ever speak to me again? Won't blame you if you don't. Fondest love, W.' then I went to my desk and started bashing out the Susie Smiles story. JB had left a neat transcript of the conversations he'd had with her and the honest comedian. He'd left a note too, a less emotional one than mine. 'Susie phoned again on Friday afternoon and said she'd "make it worth my while" if we didn't publish the story. So now we can bring attempted bribery as well as fraud and threats with menaces into the tale. Try not to sound too self-congratulatory!'

I knew what he meant. A whiff of odious smugness can so easily pervade stories like this. I decided to keep strictly to the facts, and firmly resisted the temptation of writing '*Theatre World* will never be bought or intimidated'. The bald account, coupled with the excellent quotes from Kinda Kinky's Roy Davis, the honest comedian and the female vocalist, not to mention Preston's performance in the car park, made the point strongly enough without pious editorializing. I wondered whether the police would take an interest. I certainly didn't see it as my duty to tip them off. Quite the reverse. If they charged Smiles before we went to press the whole piece would become *sub judice*.

Angela and Mirza came in, then Kevin. 'No sign of the star reporter,' said Mirza with a grin.

'No sign of the star sub-editor,' said Kevin dolefully. Monday was a heavy production day and he knew I'd have to spend at least the first part of it on the Susie Smiles tale when normally I'd be helping on the sub's desk. I pressed on at my typewriter and JB returned from his confab with Mr Torrington and read what I'd written so far.

'That's the stuff, Will,' he said. 'Keep it dead straight.'

At about eleven Kim came in looking shattered. Not a long night of passion with a celebratory Colin, I thought. Oh please God, not that. She didn't look at me as she went to her desk.

'Sorry I'm late, JB, I had a rough night.'

She saw the flowers and read the note and still she didn't look at me.

'A secret admirer?' said JB archly.

'Yes, I suppose you could say that,' said Kim. She went out and came back with a vase borrowed from the accounts department and arranged the flowers in it. Then she came over to my desk, stood behind me and put her arms round my neck and kissed me gently on the cheek. Everyone pretended not to notice.

'You're forgiven,' she said. 'I ought to make you suffer a lot longer but I can hardly do that after the way Colin's stitched you up.'

'Lunch?' I said.

'Come on, Will, you know what it's like on Mondays. And I didn't get much done on Friday afternoon thanks to you and all that drink.'

She put her hands round my throat and pretended to strangle me and I could feel her breasts pressing against my back. She could have gone on strangling me all day as far as I was concerned.

'Drink after work?' she suggested.

'Anything, so long as it's not Calvados,' I said.

She went back to her desk and I continued with the story.

'Where's the boy wonder then?' said JB after a few minutes.

'I thought you'd never ask,' said Kim.

'Boardroom,' said JB. 'You'd better come too, Will.'

Kim had had a rotten weekend. Colin hadn't come back to the office on Friday but had arrived at her flat in Brixton at midnight, uncharacteristically pissed out of his head. He had spent all day at the *News of the World*, working on the story with a couple of their hacks. The paper had been so impressed with the tape they'd offered him a grand for the story and a six-month contract. When they heard he'd stolen the tape 'from some wally who wouldn't do anything about it' they'd made it two grand and a year contract. There had been many congratulatory bevvies down the pub afterwards.

'Just as a matter of interest, Kim, why did Colin come round to your place to brag?' asked JB. He could never resist a bit of scandal.

'No comment,' she said, blushing prettily.

'So how did you get rid of him?' I asked, desperately hoping that she had. I shouldn't have asked the question in front of JB but I had to know. Kim didn't seem put out.

'I told him he was a louse,' she said. 'Good word that.' She savoured it. 'Louse. And I told him to piss off back home and leave me alone.'

'Poor Kim,' said JB with paternal fondness.

'I'm not quite finished yet,' she said. 'He came round again last night, with his copy of the paper. I'd already read it.' She wrinkled her nose with distaste. 'I told him to get lost but he barged his way in. Getting into practice for interviewing the recently bereaved, I suppose. He wanted me to clear his desk for him. And he gave me this.' She slid a white envelope over to JB. 'His last scoop for *Theatre World*, he called it, his legacy to the sinking ship.'

'Nice,' said JB. 'What a delightful young man he is.'

He opened the envelope and read the contents, a couple of sides, neatly typed, double spaced.

'Strong stuff.' He passed the copy over to Kim and me.

'Stephen Regis's national tour of *And Then There Were None* has collapsed amid mounting debts and the impresario has gone into voluntary liquidation,' it began. The report described how the actors hadn't been paid, with suitably petulant quotes from Jason Maxwell, and said the last two performances in Leamington had been cancelled. There was a quote from Regis saying he had spent more money than he could afford seeking a 'miracle cure' for his terminally ill daughter. The cast were inevitably described as being 'devastated'.

'Page one stuff,' said JB looking aggrieved. 'I'd just made up my mind to sack Colin today. I've never sacked anyone before. I was rather looking forward to it.'

Kim insisted that we should check the story out. 'I don't trust Colin as far as I can spit. He had an evil look when he gave it to me.'

'Oh come on, he can't be that bad,' said JB.

'You wanna bet?' said Kim.

'Oh, just one more thing,' I said. I nipped back into the newsroom to fetch the office copy of the *Daily Mail* and showed them the diary item. 'More or less true I'm afraid,' I said.

'My poor baby,' said Kim, and JB looked at her quizzically.

We went back into the newsroom. Mirza, Barbara and Kevin

looked expectant and a little hurt. It's horrible knowing there's a big drama going on and being kept out of it. JB told them the news about Colin without mentioning his nocturnal visits to Kim.

'Can you check the story, Mirza? I'd phone the theatres first. Leamington and . . .' He paused and consulted his extraordinary memory, '. . . and the Yvonne Arnaud in Guildford where it's meant to be playing this week.'

'Will do, chief,' said Mirza, only half taking the piss. It would be 'get me rewrite' next, like a newshound in *The Front Page*.

I finished the talent contest story by lunchtime and showed it to JB, who strengthened it with a couple of cuts, and then went and joined Kim and Kevin on the subs desk. There was a lot to do after the hiatus on Friday and we had sandwiches in the office for lunch. It was a good feeling working through the piles of copy, designing a couple of inside pages, making corrections to the proofs. I realized with a shock of happiness that there was nothing I'd rather be doing, nowhere I'd rather be, than working industriously beside Kim.

The peace was suddenly broken with a triumphant cry of 'What a fucking pillock!' from Mirza as he put down the phone.

'*And Then There Were None* opens in Guildford tonight, as planned,' he announced. 'All the shows went ahead in Leamington, as scheduled. The cast were all paid on Friday with an extra hundred each to make up for the delay. The reason they hadn't been paid is that Regis was on holiday for a fortnight and his assistant who was meant to pay the wages went off sick almost as soon as he'd gone. That only left a temp in the office and she didn't see fit to contact the boss until the complaints from the actors became really vitriolic. As soon as he heard from her, Regis got a plane from Florida and sorted it all out. I've got confirmation from Jason Maxwell. Colin didn't go to see Regis on Friday, indeed Regis hasn't spoken to him at all. Nor has he got a terminally ill daughter.'

'Fine, good work, Mirza,' said JB. He looked a little shaky as he went over and patted Kim on the shoulder. 'Thanks,' he said. 'I just might not have checked that tale if you hadn't insisted on it. A libel like that could have put us out of business. I'm always telling Torrington our insurance is pathetically inadequate in view of the ludicrous awards juries are making nowadays. Christ, and that nasty bit about the terminally ill kid. Talk about twisted.'

Kim looked miserable rather than pleased about her role in saving the firm's bacon. I winked at her and she smiled wanly.

'A louse,' she said, and went back to her subbing.

Kevin left at seven, surprising us by announcing that he was going off to sing in the *St Matthew Passion*. 'Only a scratch choir but it makes a change from Benny Hill.' Kim and I called it a day an hour or so later. Everyone else had gone home long since. There would be more than usual to do the following day but we'd manage. We packed everything we'd need at the printers into a large photographic box and left it down at reception for the motorcycle messenger to take to Clerkenwell early next morning.

'I need that drink,' said Kim, locking the office door behind us.

'The Perseverance, the Old Three Master, a little light supper at the Pagoda?'

'Let's get off this bloody island,' she said. 'If we hurry, we'll be able to get the eight-thirty boat.'

We walked through the backstreets, well off the red brick road of the enterprise zone, past abandoned warehouses and derelict terraced houses. The boat was waiting at the quay, a fifty-seat riverbus. It was a great way to go home and yet we did it surprisingly rarely.

You could smell the river and, this far downstream, it was wide and dark and mysterious. And even though they'd now been converted into trendy flats, the old wharves still looked faintly menacing. After Tower Bridge there were more lights that danced on the black and oily surface of the water. Kim seemed disinclined to talk and stared out of the window, picking up my hand and cradling it between her own, which were cool and soft. We passed Hays Galleria, with its splendid vaulted roof, and the Oxo Tower. 'Let's get off at the Embankment

Pier and go up West,' said Kim, breaking the easy silence between us at last. 'I want to see the bright lights tonight.' The great Richard and Linda Thompson song was a favourite of hers and she began singing it quietly, close to my ear, like a lullaby. She had a sweet and gentle voice and, close like that, it sent powerful shivers down my spine.

At the Embankment I asked if she could face a Tube ride. 'Only three stops on the Bakerloo. It's worth it, honest.'

We got off at Oxford Circus and walked up Upper Regent Street to the St George's Hotel near Broadcasting House. We took the lift up to the 15th floor and came out in the bar and restaurant. The west facing wall is almost all glass and on a clear day, from the centre of town, you can look out over the capital and its straggling suburbs to the open countryside beyond. At night, with all the twinkling lights spread beneath you, the word fairyland comes cornily to mind.

I've never been able to understand why the bar with the most spectacular location in London is so often deserted, but who's grumbling apart from Forte Hotels? The prices aren't even much more expensive than the average West End pub. We sat down on a sofa by the window.

'Wow,' said Kim. 'How did you find it?'

'Cathy brought me,' I said, feeling a little awkward. 'She came here after work with some of the other bankers and liked it so much she brought me along a few days later.'

Kim didn't seem at all put out. 'Clever Cathy,' she said. 'And clever you for spotting a good thing when you saw it.'

God, I want to take you to bed, I thought.

'What would you like to drink?' I said.

'Large gin and tonic, please,' said Kim.

I went over to the bar and ordered the drinks and the barman said he'd bring them over. You don't get that sort of service in the Perseverance.

There was another silence between us. It was one of the nicest things about Kim. In her company you never felt the need to keep burbling on just to fill in the pauses. Sometimes she rabbited non-stop herself, but more often she was quiet, creating a feeling of companionship in the spaces between words. The hotel pianist was playing 'Night and Day' and Kim hummed along to it unselfconsciously. The drinks came. With any luck, heaven will be sitting in the bar of the St George's Hotel with the girl you've just fallen in love with, eternally taking the first sip of the first drink of the day, looking down at the lights of London spread silently below.

'It's heavenly,' said Kim, then looked anxiously into her glass. 'It was fucking awful with Colin. The first night he was just pissed, though he got very bolshie when I showed him the door. He was sure I'd be thrilled to bits he'd sold the story and got a job in Fleet Street. He couldn't understand it when I wasn't. Last night, though, he was vile.'

'You don't have to tell me about it,' I said.

'Yes I do. I want to and you ought to know anyway. He hates your guts.'

'Well, we've never been bosom buddies.'

'No, I mean he really hates you. Beyond all the reasons you've given him, beyond logic. He said the only reason he got off with me was because he guessed you fancied me and would be dreadfully upset when you found out.'

'As I was.'

'As you were,' said Kim. She took another pull at her gin and tonic.

She looked up at me from under her fringe, just like Lady Di used to do in those photographs taken at the kindergarten before she married Prince Charles. Unlike Lady Di, there wasn't a trace of innocence on Kim's face. It was the sexiest look I'd ever had from her.

'Quite a compliment, really,' she said.

We had another drink at the hotel then found an Italian place in Fitzrovia and ate parma ham and melon and comforting plates of pasta, accompanied, and it went down unusually slowly, by a bottle of Chianti Classico. For once we didn't talk about work. Kim had become particularly enthusiastic about the Victorian poets on her Open University course and recited bits of 'In Memoriam' and 'Dover Beach' at me, and they were very nice too.

'Do you mind if we don't go to bed together tonight?' she suddenly blurted out, embarrassed and abrupt.

Of course I did. 'No, of course not,' I said, puzzled. If ever a girl seemed to have turned on her lovelight it was Kim.

'I hardly slept last night after all that malarkey with Colin. I haven't got the taste of him out of my mouth yet.'

I raised an insufferably Roger Mooreish eyebrow and she gave one of her dirty laughs.

'I don't mean like that, you bastard. I just don't want to rush it. It's too easy to tumble into bed. I want to savour it for once, build up to it.'

'I've never found it easy to tumble into bed with anyone,' I said feelingly. 'How long do you envisage this chivalric wooing going on for?'

'Do you think you could bear to wait till Friday?' she said earnestly. What a girl. I'd been expecting a far longer sentence of celibacy.

'I might just manage that,' I said, and she leant over the table and kissed me on the nose.

'Thanks, Will. I thought we might go away for the weekend. A real old fashioned dirty weekend. That's if you're not doing anything. You're not doing anything, are you?' She sounded flatteringly anxious.

'Of course I'm not and if I was I'd cancel it. Where shall we go? Paris? Or is that too much of a cliché?'

Kim stared at me in silence for a few moments. Her eyes were a deep delphinium blue but even in her elated mood they still held a hint of vulnerability and of hurt.

'Blackpool,' she said decisively. I'd never been. 'It's funny and greasy and grimy and gimcrack, and the whole place reeks of sex.'

'You've converted me,' I told her.

'And no posh hotel. I want to stay in a proper landlady's with the gong going for breakfast and dirty looks if you miss it.'

I could hardly wait.

After paying the bill we got a taxi and I told the driver to go to Brixton and then back to Vauxhall.

'You've no need to see me home, I'm a big girl now.'

'Chivalry and courtly love,' I told her sternly. 'Until Friday, anyway. Enjoy it while it lasts.'

In the cab it became clear that Kim's idea of courtly love was rather different from Chaucer's. She launched herself at me with enthusiastic abandon and kissed with a passion that verged on desperation. There was a lot of suffering in that violently searching tongue. Colin had wounded her badly. She needed healing. I did my best and we came up for air after about five minutes.

'Blimey, if this is your view of platonic romance, I'm looking forward to the real thing,' I told her.

'No one ever said anything about not kissing,' she said, more playful now, reassured. She moved her hand between my legs and gently rubbed me. 'Or a bit of heavy petting, either,' she added. 'Up to eight and back again.'

I put my hand up her rugby shirt and felt clumsily for the breasts that had populated my fantasies so often, so obsessively and for so long, fumbling like a fifth-former as I attempted to undo the catch of her bra.

'Hang on a minute,' she giggled as my fruitless labours became more violent and less effective. With astonishing ease she had her bra off and stuffed inside her handbag in a flash. I looked nervously into the driver's mirror but he seemed to be entirely occupied with the road ahead. He'd probably seen it all before.

I put my hand up her shirt again. Her breasts were every bit as big as I'd imagined, firm and heavy, and her nipples were hard. I cupped them gently, and stroked them. 'Squeeze me, Will,' she breathed in my ear. 'Squeeze me really hard, so hard it hurts.' I did as instructed. 'Christ, that's good,' she whispered and pulled my face back to her mouth. I realized that in my limited sexual experience I'd never encountered anyone before who seemed to enjoy it all as much as I did. With far greater dexterity than I'd displayed, Kim had undone my trousers and got her hand inside. After a couple of minutes I reluctantly told her she'd better stop.

'I don't think ejaculation in a licensed taxi cab falls within the rules of courtly love.'

'Certainly not,' said Kim with a fair attempt at prudishness. She withdrew her hand, provocatively licked her fingers and then stroked my cheek. I felt stunned with happiness and lust.

The taxi driver turned round to ask the number of Kim's flat just as I was doing up my flies. Kim told him without a blush, and kissed me almost chastely on the lips as she got out of the cab. 'I can't wait for Blackpool,' she said. 'See you at the printer's tomorrow.'

I spent the journey back with a silly grin on my face and gave our tolerant Pandarus a two-quid tip. 'Looks like you're well in there, mate,' he said pleasantly.

It was clear Cathy had been in the flat over the weekend. She'd made the bed and done the washing up for a start, and replaced my note with one of her own. 'I expected to find the place knee-deep in empty whisky bottles and old fag ends. Not too bad, Will. Keep it up.' She'd missed her vocation, had Cathy. She should have been a schoolmistress. 'I played the messages on the answering machine in case there were any for me and have saved them all. There's a very odd one – hope it makes sense to you. Have taken my post. Please forward anything else that comes to me to the bank. Will ring next week. Don't forget you owe me for the furniture. Am feeling all right and hope you are too. Love, Cathy.'

'Just 'love'. Not 'all my', not 'fondest', not even 'lots of'. No kisses either. Fair enough.

The shelves looked sadly depleted without Cathy's books but I was pleased to see she had taken the particularly obnoxious china poodles that used to stand on either end of the mantelpiece, horrible lifelike things which looked as if they might start yapping at any moment. The desk in the spare room had gone, too, and her bookcase, and I found myself furiously fighting off the tears when I noticed that her disreputable one-eyed teddy bear had gone from his perch at the top of the wardrobe in our bedroom. The bedroom.

I poured out the remains of the quarter bottle of Bells, and went into the kitchen for ice. Most of the pots and pans and crockery were gone, which suited me fine. The only act of spite appeared to be the loss of the teapot. One of Cathy's peculiarities is that she never drinks tea, only coffee, while I get through the stuff by the quart. I had a soft spot for the teapot, the only one I'd ever come across that didn't drip when you poured. Even then Cathy hadn't quite had the courage of her vengeful convictions. She'd left a box of tea-bags, knowing the leaf tea would now be useless. It was Cathy all over. Strict but fair. Making a point with a hint of compassion.

I switched on the answering machine and sat down on the sofa with my drink. I'd have to change the message, take Cathy's name off, but not yet, not tonight. The fluttery, posh tones of Ethel Henderson, Chief Squealer of the Venerable Society of Water Babies, one of the more self-congratulatory show business charities, came on. She'd been phoning me at work for weeks. Martha must have given her my home number. 'Oh, one of these dreadful machines,' she trilled with a show of false panic. 'Just another little reminder, Mr Benson, about our annual ball at the Savoy next Wednesday. I do hope you'll be coming as promised . . .' I hadn't promised a thing. I'd spent several phone calls carefully not promising.

Then there was a message for Cathy from some creep at the bank about her badminton night, Henry someone or other, one of the low-alcohol shandy brigade, and then a rather long silence, followed by a few metallic clicks. These were followed by a voice like a robot's in some fifties science fiction B-movie, metallic, sexless and almost comically quavery.

'"I know death hath ten thousand several doors for men to take their exits,"' it said.

That was it. The line went dead with a click as the receiver was replaced, and then the answering machine started playing the end of a rambling old message from Cathy's mother. Feeling more rattled than I cared to admit, I rewound the tape. The metallic clicks, the inhuman voice and its disturbing message. Could you get a sound like that with a synthesizer, I wondered. I remembered Meadows hadn't phoned all day, and had a reprise of the panic I'd experienced the night before. But if it was a threat, and it certainly sounded like one, it seemed a bit arty for Meadows or the Big Cunt. Shakespeare? If it was, I couldn't place it, but it was vaguely familiar. I'd ask JB in the morning. Just then the phone rang right next to me. I twitched with terror and someone seemed to have switched on a liquidizer in my stomach. I wondered whether to leave the answering machine on and simply monitor the call, then told myself not to be a wimp and picked up the receiver with a hand that trembled like an alcoholic's negotiating the first drink of the day. 'Yes?' I said. It was all I could manage. No 'Will Benson's residence, Benson in person at this end.' Not after that robot voice.

'It's only me,' said Kim. 'I just rang to say goodnight and thanks for a wonderful evening.'

'Oh, right,' I said distractedly.

'You sound a bit odd,' said Kim. 'Your voice is all tight. You're not having second thoughts? God, Cathy hasn't come back has she?' She sounded pretty anxious herself now.

'No, it's not that,' I said, trying to get a grip. 'I've had a funny message on the answering machine, nothing to worry about. I'll tell you about it in the morning.'

'Are you sure you're OK? Forget the chivalric code. You can come over here if you want.'

I was tempted, I was certainly tempted. A warm body, her warm body, to hold in the dark would have been better than a Valium. I put a bit of bogus brightness in my voice. 'No I'm fine. Honestly. It'll be a hell of a day tomorrow and it'll be much more exciting to wait for Blackpool.'

Kim made some suggestions about just how exciting it might be in Blackpool, and my cock, which had curled up and died when I'd heard the metallic message, began to make its presence felt again. I'd never been talked dirty to down the phone before. It had a lot to recommend it.

'Goodnight then,' said Kim just before lust got the better of me. 'Dream of me.'

'Goodnight, my lovely.'

'Sleep well, fatbum,' she said, and put down the phone.

The panic had passed now. Just some crank, I thought, or some bored kid with a new toy dialling at random. Deep down I wasn't convinced by this at all, but the more superficial part of my mind accepted the comforting evasion. What's more, I was aching with unfulfilled sexual excitement. It's hard to fret about sinister messages when you've got a hard on.

There was only one thing for it. Noel Streatfeild. It was about two o'clock when I finally fell asleep with the light on. The final pages of *The Painted Garden* followed by a hefty shot of *Thursday's Child* had done the trick. My seed remained unspilled.

Tuesday

The phone rang at 7 a.m. and I stumbled over to it, swearing. I'd been in the middle of a highly erotic dream. Not about Kim but Cathy, a girl I hadn't dreamt about for years even though we shared the same bed. Probably because we shared the same bed. There was silence on the other end of the line when I picked up the receiver and said, 'Hello, hello,' a couple of times, irritably. Then the memory of the message of the previous night finally penetrated my sleep-and-dream-befuddled brain and I got an attack of the shivers. I wanted a fag but they were on my bedside table. 'Is anyone there?' I said loudly. Very butch it sounded, apart from the tremble in my voice. There was a click and I braced myself for the robot voice. What I got was the Police, to be specific the Police singing 'Every Breath You Take'. Great stuff, if a little early in the morning.

It was a record I'd half-listened to countless times in pubs and on the radio. Listening to it now I realized it wasn't quite the loving, protective song I'd always mistaken it for, but the song of an obsessive, vowing perpetual vigilance on a girl who'd broken faith. Not so nice. I remembered that it was a particular favourite of Cathy's and wondered whether she'd taken its darker meaning on board or missed it altogether like me. The record stopped after a couple of minutes and I fancied I could hear faint breathing in the electronic silence. 'Hello, hello, who's there?' I shouted again. More silence without even the breathing now. I was about to put the phone down when the robot voice started. 'I'll be watching you,' it said over and over again in a ghastly metallic parody of Sting. And then, most worryingly of all, 'Watch out yourself, Will Benson, watch out on your way to work today. We wouldn't want you having any nasty accidents, would we?' I tried a bit more of the 'who's there?' routine but almost at once heard the click as my tormentor put the phone down.

I went into the bedroom, lit a Camel and started coughing so violently I felt sick. 'Sticks and stones, Will,' I told myself firmly when I'd stopped spluttering and got a couple of lungfuls down. Neither cigarette nor pep talk did much good. I couldn't face the sanctimonious politicians on *Today* and switched over to Radio 1. I made a cup of coffee, smoked three more cigarettes while I drank it and began to feel worse rather than better.

With a great effort of will I shaved, washed, dressed and went to the front door. Let myself out and then let myself in again to fetch the walking stick I'd acquired the year before when I'd done my knee in after a fall (not a drunken one, oddly enough). It was some protection and it gave me something to hold on to.

On my way to the Tube, I was keenly aware that I might be being watched and I didn't like it one bit. I imagined heavies in raincoats, chain-smoking in their cars, drinking coffee out of a Thermos after their long night vigil, and one of them turning to his equally burly neighbour and saying, quite calmly, 'There he is. Let's get him.' But nothing had happened by the time I'd reached the station.

The idea of going down the Tube seemed a hundred times more repugnant than usual. All those people, all those faces, all those eyes. I'd get a taxi. I lingered despairingly on the pavement for about ten minutes and saw two cabs with their lights on but both ignored me despite my desperate waves. Eventually I forced myself into the station, through the ticket barriers and on to the escalator, trying and failing to fight off the gathering panic. I felt sick, then I felt I couldn't breathe properly, then I thought I was going to have a heart attack. That pressure across the chest, those tingles down the arm, it couldn't be anything else, could it? All this in the time it took to get to the bottom. Death threats could be the death of a hypochondriac like me. 'I must give up smoking,' I told myself, out loud, as I tottered along to the platform. It was almost empty but not quite empty enough to be scary. But the train was an interminable time coming and before long the place had become very crowded indeed. I found I was standing uncomfortably close to the edge and thought of fighting my way back through the throng, but then there was the clatter of the wheels on the tracks, the gust of hot, stale Underground air. And then I was pushed, very hard, just below the shoulders. I felt myself stumbling forwards and the stick fell out of my hand and into the gulley below the tracks. For a heart-stopping moment I thought there was no way I could avoid following it, and then I was grabbed violently by the arm and instantly regained my balance.

'Don't even think about it,' a smartly suited man told me angrily. Where was the sympathy and the hot sweet tea?

'If you want to commit suicide that's fine by me but pick a way that doesn't screw up everyone else.'

The train was rushing past us now, drawing to a halt. 'I wasn't going to jump,' I screamed at him. 'I was pushed.' I looked wildly around me, dreading seeing a face I recognized, but passengers were already surging out of the train. Anyone could lose themselves instantly in this crowd. Indeed I'd already lost sight of my rescuer. No, there he was, climbing on board. I barged callously in front of a woman who was having terrible problems with a pushchair and followed him down to the relative calm of the passage between the seats. He looked embarrassed when I came and stood next to him and wouldn't meet my eye. Who wants to talk to a potential suicide at eight o'clock in the morning?

'I wasn't going to jump,' I said. 'Thanks a lot for stopping me going over. I was definitely pushed, deliberately, in the back. You didn't see who did it, did you?'

'I didn't see a thing. How could I?' He gestured at the packed carriage as the doors closed. When the train started, I stumbled again, though with less potentially fatal consequences this time. One of my filthy trainers landed on one of his brightly polished black shoes. You could see the ludicrously flamboyant pattern of my sole quite clearly on his gleaming leather. He winced.

'You're a bit of a pain in the arse, one way and another,' he said, surprisingly pleasantly.

'Sorry.'

'It was probably just someone behind you, who was pushed by someone behind him and lost his balance. I'm surprised it doesn't happen more often with the disgraceful overcrowding down here.'

I nodded. 'Yes, I suppose you're right.' I was sure he wasn't. There had been a frightening force in that shove. I felt weak again as I thought about it.

He nodded to signal the conversation was now over, and went back to his *Financial Times*. I began to think about the people who might want me dead and didn't much like my conclusions. I changed at King's Cross and got out at Angel, then one of the most exposed Underground stations with lines on either side of a single, not particularly wide platform. I don't much care for it when it's crowded on a normal day. That morning I crept agonizingly along the middle, desperately trying to ensure there were plenty of people on either side of me. I made it to the lift and then a new possibility for paranoia opened up. It was packed and I imagined just how easy it would be to sink a knife into your neighbour. Most people wouldn't even notice, even the victim might not know who'd wielded the blade. And then I felt a jab in the small of my back, the kidneys, and swung round violently, viciously. It was a woman and her handbag. 'Sorry,' said the middle-aged face, her eyes reflecting back my own panic. 'S'all right,' I mumbled.

The doors swung open and I walked gratefully out into the fresh air. It was five minutes' walk to HighTechnoSet and I was beginning to feel a little calmer. There were plenty of pedestrians, as far as I could see, and no parked cars with big men in them.

It was 8.30 as I climbed the stairs to the third floor of the converted warehouse and sketched a wave at the copy-setters. In the partitioned cubby hole we used as our office on press day Kim was looking briskly efficient with a pile of page proofs. I looked to see if anyone was watching and gave her a quick kiss.

'God, it's good to see you, Kim. It's good to be alive.'

'What's up, Will? You look terrible.'

I told her about the phone calls and the push on the platform at Vauxhall. She got up and gave me a hug.

'Who'd want to kill you?' she asked.

'One or two people, I'm afraid.'

She nodded and looked glum. 'I've had Colin on the phone again. He called at midnight, just after I'd gone to sleep. I think he's gone mad. He wants to take me away for the weekend.'

'Who wouldn't?'

'I gave him an earful about the Stephen Regis story and he said it was a joke, he knew we'd check it out. I slammed the phone down, then he rang again this morning. All sweetness and light, said he felt guilty about nicking the Joe Johnson tape and wanted to apologize to you, and could he come round to the pub tonight. Then he started on the romantic crap again, despite all the vile things he's said earlier. He claimed he'd only said them because I was so sniffy about his scoop. "You and me, babe, we've got something special. Why don't we jet off to Amsterdam for the weekend?" I could have puked.'

'What time did he call?' I asked.

'Just after seven o'clock. They'd just started the news on *Today*.'

'Well, well. That puts Colin out of the picture then. That was the same time I got my wake up call this morning.' He'd been my favourite suspect. It wasn't so bad receiving death threats from a wally you hated. Well, not quite so bad.

'Not necessarily,' said Kim. 'You know that snazzy tape recorder of his. He could have pre-recorded it all and left it running by the phone when you answered, then nipped out to a payphone and called me from there with the deliberate intention of giving himself an alibi. Colin knows that you and I talk, and we know that he likes playing us off against each other.'

I thought back to the phone call. I'd received a strong impression of a human presence on the other end of the line. I couldn't explain it, just felt it.

'I still don't think it's him. Attempted murder's going a bit bloody far, however much he hates me. After all, it's thanks to me he's got this new job.'

'Well, you'll be seeing him tonight. You and Mirza and Kevin can beat the shit out of him until he talks.' She sounded half serious.

'You sound like a ganster's moll.' I said.

She grinned. 'I don't want you dead,' she said solemnly. 'Not till after Blackpool anyway.'

It was a busy day and I pushed thoughts of impending doom to the back of my mind.

Barbara had come up with a lovely story about a dwarf-throwing contest in a night club in Cleethorpes. Some old bag from the council said it was an affront to human dignity and wanted the club's licence revoked. The dwarf, who called himself the Supersonic Atom, was furious. 'It's no worse than being a human cannonball in the circus, and a damn sight better than signing on,' he'd told Barbara. 'I'm a fully paid-up member of Equity and there's not a lot of work for little people like me outside the pantomime season.'

We had a picture of the Supersonic Atom flying through the air in his crash helmet, both hands giving the thumbs up sign.

Kevin arrived, looking cheerful after what he described as his night of Passion and about noon, when we'd passed most of the inside pages, JB arrived with a couple more stories that Mirza and Barbara had written in the office that morning.

'I don't suppose Harry Meadows has been in touch?' I asked.

'Not a dicky bird,' said JB. 'But there was another funny call. Martha put it through to me because the caller had asked for you by name and said it was a matter of life and death.'

I winced but said nothing.

'She just said "Tell that Will Benson 'e's 'ad a lucky escape but 'is luck won't 'old out much longer."' JB had adopted a high-pitched voice and a dreadful cockney accent. Kim and I looked at him in wonder and giggled nervously.

'No, seriously, it was just like that,' said JB, colouring slightly. 'Like some godawful Eliza Doolittle in *My Fair Lady*. A well-bred young actress trying to do a cockney.'

That struck a chord. 'Oh bloody hell,' I said. 'Harriet Smythe's a well-bred actress and I can't imagine her making a terribly good Eliza Doolittle.'

I told JB about the phone calls and the Tube. 'I've been racking my brains about the quote. "I know death hath ten thousand several doors for men to take their exits." It's ringing a bell somewhere but I can't put my finger on it.'

'*Duchess of Malfi*,' said JB, and looked at me quizzically. 'And you know what Webster specialized in?'

'Revenge tragedies,' I said. 'Oh shit.'

'Sounds like your friendly Bloody Mary thrower.'

'I still can't understand why her agent hasn't calmed her down. He promised he would. I don't suppose he's rung either? I left him a message.'

'I'll try him myself,' said JB. 'I'll fish around a bit and say we're worried about her state of mind.'

He put the phone down after just a few seconds. 'He's on holiday. Touring France. Uncontactable all week. No wonder he didn't reply to your message. He probably hasn't got it yet.'

'Do you still want to run the picture of her?' asked Kim. 'You never know, it might pacify her.'

'I suppose so,' I replied. 'Goes against the grain.'

'I'll write it,' said JB. 'I won't make it too much of a crawl.'

He started bashing away at HighTechnoSet's ancient manual typewriter and about ten minutes later handed me the piece on the Smythe girl.

'I think we should headline it TAKING A BLOODY LIBERTY,' he said with a grin. 'It'll fit across a couple of columns in eighteen-point.'

'"Our apologies to Miss Harriet Smythe, a fine young actress who is clearly going places,"' I read aloud, so Kim could hear.

'Yeah, round the bend,' she interrupted.

'"Our reviewer William Benson was highly impressed by her performance as Juliet in the new production of Shakespeare's great love story at the Camden Basement. Unfortunately our old friends, the printer's gremlins, ensured that his kind words were cut from the review. This was unfortunate, but not unfortunate enough to warrant the Bloody Mary that Miss Smythe threw into our reviewer's face at a reception to launch the new Lloyd Webber version of *Macbeth*. *Macbeth* is a traditionally unlucky play and so it proved for our critic who was attempting to apologize at the time. We hope it will prove luckier for Miss Smythe who will be one of the all-singing, all-dancing and occasionally, we gather, all-naked witches. But should Miss Smythe take exception to any reviews of the show we trust she will exercise a modicum of self-restraint, particularly if she has a drink to hand. She should echo the words of Eliza Doolittle and tell herself 'Not bloody likely'. Meanwhile, the dry-cleaning bill's on its way, Harriet."'

Kim chuckled appreciatively. 'Nice one, JB. The bit about Eliza Doolittle will let her know we've got her sussed.'

We ran the piece in Victor's diary. JB wanted to make it the lead but I knew the silly old buffer was very taken with a story about Ralph Richardson's pet rat so we bunged it in the middle with a mug shot of Harriet as Juliet. She really was very beautiful, I thought, as I signed the page proof a couple of hours later. Beautiful but entirely lacking in Kim's good humour and warm sexuality.

We finally signed off the front page at about seven. The talent contest story, with mug shots of Susie Smiles, Eric Preston and the honest comedian looked very strong across six columns at the top. The Supersonic Atom flew across four columns below, under the headline BEWARE: LOW FLYING DWARFS, and there was a boring arts funding crisis story to add a touch of *gravitas*. JB looked pleased and Kim, Kevin and I felt a glow of honest achievement. Kim asked JB if he wanted to join us for a drink and warned him that Colin had threatened to put in an appearance.

'Has he indeed?' said JB. 'I'd have enjoyed a few words with him.' He shrugged. 'Still, I've got to see the new Howard Barker down T'Pit. Four hours of blood, anarchy and foul language. Just my cup of tea.' The amazing thing was he meant it. 'Might catch the Umbilical Chord Orchestra at the Rock Garden afterwards. They've re-formed for a one-off gig.'

After packing up our stuff we walked up to the pub, Kevin gallantly offering 'to see off any footpads with his umbrella' should we be so inconvenienced. 'Though come to think of it, a bit of rough with a couple of nice footpads would be just the ticket,' he added.

'Tell us about the *St Matthew Passion*,' said Kim brightly. Kevin was inclined to get maudlin about his unfulfilled sex life, though I suspect his chastity was a result of religious conviction rather than lack of opportunity.

'Lovely tenor two along from me,' he said dolefully. 'Straight of course.'

'I'll buy you a drink,' said Kim.

'A double self-pity on the rocks will do me just fine. Mustn't have too many though. I want to go to early Mass tomorrow. I've been troubled by Doubts.'

'Silly bugger,' said Kim.

'Would that I were,' said Kevin.

Mirza and Barbara had beaten us to the pub, and Barbara was already giggly after a couple of lager-blackcurrants.

'We've put the dwarf on the front, Babs,' Kim told her.

'Oh good. He was ever so sweet.'

As always on Tuesdays, the drinks seemed to go down with almost eerie speed. Normally none of us could face eating anything until it was too late to make any difference. Kevin, however, volunteered to get a load of sandwiches in. Delicious they were, rare beef and home-cooked ham, on none of your wholemeal rubbish but lovely sliced white.

I looked at my watch. It was nine o'clock. 'No sign of Colin, then,' I said, relieved. We'd all been half dreading his arrival.

'Probably up on Hampstead Heath bashing a few queers,' said Kevin viciously. I was so bound up with my own furious feelings about Colin that I hadn't seen it from a wider perspective. To Kevin, the *News of the World* story was a particularly nasty piece of homophobia.

'Bloody creep,' said Babs loudly, and naturally Colin chose that moment to make his entrance. If he'd heard her, he ignored it. He was wearing a flashy new suit, absurdly baggy and of a

135

thoroughly obnoxious shiny material. He already seemed to have acquired the superficial gloss and the glossy superficiality of the tabloid hack, but then he'd been in training for years.

'Hi, deadbeats,' he said, then fingered his revolting suit. 'Fance, eh?'

'I expect you'll grow into it,' said Kevin.

No one offered to buy him a drink and there wasn't a spare chair for him. He hovered by the table, looking anxious and awkward. He wasn't nearly as tough as he thought he was.

'Well, I'll get some drinks,' he said after a few moments of uneasy silence. He didn't ask what we wanted before strutting over to the bar.

Babs took a swig of her lager-blackcurrant. I'm sure she'd have preferred it through a straw.

'I'm not taking a drink off him,' she said firmly in a Lancashire accent that became thicker when she'd had a few.

'Nor me,' said Kevin.

Colin came back with two bottles of champagne and six glasses, then went off and found himself a chair.

'Thought we'd celebrate my success,' he said, sitting down.

'Oh, what success was that, Colin?' said Kevin, very cool, very camp. 'Your successful theft, your successful descent to the gutter, your success at ruining someone's career? Do tell me, I really am most interested.'

'Don't be such a prick,' said Colin, 'the job, of course.'

He looked at me, half bashful, half cocky. 'No hard feelings about the tape, then? I knew it had to be something good after you spent so long with JB, and my God it was. Much too good to waste. And it was my tape recorder after all. Here's the tape by the way. Don't worry, we took a copy.'

I opened the cassette. There was some money wedged inside – four fifty pound notes.

'You're too generous Colin. I was only expecting ten per cent of thirty pieces of silver.'

'Shit, you really are a wanker, aren't you,' he said, thoroughly riled now. 'Joe fucking Johnson's fucking Jesus Christ is he?

You got a great scoop and you were going to sit on it like a great fat git.'

I unfolded the notes and put them in a neat pile by my glass. Colin finished his second glass of champagne and poured another. The rest of us sat with our full glasses of fizz untouched.

'Anyone want a drink?' said Barbara cheerfully. 'Colin can I get you anything?' Anyone else would surely have left by now and I couldn't help admiring Colin's guts. 'No thanks, Babs babe, I'm doing fine.'

I picked up one of the fifties. I should have sent the money to charity, I suppose, but I couldn't resist it. I lit it with my lighter and watched it burn with a nice blue flame. Everyone watched, fascinated. When it was all gone apart from the bit I was holding, I dropped the remains into an ashtray.

'Can I have a go?' said Mirza. 'I've always wanted money to burn.' He gave Colin a look of fierce dislike that would have scared the hell out of me, the sort of look you could imagine an Islamic fundamentalist giving Salman Rushdie after bumping into him at a cocktail party.

'I checked your Stephen Regis story,' he said. 'What kind of sicko invents terminally ill children just to spite their colleagues?' He set fire to the fifty then collapsed into boyish giggles, the thunderous intensity disappearing as fast as it had arrived. 'Anyone want a light?' I shoved a Camel in my mouth and he lit it with hands that shook with laughter. Kevin picked up one of the notes and Barbara the other and all three were burning nicely in the ashtray when the barmaid came round to fetch the empties.

'Have you gone out of your tiny minds?' she asked.

Colin was pale with anger. He'd finished one bottle of champagne in fifteen minutes and was making inroads into the second. Almost up to Kim's standard, I thought. I had a momentary twinge as I envisaged them together and Kim must have sensed it because she reassuringly squeezed my thigh. After the burning of the two hundred pounds there didn't seem to be a lot to say. Colin looked round the table.

'You're a smug bunch of bastards,' he said quietly. He was right, of course. Five against one, the big moral gesture. Not very appealing. 'And you could at least have given the money to charity.'

'Absolutely,' said Kevin. He got out his chequebook and wrote a cheque for two hundred pounds to the Imperial Cancer Fund, rolled it up and went to put it in the collecting box on the bar. 'Next to sex, of course, and I know very little about that, there's nothing quite so liberating as spending money you can't afford,' he said when he came back. 'Can I have a gasper, Will?'

He rarely smoked and as I passed the packet to him he gestured towards the charity box. 'I've paid my insurance premium after all.'

It was a small joke but it broke the tension. Even Colin managed a wintry smile. I felt a sudden surprising warmth for him. Perhaps Kim was right, perhaps he really was vulnerable beneath all the bullshit and the bluster. 'Let's call it quits,' I said, picking up my as yet untasted glass of champagne and raising it in a toast. 'To a glittering career on the Street of Shame.' We all drank to him at last. But he remained the terminal prat. To Kim's obvious distress he went and stood behind her and started massaging her shoulders.

'What say we leave this bunch of dickheads and go get us a candlelit dinner somewhere, babe?' he said. It was pathetic. Where *had* he learnt to talk like that?

'Fuck off, Colin,' said Kim, more or less equably. 'And get your bloody paws off me.'

'Come on, babe, let's go,' he said, now attempting to drag her to her feet by force.

'Leave me alone,' shouted Kim, genuinely upset now. I stood up feeling self-conscious.

'Lay off her,' I said. He didn't, so I started moving round the table towards him. Kevin was quicker than me. With a deft flourish, and without even leaving his seat, he poked Colin hard in the stomach with his umbrella. Colin gasped and let go of Kim who came and stood next to me, her tardy defender. I

138

hoped it wouldn't come to a fight. I'd never been in a fight before, not even at school.

'Christ, that hurt,' said Colin at last, rubbing his stomach ruefully before sitting down again.

'Never underestimate the power of a little prick,' camped Kevin, waving an admonitory finger at his victim.

Colin ignored him. 'You sure you won't come for a meal then, babe?' he asked Kim. There was something almost heroic about his refusal to take no for an answer. A brilliant career on the *News of the World* clearly lay ahead of him.

'Not even if I was starving,' she said.

'Well, that's nice after all the good times we've had together,' he replied.

The others went very quiet, as they took in the information that Colin and Kim had had something going.

'Don't bandy a woman's name,' I said. I'd always wanted to say that.

Kim looked embarrassed. I wanted to hold her hand and tell her not to worry, but another declaration of internal affairs on *Theatre World* would have been *de trop*. More to provide a distraction from the uncomfortable silence that was developing than in the hope of eliciting a guilty reaction, I stared at Colin for a couple of seconds and then declared, in a voice ringing with defiance: 'I am Duchess of Malfi, still.'

He looked startled but there was no shock of recognition. The others looked understandably embarrassed.

'You've been drinking too much of that Jack Daniel's, mate,' he said. 'You'll be thinking you're Danny La Rue next.'

Not Colin then. I realized that I'd really wanted it to be Colin. Colin, the sexual athlete who'd taught me what sexual jealousy was and who had betrayed the Big Cunt. Kim covered for me.

'Will's got to review the play next week,' she said gamely.

'Yeah, I've just been reading it,' I said, blushing with embarrassment. 'Marvellous stuff.'

Colin bought another bottle of champagne and not to be

139

outdone, shoved another £50 into the charity box. The Imperial Cancer Fund wouldn't know what had hit them.

'Conscience money,' he said.

'Shake?' I said.

'Shake,' he said. We shook hands. With a bit of luck I'd never have to see the slimeball again.

He left soon afterwards, tomorrow was his first day and he wanted to get 'his head down in the sack' as he put it. He suddenly looked apprehensive, like a young boy standing on the platform and waiting for the train that will take him to boarding school for the first time. We wished him good luck and I think we meant it. Shortly after he'd gone, Kevin decided he'd better go if he was to make it to early Mass the following morning and he offered to share a cab with Barbara who lived nearby. Mirza had one for the road and then drifted off as well.

'Just you and me now then, babe.' I said. 'What say we hit Upper Street and find us that candlelit dinner for two?'

'Don't, Will,' she said. 'Not even as a joke.'

She moved her chair closer to mine and put her arm round my shoulder, and I kissed her briefly, gently on the lips. 'Tobacco and bourbon,' she smiled. 'All true man.'

'I thought Kevin was the star of the evening. Dead nifty with the umbrella.'

'Mmm,' she said. 'It doesn't look like Colin, then. Not unless he's a much better actor than I'm prepared to give him credit for.'

'No. It looks like it's Harriet fucking Smythe,' I said gloomily. And I'd fancied the bitch too.

'I've had an idea,' said Kim. 'Why don't we go up to the Camden Basement now.'

We had a final drink to get our courage up and hailed a cab to the theatre. No hanky panky this time. Kim was now the determined private investigator.

Mr Simon hadn't been quite right. The show had received one other review apart from mine, in the *Independent* ('a brilliant interpretation of the Bard's ballsiest play'). Several blown-up copies of it had been stuck in the window of the pub. Of *Theatre*

World's piece there was, naturally, no sign. The show hadn't come down so I crept into the darkest and most obscure corner of the cheerless pub above the Basement, and Kim bought the drinks. A large Jack Daniel's for me, a Coke, I noticed with surprise, for her.

'My God, you are taking this seriously.'

'My future happiness may depend upon it.'

After about ten minutes a dozen or so people came up the stairs from the theatre. Most of them, I was delighted to see, looked thoroughly depressed, a couple of them positively ashen with rage or boredom.

'I'll go down now, then,' said Kim bravely. I hugged her tight for a moment.

'Take care.'

'She can hardly pull a knife. Or at least I hope she can't. Try not to be noticed by anyone.'

She clattered off down the stairs into that benighted hell-hole and I hid behind my *Spectator*. After a few minutes Kim came back.

'What's the news?' I asked urgently.

'She's in the clear, definitely in the clear.'

I felt a great wave of relief. Perhaps the threats were all a joke after all, perhaps I hadn't really been pushed on the Underground platform. Through a blur of beer, champagne and Jack Daniel's it was easy to take a sanguine view. It was very dark in our little corner, so I put my hand on Kim's breast and gave her a proper kiss for the first time that day. Once again the fervour of her response astonished and delighted but after a couple of minutes she withdrew and tried to look cross.

'Now get your hand off my tits and I'll get some more drinks and tell you what happened.' I did as instructed.

'It really is a disgusting little theatre, isn't it,' she said, returning with a well-deserved gin and tonic for herself and a less well-deserved large Jack for me. 'It smells of cats' piss apart from anything else.'

'Get on with it,' I said testily.

'Right. Well the auditorium was empty apart from a girl

sitting in the prompt corner so I introduced myself and asked if I could speak to Harriet Smythe. There was a definite *froideur* when I mentioned *Theatre World* but I pressed on and said we'd come to apologize. I kept it vague. I hoped she might think I'd come to apologize for the whole review.'

'Thanks, Kim,' I said indignantly and rather loudly. 'Most of the review was spot-on for fuck's sake.'

'Keep your voice down, you twat. There's a group at the bar who look like actors.'

I sneaked a look. They were. Women amongst them. I moved my stool even further back into the corner.

'This girl was the stage manager. She said when Smythe came back from the Alhambra and told the rest of the cast about the drink-throwing they were all thrilled to bits and treated her like some kind of guerrilla freedom-fighter. The stage manager wasn't so bad though. She said she'd had to sit through the show every night for the past two weeks and phrases from your review kept going through her mind while she was watching it. She said it made it more bearable.'

'I'd like to meet this Solomon among stage managers.'

'I thought you might say that,' said Kim. 'She's got acne and greasy hair and a flat chest.'

'Oh yeah?'

'For Christ's sake, Will, let me get on with the tale.'

'Right. Sorry.'

'So I should think. Here we are at the start of an epic romance and you start lusting after one of the minor characters.'

'Sorry,' I said again.

'Anyway, that was Friday, Harriet's triumph. Yesterday morning she came in at eleven for rehearsal. The director, Tony Blaze, is insisting that they keep rehearsing right through the run so he can try out new concepts. Apparently the tomb scene is now staged in a supermarket with Romeo and Juliet lying in freezer cabinets. The stage manager said she'd done her back in when she and the other techies were trying to lug them down the stairs.'

'Oh do get a move on.'

'I think I might like to see it. It sounds like a real collector's item.'

'Kim, do you want me to hit you very hard indeed?'

'Might be fun,' she said infuriatingly. 'But not till we get to Blackpool. Anyway, as I was saying, Harriet arrived yesterday in floods of tears and said she was being punished for throwing that drink in your face. Her mother's been taken ill – hospital, intensive care, the full works – and she said it was God's judgement and she couldn't forgive herself. She said she was going to write to you, begging forgiveness and she just hoped that might save her mother's life.'

'She must be barking.'

'Just what the stage manager said. "Brilliant but off her chump." The SM said it was frightening to see her in such distress, pouring out all this paranoia about guilt and divine retribution.'

'So did you see her yourself, tell her all's forgiven?'

'That's just it. I couldn't. She's gone home to be at her mother's bedside. In Edinburgh. The stage manager says Harriet was so upset she went with her in a taxi to King's Cross yesterday morning and saw her on to the train.'

'So how did they do the show, yesterday and tonight?'

A smile of pure happiness spread over Kim's face.

'They thought they were going to have to cancel because they've got no understudies. Then what's his name, Blaze, announced that he'd do Juliet, reading from the text. The stage manager says its unbelievable. He's got himself up to look like Quentin Crisp, all foundation and mauve hair, and he plays Juliet as if she was a fifty-year-old faggot, with Romeo as a young boy he's trying to seduce.'

'Unless we're very lucky indeed, Mr Blaze looks all set for a glittering career with the RSC,' I said grimly.

'Let's go,' said Kim. 'I suddenly feel worn out.' As we went out, with me attempting to hide behind Kim as we passed the actors at the bar, I noticed a particularly pretty girl with a notably fresh complexion and tits that were almost in Kim's class. She nodded at Kim and winked at me, then turned back to her colleagues.

'The stage manager?' I said when we got outside.

At least Kim had the grace to blush.

'I see what you mean about the acne and the flat chest,' I said. 'I'm surprised you didn't mention the club foot.'

We had to wait ages for a cab and didn't increase our chances because Kim kept dragging me into a shop doorway for a snog. I was glad she had when we finally got into a taxi. Another talker. All the way to Brixton he rabbited on about the traffic, lorries, the fucking blacks, the fucking Muslims and, worst of all, the fucking cyclists who all ought to be locked up. Kim guided my hand into the interior of her jeans under cover of her trusty rugby shirt and nodded intelligently at him as I explored the damp declivities within.

'You mustn't come, Kim,' I whispered.

'Girl Guides' honour,' she said. Half-way to Brixton she told me to stop and we cuddled up close together and tried to ignore the vile ramblings of our driver. 'Give me a ring when you get home,' she said as she got out of the cab.

After paying off the driver in Vauxhall I found myself praying as I climbed the five steps to the front door and put the key in the lock. 'Please God, don't let there be any more messages. Not tonight, please God . . .'

The green light was flashing once on the answering machine and I went into the kitchen and made a cup of tea, fearful and furious with myself for being fearful. What would it be this time, I wondered miserably. A gloat about this morning? More quotations from Webster? I couldn't put off listening to it much longer. Kim would start worrying if I didn't phone soon. I lit a cigarette, and flipped the switch to play. The tape rewound and clicked into life. 'Oh, Mr Benson, you are a very naughty young man indeed,' trilled the Chief Squealer of the Water Babies. I didn't know whether to laugh or cry. Ethel Henderson was 'absolutely desperate' for confirmation that I'd be coming to their 'night of nights' as she wanted to put me and 'naturally your good lady' on the top table.

I grinned and phoned Kim. She sounded a bit slurry but despite a medium-sized skinful myself I realized I felt OK. Very OK indeed for a Tuesday. Sandwiches, fear, and a spot of sexual stimulation were clearly a good foundation for sobriety.

'Kim, I've a favour to ask you. I've got to go to the Water Babies annual dinner and dance at The Savoy tomorrow. Will you be my "good lady" as the Chief Squealer puts it?'

'It's my night for doing my hair,' said Kim mournfully. With her close-cropped style it couldn't take her more than ten minutes, and I was about to start remonstrating with her when she gave one of her soda-siphon snorts of laughter. 'Only kidding, of course I'll come. Will it be very grisly?'

'A modicum of gristle will almost certainly be involved, I'd imagine. Thanks, Kim, I couldn't have faced it on my own.' I felt an ache for her, like a dagger in the heart. 'I love you, you know that don't you?' I said. It sounded quite fierce.

'Yes,' she said simply.

'God bless, then, see you tomorrow.'

'God bless.'

I put the phone down and thought about going to bed. A bit of music first, though, the traditional Tuesday night ritual but quieter and more sober than usual, with tea instead of Scotch. I made a mug in the kitchen, cursed Cathy for the great teapot theft and wondered which record to play first, the Grateful Dead's *American Beauty* or Van Morrison's greatly underrated *Veedon Fleece*. Always a tough decision on Tuesdays this one, but Van the Man won it by a whisker. Or would have done. Getting the record out of its battered sleeve, I saw it had been scratched, deeply, on both sides. All my records are scratched of course; in my view, or so I try to persuade myself, the snap, crackle and hiss adds to the atmosphere. But not scratched like this, just one great gash, obviously made with a sharp blade, right from the rim to the centre of the disc, on both sides. I looked at *American Beauty*. The same cruel, determined incisions. Cathy had left a little surprise behind.

I waded through my entire collection. I was only three at the height of the Summer of Love but my heart belonged to San

Francisco, circa 1967. I'd been introduced to psychedelia by an amiable old hippy I'd run into while working as a washer-up in the year off between school and university, and although I occasionally bought newer stuff on CD, nothing quite hit the spot like the old vinyl records from the sixties and early seventies. Cathy had been most discriminating. She may not have liked my music but she certainly knew what I liked. All the Grateful Deads and Van Morrisons were ruined. So were the two Syd Barrett solo albums, those haunting cries of a drowning man, and *Piper at the Gates of Dawn*, which he'd recorded in his prime with Pink Floyd before the acid finally fried his brain. The complete works of Janis Joplin, the Beach Boys' *Pet Sounds*, The Cream's *Disraeli Gears*, Jefferson Airplane's *Crown of Creation*, Neil Young's *After the Goldrush*, the Doors' *Strange Days*, the Beatles' *Revolver*, Love's *Forever Changes* – all bore the savage scratch on both sides. To add insult to injury, Cathy had spared a few records I hadn't played for years, records I was embarrassed even to admit to owning. Yes's *Tales from the Topographic Oceans*. *Tarkus* by ELP. Jeff Lynne's *The War of the Worlds*. You know the sort of stuff. Cathy had at least missed one of Van's more recent efforts, I discovered, *Poetic Champions Compose*. There's a great version of 'Motherless Child' on it in which a world of infinite pain and loss seems to have been distilled into five minutes and 22 seconds. It suited my mood. 'The bloody bitch,' I kept saying to myself, 'the bloody bitch.'

It was a deliberate incantation, an attempt to block out rational thought. Cathy, who knew how much I loved these records, was normally the least violent of people. As in the shove on the Tube, there had been a frightening fury in these great gouging scratches. If that fury was still burning, I was in real trouble. She knew my habits, knew my routines. I remembered the Police record and realized that Cathy's copy of it, one of the few records she owned, was missing. Cathy, it dawned on me, was now number one suspect in the campaign to terrify and perhaps eliminate me.

Wednesday

I sat up late, drinking endless cups of tea. By three o'clock I was reduced to Emerson, Lake and Palmer, and a couple of minutes of that bombastic claptrap sent me scurrying to my bed. I didn't expect to sleep but drifted off after about twenty minutes with the light on, thanks to another dose of *Thursday's Child*. I was getting near to the end of my stock of Streatfeild. Only *The Growing Summer* to go.

I woke with a jolt when the phone started ringing and fumbled for my watch. It was 10.30, far later than I'd expected. I decided not to answer it, just monitor the call on the answering machine. There was silence as it went through its rigmarole about Will and Cathy being unavailable at the moment, and I guessed that Cathy certainly was available – at the other end of the line. Then the robot voice came on. Cathy concealing herself, I thought, sick at heart.

> The grave's a fine and private place,
> But none I think do there embrace
> And yonder all before you lie
> Deserts of vast eternity.

No trouble placing that. Marvell's 'To His Coy Mistress'. One of my favourites. The lines had been chopped around a bit. And surely it was before 'us' lie in the original? The 'you' made it sound even more threatening and lonely.

'You're not there, then,' said the voice. 'Enjoying the bit of skirt in a taxi.' Another literary echo? MacNeice, that was it.

Worrying. It meant that on at least one night Kim and I had been followed. I didn't like the thought of that at all.

I switched off the answering machine and picked up the phone. 'I'm here,' I yelled. 'Just fucking cut it out, Cathy. This has gone on long enough.' There was silence at the other end.

'I know it's you, Cathy,' I shouted, but already I was beginning to have my doubts. She had no real interest in poetry, had never, as far as I knew, seen or read *The Duchess of Malfi*.

'Remember *Julius Caesar*,' said the voice.

' "It seems to me most strange that men should fear;
Seeing that death, a necessary end,
Will come when it will come."

'Mind you,' continued the voice, with a grotesque metallic laugh. 'Ceasar was kidding himself and he died that day. Perhaps you'll die today. Or perhaps not. Perhaps tomorrow. Or perhaps not. It will come though. "Cowards die many times before their deaths." '

'Cathy, please stop it,' I pleaded, and then the line went dead.

I started to light a cigarette, then realized I'd got to get to the lavatory very fast. Trying to engage in conversation with the voice had shaken me more than anything so far; the thought that it might be Cathy was unendurable. I made a run for it and emerged from the loo after a *mauvais quart d'heure* to find that my fag had burnt a deep dark scar on the table where we kept the phone, a table Cathy and I had bought together at an antiques fair in Lyme Regis. That made me angry, and being angry was a great deal better that being scared.

I decided to try phoning her at the bank. She usually started at 9.30. It was an open-plan office and it was hard to imagine her setting up her electronic gadgetry and making the call from there. If she was at her desk now, perhaps she was in the clear.

A man answered her extension and asked if he could help.

'I need to speak to Catherine Williamson,' I said. 'It's quite urgent.'

'I'm afraid she's not here at the moment. Dental appointment. Ouch!' He made a noise like an electric drill. The office card, evidently. I was surprised Cathy had never mentioned him. Or perhaps she had and I hadn't listened.

'Can I take a message?' said the jester, abandoning his high-pitched whine. I told him no, I'd try later and put down the phone.

I made a cup of coffee and smoked a lot and wished that my persecutor was Joe Johnson or Harry Meadows or Harriet or Colin or Susie Smiles. Someone I hadn't shared a bed with. I had a bath and listened to Radio 1 in the hope that the inane chatter would put me in such a bad mood that I'd forget about Cathy for a bit. It did. After my bath, I phoned for a minicab and sat in a chair near the window as I waited for it to arrive. This was a mistake, as any reader of Sherlock Holmes could have told me. As I should have told myself. A car stopped in the middle of the road. That's quick, I thought. The DJ was just telling us that it was 11.15 as I leant forward to switch him off. At the same moment there was a crash of smashed glass, a hiss and a clunk. I leapt up and looked out of the shattered window. The car was already heading off down the road and I only caught a glimpse of the driver, who was wearing a puffy anorak with the hood pulled over the head. As it turned the corner I realized that not only had I failed to take its number, I hadn't even noticed the make. It was red. On that point I was positive. Pathetic, really.

Fragments of glass were scattered over the carpet. What had caused the damage? There had been no sound of a shot I realized with relief, but what about the hiss and the clunk? Then I saw it, up near the ceiling, a crossbow bolt embedded in the wall. I thought about fingerprints and didn't touch it, then thought about Cathy, climbed on to a chair and yanked it out. It was lethal, fourteen inches of sleek yellow metal, and it was a real struggle to wrest it from the plaster. I'd read articles about crossbows, stories of people who had been killed or horribly wounded by them. You can buy them at those sinister survivalist shops without a licence.

What if my assailant came back for a second shot? I felt sick at the thought, dropped to my hands and knees and crawled back to the window, trying to avoid the broken glass. I raised my head a few inches and gazed warily over the edge of the sill. No red car. Then I forced myself to go outside to where the car had been, crouching down in the road to what I guessed would be the level of a seated driver to visualize the upward trajectory of the bolt's flight. There was no doubt. The line of fire crossed just over the seat where I had been sitting. If I hadn't leant forward to switch off the radio, it could have hit me anywhere between the chest and the head.

I ought to go to the police. I knew that. They'd probably have dismissed a few messages on the answering machine and a shove on the Tube. But the crossbow bolt couldn't be brushed aside. This was attempted murder. But if it was Cathy who was playing *The Golden Shot* I couldn't possibly call them in. I got up and dialled her at the bank as fast as I could. It was 11.22. The bolt had only been fired seven minutes earlier. If she was back at her desk now she had an alibi. But all I got was the office wag.

'Still no sign of her. She must be having a terrible time,' he said, giving me another blast of his dentist's drill impersonation. The life and soul of the small business loans department.

I didn't want to leave the flat with the window smashed. Thieves or squatters would be in like a flash. As I was looking up the glaziers in *Yellow Pages*, the minicab arrived. I explained someone had just thrown a stone through the window and I'd got to get it boarded up. He was sympathetic, which was magnanimous since he'd lost his fare, and toddled off without complaint. I explained to the emergency glaziers that I needed to get to work as soon as possible and they were round in no time at all, took the dimensions of the window and neatly boarded it up. They said they'd come back whenever it was convenient to replace the glass and they didn't even want paying on the spot. Efficient service with a smile. I couldn't remember the last time I'd encountered it, apart from at McDonald's and that doesn't count. All that cheerfulness for three quid an hour? They'd either been brainwashed or were androids from outer space, waiting to take over the world.

Once the glaziers had gone I phoned the office. I'd already phoned once, straight after trying to reach Cathy for the second time, but had put the phone down as soon as Martha answered. This time I asked for JB and explained that I was going to be even later than usual for a Wednesday because my front window had been smashed by hooligans.

'Sure it's nothing to do with the previous trouble?' he asked.

'Quite sure,' I lied. 'I saw the little bastards running down the street. Only about twelve, they were.'

I had a belated spasm of anxiety about Kim. I hadn't liked the crack about the bit of skirt in a taxi and if Cathy had been following us, she'd almost certainly know where Kim lived. By now she would have had time to drive to Brixton, and be ready to shoot her bolt when Kim showed her face at the front door. I realized I was already thinking of Cathy as the only possible suspect. A bit of skirt in a taxi sounded like sexual jealousy to me, and I now regarded myself as something of an expert on the subject.

I asked JB if Kim was in yet.

'Before noon on a Wednesday?' he said incredulously. 'You're joking. No hang on a minute, I tell a lie, she's just come in now.'

He called her over.

'Will?' said Kim. 'What's up?'

'Are you OK? No trouble last night or this morning?'

'Nothing apart from a bloody awful hangover. What's the matter, Will? Nothing else has happened has it? You are all right?'

'Everything's fine now. I'll tell you later.'

I remembered I had to call Ethel Henderson about the Water Babies do.

Mercifully she didn't want to natter as she usually did when she phoned me at the office. 'Must dash, the girls are rehearsing the cabaret here,' she said, all of a flutter.

I called another cab, and had my umpteenth cup of coffee. I'd calmed down at last. It was only an overdose of caffeine that was making me tremble. Nevertheless, when the cab arrived I found myself going down the front steps sideways to present a smaller target. Though considering the size of my beer-gut this was probably a waste of time.

'You all right, mate?' said the driver. 'Whassamatter? Done your leg in?'

'That's right,' I said. It was easier than telling the truth. 'Torn cartilage.'

'Tricky things, cartilages,' he said sagely. Once inside the cab I stretched out on the back seat, legs splayed to the right and left, bum right on the edge, back at an angle of 45 degrees. In this excruciating position my head was just below window level. The driver, who had been keeping up a monologue on every leg injury he and his large family had ever experienced, looked at me with some incredulity in the rear mirror.

'Done your back in and all?' he asked. 'Tricky things, backs.'

'Just the odd twinge,' I said bravely. Bad backs kept him going all the way to the Isle of Dogs; by the time we got there, my anti-crossbow position had given me a very bad back indeed. I paid him off in a crouching position using his car for cover, then made a speedy, crab-like progress to reception, remembering to limp all the while so the driver wouldn't think I'd been telling him lies. I could see Martha watching me with distaste through the plate glass window, so as soon as I got inside I went on the attack.

'Did you give Ethel Henderson, Chief Squealer of the Water Babies, my home number?' I said, making it sound as offensive as possible. 'She's been hassling me for days.'

Martha pursed her lips. 'No, why should I do that?'

'That's what I want to know. No one in the newsroom would have done it and my number's not in the book.' Martha was looking distinctly furtive now.

'Just a minute. There was a nice sounding woman, middle-aged, a few days ago. She seemed very anxious to get your number. I thought it must be your mother so I gave it to her.'

'I haven't got a mother, Martha. And if I had, don't you think it's likely she'd already have my home number?'

'Not necessarily,' said the stupid old boot unconvincingly. One up to Benson. I skipped merrily up the steps before she had time to think of a stronger riposte.

I blew Kim a kiss then went and sat at my desk. JB came over, looking smug, and handed me an old theatre programme.

'I dug it out of the attic last night.' JB keeps the programmes of every show he has ever seen, thousands of them by now, all immaculately filed away. This was one for the Thorndike Theatre, Leatherhead, the autumn season of 1971. And the play was *The Duchess of Malfi*.

'Wow,' I said as I spotted the name Susie Smiles way down the cast list. She had a small part, as the courtesan. 'Embarrasingly over-the-top,' JB had written in his tiny neat handwriting next to her name. 'Makes Fenella Fielding seem subtle.' At the back was a list of forthcoming productions. No mention of *Julius Caesar*. But one Sunday night there was an *Anthology of Great Love Poetry* to be presented by Susie Smiles and an actor I'd never heard of. Any anthology of love poetry worth its salt was surely going to include 'To His Coy Mistress'. I could just imagine Susie's horrid simper as the unknown thesp read it to her. It wasn't anything like proof, of course, but I fell on the circumstantial evidence with glee. Maybe Cathy wasn't taking pot-shots at me after all.

'Intriguing, eh?' said JB, over my shoulder.

'Even more intriguing than you might suspect.' I pointed to the advert for the poetry recital. 'I had Marvell's "To His Coy Mistress" this morning. And also a bit of *Julius Caesar*.' I turned to Susie Smiles's biography. A lot of Agatha Christie, all of it in rep or on tour. Wilde's *A Woman Of No Importance*, a couple of pantos. *Much Ado About Nothing*, not as Beatrice but as the maidservant Ursula, I noticed with pleasure. Susie Smiles had been doctoring her c.v. just like she'd been doctoring the talent contests.

'Shame there's nothing about *J.C.*,' I said. 'That would have clinched it for me. Do you think the woman who phoned you up, the Eliza Doolittle soundalike, could have been Susie? You've heard her voice recently on the phone.'

'I've been thinking about that and I'm not sure. The Doolittle voice sounded younger, certainly not kippered by fifty St Moritz a day. But then she was an actress, a bloody useless one but still an actress. She ought to be able to do younger voices. And the stab at cockney sounded like authentic Smiles incompetence to me.'

I remembered Susie's girlish enthusiasm about 'darling Gerald'.

'She can sound young, she did sound young at the talent contest. I think it's her.'

'I think you should go to the police. Mind you, they'll probably be on to her for fraud anyway as soon as we publish.'

I shook my head. I kept thinking about the records, of the knowledge of my home number (though any potential threats-with-menaces merchant had a ready ally in Martha), about the sexual jealousy that underlay MacNeice's line about the bit of skirt in a taxi. If there was any chance at all that it was Cathy, I couldn't risk calling the cops.

'I'd just like to give it a day or so, JB.'

'It's your funeral,' he said, then grinned ruefully. 'Sorry, Will, that was tactless.'

I was glad I hadn't told him about the William Tell routine that morning. He'd probably have frog-marched me down to the local nick. I'd got to see Cathy. Talk to her and judge for myself. On neutral ground. In a crowded public place.

Most of the newsroom were going to lunch at the Perseverance but I caught Kim's eye and said we'd join them later. We went to the Bricklayer's on the corner of Westferry Road, a cosy, companionable pub with none of the squalor of the Perseverance.

'Why don't we come here more often?' I asked.

'The jukebox is no good,' said Kim. 'It's got a few decent records on it.'

We settled at a small table with our drinks, low-alcohol shandies for both of us, and I told her about the morning's excitements at Rita Road. She went impressively pale.

'Will, you really must go to the police now.'

Then I told her about the records, and JB's discoveries about Susie Smiles. 'I'd go to the police like a shot if I was sure it was Susie, but I can't risk it if it's Cathy. You see that, don't you?'

She nodded miserably.

'I'm worried about you too, Kim. You're the "bit of skirt in a taxi." Whoever it is probably knows where you live now.'

'We'll just have to be careful,' said Kim. 'I'll start taking cabs as well. When are you going to see Cathy?'

'Tomorrow, I hope.'

'It won't be easy. And what will you do if she admits it?'

I shook my head. I hadn't a clue. Try to make her see reason, I supposed. I simply couldn't square this cold, murderous fury with the Cathy I'd known and loved so inadequately.

'Could it be anyone else apart from Cathy or that horrible Smiles woman?'

I munched up the last of my cheese and onion toasted sandwich and lit a cigarette.

'Well, there's Joe Johnson and/or Harry Meadows. If they think I sold the story to the *News of the World* they'd be the most likely of all in some ways. I mean Harry Meadows actually threatened to kill me and the silence from them has been deafening since Sunday. And they must have a secretary or some other loyal female retainer on the staff who could have made the Doolittle call.'

'None of the other papers seem to have found them yet,' said Kim. 'The story's gone cold. They must be staying with friends. In a safe-house. They could be phoning you from there and nipping round to your place for a bit of target practice.'

'It's possible, I suppose, but I don't think it's their style. A quick duffing up down some back alley's more their line. I can't see them using all these literary quotations either. Webster would just be a brand of beer to them.'

'And Marvell powdered milk.'

'What about the Godfather? After all, you did tell him you'd been seeing me,' I said, putting elaborate emphasis on the 'seeing'.

Kim laughed out loud. 'Dukie wouldn't know the Duchess of Malfi if she bit him on the bum. Anyway, I've been in touch with him. He phoned the other day. Knowing your lamentable tendency to jealousy I didn't tell you at the time. Relations are entirely cordial. He's seeing, sorry, going out with, fucking, his secretary. He says he didn't realize how much he fancied her until after we'd split up.' She winced. 'He says they're already trying to make babies. And he sent you his best wishes. As you'll remember, he doesn't know about Colin. Only, somewhat prematurely, about you. He suggested that we might all go out for a meal together. Do you think you could bear it?'

'Yeah. Of course. I've fought off the green-eyed monster now. At least I hope I have.'

'You better have done. Once is quite flattering. Any more and it becomes a pain.' She kissed me quickly on the lips. 'There's no cause, Will. I'm a one-man girl.'

I started babbling out further apologies for my disgraceful behaviour but she put a finger over my lips.

'Forget it,' she whispered. 'I don't mind a bit of bile. It shows you're alive. Now, back to the investigation. Is there anyone else?'

'I toyed with the idea of Martha this morning. She really hates me and I don't like her so it would be lovely if it was her. But she's got a rock-solid alibi. I phoned almost immediately after the crossbow was fired and she was on the switchboard. There's one other possibility, though. Colin. I know we're meant to be friends again after last night, but he's clearly still got the hots for you. And I've got a feeling he shares a flat with his sister.'

'He does,' said Kim. 'He's devoted to her. I think she's the one person he actually likes. He sounds almost human when he talks about her. She works at home. Computers or something.'

'So presumably he could have persuaded her to make the cockney call? It would be nice to know that he really was at the

News of the World at eleven-fifteen this morning rather than sitting in a car in Rita Road.'

A grin lit up Kim's face. 'Let's phone the *Screws*. Not Colin, the news editor. I'll pretend I'm his mother. Serve the bugger right if they think he's a mummy's boy.'

We crammed into the phone cubicle, and Kim got through to the desk.

'Is that Colin Sneath's boss?' She said, suddenly sounding very Newcastle and credibly middle-aged. 'It's Mrs Sneath here. I'm ever so sorry to bother you and please don't tell Colin I phoned but I just wanted to know if he arrived safely this morning. He's been staying at home for the past couple of days and it's a long drive from Newcastle . . . He did. What time? About ten-thirty. That's early. He must have been driving too fast. You've not sent him out this morning have you? What do you newspaper people call it? Doorstepping or something. It's coming down cats and dogs up here. I don't want my Colin standing out in the rain all day, not after a long drive like that.'

I was finding it hard to suppress the giggles but Kim ploughed on with an admirably straight face.

'He's been working on a story from the office all morning has he? Oh I am glad. Listen Mr, what did you say your name was, Mr Levington, I'm not at all sure I'm glad Colin's got this new job but don't tell him I said so. I mean, it's sleazy the *News of the World*, isn't it, if you'll forgive my saying so. I was just wondering whether, as a special favour to me, you could keep him off the nastiest stories. I don't like to think of a son of mine mixing with prostitutes and homosexuals and gangsters. If you could just keep what you might call a fatherly eye on him. You know, make sure he doesn't fall in with a set of hardened drinkers and the like. What was that? Well really, I don't call that civil, Mr Levington, not civil at all . . .'

Kim hung up the phone and I hugged her as she snorted with laughter in the tiny phone box.

'I suppose I shouldn't have done that, but after all the hassle he's given me over the past few days I couldn't resist it. He was quite patient at first, Mr Levington, in a brusque, hacky sort of way, but in the end he lost his rag and said Colin was a grown man, that the *News of the World* expected its reporters to be able to look after themselves without interference from their mothers and that Colin would have to do whatever the paper required of him to earn his, and I quote, "not inconsiderable" salary. Then he slammed the phone down. Anyway Colin's not been out of the office all morning. But I expect he cán look forward to a good deal of doorstepping after this.'

'Well, we've narrowed the field,' I said. 'It looks as though it's got to be either Cathy or Susie Smiles, with Joe Johnson and Harry Meadows as an outside chance. I can't bear it if it's Cathy. It's got to be Smiles.'

But in my heart I thought it was Cathy and it depressed me immensely. 'I wish we were out of all this and up in Blackpool. You don't think we could leave early on Friday do you?'

'It'd look a bit obvious if we both left at lunchtime with our little suitcases. I couldn't bear all the cracks about going off for a dirty weekend. And what if it doesn't work and we come back and can't even look each other in the face?'

I took her hand. 'You don't think that will happen, do you?'

'You might hate Blackpool. Or be bored by me.'

'I might hate Blackpool. I won't be bored by you.'

'I get moody sometimes. Just promise you'll buy me a bar of chocolate and pat me on the head when I get mardy. It always works.'

'Right. What sort of chocolate works best?'

'Almond Yorkie.'

Back at the office, with little to do, I tried Harry Meadows's office again, without success. There had been an answering machine before. Now even that wasn't working. Then I rang Cathy's bank and she picked up her phone on the first ring.

'Small business loans,' she said. She sounded dreadful.

'Cathy, it's Will,' I said. I couldn't think of anything else.

'Oh,' she said dully. She didn't seem inclined to chat either.

'I was wondering if we could meet tomorrow.'

'When?' Her voice lacked all expression. I'd never heard her speak like this before.

'I've got to go to the theatre tomorrow night. What about lunchtime? We could meet in that brasserie near your bank. About one o'clock.'

'Right. Bye.' She hung up immediately. She sounded either very depressed or full of guilt. I tried to put her out of my mind until the following day, but kept remembering her drained, dead voice.

Apart from that the afternoon passed peacefully, compiling the paper's listings section of new shows from an alarmingly thick pile of press releases. Not for the first time it struck me that there was altogether too much theatre in Britain. Did we really need a new play called *Vermin*, 'a savage indictment of privatization in local authority refuse collection services'? Or Tommy Steele touring in a 'sparkling new musical version of the Hollywood classic *Citizen Kane*'? No, we didn't.

At about 5.30 Kim disappeared into the Ladies to change for the Water Babies do and emerged, half an hour later, looking as stunning as I'd ever seen her. She was wearing a man's dinner jacket (one of Dukie's cast-offs, I wondered with an admirable lack of jealousy), a white blouse and black bow-tie, clinging black silk trousers and black stilettos. There was a pair of dangly *diamanté* earrings I'd never seen before and, to add a touch of colour to the austere ensemble, she'd tied a blood red scarf round her trousers instead of a belt. The usual sexy urchin with the crooked grin had disappeared. With the masculine clothes and short hair she might have looked androgynous, but that was only until you noticed that splendid chest, and you noticed that first of all. Or I did, anyway. Kevin wolf-whistled, JB gave an ironic round of applause, Barbara said 'Ooh, you do look lovely' and I just stared in delight. Kim looked embarrassed at all the fuss, sat down at her desk and pretended to get on with her subbing. I went off to change myself. I hadn't worn my dinner jacket since the *Royal Variety Show* the previous year and as I squeezed myself into it I realized I'd got a lot fatter since then. When I'd first bought the suit three years earlier I used to tighten up the tags on the side of the waistband. I couldn't even connect them with the buckles now and they dangled forlornly like badges of shame. With any luck I'd be able to undo the top of my trousers under cover of my napkin during dinner. What a terrible thing to look forward to doing. How could Kim fancy this tub of lard? I thought despairingly about trying to lose some weight and even as I said it I knew I was kidding myself. I buttoned up the jacket to cover the worst excesses of my stomach, snapped the ready made bow-tie into place and went back into the newsroom feeling hot and self-conscious.

Kim came over and ruffled my hair. 'You look sweet,' she said. 'Like a cinema manager.' Well, it wasn't quite the same as suave and sexy but it would have to do.

JB ambled over and pretended to inspect us like a sergeant major on the parade ground.

'Stomach in, Benson,' he ordered. I did my best and saluted.

'You look smashing, Kim,' he said fondly. 'Keep an eye on this old scruff. Any wandering hand trouble in the cab, report to me first thing in the morning.'

Kim blushed prettily, and JB leered. 'Or not, as the case may be,' he added.

Martha rang to say our cab had arrived and we went down the steps like a couple of kids let out of school. Just before we turned the corner and came in view of the dragon, I pulled Kim to me and kissed her gently. She tasted of lipstick and peppermint.

'He guessed, you know, JB,' said Kim after a while.

'Do you mind that much? It must be horrible for you going out with a fatty like me.'

'No, I don't mind and it's not horrible. Remarkable as it may seem, I love you, Will Benson, just the way you are.'

So that was all right, then.

We went decorously down the rest of the stairs, a chaste foot apart. Martha said a cheerful goodnight to Kim, pointedly ignoring me. Then she gave Kim a sour look too.

We climbed into the cab and I told the driver the Savoy. Kim looked at me and laughed.

'Your face is covered in lipstick,' she said. 'No wonder

160

Martha looked so sick. She always thought I was such a nice girl.'

She spat on her handkerchief and cleaned me up, just like my aunt used to do when I was covered in chocolate as a young child. I almost cried with the sharpness of the memory and the tenderness of it all.

The taxi dropped us off at the Riverside entrance and we were directed to the pre-dinner reception. A toastmaster in a red jacket asked our names, then bawled them out to the assembled throng. There was a line up of Water Baby officials to negotiate, with Ethel Henderson at its head. For her night of nights, the Chief Squealer had swathed herself in a great balloon of scarlet taffeta which ended just above her plump white knees. She looked like a cheerful toadstool. Round her neck hung her gold badge of office, a baby with its mouth open, squealing presumably. She greeted us with the mixture of effusiveness and panic that is the hallmark of the inveterate publicity seeker.

'So pleased you could come,' she gushed, 'and I do so much hope you'll give us a lovely, lovely write-up. I've engaged a photographer,' she added, gesturing at a harassed lensman with no fewer than three cameras round his neck. 'I'll send round the prints tomorrow morning with all the names on the back. Do you think your wonderful paper might run to a page?'

I'd been thinking of a picture caption. Still, needs must. 'If you took one of those Thank You adverts of say, half a page, we could probably guarantee to fill the other half with editorial. Otherwise I fear it will just be a short mention.' I twisted the knife. 'Maybe not even a photograph.'

Mr Nasty. Kim was Miss Nice.

'But just think of a full page, Mrs Henderson,' she beamed. 'Our Mr Hastings in the advertising department would be delighted to help you with the words and we could run a big picture of you in that gorgeous frock welcoming your distinguished guests.'

A lengthy queue of them was already building up behind us as Ethel found herself racked between money and vanity. Vanity won, as we knew it would, but you couldn't help liking the silly cow. 'I'll have to pay myself,' she said firmly. 'Couldn't possibly take it out of funds. How much?'

'Very reasonable, really,' said Kim. 'Five hundred for the half-page.'

The Chief Squealer shuddered, then flashed a generous smile. 'You've talked me into it,' she said. 'The price of conceit.' She turned to her next guest and we moved on down the line.

The Water Babies had been started at the turn of the century as a club for female entertainers, particularly music hall turns. Actresses, singers and dancers still joined, but so did a lot of other people, middle-aged housewives mostly, who in exchange for fairly substantial dollops of cash (which all went to charity) were allowed to rub shoulders with celebrities at dos like this. JB called it the 'monstrous regiment of Essex women', and it was indeed very Essex, a bit flash, a bit glottal-stopped. Billericay ruled. But at least the women of Billericay knew how to have a good time. Or so at least JB had assured me.

I was beaming fatuously and shaking an endless succession of hands when Kim gave me a sharp kick in the calf.

'I think we should give the courtesies a miss,' she hissed. 'Susie Smiles is here, about six people down.' I looked. She was indeed.

'Let's tough it out. I want to look her in the eye,' I said.

Despite the toastmaster's earlier vocal endeavours, Susie clearly hadn't realized we were there and our arrival was evidently an unpleasant surprise. She just stared in silence as I shook her dead fish of a hand.

'You little shit,' she managed to splutter out at last. Kim gave her the sweetest of smiles, but Susie withdrew her hand as if stung when Kim tried to shake it.

'Why don't you just piss off,' she snarled, shocking the matronly lady standing next to her who seemed distinctly flustered as Kim and I presented ourselves. At last we reached the end of the line.

'God, who are we going to meet next?' I said as we set off in

162

search of a drink. 'With my luck they'll probably have invited the Big Cunt to do the cabaret.'

Waiters were moving round with trays loaded with glasses of champagne, Scotch, gin and tonics and Bloody Marys, and after fairly vigorous pursuit I managed to collar a Scotch for myself and a G and T for Kim. I usually feel a bit of a prick at these kind of functions, overcome with an uncharacteristic shyness, but standing there celebrity spotting with Kim (Barbara Windsor, Anneka Rice, old uncle Frank Bough and all) I found I was enjoying it. I spotted Stephen Regis, and waved at him. He strode over looking affable and tanned from his Florida holiday, and was wearing, I was delighted to see, his gold medallion outside his lacy lilac dress shirt.

'Will Benson, isn't it?' I assured him it was. 'And who, may I ask, is your delectable lady companion?' I introduced Kim and he kissed her hand.

'Thanks a million for not printing anything about our temporary cash flow problem,' he said. 'I don't know what that reporter of yours was playing at.'

'He no longer works for us,' said Kim.

Regis grinned. 'Like that, is it? Mind you, there's part of me wishes you had printed it. They pay well in the libel courts these days.'

Susie Smiles was advancing on us. I knew I'd have to confront her at some stage, but couldn't face it until I'd got a few drinks inside me. 'I'm afraid I must go,' I said. 'I've just seen someone I want to avoid.'

'I spend most of my life doing that,' said Regis equably. 'Make a run for it.'

Kim and I thanked him, and went and lost ourselves in the crush at the bar.

'All on the house,' said the barman as I waved a limp tenner. Bliss was it in that night to be alive. As I negotiated my way back to Kim, I was jovially nudged in the ribs and spilt half of Kim's gin and tonic down my trousers. It was Billy Walter and he was entirely unrepentant.

'Christ, it looks like you've just pissed yourself,' he said predictably.

'Very witty. How are you?'

'All the better for seeing you here. Is the lovely Kim with you?'

I nodded. 'I expect that was her gin and tonic. I'll get another one and see you over there,' he said, pointing to an area of relative calm at the edge of the bunfight. I gestured to Kim and she followed me over.

'What's this then?' she said as I gave her what was left of her drink. 'Half-rations?'

'Don't worry, a replacement's on its way.' Billy returned with Maureen, Miss Wet T-Shirt, in tow.

'Well, here we all are again,' I said inanely. 'You've seen Susie Smiles is here?'

'Not only seen her but spoken to her,' said Billy. 'She's spitting tacks about you and *Theatre World*.'

'Has she seen the piece yet?'

'You bet she has. I've news on that front. She and her husband are flying to Spain first thing tomorrow morning. They own a club out there and apparently they feel it's time they took a keener interest in its management. In other words, they're ducking out before the old Bill has a chance to interview them. She must be relying on the fact that most people don't see *Theatre World* till Thursday. This will be her last appearance in dear old Blighty for some time to come.'

'She must have realized you gave us some help, I'm afraid.'

'Oh, she knew all right. I got all the stuff about Spain when she was with some of the other Water Babies. But then she got me on my own and started spurting her usual venom. Called me a duplicitous cunt and a fucking child molester. I do love Susie's way with words.'

Maureen looked at him affectionately. 'I'm not that young,' she said in a little girl's voice. 'And what does duplicitous mean?'

They seemed very happy together.

I told them about the threats and phone calls and the

crossbow attack and they both looked gratifyingly shocked. 'I think it's Susie and I'm going to tackle her later when I've got enough booze inside me.'

'I'll come with you, be your minder if you like. Safety in numbers and all that.' He was a good sort was Billy.

'My Lords, Ladies and Gentlemen, dinner is now being served,' bawled the buffer in the red coat.

We checked the table plan. Mercifully they hadn't split Kim and myself up. We were near the end of the top table, Kim sitting next to a rather endearing alternative comedian, well off his usual beat in this company, while I'd been placed next to a singer called Dolores who'd come sixth in the Eurovision Song Contest in the early seventies and had been singing the same dreadful number in summer shows and pantomimes ever since. It could have been a lot worse. Susie Smiles was safely situated at the other end of the table.

Dinner with the Water Babies was rather different from dinner with anyone else. After a lengthy grace from a bald and stammering clergyman and a quick chomp on the smoked salmon, all the showbiz members (who paid far less hefty subscriptions than the celebrity-seeking housewives) got up from their tables and performed a conga round the Lancaster Room, with many an old chorus girl's leg gamely flashing. Then after the main course and the loyal toast (nice to be able to light up before the pud) the Chief Squealer announced the auction and a smooth young man from Sotheby's called Rupert took to the podium.

'Lot number one, Ladies. Mr Bob Monkhouse, a most distinguished and talented gentleman as I think you will all agree.'

Poor Monkhouse stood there with a foolish grin on his face as the tables started bidding for him. Only women were allowed to take part, but the women in the room outnumbered the men by about three to one.

'Do I hear one hundred pounds? asked Rupert. He did indeed. He heard £150, £200 and Bob was finally knocked down for a respectable £250. Nor did the Water Babies get much for such largesse. Monkhouse strolled over to the successful table, planted a chaste kiss on each female cheek and 'took wine' with them. His duty done, he returned to the top table. The weatherman Michael Fish raised an astonishing £750, Christopher Biggins an embarrassing £100. With a sudden spurt of panic, minor stuff to what I'd been through recently, I realized that every man on the top table appeared to be going through this humiliating ritual. The pink-faced vicar from the Actors' Church Union was sweating it out even now (no wonder he'd stammered through grace). I turned to the amiable Dolores.

'They won't make me do it, will they? I mean not some poor hack from *Theatre World*?'

'Oh yes,' she said pleasantly but far from reassuringly. 'All the chaps on the top table.'

'Your wretched Chief Squealer never warned me,' I said petulantly.

'Well, she wouldn't want to put you off, would she? You might not have come if she had.' Too bloody right.

The friendly alternative comedian went for £150 and drained a glass of wine in one swallow before sitting down.

'God, it's horrible. All those bloody women ogling as if they were mentally undressing you.' He stopped for another swig of wine, taken this time from Kim's glass.

'God, I almost forgot, I'm meant to be a non-sexist comedian, aren't I? I'll be telling mother-in-law jokes next.'

The auctioneer, unfortunately, was moving on to the final lot, Mr William Benson, a journalist on *Theatre World*. He managed to make this job sound only marginally more appealing than that of rodent exterminator and there were a few jeers and catcalls.

I got up and made my way to the podium, furious to find that I was blushing. I tripped as I went up the steps, and Rupert had to beg for calm from the audience of baying Water Babies. The jeers I now realized, as I blinked against the lights, had given way to hysterical laughter from almost every corner of the room. I looked down and I nearly died. Understanding that the ordeal to come was unavoidable, I'd gone to considerable pains re-fastening the buttons on my trousers after an hour of blessed relief from the excruciating waistband. What I hadn't noticed as I performed this delicate operation under cover of the tablecloth was that a longish section of my shirt was now dangling from my flies like a limp white phallus. Did I stand there and leave it all hanging out, or turn my back on the audience and adjust my dress?

'Yer willy's hanging out, Willy,' cried one old dear who should have been suffering pindown treatment in an old folks' home as far as I was concerned. It was a cry other sections of the room seemed eager to echo. I turned round and tucked my shirt back in, the gleeful shouts of the Water Babies showed no signs of abating. The new refrain was 'Get 'em off, get 'em off, get 'em off.'

'Ladies please, a little quiet,' said Rupert feebly. The sweat was pouring down my face as I turned back to face my tormentors.

'Lot twelve,' said Rupert when the room had finally calmed down. 'Mr William Benson of *Theatre World*. Do I hear fifty pounds?' Rupert didn't hear £50, nor did he hear £40 or even £20.

'Now come on ladies, I must have a bid.'

I stood there, my mouth aching from the effort of keeping my desperate grin intact. The urge to run was strong, but where to?

'Ten pee' cried a kindly looking granny with silver hair. Had *Theatre World* stitched up every silly cow in the room, I wondered glumly. I turned round, desperately seeking a friendly face, Kim's for preference, but she was deep in conversation with Dolores, apparently oblivious to my plight, and I caught Susie Smiles's eye instead. She looked as though she was approaching the final stages of sexual ecstasy, her mouth hanging open with the pure pleasure of it all. Like some Roman Emperor she gave me the thumbs-down sign. I studied my shoes and the bidding began to crawl up in risibly small amounts. After several years Rupert decided to stop his futile pleading and knocked me down for £3.48. I now had to go over to the table that had put such an insulting end to my misery, kiss the hags on their cheeks and raise a jovial glass to them.

'Don't take it personally, we always do that to the last lot, someone who's never been to the dinner before. It's just our bit of fun,' said one of the killer grannies smugly. 'It was the vicar last year.' The man must be a saint to say grace for these harpies. 'Have a drink,' she added, offering me a wine glass. 'To the honourable society of Water Babies,' I said, following past form. 'Splish splash, splish splash, splish splash, SPLOSH!' they cawed back in time-honoured tradition. I took a huge swig, about half a glassful and thought I was going to explode. Fire caught the back of my throat and burnt its way down to my stomach. My eyes bulged and watered with the effort of not choking. It was neat whisky, a peculiarly peaty malt.

'Perhaps I should have said, dear,' said the sadistic pensioner sweetly. 'We always give the last lot a nice drop of whisky. We feel he deserves it after all he's been through.'

'A most considerate gesture,' I said. 'A kindness typical of your fine society.' I'd meant this sarcasm to bite but after the onslaught of malt my voice was so husky that I sounded almost tearfully sincere.

'We like to think so, dear,' said the old crone with an intolerable twinkle in her eye.

I staggered back to the top table and took my seat. Kim put her hand on my knee. 'You poor thing,' she said. 'Dolores was telling me, apparently they always bid low for the last lot.'

'So I've heard.'

Kim giggled. 'It's quite funny, really.'

I could have killed her. 'Any minute now you'll be telling me you want to join the bloody club yourself,' I said acidly.

'Oh, Will, can't you take a joke?'

I cranked up my inane grin for one last appearance and turned it on her like a blowtorch. I felt I had been smiling all my life, Mr Bleeding Smiley. 'Of course I can take a fucking joke,' I said.

The Chief Squealer came bustling over, trilling chirpily. 'I hope you'll forgive our little jest. You see all the other brave gentlemen on the top table have been our guests before and we do like to spring a little surprise. You're in distinguished company. Back in nineteen fifty-two Arthur Askey only raised two and six. How he laughed.'

I bet he had, I thought sourly, then realized I was feeling better. The initially malign effects of the malt were expanding into a nice warm glow.

'And there's this little present as a thank you,' added the Chief Squealer, handing me a bottle-shaped parcel with a bulge on top.

It was a litre of Glenlivet and a Swiss army penknife. Ethel Henderson knew the way to a fellow's heart. I'd had a penknife like this as a child, and had cried for hours when I lost it on the way back from school one day.

'I can't think of any presents I'd rather have,' I said, and I meant it. Against all the odds I was beginning to enjoy myself once more. Puffing a cigar, drinking vintage port and with my trousers recklessly unbuttoned again under the table I felt at peace with the world. Kim poured herself another glass of port and pawed affectionately at my crotch. I felt a faint stirring.

'Well, you're obviously feeling better,' she said.

The cabaret started. Dolores left to do her Eurovision number ('Wacka-Wacka-Whizz-Bang') and three septuagenarians performed an astonishingly nimble tap routine. Then a blonde and busty comedienne, whose jokes found little favour with our alternative neighbour, came on.

'Stevie Wonder was on this chat show the other day and the host asked him what it was like to be blind. Stevie sat and thought for a minute and said, "Oh, you know, it could be worse, I might be black." Last year someone gave him a cheese grater for Christmas and he said it was the best book he'd ever read. And did you hear about the time he went shopping? He was standing in the middle of Bloomingdales and suddenly he picks up his effing guide dog by the tail and starts swinging it round and round his head. An old woman comes up and taps him on the shoulder and asks him what the hell he thinks he's doing with the poor creature. "Just looking around," says Stevie.'

She changed gear and suddenly her tone was breathily sincere. 'And now in honour of a very great entertainer, I'd like to give you my version of one of Stevie's loveliest numbers. It's a beautiful little love song and it's called "My Cherie Amour." Very nicely she sang it, too. Prejudice and schmaltz, the twin pillars of light entertainment.

The dinner ended with a speech from the Chief Squealer, in which she contrived to thank everyone from the prime minister to the Savoy's cloakroom attendants, ending with the threat of dancing till the wee small hours.

Many of the Water Babies and their gentlemen guests started drifting towards the dance floor and much to my horror Kim started dragging me by the arm towards it as well. Just as the evening seemed to have exhausted its stock of humiliations, here was a fresh one.

'No, Kim, I really can't dance. I won't dance,' I said. Pretty forceful stuff, I think you'll agree, but all in vain of course.

'No excuses, Will. I learnt ballroom dancing at school. I'll lead, you can just follow.'

She allowed me time to do up my trousers and steered me round the floor a couple of times, and I trod on her toes and collided with another couple, but it didn't matter. It was enough to be there, holding her close, smelling her perfume and feeling her breasts against my chest. I kissed her gently on the cheek.

'I'll take lessons.'

'Too bloody right you will.'

As we made our way back to the top table, we spotted Billy Walter with Maureen wrapped around him, whispering in his ear. I tapped him apologetically on the shoulder. 'Sorry to interrupt.'

Maureen was comically aggrieved. 'I was just trying to tell this fat bastard what a good idea it would be if he took me to Paris for the weekend.'

'Just saved me in the nick of time,' said Billy.

In Ken Dodd's great phrase, I was full of plumptiousness

and fizzing like a bottle of pop with the cork out. The idea of putting an end to all this crossbow nonsense seemed ludicrously easy with so much wine, port and whisky sloshing cheerfully around my bloodstream. It had to be Susie, didn't it, and Susie was going to Spain tomorrow, out of harm's way. It was time to tackle her at last. I dragged Billy from his doting companion and we set off in search of Smiles. She was over by the bar with old death's-head.

'Susie, nice to see you,' I said, infuriatingly hail-fellow-and-well-met. Billy was right behind me.

'Bugger off,' she hissed.

'No, I thought we'd have a little chat,' I said, the smile still in place. I had, after all, had plenty of practice over the last couple of hours.

'Shot anything interesting with your crossbow recently?' I asked politely. 'Apples, journalists, you know the sort of thing.'

If I was expecting Susie to pull a button off her jacket, swallow it and fall instantly to the floor, with a doctor conveniently to hand to diagnose death by poisoning ('The bitter-sweet smell of almonds is unmistakable') I was to be disappointed. Susie looked blank, then affected a shrug of massive boredom.

'He's drunk again, Bernard, let's go.'

'"Had we but world enough, and time, this coyness, Lady were no crime,"' I babbled.

'What on earth are you on about now, you silly little man?' She sounded genuinely puzzled.

'"Cover her face. Mine eyes dazzle,"' I tried with mounting desperation. It looked like Cathy after all.

Susie's eyes went momentarily dreamy before she remembered who was delivering the quotation. '*The Duchess of Malfi*, one of my best-ever roles, Bernard.'

'Leatherhead, nineteen seventy-one, and you played the Courtesan, not the Duchess,' I said cruelly.

'Christ, you shit.'

'These fascinating theatrical reminiscences are besides the point,' said Billy. 'What Will wants to know is whether you've been threatening him. Just like you threatened me with that underage singer.'

'We don't have to listen to all this, dear,' said Bernard, sticking up for his wife at last. 'Let's be getting on. We've an early start tomorrow.'

'We've got an early start tomorrow because of this prick,' she snapped.

'Just tell me what you were doing at eleven-fifteen this morning and you can be on your way.'

'Oh, how frightfully dramatic,' said Susie with one of her unconvincing girlish laughs. 'And just what was happening at eleven-fifteen this morning?'

I'd have to tell her if I was to get a straight answer.

'Someone shot a crossbow through my window. It just missed.'

'What rotten luck. That they missed I mean, naturally. And no doubt you're accusing me of this most public spirited of crimes.'

'You've got it in one.'

'Well, I hate to disappoint you but at eleven-fifteen this morning I was at Ethel Henderson's charming Braintree residence rehearsing tonight's cabaret. You can ask any of the acts or the Chief Squealer herself,' she sneered.

'You could have hired someone else to do it,' I said desperately. Oh Cathy.

'What, and have deprived myself of the pleasure. I only wish I'd thought of it first.'

There had been an amateurishness about both attempts on my life, an amateurishness to which I probably owed my continuing existence. I couldn't flatter myself that someone had taken out a contract on me. This was a DIY job and it now seemed certain Smiles had no part in it. I'd check her alibi like some dogged PC Plod, but I knew it would hold up.

'Any further questions, Monsieur Poirot?' she asked.

'No,' I said dully.

As she turned to go, she placed her stiletto heel carefully on my left foot and put all her weight on it. I screamed in pain, pushed her off and started hopping round the crowded bar with my foot in my hands, cannoning into people as I went. Someone spilt a glass of wine over my dress shirt.

'I really ought to have put Mr Benson into my cabaret,' I heard Smiles saying to a group of interested spectators. 'He does so love to make an exhibition of himself.'

Dear old Billy came to my defence. 'Or indeed one of your talent contests,' he said. 'I was reading a fascinating article about them in *Theatre World* this morning.' By the time he'd reached the end of the sentence, Susie and her husband were heading for the exit, fast.

The worst of the agony was over now and I stood tentatively with both feet on the floor.

'Can you walk?' he asked. I found that I could hobble and with my arm round his shoulder we made our way back to the table. Kim and Maureen were pissed and giggly but sobered up when Billy told them about Susie's parting trick. I managed a brave smile.

'What did Susie say?' asked Kim.

I told her about the alibi. 'So it looks as if it's Cathy after all . . . a former girlfriend,' I added for Billy and Maureen's benefit.

'Oh dear,' said Billy, pouring us all large glasses of port. We chatted idly for a while, but he and Maureen were making bedroom eyes at each other and it seemed a shame to keep them up.

'Let's call it a day,' I said. 'Thanks for all your help, Billy, I'll give you a ring when we get back from Blackpool.'

We parted with much hugging, and Maureen told me sternly that I was to look after both myself and Kim.

'You've got a good 'un there,' she whispered. 'She really cares about you.'

They wandered off, arm in arm, and Kim and I set off to look for the Chief Squealer. We found her holding court in the bar with an apparently limitless supply of champagne and she thrust glasses into our hands, brooking no refusal.

'Thanks for everything,' I said. 'I'll give you a ring tomorrow to check a few details if I may. There's just one thing I need to know now. Did you rehearse the cabaret at your place this morning with Susie Smiles?'

'Yes, all those lovely artistes came round this morning and Susie put them through their paces. Such a nice, talented lady, I can't think why she's going to Spain.'

'Hmm. What time did you start? How long were they all there for?'

'We started at ten, and everyone left about half past twelve.'

'And Susie Smiles was there the whole time?'

'Oh yes. Why are you so interested?'

I couldn't face another long round of explanations.

'Oh, I just thought they did a terrific job and wondered how long they'd had to rehearse,' I lied. 'But there's a story in *Theatre World* that might interest you tomorrow.'

'That reminds me,' said Ethel. 'Harry Meadows, you know, Joe Johnson's personal manager, turned up an hour or so ago. He said he was looking for the *Theatre World* reporter about a story he had for your paper. I can't think where he's got to.'

She peered vaguely around her and the liquidizer switched itself on in my stomach again.

'Christ, what's he doing here?' It sounded rude, rude and panicky, which was just how I felt. 'I'm not sure,' said Ethel Henderson. 'Joe Johnson was going to be one of our guests tonight but after all that shocking stuff in the papers I felt the teeniest weeniest bit apprehensive about having him here. Luckily Mr Meadows phoned and cancelled anyway, and I said, just a touch hypocritically, that it was a shame Joe wasn't coming because we had a very nice journalist from *Theatre World* covering the event and it would give him a nice bit of publicity, you know, supporting a charity despite all his own problems.'

'And did you give the name of this nice young journalist?' I asked, knowing quite well what she'd say.

'Oh yes, dear. Is anything the matter?'

Well, quite a lot actually but I could hardly ask for an armed guard to see Kim and me safely home.

'No, everything's fine. Thanks for a great evening.'

'Now, you will take care of him, dear?' said Ethel to Kim. 'He looks a bit peaky.'

Kim wasn't looking too hot herself. We shook hands with the Chief Squealer with a brave show of enthusiasm, declined further champagne and made nervous tracks for the exit.

'Well, there's one thing,' said Kim. 'It might not be Cathy after all. Perhaps Joe Johnson and his manager have been bettering themselves at the Open University, like me.'

'Perhaps,' I said absently. I expected to see Meadows and Johnson coming round the corner at any minute, but we reached the Riverside entrance without being ambushed and I kept a nervous watch outside the Ladies' cloakroom while Kim went to get her coat. I was trying and failing to look nonchalant when a hand slapped me sharply on the shoulder.

'Just the chap I'm looking for,' said a familiar voice with a failed attempt at cheeriness, before adding *sotto voce* in my right ear: 'Don't say a word and just walk towards the door.' There was a sharp dig in the small of my back. 'It's a gun,' added Meadows, unnecessarily. 'Start walking, nice and calm. One word out of order, any attempt to make a run for it, and I shoot.' There was no one in the foyer apart from the porter on the door who looked about eighty-two. Meadows' grip on my shoulder was so tight it was hard to turn, but I twisted my neck a bit as we headed for the door and got an unpleasant look into those dead grey eyes. He was wearing a white mac over his dinner jacket and the gun, in time-honoured tradition, appeared to be in his pocket. Just then Kim came bouncing out of the Ladies and stopped dead in her tracks when she saw us.

'Who's your friend, Will?' she said with admirable calmness.

'Harry Meadows,' I said. 'I think he wants a little chat.'

'Just move,' said Meadows, then turned to Kim. 'And you'd better come too.'

The three of us made what felt like a long, long walk to the exit, Meadows just behind, the gun occasionally nudging me in the back. 'Any trouble and I'll shoot your friend first, then you,' said Meadows for Kim's benefit. We kept walking and the doorman gave us a salute.

There was a line of cabs 10 yards up the road and I toyed with the idea of making a run for it but Meadows had his gun in the now familiar place and I changed my mind without any trouble at all.

'We've got wheels,' Meadows told the doorman to stop him whistling up a cab, and sure enough he had. A black stretch limo cruised slowly up to the door.

'In you get,' said Harry. 'Much more comfortable than a taxi. More room. And you too,' he hissed at Kim. 'We don't want you taking the number like a good little member of the I-Spy Club and phoning the police.'

Once inside, Harry kindly removed my bottle of whisky then searched my pockets and found the penknife.

'I don't think you'll be needing that,' he said.

I'd been clutching it as if my life depended on it. Perhaps it did, but it was too late now.

I'd never been inside a stretch limo before and as Harry said it was much more confortable than a cab. A Mozart piano concerto was playing on the sound system, and there were two bench seats facing each other across an expanse of carpet. Meadows, Kim and I occupied one, with me in the middle. The other was taken up by the considerable bulk of Joe Johnson and a thug with a broken nose and a beer-gut. Kim squeezed my hand.

'Don't worry, Will,' she said. Silly advice, really, but kindly meant.

'Oh I'm not,' I said in a voice whose steadiness surprised me. 'It's very kind of these gentlemen to give us a lift home.'

That was when the thug, apparently unprompted, hit me on the mouth and I unaccountably found myself on all fours on the nice white carpet. After a bit, I climbed back into my seat. There didn't seem to be anything else to do really.

'You're about as much use as woodworm in a cripple's crutch,' said Meadows, reaching, I saw with horror, into his raincoat pocket. We were bowling down the Embankment now.

'Look, you've no quarrel with Kim,' I pleaded. 'Let her out.' They all pretended not to hear. Meadows got his gun out at last. It was a child's cap gun, cheap moulded metal with a plastic handle. I'd had one myself. I looked at it with a mixture of relief and regret. It didn't look as though we were going to be shot. But then if we weren't going to be shot, why had we climbed into this preposterous limo rather than one of those lovely London cabs. Pure funk was the reason, and I'd dragged Kim into the mess as well. There was a lot more silence as we drove along, and then Joe Johnson pulled a large hip flask out of his pocket, took a long swig, offered it to the thug and Meadows, who both declined, and then to me.

'Sup up, lad, you're going to need it.' He sounded tired and there was a worrying hint of pity in his voice. I shook my head and he shrugged.

'That was a good story you had in the *News of the World*,' said Meadows at last. 'Just as a matter of interest, how much did they pay you for it?'

'I've been trying to phone you all week to explain,' I babbled. 'I had nothing to do with it.'

'Oh, don't play games,' said Harry, and hit me, rather hard, on the cheekbone with the pistol.

'Just a toy,' he said quietly as I rubbed my face and tried not to whimper. 'Just a toy,' he said again as he hit me, much harder, in exactly the same place. I did cry out then, and Kim squeezed my hand with bracing severity. She'd been crying quietly earlier but she'd stopped now and looked fierce and in control.

'Listen, you mindless apes,' she said. 'Will's got nothing at all to do with this. He came back to the office last week, told everyone the interview had been cancelled and then played the tape in confidence to the editor. They had a long chat and decided not to run the piece and, although Will would have got a lot of money for it, not to sell it to another paper either. So just leave him alone will you, and let us out of this silly car.'

'So the story just got into the *News of the World* by magic, did it?' asked Meadows. The Big Cunt had another drink and the thug stared out of the window.

'The tape was nicked from his drawer. Someone else flogged the story.'

She certainly had their attention now as we cruised aimlessly round the empty streets of the City. We had all the time in the world.

'So who did steal the tape?' asked Meadows.

Kim said nothing, and neither did I.

'Who stole the tape?' asked Meadows again.

'I'm not saying,' I said at last.

Meadows gave the thug a barely perceptible nod and he leant forward with an absent-minded smile and smashed me in the stomach with his great sirloin of a fist. I gasped, fought for breath, and tried not to throw up on the expensive shag pile. Why give them the satisfaction, I thought. They'd probably only rented the limo anyway. My eyes were watering and Kim gave my hand another squeeze. We both sat there and said nothing and tried to enjoy the ride. The Mansion House went past, for the third time as far as I could remember. Thank God I was pissed. The actual blows weren't much fun but the alcohol did a pretty good job in anaesthetizing most of the pain.

At last Meadows broke the silence. 'You're going to tell us who stole that tape if we have to keep driving all night,' he said, then crashed the handle of the gun just above my left eye. It was easily the worst blow so far, and I tried to retreat into a little world of my own and forget about the pain.

'You're a fucking sadist,' Kim screamed at Meadows, before making a lunge at Joe Johnson, grabbing him violently by the lapels and shaking his huge bulk with impressive force.

'Tell him to cut it out, Joe,' she shouted.

'Get her off him, Gary,' said Meadows calmly to the thug and for a nasty moment I thought Kim was going to get the benefit of that enormous fist as well. But Gary seemed more interested in the view.

'I'm not paid to hurt tarts,' he said flatly, gazing out of the window, and I would have shaken him warmly by the hand if I hadn't thought he'd crush mine to a pulp.

At last Kim seemed to have got through to the Big Cunt.

He'd been staring unhappily at the floor for most of the ride but Kim's shaking had forced him to sit up and pay attention. Bleary attention, but attention nonetheless. Not bad for a man who had probably been drinking solidly since he saw the papers on Sunday morning.

'Listen,' said Kim, back in her seat now but leaning forward and staring at the Big Cunt with mesmeric intensity. 'Your Mr Meadows may like playing these tough-guy games but you've got to realize it won't do you any good. You'll end up even deeper in the shit. Sure, you and your friends could beat me and Will up but what good's it going to do you? Anyone lays another finger on either of us and we're straight off to the *News of the World*. A picture of Will's bruises would give them just the follow-up they're probably looking for.'

Kim was talking to Johnson but it was Meadows who answered.

'Who said anything about letting you out of the car?' he asked icily. Rather the same question had been occurring to me during Kim's magnificent speech.

'Don't be so bloody soft,' said Kim scornfully. I couldn't actually think of anyone less soft than Meadows and he clearly didn't like the jibe one bit. Kim's Geordie accent was stronger than usual and she exuded a furious confidence in spite of the dismal circumstances. That last blow had clearly addled my brain. I found I was drifting off again, imagining an English country church and Kim walking down the aisle towards me with her father, sunshine in a country garden, children, all that sort of thing. I must have started to smile. Silly really.

'You can wipe that stupid grin off your face for a start,' said Meadows, lashing out with the pistol. Just under the eye this time, but not quite as hard. But then he followed it up with a blow to the knee, and that hurt like hell.

Johnson was studying the carpet again and looking miserable, like a man who's lost a contact lens. He didn't appear to be enjoying the fisticuffs any more than I was.

'Lay off him, Harry,' he said sadly. 'The girl's talking sense.'

'Too bloody right I am,' said Kim. 'You've only got three

options. You can kill us and dump our bodies.' I wished Kim hadn't said that. I really did. 'In which case the police will be on to you before they're cold. Or, you can carry on beating up poor Will here and every time you hit him it will just make a better picture for the paper.' God, she was full of bright ideas. 'Or,' she said finally, 'you can stop all this nonsense and drive us home and nothing more will be said.'

Joe Johnson looked up and gave me an oddly matey wink. I can only wink with my left eye, and that didn't seem to be working any more, so I gave him a grimace of a grin instead. I tried to talk.

'There's a lot in what Kim says, you know,' I said. I'd hoped it would sound as casual as someone debating the respective merits of the McDonald's Quarter Pounder with cheese and the Burger King Whopper but it came out as a desperate croak for mercy.

Meadows ignored me and kept talking to Kim. 'How do you mean the police would be on to us before the bodies were cold?' he asked. He was playing with my new Swiss army penknife, opening and closing the largest of the blades. Kim did a good job of ignoring it.

'You spoke to Ethel Henderson at the do tonight. If Will and I don't turn up to work tomorrow, our editor will be on to her at once. He knows Will's been receiving death threats and he's heard the tape. He'd phone the police as soon as he heard you were at the Water Babies do. And anyway, you know quite well you're not going to kill us.'

Meadows was playing with the corkscrew now. That would be worse than the blade.

There was another of the long pauses that were proving such a poignant, Pinteresque feature of the drive. We'd turned round and were now heading up Victoria Street, past the Catholic cathedral.

The comedian broke the silence at last.

'The girl's right, Harry.' He looked surprisingly cheerful, and offered Kim his flask. 'You're a brave lass,' he said. Kim refused a drink but I gazed at him with craven appeal in my eyes, and he handed it over. Malt whisky again.

'What's all this about threats?' Johnson asked as I gratefully returned the hip flask. 'We've not been making any threats, not before tonight, have we Harry?'

The fight seemed to have gone out of Meadows. He just shook his head and stared out of the window. The Big Cunt was right of course. This was just a side show, nothing to do with the rest of the threats. Never mind all the literary stuff, what possible sense was there in going to all the trouble and risk of picking us up at the Savoy when the real source of my recent troubles clearly knew just where I lived. As Cathy most certainly did.

'You're a popular lad, aren't you,' said Johnson with a trace of humour in his voice. 'So we're not the only ones you've wound up?'

'No.'

'What are you going to do now?' asked Kim.

'Find out who nicked the sodding tape,' said Meadows. He picked up the pistol again. I couldn't face it. I'd thought it was all over, but it looked as though Harry had just been taking a breather. 'I thought it would cheer old Joe up a bit if we beat the shit out of you but you've not really been enjoying yourself have you, Joe?' He spoke with surprising tenderness.

'Not really, Harry, no. Let's call it a day now.'

'No, 'fraid not. Work's got to be done. You may be past caring but I'm going to find the cunt who stitched you up and fix him.' I waited for the next blow.

Kim spoke very quietly. 'Don't even think about it,' she said. 'You know it won't do you any good. We're not going to tell you who flogged the story and that's that. The guy who did it may be a creep, but I'm not letting him in for this sort of treatment and nor's Will.'

I'm not sure how many more knocks round the face it would have taken before I divulged Colin's name but mercifully I wasn't put to the test. Harry pressed a button, the window slid silently down, and he dropped the pistol in the gutter.

'You've got a good 'un there,' he said to me. Vaguely I remembered that someone else had said the same thing to me earlier that evening but it seemed years ago and I couldn't remember who it was. Kim was still holding my hand and I gave it a squeeze.

'Yeah,' I said. It sounded graceless but it came from the heart. Meadows' eyes were as unreadable as ever in the street lights, but there was a smile on his face that looked less sinister than usual.

'You're no nancy boy yourself,' he said. 'Whoops, sorry, Joe.' For the first time that night he sounded cheerful. 'Give the man a drink, Joe.' he said.

I took the flask, had another swig and felt a bit better.

'You promise you won't go to the papers about this,' Meadows asked, some of the old intensity returning.

'No, I promise. It would do Joe more harm than you and he's suffered enough,' I said. 'And I'm not sure Joe's career is as wrecked as you think it is.'

'Leave it out,' said Meadows. 'How fucked is fucked?'

'All Joe's got to do is make a clean breast of it, not to the *News of the World* but to some other paper. Say how sorry he is, say how ashamed he is, bring in lots of sob stuff about how it was all brought on by the death of his wife and how he feels he's let down his fans.'

'Will's right,' said Kim. 'There's nothing the tabloid-reading public like more than a good wallow in someone else's guilt. It will be THE COURAGEOUS CONFESSIONS OF JOE JOHNSON, you just see. The British love a gallant loser. All will be forgiven.'

'What do you think, Harry?' asked Joe. 'There's that old bag on the *Mail* who did the feature on the house a few months ago. She writes that kind of stuff, doesn't she?'

'It's worth a try,' said Harry. 'I'll phone her tomorrow.'

'Give it to her as an exclusive interview, then when the other papers start ringing after it's appeared for God's sake answer the phone. They'll only keep stitching you up if you don't play ball. Then in a month or so I'd do some big gala for Aids charities.'

'Who's running the silly fucker's career, you or me?' put in Meadows sharply. I thought he was going to hit me again but then he turned on one of his disconcerting grins. 'No, you're probably right, ta.'

'Can we go home now?' asked Kim.

'Yes, home please,' I said. 'Brixton and then Vauxhall.'

Kim gently put her finger on my bruised lips.

'Just Brixton will do. You're not going home on your own tonight, Will, not after all this.'

Harry gave the driver instructions and Joe announced that he'd run out of drink. The silent thug opened a cupboard under his seat and produced glasses, ice and half a bottle of Glenfiddich. We all had one, even Kim, who usually claimed that she hated whisky.

'Good health,' said Meadows, then looked at me ruefully. 'Christ, you look terrible. Sorry. But if it *had* been you who leaked that tape I wouldn't be sorry at all.'

Joe Johnson was looking thoughtful. 'What am I going to do with all my pooftah jokes now?' he asked mournfully.

'Tell them against yourself,' I suggested. 'You're act is full of hate but it's you you hate really. Give yourself a starring role.'

'Very psychological, I'm sure. I didn't realize we were travelling with Sigmund fucking Freud,' said the Big Cunt. 'I expect you'll be wanting me to drop the Paki jokes next.'

'One step at a time, Joe. There wouldn't be much of an act left if you did that.'

'I'm going to have to rethink the whole thing. I'm fed up with it anyway. Find a few new people to put the boot into. Tabloid journalists for fucking starters.'

'Clement Freud,' I suggested.

'Richard Branson,' said Kim.

'Melvyn Bragg,' put in the thug unaccountably.

'Jeremy Beadle, Noel Edmonds, Norman Lamont, Roy Hattersley,' said the Big Cunt, entering into the spirit of the thing. 'The Archbishop of Canterbury, sanctimonious git.' He looked a genuinely happy man. 'This is going to be the second fucking coming this is. You come and see me in a few months, you won't recognize me.'

By now the car was climbing Brixton Hill.

'You like living next to all these coons?' Meadows asked Kim offensively.

'Now, now, Harry. No cheap racist cracks like that, please,' said the Big Cunt. He looked at me with concern. 'How are you feeling, Will? I'm sorry about all that rough stuff.'

'Not half as sorry as I am.' I was feeling terrible. My head was like an overripe melon that had been dropped on to the supermarket floor, and the booze now seemed to be making it worse rather than better.

Harry had got his wallet out.

'I don't want your conscience money,' I told him primly.

'Don't be such a silly twat,' said Meadows. 'If you don't want another clip round the bloody ear you'll take it.'

He stuffed some notes into my breast pocket and I hadn't got the energy to take them out again. Kim had been giving directions to the driver and we came to a halt outside her place, an Edwardian house in a side street whose pavements were covered with dog shit and crushed cans of Red Stripe.

The thug got out and opened the door for us. I climbed out stiffly and had to concentrate hard on staying upright when my feet hit the pavement.

Harry leant out of the limo and handed Kim the whisky and my penknife. 'I really am very sorry,' he said.

I stared into those grey eyes. It might have been a trick of the light, but there seemed to be a glimmer of warmth in them for once. Harry must have noticed I'd spotted it, because they suddenly went dead again.

'It's OK,' I said. 'Forget it. Look after the Big Cunt.'

'Sure you don't fancy a quick blow job?' called Johnson, and the terrible wheezy laughter began.

Kim's studio flat was in an attic room on the third floor and the long climb up the dimly lit stairs didn't do me any good at all. I'd never been to her flat before. Mind you, Kim hadn't seen much of it herself until recently.

'Don't expect too much,' she said as she unlocked the door. 'It's very small and very spartan.'

It was, but it felt immediately welcoming. Brightly coloured rugs covered the polished floorboards and there were a lot of indoor plants giving the room the atmosphere of a conservatory. The walls were white and apart from a couple of framed posters for a Matisse exhibition in Paris, quite bare. There was a huge old oak wardrobe, a big bookshelf and a desk in the bay window. And of course there was the bed, covered with an Indian bedspread. I looked at it longingly, then slumped on to the Habitat sofa.

'It's lovely, Kim.' She was in the tiny kitchen, making mugs of tea. 'It's nice to be home at last,' I added, then realized it wasn't my home at all. I curled up in a foetal position and called for Disprin.

Kim came out with a bowl of warm water and a flannel and cotton wool drenched in TCP.

'Your left eye's all swollen with a cut above it, you've got a busted lip and there's a nasty graze on your cheekbone,' she said matter of factly. 'How do you feel?'

'Honestly?' I said.

She nodded.

'Absolutely terrible,' I whimpered.

She bathed my wounds and dabbed at them with the TCP, which stung like hell. Then she gave me the Disprin and the tea, which was sweet and laced with something. Rum. As I drank it she knelt in front of me, tenderly stroking my good cheek. Her eyes held a hint of the hurt I'd seen earlier.

'What's the matter?'

'Nothing,' she said. 'I just couldn't bear it when he kept hitting you.'

I pulled her head on to my chest and stroked her hair. 'You were wonderful tonight. So brave, so strong. I was within a second or two of shopping Colin. It was you who stopped him hitting me, made him see sense.'

'You were fine, just fine,' she said, and she was crying and I wiped the tears off her cheeks with my fingers.

'It's a funny way to spend our first night together. Is the no-bonking rule still in force? I'm not up to much. Do you mind if we don't?' I'd never imagined the day when I'd be negotiating with Kim not to have sex.

'Lay one immodest finger on me and you're out of the house,' she said with a grin. 'I don't fuck cripples.'

It wasn't much of a joke, a veritable Joe Johnson of a joke in fact, but it cheered us up. Kim said she was going to have a bath and I asked if I could come and watch.

'No you bloody can't,' she said. 'You'll wait till Blackpool like you've been told.'

She brought me another cup of tea and I smoked a fag and tried not to think about seeing Cathy the following day.

Kim emerged from her bath looking pink and innocent in a big white towelling dressing gown and asked me if I'd mind using her water because the boiler only ran to one bath at a time. I went into the bathroom, which was even smaller than the kitchen, and slowly undressed, folding my clothes up carefully and putting them on top of Kim's on the laundry basket. It was a curiously intimate feeling to be climbing into her hot, soapy water and I lay back and closed my eyes as the heat lapped away some of the pain.

The door opened and Kim was standing there with a mischievous smile on her face.

'You bloody hypocrite,' I said. 'You don't let me come and look and then you sneak up on me when I'm almost asleep.'

I felt suddenly self-conscious, horribly aware of the inadequacies of my body. 'God. I'm sorry I'm so fat. Don't look. It's a horrible sight.' I submerged as much of me as I could beneath the cloudy water but there still seemed to be far too much belly on view.

'Not fat, cuddly,' said Kim.

'You've obviously taken your contact lenses out.'

She knelt down and soaped my back, then washed my neck and chest and legs.

'Do you want me to do the rest?' she whispered.

I felt a faint stirring down below and was tempted, but then the old Benson iron resolve reasserted itself.

'Better not. I'll only get all randy and I really don't think I'm up to it. I'm bruised and pissed and beaten.'

She gave me a quick affectionate grope.

'OK, Will. Come to bed soon, you can use my toothbrush.'

I felt weak and trembly again as I dried myself and thanked my lucky stars I wasn't due for a fuck. Christ, what had Harry Meadows done to me. I cleaned my teeth with Kim's toothbrush as invited, and reflected that in all the years I'd lived with her, I'd never done that with Cathy's. In the main room, there was only a single dim light by my side of the bed and Kim had left me a bottle of mineral water, a glass and a supply of Disprin. I climbed in and curled round her, my front to her back. We fitted snugly, like two spoons in a drawer. She was wearing a passion killer of a nightdress and I was glad she was. It was good to lie there, chaste and close and warm. I kissed her on the nape of the neck.

'Hold me tight, Will,' she said.

I turned out the light and held her tight and in a couple of minutes she was asleep, breathing slowly and deeply, at peace. I was sure I'd be awake for hours, lying there in the dark, fretting about Cathy and wanting to fuck Kim, a racing mind and a rigid cock. But Kim's peace was catching. Breathing in her clean smell of soap and newly washed nightdress, cradling her in my arms, I felt protecting and protected, a wonderful sense of rightness. I heard the hissing of a car on the road outside, the distant barking of a dog. And then I heard no more.

Thursday

They were giving me funny looks in the brasserie and I couldn't altogether blame them. I tried to look respectable with my cappuccino and my croissant but the waitress had visibly winced when she handed them over, and a couple of androgynous fashion victims on an adjoining table appeared to have dropped their customary cool and were shooting furtive glances in my direction, followed by a great deal of whispering and giggling. I looked as though I'd been to an S & M party that had got horribly out of hand.

I'd slept deeply, and woken at nine. My head was aching dreadfully and at first I put it down to a hangover but there were sharp persistent pains in places even a brandy hangover doesn't normally reach, like my knee. Memories of the drive with Meadows and co. came rushing back and I groaned and put my head under the pillow. Then I remembered curling up with Kim and felt more cheerful. She came out of the kitchen with supplies of tea and Disprin, and kissed me on the forehead. It felt good to have her sitting on the edge of the bed, asking how I was, chatting about the night before and not expecting me to do much of the talking. Finally I dragged myself off to the bathroom, modestly clad in Kim's dressing gown, and gazed at myself in the mirror. The bruises and cuts were bad enough, but it was the discoloured puffy flesh where my left eye used to be that impressed me most. Very *Dirty Harry* I thought. Then I got into a hypochondriacal panic that I might actually be blind under all the horror film mess and spent a painful minute trying to prise apart the two rolls of flesh with my fingers. Something

188

red and frightened stared back at me and I decided not to look any more. A man can only take so much. I climbed into the bath with some difficulty and noticed that the throb in my knee was setting up an interesting counterpoint with the one in my head. Kim came and grimaced and offered me the use of the razor that she used for legs and armpits. This I politely declined.

'What are you going to wear?' she asked, scrubbing my back. I could get used to this geisha treatment, I thought. 'I could get a cab to Vauxhall if you like and bring you some clothes over.'

'You're a saint, Kim, but no, it's much too risky. Cathy may want to knock our little chat on the head before it's even started and this morning at Vauxhall would be her last chance. I'll go like this. People will just think I'm a musician in my dinner jacket and I've got the clothes I left at *Theatre World* to change into this afternoon.'

Kim picked up my crumpled dress shirt which was still lying on the dirty laundry basket and held it at arm's length. There was quite a lot of blood on it, and it made interesting patterns with the red wine stains.

'I'm not letting you wear this,' she said, and far from feeling nagged, I felt reassured. She went out of the bathroom and came back with one of her rugby shirt collection, a huge faded garment with broad pink and green stripes.

'Take care of it, Will, it's my favourite. The Godfather was always wanting to borrow it but I wouldn't let him.'

I was touched, just as she'd meant me to be.

I asked Kim to tell JB I'd be in that afternoon and to bring him up to date on what had been going on. 'I'll do the Water Babies piece here before I go to see Cathy. Have you got a typewriter?'

'Yes, it's in the wardrobe and there's some copy-paper in the desk drawer. I'd better go, Will. Phone for a taxi and let it drop you off right outside the café and get a table in the middle of the room well away from the windows.'

'She can hardly do anything in front of all those Sloanes and trendies,' I said. 'I'm sure she'll see sense when we talk. She was relieved when we split up, for God's sake.'

Kim nodded but didn't look convinced. She kissed me gently on the lips, wished me luck and left for work. I soaked for another ten minutes and then dressed. Is there anything more sordid than putting on yesterday's socks and underpants? Well, yes, I suppose there is, actually. I made another cup of coffee and phoned the Chief Squealer, whose squeals were more subdued than usual. Her night of nights had taken its toll on her too.

I took the details of how much cash had been raised, and checked I'd got all the names of the celebrity guests, then bashed out the piece, noting that Michael Fish had fetched £750 and *Theatre World*'s correspondent £3.48. 'The Water Babies', I typed with clenched teeth, 'are renowned for their sense of humour and fun.'

By the time I'd finished it was 11.30 and I ordered a cab. I put my dinner jacket over the rugger shirt and gazed again at the smashed face and ludicrous outfit in Kim's bathroom mirror. 'The stylish man about town is wearing a black tie with matching black eye and sports accessories,' I told myself, then wondered what was making such a bulge in the breast pocket. It was Meadows' parting gift. He must have been feeling very guilty indeed – a grand in crumpled fifties. I'd never had so much cash in my hands and I could hardly cram it all into my wallet. Almost worth getting beaten up for. When the taxi driver rang the bell, I had a quick belt of Kim's rum to get up some Dutch courage and limped painfully downstairs.

'Blimey,' said the driver when he saw his fare. 'Where do you want to go – Covent Garden, Twickenham or casualty?'

'The Goat That Smokes, Sloane Square,' I said coldly.

'You going to tell me what happened?'

'No, I'm not.'

'Fair enough,' he said amiably, and kept quiet all the way to the lamentably pretentious caff.

I'd finished my coffee and smoked three plain Camel and there was still no sign of Cathy. The waitress came over and asked if I wanted anything else, her eyes riveted to a spot on the ceiling so she didn't have to look at my face.

'A bowl of French onion soup and a Sol beer, please,' I said, then remembered how awful I was feeling and ordered a large brandy as well. I'd got my head bent over the soup when Cathy arrived at the table and her familiar 'Oh, Will', half anxious, half exasperated, made me choke on all that gungy cheese they put in it. Several yards of the stuff ribboned their way between my mouth and the bowl. There was far too much to try and suck it all in, and with Cathy standing there watching in appalled fascination, I didn't feel I could spit the whole mouthful back into the bowl. I was trapped by the quivering strands of glutinous cheese, unable to move or talk. Then I remembered the Swiss army knife, and with as much grace as I could muster hacked my way through the mess with the sharpest blade. Most of the cheese missed the bowl and landed on the table. I got the rest into my mouth and chewed desperately on it. It was like cheese flavoured bubble gum. Eventually I just swallowed the lot with a shudder and reached for the beer.

'Sorry about that, Cathy,' I said at last. 'Tricky stuff, French soup.'

'Oh, Will,' she said again. 'What have you been doing to yourself now?'

'You should see the other chap,' I said. The waitress came over and gave Cathy a look of deepest sympathy. To her credit, Cathy refused to collaborate in this female conspiracy and with cool disdain ordered a spritzer and tuna salad. She was wearing the matching skirt and jacket, in a particularly unfortunate shade of light blue, that made her look like an air hostess. And she'd plaited her wonderful auburn hair and coiled it like a snake on top of her head. It was a style I'd never liked but unlike the suit, which had caused furious rows, I'd kept quiet about it. It was odd. As soon as I'd seen her, I knew Cathy hadn't been making threats, still less trying to kill me. Or at least I thought I was sure.

'Come on, Will, tell me the worst,' she said when the waitress had gone, and there was real anxiety in her voice. If she was intent on rubbing me out, she ought to be pleased that someone else was trying to save her the trouble. 'And why are you dressed like that?' she added, a hint of the old exasperation bubbling back. 'Can't you even look after yourself for a few days without me there to nag you?'

'I'm fine,' I said. 'I tried to play some of my Van Morrison records the other night.'

'Oh, Christmas,' she said. 'I thought you might have done.' I'd always hated it when she said 'Oh, Christmas'.

'Why did you do it, Cathy?'

'I just saw them. I'd packed everything up. I was about to go. It all seemed so empty and meaningless, as if I'd never really been there. Then I remembered how I'd felt about you once, and how I tried to keep you, you know when I . . .'

She still couldn't bring herself to say it.

'Gave me a blow job,' I said quietly.

'Yes, well it all came flooding back, that hurt, that love, the waste of it all. So I thought I'd do something for you to remember me by. I hated you at that moment if you really want to know. I hated you for never having felt the same as I did.'

'And now?' I asked gently.

'No, of course I don't. I mean take a look at yourself, Will, for heaven's sake. I saw a duck in a park once, when I was about sixteen, you know how things make an impression in adolescence, one little thing seems to sum up the whole of life. Well this duck had snapped the bottom half of its beak. It was just dangling from a thread, quite useless. It couldn't eat and it couldn't quack and it must have been suffering terribly. It haunted me for weeks that duck. Useless, horrible suffering. I wished I'd killed it myself but I didn't have the guts. But I should have done. You're a bit like that duck at the moment, Will.'

'Thanks a lot. Quack, quack.'

She laughed, a genuine affectionate laugh. 'The duck couldn't quack and you can. The duck couldn't eat and you can, well, more or less, though your table manners certainly haven't improved. Come on, are you going to tell me what happened?'

'Very possibly, in a moment. Listen, Cathy, you haven't been

192

trying to do to me what you failed to do with that duck, have you?'

'What do you mean?'

'Kill me.'

'Is this one of your silly games, Will?'

'No, I wish it was. Someone is trying to kill me. And until you walked in here I'd convinced myself it was you. Those records . . . that wasn't like you, Cathy.'

'Oh, come on Will, I'm sorry about the records but it's a bit different from trying to bump you off and you've got to admit they caused me a lot of grief. I mean Van the bloody Man at full volume at three o'clock in the morning with you comatose on the sofa. It wasn't a lot of fun. You can count yourself lucky I spared the hi-fi.'

'Yes, I suppose I can.'

'Spill the beans, then, what's been happening?'

I told her the tale. The Police record, the *Duchess of Malfi*, the coy mistress, the horrible computer voice, the push on the Tube and the crossbow.

'Golly,' she said when I'd finished. 'You have been going through the wars. Yet presumably whoever beat you up like that must be the same person who's been making all the threats?' She stopped and looked thoughtful. 'Don't tell me it was just a drunken fall?'

'No it wasn't,' I said indignantly, and realized I had no justification for such a response. So I filled her in on the Joe Johnson interview, and the Water Babies do and the ride home with Johnson and Meadows. Cravenly, I didn't mention Kim.

'But surely you didn't go home last night. Not after the crossbow yesterday morning. You can't have done, anyway, you wouldn't still be wearing your dinner jacket.'

'No, I stayed with a friend.'

'Big-breasted Kim?'

'Well, yes, but . . .'

'You don't have to spare my feelings, Will. You didn't remember it but you told me exactly how you felt about her last week. I've taken it on board. And I'm glad you've got someone to take care of you. Particularly after what you've just been telling me.'

'We've not actually done anything yet. Promise.'

'More fool you. And it's hardly for me to start climbing on my high horse. I've not been exactly faithful myself.'

This got right in among me. 'I thought you were staying with a girlfriend?'

'Oh I am. Most of the time. Well, some of the time, anyway.'

'You're a quick worker. Well, quicker than me.'

'Yes, but I had a bit of a start on you. I've been seeing Henry for the past six months.'

There seemed to have been a great deal of this seeing going on and the only person who hadn't been seeing anything at all was Will Benson.

'Seeing as in giving a good seeing to, you mean?'

'Oh yes,' said Cathy cheerfully.

'Well, this is a bit of a turn up for the books. You were the one who always made a big thing of fidelity.'

'There are different kinds of fidelity, Will. Very soon after we got to London you made it quite clear that you were bored stiff with me and you'd much rather spend all your time with the people at *Theatre World*. I hardly saw you. So I started seeing Henry.'

'Let's have less of this bloody seeing. Fucking's the word you're looking for.'

'Well, that's part of it.'

After the lunch with Kim, this was kid's stuff. No waves of overpowering jealousy here. Just a minor irritation that Cathy had been happily having it away while I'd been wallowing in enjoyable guilt about my unfulfilled lust for Kim. I felt peeved, not hurt. And curious.

'Yes, but we were still living together, going to bed together and all the time you were screwing this . . . what's his name?'

'Henry,' she said. She was beginning to look cross.

'Who is he, anyway?'

'You've spoken to him. When you rang yesterday.'

'Oh, the prince of jesters. He was very entertaining on the

subject of your visit to the dentist. If anyone ever needs a dentist's drill impersonator, Henry's your man. And you lied, Cathy. You said there wasn't anyone else. You said after me you were looking forward to a man-free existence for a bit.'

Cathy blushed; she did so very rarely. But then she very rarely had any cause to.

'Yes, I'm sorry about that. I just couldn't face all the explanations. I was trying to let you down gently.'

Fair enough. Compassionate too. With the kind of hangover I'd had that Wednesday afternoon the shock would probably have killed me. But I wasn't going to stop the inquisition yet. After all, I hadn't quite ruined Cathy's lunch.

'When did you and Henry find time for all this unbridled passion? Not in the bank after shutting up shop, surely?'

'Well, every Tuesday night was safe for a start,' she said sharply. 'You were never home before eleven-thirty. And then there were the badminton nights.'

'So he wields a nifty shuttlecock then, Henry?'

'Don't be cheap, Will.'

'No, seriously. I mean did you actually play badminton or was that just a cover?'

'Oh yes, we'd play and then go back to Henry's for a Marks and Spencer's supper and a couple of hours in bed.'

'Idyllic,' I said.

'Yes it was . . . is.'

She didn't sound terribly sure.

'Didn't you ever feel the faintest twinge of guilt? I mean I know I was hardly the ideal partner, but at least you knew I wasn't having it away with someone a couple of nights a week.'

She picked up my hand, which was more than I deserved, and looked at me gravely. 'I was so lonely, Will. You weren't there any more. Henry's not the great love of my life, in fact since you and I have split up properly I don't actually feel the need to see him much at all. But I felt neglected. And he was kind, and funny . . .'

'Bleeding hilarious,' I said unkindly.

'Yes, well, I suppose he's not that funny actually,' said Cathy, and pulled a very funny mournful face of her own. I felt a sudden return of all the old affection.

'Sorry about the cross-examination. It's none of my business now.'

'He really cares about me you see. Besotted. It's very good for the damaged ego.'

'Cathy, forgive me,' I said. 'You were absolutely right to go off with Henry.'

'I shouldn't have followed you up to London. It was over long before then, I know that now. But despite all this grief I'm glad I did. I've got a better job. I've got more confidence out of this affair. I've got over you at last, properly. I mean I even like you now, and I haven't felt that for a long time.'

I felt chastened. 'I like you too, Cathy. Very much. And I'm sorry.'

I leant over and kissed her on the nose.

'Best mates, then?' she said.

'Best mates,' I replied.

'Buy me another drink on the strength of it?'

This was a new Cathy. A spritzer was usually the height of lunchtime debauchery for her. I summoned the waitress and she asked for a gin and tonic, and I ordered another large brandy for myself. Just to keep her company I told myself mendaciously.

'Let's not talk about us any more,' said Cathy. 'Tell me more about the death threats.'

'Well, I've told you most of it.'

'Yes, but who do you suspect?'

I went through the list, much as I had with Kim in the Bricklayer's the day before. 'There was just a remote possibility it might have been the Big Cunt and Meadows but after last night they're in the clear. And so's Susie Smiles. And so are you now. You were my last suspect.'

'It could still be me,' said Cathy. 'I could still be trying to kill you.'

The waitress was serving us the drinks as she spoke and favoured us both with a look of frank alarm. The idea of the respectable girl in the hideous blue suit murdering the battered sot in the dinner jacket was clearly more than she could take on board.

'Wouldn't you want to kill this fat slob?' Cathy asked her sweetly. The waitress fled and Cathy looked like a girl who'd done a good day's work.

'Listen, Will, I've got a theory. But first I want to give myself a proper alibi. You may believe me now but I don't want you to start getting your dawn dreads after I've gone. I could just be putting on an act after all.'

'You never could act. Don't forget I saw you in J.B. Priestley's *They Came To a City*, Midland Bank Thespians, Bridport Leisure Centre, 1986.'

'I managed to have an affair for six months without you suspecting a thing,' she said with a flicker of pride.

There was no answer to that.

'It won't take a minute. What time did you say you were shot at exactly?'

'Eleven-fifteen. The DJ had just given a time check.'

'Right, the dentist was drilling away at my teeth then. I had an eleven o'clock appointment and I was in there for almost an hour.'

'Cathy, there's no need for this. I believe you.'

'Proof positive, Will.'

She dragged me to the phone, got out her Filofax and dialled a number. As soon as she'd finished she handed the phone to me.

'I want you to hear them answer. No funny business.'

'Bayswater dental surgery,' said an efficient voice at the other end. I hadn't got a clue what to say.

'Um,' I said. 'Er, um,' I added by way of variety.

Cathy grabbed the phone. 'Hello, this is Cathy Williamson. I had an appointment with Mr Payne yesterday. Could I speak to his nurse if she's free, please?'

I goggled. It was somehow typical of the dead waters our relationship had drifted into that Cathy had never bothered to tell me her dentist's splendid name. I hadn't found a dentist since coming to London and just the thought of all that neglect made me think I'd got toothache. Top, left hand side. I wiggled my tongue against it. Very tender. Very tender indeed. Cathy was feeding another 50p into the phone.

'Oh, is that Mr Payne's nurse? Cathy Williamson here. It's terribly embarrassing this but I've got a rather suspicious boss and he thinks I was skiving yesterday when I had my appointment. Could you confirm I was actually there, please? From eleven till almost twelve.' There was some jabbering at the other end and then Cathy handed me the phone.

'Listen, mister, I don't know who you are but I wouldn't want to work for you. Miss Williamson had two large and difficult fillings yesterday. You're lucky she came in at all. She must have been in considerable discomfort yesterday afternoon after that root canal work.'

'Right, yes,' I murmured. I felt a heel even in this masquerade. To hell with it. 'I did have grounds for suspicion though. Miss Williamson is conducting a somewhat torrid office romance with one of my junior managers and since he failed to arrive yesterday morning as well, I naturally put two and two together.'

'Yeah, and got five,' replied the doughty dental nurse. 'What kind of prick are you?' Then she hung up on me.

'You rotter,' said Cathy with a grin. I've got to go back for yet another wretched filling next week. How will I look her in the eye?'

We ordered coffees and I lit another Camel.

'You're smoking too much.'

'I know. Now tell me your theory.'

'Remember your Sherlock Holmes. When you've eliminated the impossible (i.e., me and Susie Smiles), whatever remains, however improbable, must be the truth. Now anyone could be making those calls, and the shove on the Tube just might have been an accident, though it's not at all likely after that call to your editor. But surely the critical time is eleven-fifteen yesterday morning when the bolt actually came through your window, unless someone's got a contract out on you, but as you so rightly say, contract killers don't mess around with bows and arrows. So who hasn't got an alibi for yesterday morning?'

'Well, they all have, that's just the problem.'

'Bottom of the class, Watson. There's your actress.'

'But her mother's in intensive care. The stage manager put her on a train for Edinburgh. And she's not been back in the show since. An ambitious actress like that would never miss the chance of playing Juliet, however ropey the production.'

'But she's done that part now, and she's got a much bigger break coming up in the West End. And in any case she's found a much better role than either of those. You say this girl is a dedicated, intense actress. What could give her more satisfaction than making all her colleagues believe she's distraught with guilt and grief? I bet she just loved putting on all those tears and snivels. I bet the snot was running out of her nose and she pretended she was too upset to notice. I've seen them do it. They can turn it on like a tap but that doesn't stop saps like you rattling on about what a naked, courageous performance it was in your reviews.'

'But why should she want to kill me? Just for a review that didn't even mention her?'

'Because like most actors she's got an ego the size of a barrage balloon and she's mad as a hatter,' said Cathy, who had always regarded the theatre with a loathing that bordered on the pathological. 'She probably thinks she's on some kind of mission to save the world from the philistines, that she's doing what all actors would do if they had the courage and didn't actually need the good reviews to flog their dreadful shows.'

'I still can't believe it's her. She looked so innocent and vulnerable as Juliet.'

'I bet she took her clothes off.'

'Well, yes, she did, but what's that got to do with it?'

'You know you're an absolute sucker for any actress who gets them off. You think they're doing it just for you and you start having dirty fantasies about them. How you ever became a critic is quite beyond me. You can't even follow the plots. How many more times do I have to say it. She's an actress. Therefore she's vain, deceitful and devious, with only the feeblest grasp on reality. It's her job, pretending, making a drama.'

Cathy had worked up a nice head of steam now. Down to earth, sensible Cathy, as worlds removed from an actress as anyone could hope to be.

'Are you sure you're not picking the person you'd *like* to be behind it all?' I asked. 'What with your notorious dislike of the acting profession.'

'Try and bring some logic to bear, Will. The Holmes line. She's the only person who could have done it with any kind of a motive. It might just be some sicko you've never heard of but it doesn't sound likely to me. I mean, all those quotations and the silly voice down the telephone for heaven's sake. Who else could it be but an actress?'

'So what shall I do now?' I asked. There was something about Cathy that made me feel like a small boy seeking advice from his mother.

'Go to the police of course. You should have gone yesterday.'

'I thought it was you, yesterday, in case you'd forgotten.'

'So you did. Silly boy,' she grinned.

I lit another cigarette and asked if she wanted another coffee.

'No, I ought to be getting back. And don't you have to go to work anymore?'

I told her I did.

'What, dressed like that?'

'I've got the clothes I was wearing yesterday in the office. I can change when I get there.'

'Same socks and pants I suppose. Ugh.' Cathy was a stickler for personal hygiene.

'Will, promise me you'll go to the police.'

'Yes, I will. Tomorrow.'

'Today, Will. This afternoon.'

'All right. But I'm not going like this. I'll go to work and report to the cop shop in Docklands.'

'Just make sure you do, that's all.'

I tried to catch the waitress's eye with vague flapping movements of the arm but it was clear she couldn't bear being anywhere near us now. Cathy was looking anxiously at her watch so I told her to push off. She wanted to pay her shout but flush with Meadows' conscience money I wouldn't hear of it.

'It's been great to see you,' I said. 'You're not cross I suspected you?'

'Not cross that you thought I was trying to kill you. That's flattering in a twisted kind of way. Bloody furious that you think I'd make such a pig's ear of it.'

'Touché,' I said.

'Keep in touch,' she said, standing up to go. 'Stay alive.' She looked suddenly embarrassed. 'And good luck with Kim. I hope it all works out for you.'

I was very moved and didn't know what to say. I stood up and hugged her instead. Cathy allowed me a quick squeeze, then disentangled herself quickly and efficiently.

I kissed her on the cheek, patted her on the bum for old time's sake (she'd always hated it) and watched her with great tenderness as she walked out of the brasserie. She waved at me from the door, a shy, tentative wave, the sort of wave you might get at the end of a first teenage date.

Despite Cathy's strict instructions I had no intention of going to the police and had said I would merely to put her mind at rest. Perhaps I *was* soft about actresses. I didn't want to see the delectable Harriet arrested. Committed to a loony bin yes, but not banged up in some police cell.

I paid, left the brasserie and hailed a cab in Sloane Square, and was about to tell the driver to take me to the Isle of Dogs when I noticed how big he was: thirtyish, short hair, and with huge biceps which he was obviously proud of since he was wearing a T-shirt with the sleeves cut off to display them to maximum effect.

'I don't suppose you'd like to act as my minder for ten minutes or so?' I asked him. 'There's fifty quid in it but I don't want you to ask me any questions.' This was a new strategy and one that I would adopt permanently if I ever came into any serious money. Paying taxi drivers to keep their mouths shut.

'Legal is it?' he said.

'Oh yes. It's just a matter of coming into my flat with me for ten minutes or so and then going on to the Isle of Dogs.'

'Right. Where to?'

I told him. He drove in silence and didn't try any cracks about my face or the outfit. When we reached Rita Road I asked him to drive slowly down to the end and then double back again and park a few doors from my place. No sign of a small red car. We walked to the front door together, me on the inside of the pavement, nearer the houses. It felt safer there. He was huge, 6ft 4ins at least and with a beer-gut that made mine seem like a pimple.

'How do you manage to have biceps like that and a beer-gut as well? They don't normally go together.'

'Two hours weight training every night, followed by eight pints of lager,' he said complacently. 'You work up a thirst.' I rather liked him. It was like having your own pet Rottweiler.

I let myself in and he followed. The light was winking on the answering machine in the living room. Just the once. I hit the play button and it was old robot voice again.

'Where have you been, Will? You can't go on hiding for ever.' Was that really Harriet Smythe's voice behind all the electronics?

'That really was an arrow of outrageous fortune yesterday morning,' said the voice, followed by another of the electronic laughs. Even with my friendly guard dog in the room it gave me a chill. 'But I'll not miss again. You've very little time left. Like Faustus at the end of Marlowe's play. You remember, Will?' There was a click and the funeral march came on. Not very original, Miss Smythe, I thought. 'Sorry about the corny choice of music,' said the voice as though it had been reading my thoughts. 'But it is very appropriate. And such a fine piece, don't you think?' The music played for a minute or so and the cab driver hummed along with it. Then the voice started again:

Now hast thou but one bare hour to live
And then thou must be damned perpetually . . .

The stars move still, time runs, the clock will strike,
The devil will come and Benson must be damned.

The funeral march continued for a bit after the Marlowe, and then the voice came back.

'Why should a dog, a horse, a rat have life and thou no breath at all?' inquired my robotic tormentor. 'Because you're a shit, Will Benson, an arrogant, uncaring little shit.' There was a click, the bleep and I switched off the machine.

'*King Lear*,' said the taxi driver and I slumped incredulously on to the sofa. 'The greatest play ever written if you want my opinion, though you probably don't.'

'I think I can live without it,' I said weakly.

'What now, then?'

'I'll just go and change. Then straight on to the Isle of Dogs.'

The driver started quoting lines from 'The Waste Land'. 'T. S. Eliot,' he added smugly, 'not quite as great as Yeats in my view. Did you know that T. S. Eliot is an anagram of toilets? And that "Was it Eliot's toilet I saw" is a perfect palindrome? Some smart-ass is supposed to have come up with it when he saw the bog at Faber and Faber.'

'Why don't you shut up?' I said without malice.

'All right, no offence meant.'

We drove to the Isle of Dogs with the taxi driver singing 'Weialala leia' most of the way. To get him to shut up I asked him about his interest in literature.

'You told me not to ask questions. Why should I answer yours?' he asked.

'Fair enough.'

'Too bloody right.'

Outside the office I gave him the fare and the fifty.

'I'd tell the filth if I was you,' he said, handing back the fifty. 'You've got enough problems without going broke as well. I hope they catch the silly bitch.'

'You think it's a woman, then?'

'Yeah, I know there's no way of telling with that God awful

electronic voice but this has got woman's work written all over it. I mean, showing off her erudition like that . . .'

'What about you? *King Lear*, "The Waste Land", not bad going is it?'

'Yeah, well.' To my astonishment the great bruiser was blushing. 'Sorry about that, well out of order. Best of luck and all that.'

He drove off at speed and I wondered when he had the time for reading, between the taxi job, the weight training and the eight pints a night.

I bounded through reception, not even looking at Martha but flashing my identity card in case I was challenged, and raced up the stairs. I was longing to see Kim. She looked up anxiously when I went into the newsroom but saw my broad grin and reflected it back. I went over and kissed her on the cheek and Kevin asked if he got one too. Much to his alarm, I obliged and he started rubbing at his face with his hankie. I hustled Kim into the boardroom, ignoring Kevin's raised eyebrow, and held her tight and kissed her face and neck, little kisses of relief and happiness.

'Cathy's in the clear. And we're on speakers, and I still like her and I'm madly in love with you, "that thou didst know how many fathom deep I am in love". I had a taxi driver who kept spouting *King Lear* and "The Waste Land" at me. Hence the literary quotations. Sorry, Kim. Fathom deep. I only realized it eight days ago, at the Perseverance . . .'

The words came tumbling out in my manic euphoria. The idea of Cathy plotting to kill me, with considerable provocation, had upset me more than I had been prepared to acknowledge even to myself. 'She doesn't even hate me, God bless her, and she's been having an affair for the past six months with a humorous bloke called Henry.' I was pacing round the room now, and shouting. 'It makes me feel so much less guilty. I'm a free man.'

'Calm down, Will. Sit down and tell me what happened for God's sake. I've been in suspense all morning. I haven't even been out to lunch in case you came back when I was out. A solitary sandwich at my desk. The others thought I was ill.'

I quietened down at last and told her about Cathy, and the dentist, and her affair after badminton nights and her deductions about Harriet Smythe.

'Gosh, Will. I'm sorry. It was me who thought she must be in the clear after talking to the stage manager.'

'Oh yes, the old boot,' I said. 'The beautiful old boot.'

'Fuck off,' said Kim equably. 'Cathy's quite right of course. All this would be God's gift to an actress. What are we going to do now?'

'Try to find her. I'm not going to the police unless we have to. She's obviously off her trolley.'

'I could phone the stage manager,' said Kim. 'She might just part with a home address. And you never know, the bloody girl might even be back in the show by now.'

'I've got to see the new Ray Cooney tonight. If we can get her address I could pop round, unannounced, after that.'

'I'm coming too,' said Kim.

'It'd be better if I went on my own. It might be dangerous.' I tried to sound all tough and macho but I wanted Kim to come with me very much indeed.

'You're a wally, Will. It'll be much more dangerous if you go on your own. Really confrontational.' She grimaced with distaste at the social worker's jargon. 'But if I'm there, all sweet and calm and smiling, she might actually see that you're human after all. And anyway I want to see the Cooney. I'm your best girl now, remember. You take me to the first nights. I've brought my posh outfit along with me. Now leave me in peace. I'm going to get on with the case in here and Kevin's desperate for the Water Babies story and the captions. The Chief Squealer's sent the pictures round by courier.'

'Yes, boss,' I said.

'Quite right too,' she said, blowing me a dismissive kiss.

I gave Kevin my copy and started pounding out the captions. After a few minutes Kim emerged from the conference room.

'I got through to the stage manager again. And I've got

Smythe's address. She lives in Eccleston Square, SW1. But she hasn't been back to the show, they've not heard from her and no one's answering the phone. Blaze is still making them rehearse all day apparently and they're furious. He's changed the concept again. He didn't think Quentin Crisp was sexy enough so he's playing Juliet as a gay leather freak. It's called *Romeo and Julian* now.'

Kim went back to her desk to get on with the subbing, and later in the afternoon, after I'd finished the captions, a contact phoned with a nice little tale about Paul Raymond sponsoring Covent Garden's new production of *Salome*, since on this occasion he felt they were in the same line of business. 'It's very short and if any of the audience like what they see, they can come round to the Revuebar for the late show afterwards. I'm offering a fiver off the normal ticket price to all punters with the Opera House programme,' Raymond promised. The Opera House seemed embarrassed by his largesse. 'The fact that we are now reduced to accepting sponsorship from a sex show impresario is a damning indictment of the Government's mean spirited policy towards arts funding,' said a spokesman drearily.

Kim went off to change and I borrowed Mirza's Raybans to cover the black eye which was turning a nasty purplish yellow. They didn't really go with my sports jacket and it was dusk by the time we left but what the heck? I felt dead cool.

Kim had brought her car into work. The traffic leaving the island was terrible and by the time we'd got up West, and Kim had finally managed to park in a space that would have comfortably accommodated Joe Johnson's stretch limo, there were only five minutes to go to curtain up.

'I hate people watching me park,' she said after her Herculean labours. 'And if you think I didn't see you grimacing you're wrong. And you look a prat in those sunglasses.'

'Is this the moment to pat you on the head and buy you a Yorkie Bar?'

She gave a sulky *moue*. I bought her the chocolate on the way to the theatre, patted her on the head and said, 'there, there'. She looked cross at first, then giggled.

'You see, I told you. It always does the trick.'

There was the usual first night crush of gawpers and rent-a-celebs outside the theatre and as we went in, the photographers rushed towards us, flashguns blazing. Perhaps it was the dark glasses. Perhaps they thought I was Jack Nicholson. I gave a film-star smile and put my arm round Kim, but they kept going straight past us. I turned round. It was Anneka Rice, of course.

When the curtain fell, a couple of hours later, it seemed silly to spoil the evening by making an early call on Harriet Smythe. She probably wouldn't be there anyway, and if she was I wanted to catch her in a state of sleepiness. With any luck she wouldn't have time to load her crossbow. Unless she kept it under the bed. We went to a pasta joint and sat in a glow of wine and love. Kim started talking about her family. I felt I knew her so well and yet I was almost entirely ignorant about her background. Far from being the Newcastle-Brown-swilling docker I'd always imagined, it turned out her dad was a busy GP in South Shields who had fathered an improbable number of children, seven at the last count. Kim was the eldest. She seemed to like her family a lot, and was describing them with great warmth when she suddenly stopped, embarrassed.

'I'm sorry, Will. Your parents are dead, aren't they? It must make you miserable me going on like this.'

'Not at all. I love to hear you talk.'

'No, tell me about you. All I know is that you're an orphan.'

So I told her about my solitary but not unhappy childhood in Thames Ditton, brought up by a loving aunt after my parents were killed in a car crash when I was three.

'Poor baby,' said Kim and her eyes were moist. 'Don't you miss them?'

'I can't remember them.'

'Nothing at all?'

'Only the old photographs. And the voices. I can remember lying in bed and hearing them talk in the sitting room below my bedroom. Not the words, just a murmuring. Reassuring it was, safe. Knowing they were there when I went to sleep and would be there again when I woke up. And then one day they weren't. They're just an absence, a pang that comes and then goes away again just as quickly. Especially at night. I often wish I could hear their voices again at night.'

'I'll talk you to sleep,' said Kim. 'I'll whisper to you in the dark. Come back to my place tonight. Whatever happens with the Smythe girl, come back. I want us to make love. I'm ready now. I wanted you this morning when I woke up but you looked so peaceful I let you sleep on.'

I was tempted to pay up there and then and get Kim back to Brixton in a hurry and forget all about La Smythe but Kim insisted on trying to sort it out once and for all.

'I don't want to see you with an arrow in your head,' she said.

'Bolt, actually.'

'Did anyone ever tell you you were a pedantic pain in the arse?'

'Yeah. All the girls tell me that.'

We finished the bottle of Corvo Bianco and the surprisingly good lasagne, drank double espressos and walked back to Kim's car, which by some strange miracle hadn't been clamped. I found there were butterflies in my stomach, butterflies about confronting the woman who wanted to kill me, and butterflies about going to bed at last with the woman I loved. The next couple of hours seemed alarmingly important, like some exam that could change the rest of your life. And as Kim drove hesitantly down Whitehall, Big Ben was striking midnight.

Friday

Neither of us had a clue where Eccleston Square was, so I dug the *A to Z* out of the glove compartment as Kim drove past the Houses of Parliament. It turned out to be just a couple of streets from the Pimlico Court Hotel, and I thought of the Big Cunt and wondered whether he was still on the bottle or working on material for his new act. We cruised round till we found number 34, Kim parked with uncharacteristic ease and as we climbed out of the car we were both silent and tense.

` 'Not bad for an actress on a non-existent profit share,' said Kim, looking up at the impressive white stucco façade. 'Perhaps she's got a rich daddy.'

'It's thirty-four a, probably the basement,' I said. Sure enough there was a little wooden plaque which informed us that 34a – the 'garden flat', no basements in SW1 – was down the area steps. I rang the bell, a good, long, drugs-raid-style ring, then hammered on the brass knocker for good measure. My heart was beating uncomfortably, Wacka-wacka-whizz-bang, just like Dolores's Eurovision song. What was I going to say? Would she come to the door with her crossbow? I told Kim to stand in the shadows out of the direct line of fire, then went back to the ringing and knocking routine. Nothing happened.

'Looks like we're in for an early night,' I said.

'Try just once more,' said Kim. 'She might have taken a sleeping pill or something.'

I rang and knocked again, and then, with the courage of a man who knows damn well the coast is clear, knelt down and pushed open the letter-box. 'Open up, it's the police,' I shouted, more to make Kim laugh than anything. 'We've got the place surrounded and there are armed marksmen on the roof. Come out quietly or we'll shoot.'

Kim did laugh, but much more worrying was the sound that emerged from within. I was looking down a cosy corridor, all Regency striped wallpaper, dark blue carpet and tasteful watercolours on the walls and I could have sworn I heard a voice coming from the end of it. A man's voice, not Harriet's.

I dropped the *Sweeney* impersonation. 'Hello!' I shouted. 'Anybody home?' Stupid question, really.

'Stop playing silly buggers,' said the voice, distant but clearly audible now I was expecting it. 'I'm tied up and I can't move. If you look in the cellar opposite the front door you'll find an old washing machine. Inside the drawer where the powder goes you'll find the front-door key. For God's sake get a move on.'

We found the washing machine and the key.

'Who the hell is it?' whispered Kim.

The voice was familiar but I couldn't place it. I got out my Swiss army knife and opened the biggest blade before opening the front door.

'Wait here,' I said to Kim. 'It might be a trap and if there's any trouble you can scoot off and call the police.'

'I'm coming with you,' she said in a tone that brooked no refusal.

We advanced slowly down the corridor. It was a surprisingly spacious basement, and I glanced into a sitting room and a dining room with a huge mahogany table.

'Get a bloody move on,' called the voice testily. There was a half-open door at the end of the passage. We entered a small, overheated study, with dark wood-panelled walls, a big antique desk, a green leather sofa and a lot of leather-bound books in a handsome glass-fronted case. I took this in later though. What first struck the eye was the large man dressed only in his underpants, sitting in what must have been a very uncomfortable position by the radiator.

'Are you all right?' I asked fatuously.

'What do you think? I'm handcuffed to the radiator pipe and it's as hot as hell.'

Kim went to the other end of the radiator and turned it off.

'Burglars?' she asked.

'No,' he said. 'Miss Harriet Smythe.'

He was about fifty, with greying hair and owl-like horn-rimmed spectacles. His boxer shorts, endearingly, had pictures of the Flintstones on them.

'Is there a key to the handcuffs, Mr Simon?' I asked. I'd recognized the voice at last. Harriet's agent.

He looked embarrassed. 'In the bedroom, just next door. In the chest of drawers. Top drawer on the left. You'll find a small leather box. It should be in there.'

I went out and found the bedroom, opened the drawer and discovered why he was so embarrassed. The box with the key in it was there all right. So were a lot of hard-core bondage magazines. Also a whip, and a cane that looked just like my old headmaster's except that its silver handle was a meticulously detailed representation of an erect penis. There was a leather hood with a lot of zips on it, a studded dog collar and a lead, and an extraordinary assortment of chains and padlocks. The bed was an old oak four-poster with a mirror under the handsome tapestry canopy and a large number of rings on all four posts, chains and padlocks for the use of, presumably. I flicked through the magazines, which seemed to have less to do with sexual pleasure than with peculiarly painful forms of GBH. All the pictures showed men suffering at the hands of women. Mr Simon clearly liked being on the receiving end and it didn't take much imagination to guess who liked dishing it out. The prospect of a night of passion with Harriet Smythe was an alarming one.

I went back to the study. 'By the look of things in the bedroom, you must have been enjoying yourself down there.'

'I've been here for nearly twelve hours,' he said. 'Cut out the cheap cracks and undo me.'

He was so stiff that it was tricky getting him to lean forward so I could unlock the handcuffs, but we managed it in the end.

His wrists were raw and bloody, and half his back was livid from the heat of the radiator. He might like being hurt, but this had clearly been far too much. It took both of us to haul him to his feet and when he was upright he began to shake uncontrollably. Then he limped out of the room. 'I'm dying for a piss,' he called over his shoulder. 'I had two pints of beer with my lunch before Harriet pulled her little stunt.'

He came back a couple of minutes later, clad in a scarlet silk dressing gown with a beautifully woven dragon on the back.

'Will Benson, I presume,' he said with a touch of the old urbanity. 'And you must be the young lady Harriet calls the Doxy. I'm very relieved to see you both in such blooming health. Surprised too if it comes to that. Drink?'

I nodded and so did Kim. He poured us largish measures of a pale spirit from a decanter and served himself a veritable depth charge of a drink. It was the best malt whisky I'd ever tasted, clear and complex with a hint of peat and smoke but none of the tarriness of Laphroaig. Even Kim smacked her lips in appreciation.

'How was your holiday in France, Mr Simon?' I asked nastily. 'Did you bother to speak to Harriet before you did your disappearing trick? I think you owe us both an explanation.'

'Yes I do,' he said quietly, and motioned us to the sofa, swivelling round his desk-chair to face us. He buried his face in his drink for a bit, sighed, and started talking.

'As you must have gathered, my mistress is trying to kill you, Mr Benson. She is, I imagine, lurking outside either your house or your companion's as we speak, armed with a crossbow.'

'Ah,' I said. 'I thought she might be.'

'The reason you found me so ingloriously secured to my own radiator is that I tried to stop her. She pulled the smallest of her crossbows on me. I don't know when she'll be back.'

'At the Alhambra she threw a Bloody Mary at me as soon as I announced my name.'

'You were lucky that's all she threw at you. She's gone mad. I'm only beginning to realize just how mad myself.'

Mr Simon, we learnt, had first met Harriet Smythe just over

a year earlier, at her graduation performance from drama school. She had been playing, surprise, surprise, the Duchess of Malfi; Simon had been enormously impressed, signed her up immediately after the performance and then taken her for a celebratory dinner.

'Somehow or other she picked up on my sexual preferences. She came back here afterwards and she's been here ever since.'

Mr Simon's eyes went all misty. 'She really loves inflicting pain. It was the answer to all my prayers.'

Kim, who hadn't seen the contents of the chest of drawers, was looking confused, as well she might.

'Our host', I told her, 'is a masochist.'

'Yuck,' said Kim.

'Each to his own,' said Mr Simon with considerable dignity. 'There are worse forms of deviancy.'

For many months, he continued, everything had been idyllic. Harriet had done a couple of shows on the fringe, Mr Simon had put her up for the role in *Macbeth the Musical* and she'd got it and each night she'd come home, tie him up and beat the shit out of him. Sometimes, just to be cruel, she'd tie him up and not beat the shit out of him.

'Then she did that abysmal *Romeo and Juliet* which contrary to what I told you, I saw.' He shuddered. 'The Camden Basement's no place even for a masochist. Your review by the way, apart from not mentioning Harriet who I think you'll agree was superb, was first-rate. It made me laugh out loud.'

'Not in front of Harriet, I hope.'

'As you say, not in front of Harriet. Anyway, she did phone me at work in floods of tears as I told you and I tried to quieten her down. When I got home I told her you'd phoned to apologize but she wouldn't listen. That appalling pseud Blaze had persuaded her the production was a masterpiece and she just kept screaming that you were scum. She had hysterics until two o'clock in the morning, then she calmed down a bit and started on me. She told me I was a disgusting old pervert and she wished she'd never met me. And then she went to sleep on the sofa like a baby. I can't tell you how relieved I was. It was horrible to see her like that.'

Simon, it transpired, had had enough and reckoned that his presence would make matters worse rather than better. He'd left Harriet a note and driven to Dover before she woke up, catching an early ferry to Boulogne.

'I feared you might get a rough reception at the Alhambra but I thought you'd cope. I'd no idea at that stage that she was turning homicidal. She certainly didn't mention it in all her raving, and everything but everything was pouring out that night. The idea must have come to her later. Anyway, I spent a peaceful week touring Normandy, reading Proust and eating like a pig, and only returned this morning. Harriet was affectionate and apologetic when I arrived and I thought she'd calmed down and seen sense. Then she told me she was embarked on a wonderful adventure. I'm afraid she talks like that sometimes. *Romeo and Juliet* was a wonderful adventure. *Macbeth the Musical* is almost certain to be a wonderful adventure as well, unless it turns out to be an incredible voyage of discovery. You know what intense young actresses are like.'

I nodded. 'And did she tell you just what this wonderful adventure consisted of?'

'Yes, I'm afraid she did. At first I got a bit of *Macbeth*, you know, "Be innocent of the knowledge, dearest chuck, till thou applaud the deed," but she was so hyped up she couldn't wait to spill the beans. I got the lot, the phone calls, the shove on the Tube, following the two of you around in taxis and last but not least, her shot through your front window. She says if you hadn't moved she'd have hit you. She's looking forward to trying again.'

'How did she do the robot voice?' I asked.

'Very easily. You'd better come and have a look at her work room.'

He led the way. It was a tiny room and a good deal of it was taken up with electronic equipment – a synthesizer keyboard, speakers, amplifiers, an expensive looking tape-deck and a microphone.

'I'm afraid I bought her all this stuff,' he said. 'When she's not acting she's composing. You had one clue actually. The music in *Romeo and Juliet* was Harriet's. She's credited in the programme.'

I remembered lots of doomy electronic chords and strange haunting melodies. 'But can you change a voice with one of these things?' I asked.

He went over to the table where most of the equipment was, turned a few knobs and spoke into a microphone.

'I can't tell you how sorry I am about all this,' he said, and out of the speakers came the robot voice, so near and loud it made me jump. It was a little deeper than the messages I'd received, but he turned a knob and it sounded almost identical. He twisted the knob again, and his voice was a low rumble, twisted it again, and it was a high-pitched squeak. 'So you see,' he said in that horrid metal falsetto, 'Harriet has no trouble in disguising her voice.'

He showed me the small speaker she'd probably used for sending her messages down the phone, then switched on the tape recorder. 'Every Breath You Take', followed by the funeral march. There was even a loose-leaf folder, with her messages typed out in it like a radio script, right down to technical instructions like 'Cue SFX'.

There was a pile of books, too, and I knew just which ones they'd be. *The Duchess of Malfi*, heavily annotated for her drama school production, *Julius Caesar*, Marvell, and the collected poems of Louis MacNeice, opened at 'Bagpipe Music'.

'It's no go the Yogi-Man, it's no go Blavatsky
All we want is a bank balance and a bit of skirt in a taxi'

I read into the microphone. It was quite fun pretending to be a Dalek.

'The last of the revelations,' said Mr Simon, opening a cupboard. He brought out two crossbows, one small, one big, both in matt black metal. Very sinister they looked. The big one had an integral quiver-device for storing the bolts whose viciously barbed tips looked as though they'd do more damage when you pulled them out than when they actually hit their target. One of them, I noticed, was missing. Then I remembered it was in the wastepaper basket at home.

'But I thought you said Harriet was looking for us now,' I said. 'Surely she hasn't gone unarmed?'

'She's taken the prize of her collection. One hundred and fifty-pound draw and telescopic sight.'

'A telescopic sight on a crossbow?'

'I'm afraid so. And a range of almost two hundred yards. Even this little one can fire a hundred yards. She uses it for shooting rabbits, down at my cottage near Chichester. The one disadvantage with crossbows is that the bolt tends to fall out if you move quickly. But as you can see, she's got over that by attaching these little clips. It's almost as versatile as a pistol now, though of course you only get one shot before reloading and that takes a bit of time.'

'And just how good a shot is she?'

'Excellent. She did archery instead of hockey at school, crossbows as well as longbows. Won the school cup.'

'Oh great,' I said. 'And can you really buy these buggers over the counter without a licence?'

'Absolutely. We bought both of these in a shop in the Haymarket. Ninety-five pounds for the pistol version, a hundred and ninety-five for the big one. The one with the telescopic sight was more expensive. But then it's a particularly accurate and powerful model. Harriet has considerable difficulty in pulling back the draw string. But it's got a footclaw for her to pull against, and she manages.'

'Quite a girl, isn't she, your Harriet,' I said. 'So what happened after she told you all this?'

'She went off to do her Buddhist chanting ('Wouldn't you just know she'd do Buddhist chanting,' whispered Kim with contempt), and I came in here to phone the doctor. I was going to get him to fill her full of tranquillizers and get her quietly into a psychiatric hospital. The trouble is Harriet obviously suspected something and was eavesdropping outside the door.

As soon as she heard me asking for the doctor, she came in with the little crossbow, cut me off, made me strip and handcuffed me to the radiator. Then she said she was going out to look for you. She left at two o'clock. She's not been back since.'

Kim finished her drink. 'Well, we'd better phone the police. They ought to be able to pick her up easily enough. She'll either be staking out Will's place or mine.'

Simon's face crumpled and this urbane, dignified masochist began to cry.

'I love her,' he said through his tears. 'If the police turn up, she'll probably shoot at them and they'll lock her away. She needs psychiatric help for God's sake. I don't think she'll ever recover if she's arrested and thrown into a cell.' Simon begged for a day or two's grace. 'She's got to come home sometime. As soon as she does, I'll call the doctor and get her into hospital.'

'But isn't it terribly dangerous leaving her out on the streets all night with that wretched weapon?' said Kim.

'Couldn't she take a pot-shot at someone else when she gets bored with waiting for us?'

'I don't think so,' said Simon. 'It's an *idée fixe*. She's only interested in Will and, to a lesser extent, I'm afraid, you, Kim. She seemed obsessed with the notion that you could allow such a vicious bastard to share a bed with you.'

Kim grimaced. 'Fat chance of that tonight by the look of it. We can't go home, can we?'

'I'm afraid I don't think you can. She spent all last night outside Will's place, apparently, so I suspect she'll be outside your place tonight. And if you don't turn up there she'll go back to Will's to try to pick you off in the morning. There's a strong chance she might come back here for a couple of hours' rest in the middle. I don't think she'd leave me chained to the radiator for twenty-four hours. I hope she wouldn't. Otherwise I'd offer you a bed here.'

We went back to the study and Simon poured us more of his delicious whisky but the news that Harriet might come home at any moment had put us both on edge. I think Simon was pretty keen to get rid of us as well.

'So we can't go home and we can't stay here,' said Kim. 'What do we do? Check into a hotel?'

'I've had a better idea. Let's go to Blackpool. I'll phone JB now and let him know.'

'You can't,' said Kim, 'It's one o'clock in the morning.'

'He asked me to keep him posted. We can't hang around here much longer, and I don't think it's safe to go to work tomorrow morning anyway. When Harriet realizes we're not in either of our flats she'll probably go to the Isle of Dogs. And if that weapon with the telescopic sight is as accurate as Mr Simon says it is, she could pick us off on the path from the cab to reception as easy as winking. We're lucky she hasn't tried it already.'

JB answered the phone on the second ring and didn't sound at all miffed at being rung at such a late hour. He'd been judging a talent contest and had felt an irresistible urge to listen to some Jimi Hendrix when he got home. I could hear 'Voodoo Chile' screaming away in the background as I told him the latest.

'How would you feel about us taking tomorrow off? If Simon hasn't got the girl into hospital by Saturday we'll call in the police. We thought we'd go to Blackpool until she's out of harm's way.'

'It's the most elaborate excuse I've heard for a day's skiving and an extended dirty weekend but I'll buy it,' said JB. 'Drive safely and bring me back a stick of rock.'

I put the phone down, took Simon's number and said I'd call from Blackpool to find out what was happening. 'Be careful. And for God's sake lock her crossbows away somewhere safe.'

Simon left the house first to make sure the street was a Smythe-free zone and then told us it was safe to come up the steps. I suddenly noticed how tired Kim was looking.

'I'll drive,' I said. 'The first leg anyway.' Mr Simon waved us off and I gave him a cheerful toot on the horn.

I wasn't pissed, but I was certainly over the limit so we

stopped at the all-night cafe near Westminster Bridge for coffee before driving up to the M1. Tired though she was, Kim still looked beautiful, even in the cruel glare of the cafe's harsh neon lights. We sipped our filthy beverage in silence and I hoped Harriet didn't patronize the same dive after a happy night's hunting. Much too downmarket for her, I thought. Kim looked at me shyly.

'Will, you don't want me to tie you up and whip you, do you?' she said. 'I don't think I'd like it.'

'No, I don't think I would either.'

We sat in silence, thinking of Mr Simon who seemed so straight, and Harriet, thirty years his junior, and chains and whips and padlocks.

'Strange the avenues lust leads you down,' I said at last. 'I was drunk once and asked Cathy to piss on me. She was dreadfully shocked.'

'Mmm,' said Kim primly and I thought I'd shocked her too. 'I was very drunk indeed at the time,' I blustered.

She took a demure sip of coffee and looked me in the eye.

'I could quite fancy it,' she said.

Big Ben was chiming two o'clock when we climbed back into the Mini. There was a road atlas on the back seat and I checked the route. Simple enough, M1, M6, M55. Dead easy as long as I could keep awake and didn't get stopped by the police. It was wonderful driving out of London on the empty roads, a pleasure to be leaving a city where mad actresses stalked your flat with crossbows.

By the time we reached the M1 Kim was fast asleep. I tuned to Radio 2 and the bland, nostalgic music soothed away the miles. I felt an ache of tenderness for Kim as she lay there with her head lolling awkwardly on her shoulder and her mouth open. Her sleep was a kind of trust. The Mini was a rattly old thing and 65 m.p.h. seemed to be its top whack but on the clear roads it felt like a haven, warm and safe and secure, and I managed to stop thinking for once, and drove through the night in a trance of relief and happiness.

At 4.30, I stopped at a service station and gently woke Kim

up. We dragged ourselves into the Granary Cafe, and ordered coffee. Tousled and crumpled with sleep, Kim put her head on my shoulder and we sat there in companionable silence. I suddenly realized she'd gone to sleep again. I couldn't bear to wake her so I sat there, mind blissfully empty, for forty minutes until she came to with a jerk. 'Sorry,' she said, swigging back her tepid coffee.

We hit Blackpool at 6.30, just as the sky was showing the first iron grey smudges of dawn. I nudged Kim awake and we cruised along the Golden Mile, past the Tower, the shuttered amusement arcades and the fortune tellers' booths. Apart from an old man with his dog, there wasn't a soul stirring and the place seemed mean and gritty and desolate. The railings were rusting on the prom, the pavements strewn with litter.

Kim asked me to tour the backstreets, and we drove slowly past the Boltonia ('A warm Bolton welcome assured'), The Home from Home ('Lift for elderly residents'), and the Sea Breeze ('Every night is karaoke night in our luxury bar'). Kim shook her head at each. 'Not quite right,' she said. They all looked perfectly foul to me.

'Are you sure you don't want to go somewhere posh like the Imperial?' I said. 'We've got Meadows' money.'

She shook her head. 'I want to find the place I stayed in as a child. What was it called. The Clifton. No, the Connaught, that's it. I remember my dad saying it was the same name as one of the most exclusive hotels in London. I asked him what exclusive meant.'

'How old were you?'

'Eight. We had a huge family room. Mum, Dad and all us little ones.'

'All seven of you?'

'The twins weren't born then. They were a bit of an afterthought.'

'And you've no idea where it was? There must be hundreds, thousands of hotels here.'

Kim was looking rapt, gazing back through the years.

'It was near the Tower, round the back of the Tower. I

remember walking down the road to the circus. It was wonderful, that circus, Will. The sods have closed it down now, turned it into some lousy puppet display, but it was beautiful, a huge gilded auditorium, with a cage for the big cats, and a knife-thrower and a proper ringmaster in a red coat. And at the end, I don't know how they did it, the whole ring sank and filled with water, and there were coloured fountains. And then they shot a man out of a cannon into a net. God, I'd love to see it again. I remember there was a baby tiger that leapt fifteen feet into its trainer's arms. It wouldn't have done that if it had been mistreated, would it? Bloody animal rights people.'

Her eyes were shining and I hoped we'd find the hotel. But would it still be here after more than fifteen years? And if it was, would it still have the same name?

I turned off Albert Road down a side street and Kim started screaming. 'Look, there on the corner, on the right.'

The Connaught was marginally grander than its neighbours – the same red brick and hideous plastic sign, of course, but four storeys high and with a rather fanciful turret at one end.

'My fairytale tower, that's what I used to call it.'

I tried to smile but it must have looked more like a scowl.

'Sorry,' she laughed. 'There's nothing quite as yucky as other people's memories of childhood.'

It was seven in the morning and we had no luggage. I looked at my purple eye and put Mirza's Raybans on, then took them off again. If we were going to get into the hotel, it would probably be wiser to look like the victim rather than the threat. Kim jumped out of the car and was ringing frantically on the bell. Nothing much stirred inside for a minute or so, then there was the sound of footsteps and a voice saying, 'All right, all right, no need to wake up the whole hotel.'

The door was answered by a roly-poly woman in her early sixties, with fluffy slippers, a hideous floral dressing gown, and thin hair dyed a candy-floss pink.

'We wondered if we could have a room for a couple of nights,' said Kim, pointing at the vacancies sign hanging in one of the front windows. 'Mrs Robinson, isn't it?'

'You're not one of my regulars. I've never seen you before in my life,' said Mrs Robinson, producing a packet of Players Number 6 from her dressing-gown pocket. I hadn't seen anyone smoking those vile little cigarettes for years. I thought they'd stopped making them.

Kim was impressively beseeching. She churned out all the stuff about staying there as a child, how she'd never forgotten the place, how we'd driven through the night to get there early. 'I've been telling my husband about it all the way up here,' she said.

Mrs Robinson looked at the finger where Kim's wedding ring ought to have been and wasn't, then at my black eye. Then she gave a leery smile.

'Aye. And I bet you were a virgin bride and all,' she wheezed through a cloud of blue smoke. 'Where's your luggage?'

'We left in a bit of a hurry,' I said.

'Not a police matter is it?'

'No, I can pay in advance if you like. Cash.'

'That'll do nicely,' said the landlady. 'Normal checking-in time's two p.m. but I've got a room spare. Thirty pounds a night with full English breakfast. Say an extra tenner for the early booking.'

I peeled seventy quid from my wad and realized I'd miss it when it was gone. She finally let us in and led us up the stairs, which were carpeted in a retina-burning sunburst design. Little plastic notices were screwed to the red flock wallpaper: 'To prevent ANNOYANCE and INJURY, parents are asked to prevent their CHILDREN playing on the STAIRS,' said one. 'In the interests of HYGIENE, we respectfully ask guests not to bring food, I.E. TAKE-AWAY, FISH AND CHIPS, etc into any part of these premises,' read another. 'FIRE DANGER' warned a third. 'On the advice of the fire authorities, we have to ask our visitors NOT TO SMOKE IN BED.'

'Strict here, isn't it,' whispered Kim. 'I'm surprised we aren't respectfully asked to use a condom at all times.'

'What's that about condoms?' said Mrs Robinson, quick as a flash.

'Er, nothing,' I said, blushing.

'For the convenience of guests, a CONDOM MACHINE is located in the Gent's TOILET,' said the old battle-axe, speaking in bold capitals just like one of her signs.

'Christ, that's a thought,' I whispered to Kim as our landlady went round a corner.

'It's OK, Will. I'm on the pill. Remember?'

At last we reached the fourth floor and Sherpa Robinson came to a halt, produced a key and threw open the door with a proud flourish as if she was showing off a suite at the London Connaught. She didn't go in, and as Kim and I edged past her we realized why. There wouldn't have been room. The double bed, not an especially big one, took up almost all the available floor space. On two sides of it there was a gangway about two-feet wide, and on the left-hand wall a door led into the windowless bathroom. Here, a lavatory, a wash-basin and a shower unit had somehow been installed with the cunning use of advanced geometry. On the bedroom window-sill there was an electric kettle, two chipped tea cups, a single tea-bag and a little tub of artificial milk. There was another notice as well. 'Further supplies of our refreshing TEA and COFFEE may be purchased at reception for a nominal charge.'

Kim and I gazed at the room, at the coy little pictures of ragged, huge-eyed urchins taking a leak in a Disneyfied version of Venice, at the view over the rooftops. It was just fine.

'We'll take it,' said Kim.

'Breakfast is at eight on the dot,' said Mrs Robinson. 'You'll hear the gong. If you're down more than ten minutes after that, you'll not get served.' She looked at her watch. 'But you've got almost an hour. That should do you for the time being.' The sight of Mrs Robinson, down to the last quarter of an inch of her fag but still dragging away gamely before favouring us with the most lubricious of smiles, will stay with me for some time. 'You'll find the bed very comfortable but for the CON-VENIENCE and SAFETY of other guests, please keep noise to a minimum. The walls are thin and there's a dirty old man next door with a dicky ticker.' I found myself warming to our landlady.

When she'd lumbered off I felt suddenly shy.

'Well, here we are,' I said nervously.

'Here we are,' said Kim, and she didn't look shy at all.

'Cup of tea?' I asked.

Kim came over to me by the window and kissed me, long and softly, and when she stood back I looked deep into her eyes; they were warm and shining and at peace. The hurt had gone. She knelt down and undid my trousers, clumsily, endearingly.

'There's no need,' I said, excited, erect at once but thinking too of that horrible blow job with Cathy. She held me gently, with cool hands, like a nurse.

'There's every need,' she whispered. 'I've been wanting to do this for months.'

'Months?'

'Months,' she said, licking her lips. 'Now shut up and enjoy it.'

Her mouth was warm and soft and receptive and I stroked her hair and gazed, with a curious feeling of detachment, over the roofs and chimney pots to the Tower. She made little sucking noises, and was doing wonderful things with her fingers and tongue, and very soon I didn't feel detached at all as I thrust into the wonderfully welcoming wetness of her mouth while she knelt in front of me like some debauched religious votary. I cried out with the sheer wonder of it all as I came, again and again, into her mouth, the mouth that so often wore a crooked grin and was now full of cock and spunk. I remembered Cathy's tear-stained face but Kim lifted smiling eyes when it was over and winked and climbed to her feet. Her mouth was wet with dribble and she smiled like a mucky child. Unlike Cathy, she swallowed the come with every appearance of pleasure. 'Wonderfully nutritious,' she said. 'Who needs breakfast?'

Kim made hungry where most she satisfied. She kissed me again and I could taste my own sperm and began fumbling desperately with the buttons of her blouse. She stepped back, and slowly, tantalizingly, undid it, button by button. Standing there with my trousers round my legs I watched as she took off her bra. The breasts I'd fantasized about and groped but never seen were exposed in all their plump glory. She looked so proud standing there, naked to the waist in her black silk trousers, but small and vulnerable too, her breasts like some wonderful afterthought of a God who'd suddenly tired of a due sense of proportion.

'Kiss them, Will, suck them,' she said. I took her in my arms, and kissed her mouth and then her breasts and sucked, and sucked, and Kim kept whispering 'harder', and then we fell in a heap on the bed. There was a squelching sound as our bodies hit the grubby candlewick bedspread.

'Oh Christ,' Kim giggled. 'A rubber undersheet for the incontinent. I remember that from last time.'

We struggled out of what remained of our clothes and Kim pushed me down and knelt astride my face, and I licked and sucked, and her juices seemed like the distilled essence of lust and love. She moved against my mouth and my tongue, faster, harder, wetter, and I reached up and held her breasts and her back arched and she wasn't whispering any more, she was shouting that she was coming, oh fuck she was coming and fuck, she never came in the mornings. She collapsed in a sweaty, smiling bundle beside me and I kissed her neck and her cheeks and her lips and her eyes.

'Let's get between the sheets,' she said. 'I want you inside me, Will.' We stood up awkwardly and pulled back the disgusting bed-cover and lay down on the squeaky rubber beneath the thin sheet.

'A perve's delight,' I said.

'I'm taking it off straight after breakfast,' she said, 'It gives me the willies.'

She guided me in and it was like coming home, warm and tight and tender. I held her bum and nibbled her ear and she moved like an angel, drawing me in and on, undulating, her nails scratching my back. I felt myself on the edge of coming again and rolled her on top to slow myself down, and she laughed and took charge herself, writhing on top of me, half lying, half crouching on her knees. She swung her heavy breasts against my face, again and again, more and more violently, and then she pulled back and there was a new urgency in her movement. I moved with her, deep inside her, and when she came, she called to Christ and the tears streamed down her cheeks. I rolled on top of her and came again in a few deep thrusts, then lay exhaustedly on top of her, grinning, and licked her tears away.

'Bloody hell, that was far better than either of us had any right to expect,' she said. 'I told you, it's the Blackpool air. It's full of sex.'

'I hope the dirty old man next door's OK.'

We held our breath, and listened to the silence. Then there was the sound of a match being struck and a bout of hideous coughing as he took his first drag of the day.

Kim giggled. 'First he has the vicarious fuck, then he has the real post-coital cigarette. Do you want one? I don't mind. And I promise I won't tell the Blackpool Fire Brigade.'

For once I didn't. I pulled myself out of her, she turned on to her side and I curled round her and held her tummy. She extricated her arm and looked at her watch.

'It's quarter to eight,' she said. 'Brekker in a quarter of an hour.'

'I thought you'd had yours,' I mumbled.

She didn't reply. Fast asleep again, and I felt myself drifting away as well, down into that deep, sweet, post-sex sleep, the very marrow of sleep. It didn't last long. There was a terrific clanging outside, like an old fashioned fire engine coming up the stairs. Old Ma Robinson was banging her gong and making as fine a fist of it as the muscle-bound chap at the start of the old Rank films.

'Oh hell,' said Kim. 'Push me out of bed will you?' I took her at her word and she ended up on the floor. 'Bastard,' she grumbled, crawling on her hands and knees and searching for her knickers.

Sweaty and dazed with sleep and sex we legged it down the

226

stairs to the dining room. All eyes were down for a full house. There was just one empty table by the window and we sat there and drank the tiny glasses of tepid, watered-down orange juice that were sitting forlornly in the middle of our cereal bowls. Most of the other guests seemed to be middle-aged couples, but there were two ridiculously young kids, the youth blushing furiously, the girl pregnant, tense and tight-lipped, neither of them more than seventeen and both of them looking so unhappy that they could only have been on their honeymoon. Two harassed parents fussed over a peculiarly ugly baby which was dribbling all over the tablecloth and there was a solitary buffer of about seventy who kept grinning and winking at us. The dirty old man from next door, presumably. Kim gave him a regal little wave and he choked on his tea.

The fried eggs, bacon, sausage and baked beans were surprisingly good, and so was the coffee.

'Looking after you all right, is he?' said Mrs Robinson as she came with a second pot.

'Mustn't grumble,' said Kim

I wondered where Harriet was.

'Forget her,' said Kim, reading my mind. 'We're on our hols. Three whole days together. We'll go and buy some clothes after breakfast, then you'd better have a sleep. Then I want you to take me to the Pleasure Beach.'

The sun had appeared after the grey dawn, but there was an autumnal nip in the air and our breath made clouds of mist. Kim shivered in her skimpy trousers and blouse, and hugged her old dinner jacket around her. We bought the basics in Marks, knickers and socks, shirts and jumpers and jeans. Kim inevitably found another rugby shirt and bought a pair of trainers to replace her dizzy high-heels. She wanted to pay for her own stuff but I insisted that Mr Meadows should foot the bill. 'It's not my money. It's ours. And who wants to keep it anyway? I want to blow some of it on a proper present for you, as well. Something you've always wanted. You deserve it.'

'There's no need, Will.'

It's so much easier to give than to receive, but Kim had the real generosity of those who can accept a gift gracefully. We walked down the street a few paces and she looked thoughtful.

'I'll think of something,' she said and squeezed my hand. 'I do deserve a present, don't I?'

In Boots we bought toothbrushes, toothpaste and deodorant, plus Bisodol, Disprin and Vitamin C in case of hangovers to come. 'Hung-over sex', said Kim dreamily, 'is almost my very favourite sort.'

She shivered in the street outside and I said she should have bought a jacket in Marks.

'You know my present. That's what I want. A black leather biker's jacket, all studs and buckles.'

We toured the drab streets and Kim finally found a shop so formidably trendy that I felt a fool simply going into it. A girl with a shaved head and, rather spoiling the effect of screw-you cool, a Jason Donovan T-shirt regarded us with all the enthusiasm of someone welcoming the VAT inspectors.

'Yeah?' she said at last, just a fraction short of insolence. There was rap music on the sound system and I realized I really was getting old. Rap was the first form of pop music I actively, violently disliked. Kim entered into urgent negotiations with the assistant and I realized the noise was so unpleasant I couldn't bear being inside the shop any longer. I stepped briskly outside, discovered a newsagent, and bought a *Daily Telegraph* and a packet of Capstan Full Strength. After lighting up I caught myself turning to the sports pages first. Perhaps there were compensations in growing old after all.

After about five minutes Kim came out in a jacket that had all the buckles anyone could possibly want, plus a skull and crossbones and the legend 'Hearts on Fire' picked out in studs on the back. She looked smug and shy, defiant and lovable and she launched into a Pete Townshend impersonation on the pavement, playing an imaginary electric guitar, whirling her arm like a windmill and leaping into the air.

'Is this as cool as fuck or what?' she shouted in delight, then looked suddenly anxious. 'It's terribly expensive, Will. Three hundred smackers.'

'It's fine,' I said. 'Cheap at the price.' It was nice pretending you were rich for once, and I braved the gangsta rap and peeled off the notes for the improbable Jason Donovan fan. We still had almost £400 left in the kitty.

'You better phone Meadows and book a bashing up next week to keep us in the style to which I've grown accustomed,' said Kim.

'Your turn, next,' I replied.

We walked down to the front and along the Golden Mile. It was ten o'clock and there were a few people about now, kids riding donkeys on the beach, grown-ups killing time before the pubs opened. We wandered into a shop selling naff novelties – rock in the shape of false teeth, peaked caps with beer cans stuck on top, huge and lurid lollipops.

'Go and have a look at the sea for a minute,' called Kim from the back of the shop. 'I want to buy you something.'

I crossed the road, and narrowly missed being run over by a battered corporation tram that seemed to come out of nowhere. The famously filthy sea was a long way out, turbid and still, and on Central Pier the huge ferris wheel was beginning its first ride of the day. I felt wrung out and deliriously happy at the same time. I thought about Kim and how lucky I was, and said a little prayer of thanks to the God I wished I had a stronger faith in. It was nice to be saying thanks for once, rather than the usual panicky dear God get me out of this mess. Perhaps we'd go to church before going home on Sunday.

Kim returned in a Kiss Me Quick, Squeeze Me Slow hat and handed me a carrier bag. There was a stick of rock in it; a T-shirt advising that the best way to avoid hangovers was to stay drunk; a horribly realistic plastic model of a severed arm and hand ('Astound your friends! Trap it in the fridge door or the boot of your car!!') And another Kiss Me Quick hat. Or so I thought. In fact the slogan was rather different. Get Your Lipstick Round My Dipstick, it read.

'Time for bed said Zebedee,' said Kim.

I put my hat on and we walked arm in arm back to the hotel,

a couple of wallies in love. By the time we got there I was dead on my feet.

'It's all right,' said Kim as I puffed up the stairs after her. 'I'm not going to make you worship at the temple of my body. Not yet anyway.'

I dumped the carrier bags, undressed as fast as I could, thought about cleaning my teeth and then thought better of it, and climbed into bed. I was almost asleep in the couple of minutes it took Kim to join me.

'Shove over, you great lump, you're not on your own any more.' She curled tightly around me and kissed the nape of my neck and that was the last thing I knew until I heard the chink of the tea cups and opened a gummy eye. Kim, naked, was waiting for the kettle to boil and humming softly to herself. I watched her unselfconscious movements, the curve of her back as she bent over the tea things, one breast just visible, hanging heavily and, to me, almost unbearably beautifully. I wished I could draw her like that, against the light. I wanted to hold the moment for ever. I pretended to be asleep when she turned round, and pretended to wake up when she hammered on the door and shouted room service.

'You're every old goat's fantasy of the perfect chambermaid,' I said as Kim handed me a cup of tea. 'What's the time?'

'Half past one. We've slept for three hours. How do you feel?'

I took a sip of tea. Not too hot, not too strong, not too weak, not too sweet. Just like Jeeves used to make it.

'Wonderful.'

'Drink and a snack on Central Pier suit you?'

'Wonderful,' I said again.

We sat in silence and drank our tea, Kim on the edge of the bed, me inside it.

'I'm going to have a shower. Do you want to come and scrub my back?' she said.

'Just try and stop me.'

There wasn't much room in the shower and we kept dropping the soap. One thing led most satisfactorily to another and in the end Kim said that if we went any further we'd smash the glass and ordered me to carry her to the bed forthwith.

'We're soaking wet,' I said

'What do you think the rubber sheets are for?'

An exhausting, ecstatic hour later found Kim in the shower again and me trying not to cut myself as I watched her through the frosted glass while attempting to shave at the same time.

She emerged dripping and tried to dry herself on one of Mrs R's tiny and ingeniously unabsorbent towels. I went into the shower myself, and got a mouthful of water as I sang a celebratory 'I Feel Fine'. The memory of Kim on all fours, groaning and swearing like a navvy in the heat of her passion, made me smile like a village idiot. Kim opened the door.

'What are you grinning about so slyly in there?'

'You,' I said, 'Just you, little Kim.'

She blushed. 'It wasn't too much was it? I've never given myself to anyone like that before, not absolutely abandoned like that. I love you so much, Will.'

She was crying. I picked up the least damp of Mrs Robinson's toy towels and dried her eyes.

'I love you too, Kim, so much it hurts.'

She sniffed, then laughed. 'For a man with a beer-gut and a black eye you're a terrible old softy. And girls with new leather jackets don't cry.'

Out on the streets, Blackpool was bustling at last. Middle-aged couples, couples with kids in tow, youngsters on the prowl for a good time, oldies looking back on the good times they'd had and wondering where they'd gone. Seen *en masse* they were an ugly bunch. You couldn't imagine an Italian crowd with so much bulging white flesh on show, so many tattoos, so many pinched and anxious faces. Almost everyone seemed faintly unwell, short of sun and green vegetables and the money that could buy them a decent set of clothes. Walking through the stink of hamburger fat, listening to the hypnotic mantras of the bingo-callers – 'Red, three and four, thirty-four, Scooby Doo, yellow, two' – eyeing up the alarming bouncers on guard outside the pubs at three o'clock in the afternoon, I realized that what made Blackpool different was that it was a place from which the middle-classes were almost entirely excluded. And yet I, public-school posh, an easily embarrassed tight-ass, felt a curious communality with these graceless pleasure seekers as they stumbled along, searching for happiness and cheap thrills and alcoholic oblivion, counting out the long hours of their holiday, waiting for the time to pass.

On the pier we bought pieces of bread shaped like hedgehogs, filled with turkey, stuffing, onions and grease, and then I had half a dozen oysters from the seafood stall.

'You and your sea-flavoured snot,' she said, wrinkling her nose.

We passed the screeching, flashing fruit machines and climbed the stairs to the Wheel House Bar on the first floor. Kim found a table on the terrace, just under the revolving cars of the big wheel, and you could feel the last hint of the summer's warmth in the weak, lemony sunshine.

When Kim had finished her drink she said she wanted to go and buy presents for the twins whose birthday it was the following week. 'Don't come,' she said. 'You were very good this morning but there's no quicker way to take the shine off things than to drag a bloke round the shops. I'll meet you at the entrance to the Pleasure Beach at four-thirty.'

'Right. I'd better phone Mr Simon, I suppose. We said we'd phone when we got here.'

'OK. But have a couple more drinks first. I'm worried about you, Will. You're not drinking enough. You've got to keep topped up in Blackpool or it all begins to seem quite horrible.'

I had another pint, and a ride on the big wheel and wondered whether to have my fortune told by Gypsy Rosa Lee. Shagged out with sex and booze and lack of sleep, the world was a beautiful blur. I must have dozed off for a bit, and woke with a start and saw it was already quarter to four. Walking towards the Pleasure Beach I was delighted to see a pub advertising striptease and toyed with the idea of going in for twenty minutes.

'Three quid,' said one of the gorillas at the door. I thought of Kim making the tea, of Kim in the shower, of Kim kneeling on the bed and realized that for once in my life the idea of watching an unknown woman taking her clothes off held little appeal. I shook my head, and walked on with the crowd, fervently hoping this wasn't going to be a permanent disability. I hadn't taken more than half a dozen paces when I spotted her, Harriet bloody Smythe, dolled up in a dinky red designer suit and a silly pill-box hat, looking ludicrously out of place amid the jeans and T-shirts. She was staring hard into the window of a fish and chip restaurant a couple of yards away and was toting a Louis Vuitton bag that doubtless contained the smallest of her crossbows. I stopped dead in my tracks and a large man cannoned into me. His furious 'Watch where you're bloody going mate' was loud enough to make her turn round and I saw the sudden shock of recognition in her eyes. I turned on my heel and ran straight back to the strip club.

'Changed yer mind, eh?' said the friendlier of the two doormen. His mournful mate looked as if he'd just lost his religion. I got their reassuring bulk between me and the narrow door and nodded.

'You don't let women in here, do you?'

'Nah, course not. What woman would want to come down here apart from the sodding dykes? And in any case it would cause a riot. We have to have two blokes guarding the strippers as it is.'

I thrust a fiver at the woman on the cash desk and didn't wait for my change. Half-way down the stairs I turned a corner, stopped, stuck my head tentatively back round it. Miss Smythe was having a little chat with the bouncer and laying on the Roedean vowels with a vengeance. In *Romeo and Juliet* and at the Alhambra her voice had been neutral, democratically class-less. This was the real Harriet Smythe. She'd just seen a dear friend entering the premises, she said, and it was vital, absol-utely vital, that she had a word with him because he was a diabetic and he'd forgotten his insulin injection that morning. He could, she said, go into a coma at any moment. The bouncer's words were just a mumble

'You've got to let me in,' she said, tearful now and shamelessly raising the ante. 'He could die if I don't get to him in the next few minutes.' She was a credit to RADA. One of the bouncers must have asked her what I looked like.

'Short, balding, running to fat. Oh, and he was wearing one of those silly hats.'

Thanks a lot, I thought. I just hoped the bouncers didn't have hearts of gold under the rough exterior. Be tough, I mentally urged them. So what if some poor sap's got diabetes. Don't let the silly bitch in. There was a clatter on the stairs and I pressed myself up against the wall. I might be able to grab her I thought. But it was only the doorman. I put a finger to my lips and we went a few more steps down the stairs. The music was louder now. The Stones, 'I Can't Get No Satisfaction'.

'You've forgotten your insulin, mate,' he said, looking rattled. After a couple of minutes of La Smythe the toughest-looking nuts cracked, it seemed. Give them a drunken stag night any day.

'Listen, can you do me a favour,' I said, pulling out Meadows' money and peeling off a twenty. 'The girl's a fucking headcase.' I tried to think of a story shocking enough to get through even to his seen-it-all, heard-it-all brain. I'd have to do a bit of acting myself.

'I pulled the slag last night and took her back to my hotel. You should have seen her in the taxi, right little raver. Knickers wringing wet, hand down my jeans, the lot. Anyway we get to my room and she suggests a blow job.'

He nodded, he was enjoying it. 'The hat?' he said eagerly.

'Probably. I get it out and whang it in and it's fine for a minute or so and then I tell you, I'm not kidding, she tried to bite the fucker off. Not a little affectionate nibble, a vicious great bite. Agony it was. I gave her a good slap, and she opens her mouth to cry out and I got it out, thank God. Then she starts screaming the whole hotel down and the landlady comes in and it takes for ever for me to persuade her I hadn't fucking raped her. Anyway, I got shot of the bitch at last but this afternoon there she is again, standing outside the hotel. I

234

jumped into a cab and thought I'd lost her but she must have seen me coming down here. Can you get rid of her?'

'I don't know about getting rid. We can't stop her standing on the pavement outside. But we won't let her in.'

'You're a pal,' I said.

'Tried to bite your bleeding winkle off. Jesus Christ,' he chuckled. It tickled him, it really did.

'I'll come up and see if the coast is clear in half an hour or so,' I said.

He nodded. 'Enjoy the show. They're mostly dogs but at least they don't fucking bite.'

It was cramped and hot downstairs and the Kama Sutra Klub didn't even run to a stage. The performing space was a bit of lino in the middle of the floor, with the punters, all eyes, all quiet concentration, seated at tables on three sides and, further back, standing on their chairs to get a better view. I caught a glimpse of the girl's face. She looked miserable as sin. I pushed my way through a few standees to the bar, which, with a stripper in mid-act, was virtually empty. A woman with hennaed hair looked up from her Jackie Collins. A bit old for stripping now, but a still not inconsiderable eyeful.

'Pint of lager,' I said. 'And have you got a phone?' She reached for a portable payphone from behind the bar and put it on the counter.

I fed in a couple of 50ps and dialled Simon. He answered after the first ring.

'It's Will Benson,' I said.

'You've taken your time. Bad news I'm afraid. She's on her way to Blackpool.'

'She's already here.'

'Oh, Christ in heaven.'

'Quite. What happened, Mr Simon?'

It was a long story and it was hard to hear all the gory details over the racket of 'How Much Is That Doggie In The Window' which the DJ was cruelly playing for the stripper. Poor girl. Humiliation heaped on misery.

Harriet, it seemed, had returned at 10 o'clock that morning

after a fruitless vigil. Simon's plan had been to wait up for her, get back into his position by the radiator as soon as he heard her key in the lock and overpower her as she bent down to free him. He'd reckoned that at that moment at least she wouldn't have her crossbow to hand. But at about eight he'd drifted off on his sofa and hadn't heard her coming in. He'd woken to find her standing in the study, weapon loaded, and impatient to learn how he'd managed to free himself. When she heard about Kim and me she went apeshit. Harriet had made him hand over the handcuffs, which he'd kept in his dressing-gown pocket to immobilize her with, and in a couple of minutes he'd found himself tethered helplessly to the radiator again.

'She said this time she'd leave me there for at least forty-eight hours,' said Simon.

The act was over now and the bar was filling up. 'But if she manacled you again, how are you speaking to me now?'

'Harriet forgot that the cleaning lady comes today. A mixed blessing as you can imagine.'

'Blimey. Did you have to take all your clothes off again?' I shouted, to the evident interest of an old codger who was ordering a large rum and blackcurrant at my elbow. It was, I suddenly realized, the man in the room next door. He was having quite a day.

'Underpants as well this time,' he said mournfully. 'And Harriet had put the key back in the box in the drawer again. I had to tell the cleaner where to find it. Naturally I normally keep that particular drawer locked when Maria's in the house. She was a long time gone, and when she came back to free me she wouldn't look me in the eye. Handed in her notice on the spot and cleared off there and then.'

'I'm sorry. I don't blame you at all for telling Harriet where we'd gone.'

'Oh, but I didn't. I said you'd gone to Bournemouth. But she decided to check. She phoned *Theatre World*. Someone there told her Blackpool. She wasn't pleased. She decided to punish me.'

How do you punish a masochist, I wondered. Simon

answered my unspoken question. 'It was nothing pleasurable, I can assure you. Two really vicious kicks in the balls. The whole thing about S and M is it's about control and trust and knowing your own limits. There was no control in those kicks.'

'Are you OK now?' I yelled.

'Very sore but just about ambulant. Listen, I'm coming up. Where the hell are you by the way? I can hardly hear you speak.'

'In a strip club on the Golden Mile. The silly bitch is outside but they won't let her in. All I've got to do now is get out without her seeing me.'

'Assuming you do, where can I find you? I should be there about nine.'

I gave him the address of the hotel.

'Right. I'm bringing the handcuffs and one of her crossbows. We can cruise round town together and if we spot her we ought to be able to bundle her into the car and get her into hospital. She's only taken the small one by the way, and it's not so accurate. Mind you she can still hit a rabbit with it at thirty yards.'

'Gee, thanks,' I said.

'But sometimes even the rabbit isn't killed outright.'

'Thanks again.'

'Good luck, Mr Benson. Give my regards to your young lady. And I'll hope to see you, safe and sound, at about nine.'

I redialled immediately and phoned *Theatre World*. As soon as Martha answered I let her have it with both barrels.

'Listen, you sour old cow, you've endangered both Kim's and my life by blabbing about us being in Blackpool.'

'That's Mr Benson I take it,' she said coldly.

'Of course it is,' I spluttered.

'I can assure you I had no idea that you were in Blackpool and therefore can't have told anyone that you were there. And I'm complaining to the editor about your disgraceful language.'

'Fine, just put me through to him first.'

When I got through to editorial, I assumed Martha had pulled another of her mean little tricks. Victor answered the phone in his ventriloquist's voice.

'*Theatre World* newsroom. Lord Marmaduke at this end. Can I possibly be of any assistance?'

'Victor, it's me, Will,' I said, trying to make contact with the journalist rather than the ventriloquist. 'Can you put me through to JB? It's urgent.'

'Oh, I do like to be beside the seaside,' sang Lord Marmaduke.

'Victor, how do you know I'm beside the seaside?' I shouted.

'JB told me you'd gone to Blackpool this morning. He's having to spend a lot of time with young Mr Torrington today and Barbara and Mirza are at news conferences. All the calls are coming through to me.'

And all being answered by Lord Marmaduke, I thought.

'JB said it was a secret you were in Blackpool. He said that nice little Kim was with you too and I wasn't to tell anyone where you were. Got your leg over yet, hee, hee?' The last question was from Lord Marmaduke again.

'Mind your own business,' I said icily.

'Keep your hair on, you silly old beezer,' said Victor, still in Marmaduke mode.

'Listen, Victor, this is important. Have you told anyone we are in Blackpool?'

'No, of course not,' he said, back in his own voice now. He sounded hurt. 'Apart from your solicitor of course.'

Oh shit. Another role for Miss Smythe.

'What did she want, Victor?'

'She said she needed to speak to you urgently. Regarding an inheritance. A substantial inheritance. Exciting isn't it?'

'Oh dear,' I said.

'What's the matter? I thought you'd be pleased.'

'I don't think it was my solicitor, Victor. To be perfectly frank, I haven't even got a solicitor.'

'So you don't think there will be an inheritance then?'

'No, I'm afraid not.'

'I'm sorry, Will. I hope I haven't spoken out of turn.' He knew he had, and I felt sorry for him.

'No, it's fine,' I said brightly. 'Just a practical joke I expect. No harm done.'

He wasn't convinced. 'I've put my foot in it,' he said sadly. 'What's all the noise by the way?'

'I'm in a strip club. On the Golden Mile.' I hoped this would cheer him up a bit.

'Oh, my paws and whiskers,' said Victor, then Lord Marmaduke came quavering down the line again. 'Tits and bums, tits and bums, I like 'em whatever size they come. Eh, Will?'

His heart wasn't in it. He sounded tired and old and depressed.

'That's right, Victor,' I said as cheerfully as I could. 'Wish you were here to see them yourself. You'd liven the place up a bit. Take care and see you on Monday.'

I put the phone down and hoped that I would. I ordered another pint and asked the barmaid to keep an eye on it, then went back up the stairs. I gave a wolf whistle from my favoured position just round the corner and the doorman came down the steps.

'She's still there. Just standing there, staring at us both like we'd just farted. Gives you the creeps it does.'

'I've got to get out of here. I'm meant to be meeting someone. It's urgent. Isn't there a fire exit I could nip out of?'

The bouncer looked embarrassed. 'Well there is, of course there is, it's regulations, innit? The trouble is we lost the key a couple of weeks ago and we haven't got round to changing the padlock yet. You won't breathe a word, will you? They'd shut us down just like that.'

I promised I'd keep my mouth shut and the bouncer nodded and looked at his watch. 'We close for an hour at four-thirty to clean the place up a bit. The last girl's just coming on now. Cindy.' Even this old thug's voice softened at the mention of the name. 'You shouldn't miss Cindy, you really shouldn't,' he said. 'Anyway, after she's finished we'll be chucking 'em all out. There'll be a big crush coming up the steps. Try and get somewhere in the middle of it and just steam out with them. We'll hold her back for as long as we can.'

'You couldn't arrange to break her leg, could you?'

He seemed to give it serious thought.

'Not a bird, no, whatever she's done,' he said at last.

'Oh well. Thanks for everything.' I gave him another twenty, and went back to the bar to pick up my pint and found a surprisingly good vantage point, squeezed between two tables near the front. Cindy was wearing a lot of white lacy underwear, white stockings and white high-heeled shoes. She had abundant golden hair, fantastically braided, and an expression of pure mischief on her face. I lit a fag and managed to forget all about Harriet Smythe at the top of the stairs.

Cindy sat on a chair with her legs splayed and her hand moving up and down inside her knickers. From here she finally produced a lollipop which she sucked provocatively.

'Christ, I can't stand it,' said a young lad standing next to me.

'She's lovely,' I said.

'Best of the day. We've been down here since noon. Party of us over from Wigan.'

He was swaying slightly on his feet, though whether from drink or lust I couldn't tell. I offered him a cigarette and he shook his head. 'Gotta concentrate.'

Cindy removed her bra to cheers, and I smugly congratulated myself that her breasts weren't quite as terrific as Kim's. They were still pretty good though, and as she rubbed baby oil into them I realized that my tired old cock was managing yet another hard-on. She got a guy in the front row to help her with the massage and when he was fully occupied, squirted the oil all over his glasses. The place erupted into cheers as he grinned sheepishly and wiped his spectacles with his hankie, but then the record changed to Tina Turner's 'What's Love Got To Do With It?' and everyone settled down to a bit of serious voyeurism. Cindy got down on all fours and waved her bottom at all sections of the audience, lollipop still in mouth. Then, in a moment of exquisite erotic grace, she rolled on to her back, bent her legs right back over her head, removed her stockings and knickers in a single arching movement, and threw them with astonishing accuracy straight into the DJ's face. There was a gasp of communal delight and disbelief as she removed the lolly from her mouth and, spread out on the filthy floor, began to use it as a tiny dildo.

'I'm going to get down there and shag it now,' said my friend from Wigan with such violent intensity that I put a restraining hand on his arm and Cindy, who clearly counted excellent hearing among her many other attributes, gave him a slow, sly wink. She got to her feet, withdrew the lollipop and offered him a suck. Blushing to the roots of his dyed blond hair, the lad took up the challenge to ribald cheers from his mates, but Cindy hadn't finished with him yet. She knelt in front of him, undid his belt and the top button of his trousers and then, slowly, with the whole audience holding its breath, unzipped his flies. With an innocent smile, she looked round the room she had so effortlessly transfixed, then theatrically licked her lips, just as Kim had done. The young lad was sweating now, and muttering 'yes, yes, yes,' under his breath and I almost found myself envying him, though not for long. With the same grace and speed with which she'd removed her knickers Cindy reached for an almost full pint on a neighbouring table, and carefully poured the contents inside my friend's trousers. She was on her feet just before he had time to react, licked her finger and chalked one up to herself in the air and disappeared through the door next to the DJ at exactly the moment the Tina Turner record ended.

'A big hand for the sensational, sinful Cindy,' said the DJ, and the crowd clapped and cheered desperately in the hope of an encore. But Cindy didn't return as we all really knew she wouldn't. She was a girl who knew that the tease was every bit as important as the strip.

The barmaid came over with a towel for the luckless Wiganite who resolutely refused to see the funny side and was now muttering 'the fucking bitch' over and over again.

'Never mind,' said the raddled beauty maternally, giving him a vigorous rub down which he might have enjoyed if he'd been in a better mood. 'It'll all come out in the wash.'

The DJ announced the club was closing for an hour but would

be open again from five-thirty until two in the morning 'For the hottest non-stop erotic entertainment on the Fylde Coast'.

The shutters were down on the bar and I tried to make myself inconspicuous among the throng making their way to the stairs. It was twenty to five and I hoped the bouncer was a man whose word was his bond.

He was. He and his companion were standing just inside the entrance, with the actress securely though not violently pinioned to the wall between them. She was kicking against the wall and screaming about male brutality and the police. The punters eyed her curiously but kept moving. She wasn't their problem after all.

My friend was in grotesquely emollient form. 'I'm sorry, madam, but you must understand. We're only doing this for your own protection. We've got two hundred aroused men coming out of here and if they see you hanging around outside they'll think you're soliciting. It's against the law, you know, soliciting. The police would close us down if they thought we countenanced it.'

I was just wondering where he got a word like countenanced from when Harriet spotted me. 'That's him, that's my friend,' she screamed. 'Let me go.' The bouncer looked at me mournfully. 'Make a run for it, mate,' he said. 'I should be able to give you a three minute start but I won't be able to hold her once the club's empty.'

I legged it down the Golden Mile. A hundred yards away, on the other side of the road, a tram was drawing to a halt. I sprinted towards it and prayed that the conductor was of a less sadistic bent than the Train Captains on the Docklands Light Railway. My chest felt as if it were about to explode as I staggered on board.

'Nice run, mate,' he said, closing the door as I slumped into the nearest seat. I looked back but there was no sign of Harriet's red suit on the other side of the road. Perhaps she was still in the club, perhaps I'd really lost her after all. By the time we reached the Pleasure Beach I felt better enough to chance a cigarette.

I climbed out of the tram warily and prayed Kim would be at the entrance as planned. The idea of hunting for Kim with Harriet hunting for us both didn't appeal at all. I spotted her from half-way across the road, standing by a fast-food stall and stuffing her face with a baked potato filled with bright orange cheese, an orange that had never featured on God's colour chart. 'You're late,' she said without rancour, giving me a quick, cheesy kiss. Just seeing her stopped me panicking.

'You'll never guess who I've just seen. Harriet's in town.'

'Tell me all,' she said calmly, taking another bite of her potato.

I told her about ducking into the strip club to avoid the Smythe girl, and my calls to Mr Simon and Victor.

'How were the strippers?' was all she asked when I'd finished.

'Good. One of them was almost as sexy as you.'

We walked into the amusement park, past the model camel-racing stall with the showmen dressed as Arabs, past Hiram's Flying Machine and the Octopus. The sun was stronger now, casting long shadows and bathing the gimcrack scene in golden light.

'Did you find anything for the twins?'

'Yes I did,' she grinned. She opened the bag she was carrying and produced two plastic bow and arrow sets, with nice safe rubber suction pads on the arrows.

'Ho ho, very witty,' I said.

'They didn't have crossbows. I don't see why Harriet should have all the fun. They'll love them.'

'I suppose we ought to get a cab to the hotel and wait for Mr Simon,' I said. 'This is one place Harriet's bound to look for us.'

But we both kept on walking, past the Ghost Train, the Wild Mouse, the Tunnel of Love and the Hall of Mirrors.

'Do you really want to go back, Will?' Kim asked at last.

I didn't. I was tired of running, tired of hiding, tired of having the terms dictated by a sadistic loony of an actress who handcuffed her lover to a hot radiator and then booted him in the balls. Twice. There was something especially nasty about that second kick. Once wasn't enough for Miss Smythe. There were so many people about on the Pleasure Beach, so many children, that I didn't think that even she would try anything here. If she turned up, it would be as good a place as any to collar her, and the idea of handing her over to Mr Simon, tightly bound and gagged, gave me such pleasure that I wondered if I might not have a touch of sadism in my own personality.

'I'd like to stay,' I said at last. 'But we'll certainly go if you want to.'

'Sod her, Will. I want you to take me on the Grand National.'

'That's my girl. What is the Grand National anyway?'

It turned out to be an old wooden roller-coaster, dating, said Kim, who appeared to be something of an expert in these matters, from the early 1930s, the great age of the traditional big dipper. This one had a difference though. Instead of one track it had two, and two different sets of cars raced each other to the finishing line.

We paid our money at the turnstile and went through on to the platform.

'Are you sure it's safe?' I asked pathetically. 'I think I'll have a heart attack if I get on this thing.'

'Wimp,' said Kim unfeelingly, and dragged me down the platform. 'I'm glad we got here early. It's best at the back. You get all the G-forces from the whiplash effect here.'

'I can't tell you how happy that makes me.'

Kim had to drag me into the tiny car, and once we were inside, there was no escape. Someone came and pushed the safety bar down over our knees, and when I tried to lift it, it was locked into position. Kim gave my thigh a reassuring squeeze and told me I'd love it.

The rest of the cars were filling fast, and so were those on the other side of the platform. With a familiar sickening lurch of the stomach I saw that Harriet Smythe was among them, her Louis Vuitton bag swinging from her shoulder. She climbed into a car and if she saw us she gave no sign of it.

I broke the news to Kim.

'You're joking,' she said in the appalled tone of voice of someone who's quite sure you're not. 'Which one is she?'

I realized she'd never seen Harriet in the flesh, only the headshot we'd used with the apology.

'In the middle of the carriages,' I hissed. 'In the red suit and that damn silly hat.'

'If we could get out now, we could head out through the exit and nab her as she comes out after the ride,' said Kim. I gave the bar a violent heave, but it was useless. With only one person in the car it might have been possible to twist your legs out sideways on to the seat, but Kim and I were jammed together like sardines in a tin.

'We'll just have to sit tight,' said Kim.

'And if you see a crossbow bolt, duck.'

A bell rang and we were off. At first, as we dived under a tunnel, the two trains went their separate ways, but they converged again for the long slow haul to the top. The other train was just ahead of us, and since we were in the back seat this suited me just fine. Harriet was too far ahead to try anything. I held tight to the safety bar with one hand and held Kim with the other. The track bent round at the top on the way to the first big drop, and suddenly I realized our nice safe position at the back was changing. We were on the inside track and gaining fast as we lurched round the corner. As we came closer to the other cars, I could see that Harriet had taken her shoulder bag off and was fiddling with something on her lap. Please, God, I prayed, don't let her shoot here, not at this speed, not with so many potential targets. I tried to shout at the people in front but the two girls were screaming so loudly and so pleasurably that they couldn't hear.

Both trains were travelling fast but ours seemed to be passing the other painfully slowly. Time itself seemed to have wound down to a crawl. You felt you could lean across and shake hands with the people in the adjacent carriages as you overtook them. At last Harriet looked up and raised her hand-held crossbow. The girls who had been screaming so enjoyably before fell silent as they spotted her. She was just ahead of us but we were gaining, gaining. Kim was nearest to the other train and I pushed her head roughly down so her face was bent over her knees, and stared Harriet in the eye as we drew level with her. She looked calm and deadly, but a trickle of saliva was dribbling down her chin. 'Don't, Harriet, don't,' I cried as we rounded the second bend together, but it was too late. At the very moment that we lurched on to the vertiginous descent Kim's body thudded against mine and she screamed. She'd been hit.

'Are you all right?' I shouted in Kim's ear as we roared down the tracks. Her face was white and she didn't speak. Then I saw the bolt, three pink feathers and a couple of inches of metal the thickness of a pencil sticking out of her shoulder. Not a fatal wound, thank Christ. We were well in the lead now and suddenly Kim started shouting that she'd murder the bitch. It cheered me up no end.

'Are you sure you're all right?' I yelled again as the ride momentarily slowed a little as we climbed up to the next drop. 'Can you move your arm? Does it hurt?'

'I'm fine,' she yelled. 'I can hardly feel a thing. Just a graze if that. But she's ruined my bloody jacket.'

She yanked at the bolt with her free hand and pulled it out. 'Just stuck in one of the shoulder pads, I think.' But her white face was twisted with pain. We were racing downhill again now, then whipped round a series of tight bends, before another upward climb.

'She won't be able to load again, not at this speed.' I shouted. 'And we'll grab her as soon as we stop.'

'Too bloody right we will,' said Kim. 'And she's a dead woman when we do.'

I looked back and saw the other train was catching up with us. Far, far worse, Harriet was no longer sitting but crouching on her seat, gripping the safety bar with one hand. And as her car rattled past ours, she made a lunatic leap.

There was a gap of about five feet between the two tracks, and she landed half in, half out of our compartment, legs waving in the air, her head and chest in our laps. She was writhing with such mad desperation that we almost lost her as we went round another tight bend, but I grabbed hold of one of her arms, and Kim got her arm round a thigh. Harriet's other arm was free and she lashed with it wildly, scratching at my face and hissing 'bastard' through clenched teeth. Kim slapped her, hard, and we rounded another corner and raced downhill yet again. 'Just shut the fuck up and keep still,' Kim screamed, but Harriet didn't listen. She never did. She kept twisting and screaming and scratching for the rest of the ride. I had a nightmarish feeling that it would never end, that the three of us would be locked together for ever, up and down, round and round, the wheels clattering on the metal tracks. The cars bounced sickeningly over a few low humps, swept under a concrete bridge and suddenly we started slowing down. It was over at last. As we drew to a halt, all the fight seemed to go out of Harriet and she lay flaccidly on top of us, whimpering pathetically and covering my trousers with saliva and snot.

'A quick exit, I think,' said Kim. There was a click; the safety bars had been released automatically. Kim and I dragged the almost inert actress out of the car with more violence than was actually required and half carried, half dragged her to the exit.

Most of the ride was invisible from the platform and the attendants can't have seen what an exciting Grand National it had been. But one of them belatedly realized that three people had emerged from a car designed for two and bawled at us to stop. Fortunately his surprise seemed to have immobilized him and we kept going unhindered, down the steps and out through the turnstile. We kept a brisk pace and a firm grip on Harriet who appeared to have recovered the use of her legs.

'How are you feeling?' I asked Kim as we passed the Avalanche. She gave a brave smile.

'Fine. I'm not so sure about Harriet though.'

Harriet was moving like a sleepwalker. I looked into her eyes but there was no one at home. She'd gone somewhere else for a while and I must say I was glad of the peace.

'Shock, I expect. We'd better get a cab to take us to the hospital.'

'I think I could do with a quick check-up as well,' said Kim.

She held up her hand which was covered in blood. 'It's funny, I can feel it running down my arm.' I looked behind and she had left a trail of bloody drips in her wake.

'Christ, are you sure you're OK? I thought you said it was just a graze.'

'It's nothing, just a flesh wound. That's why it's bleeding so much. And I expect the rough and tumble with our friend here opened it up a bit.'

I wanted her to take off her jacket so I could try and staunch the flow with a handkerchief but she shuddered at the very idea. 'It hardly hurt at all at first,' she said and now there were tears of pain in her eyes.

We reached the exit and I spotted a cab almost at once. Kim climbed into the front, and I pushed Harriet into the back and closed the door after us. I asked for the nearest hospital with a casualty unit.

'Meter's bust, I'm afraid. Couple of nuggets be all right?'

'That's very kind of you,' I said. I hadn't a clue what a nugget was.

'What's been going down?' the driver asked Kim, looking at the drenched red handkerchief she was holding in her hand.

But that was when Harriet started her astonishing variety turn. In a deafening shriek she started reciting poetry. She really loved her literary quotations.

'"O the mind, mind has mountains; cliffs of fall
Frightful, sheer, no-man-fathomed. Hold them cheap
May who ne'er hung there."'

Then she was off again, repeating the lines over and over in a strangely mechanical voice, just like, it suddenly dawned on me, a recorded message on an answering machine, amped up to heavy-metal volume.

'Can't you shut her up?' said the driver.

I shook her and slapped her and shook her again, but I hadn't the heart to put much strength into it and it didn't do the least bit of good. Finally I put my hand over her mouth and she bit it.

'What's she on about anyway?' said the driver when he realized he'd have to live with the screaming for the next few minutes.

'Poetry of some sort, but I don't recognize it,' yelled Kim. 'Quite appropriate though. She nearly fell off the Grand National at the Pleasure Beach.'

'What's that about the Grand National?' he shouted. Kim told him as best she could above Harriet's racket and he patted her knee with sympathy and respect when she'd conveyed the bare details of the dreadful ride.

'Soon be there now. Don't worry too much about getting blood on the carpet.'

Naturally Harriet wouldn't get out of the car when the driver pulled up in front of casualty, and he and I had to drag her out by force and virtually frog-march her into the waiting room with Kim, who looked worryingly weak now, bringing up the rear. There's one thing to be said about arriving at an accident and emergency department with a screaming lunatic in tow – it gets you prompt attention. You can sit there for hours with a broken arm but the wailing Harriet couldn't be ignored.

'She won't stop I take it?' said the nurse behind the reception desk.

All three of us shook our heads forlornly.

'You'd better go straight through then.'

I turned to the driver. 'Those nuggets?' I began.

'Forget it, no charge,' he said, and stalked off before I had a chance to protest.

In the ward a Malaysian doctor came bustling over with a broad smile on his face and gazed at Harriet with admiration. It was nice to know someone appreciated her.

'The great Gerard Manley Hopkins,' he said, leading us into a curtained cubicle. 'One of the dark sonnets when he felt abandoned by the God he had served for so long. He should never have become a Jesuit, you know. Quite the wrong religion. Buddhism, that's the faith the great G.M.H. should have

249

followed. Not', he added gnomically, 'that I'm a Buddhist myself. Sometimes I wish I was.'

Harriet gave us a couple more renderings of the now hideously familiar lines and even the doctor seemed to tire of them. 'Doesn't she know any more? I can only remember the last words. "All life death does end and each day dies with sleep." Not much comfort there for a junior doctor on a sixty-hour shift in casualty. If only each day did die with sleep—'

'I wish you'd put her to sleep,' cut in Kim, who seemed understandably narked by this delightful but loquacious medic. 'We've had her non-stop for the last fifteen minutes and I'm sick of Hopkins. Also I'm bleeding to death.'

'Seriously?' asked the doctor.

'Well, not quite to death,' said Kim with a grin. 'But I've lost very nearly an armful.'

Once he got weaving he was terrific. I filled in some of the background about what had brought Harriet to this pitch of hysteria and he went and got a syringe and injected her in the arm. In a few seconds her Hopkins delivery was slowing down and in a minute it had stopped. A nurse arranged her tidily on the bed and I looked down on her, knowing she was safe at last. She looked at peace and almost unbearably young, like Juliet in the tomb.

'We'll keep her in overnight. Are you bringing the police into this?' he asked.

Kim and I glanced at each other and shook our heads.

'No, a nice secure loony bin will do nicely,' I said.

'Not many of those left,' said the Malaysian cheerfully, and turned to Kim. 'Now young lady, can you get that most excellent jacket off?'

With his help, she managed it at last and the sight of all the blood on her rugby shirt made me feel ill.

'Get lost, please, Will,' she said through clenched teeth. 'This isn't what dirty weekends are all about.'

I sat in the ramshackle waiting room amid the other anxious faces and tried to read the evening paper, but jumbled images of the Grand National, Harriet Smythe and the terrible pain I'd just seen on Kim's face kept imposing themselves between my brain and the words.

After half an hour Kim came back and managed a smile.

'Twelve stitches,' she said proudly.

'How bad was the cut?'

'Only a couple of inches long. But the bolt had ploughed quite a deep furrow in my shoulder.'

'And how are you feeling? Is it agony?'

'No, they gave me a shot. And some super-duper painkillers for when it wears off.'

I hugged her and she screamed.

'Not my shoulder, Will, you idiot. Get a cab.'

There was a rank outside and I gave the address of the hotel but Kim said she wanted to stop off on Central Pier and watch the illuminations being switched on. It was six o'clock, the dusk was deepening and there was a touch of mist in the air. We walked down the boardwalk and stood on the end.

'I'll get you a new leather jacket tomorrow,' I said.

'No, I've been thinking about it. Most of the blood will come out at the cleaner's. And I can get the hole stitched up. It's kind of cool to wear a leather jacket you've actually been shot in, isn't it?'

'I can't think of anything cooler.'

The lights were slowly coming on down the whole length of the Golden Mile. The tide was in and you could hear the water gurgling and sluicing beneath your feet.

'The illuminations look better at a distance,' she said. 'The whole of Blackpool looks better at a distance.'

I put my arm round her waist, careful to avoid knocking her shoulder.

'I'm sorry I got you into this mess, Kim.'

'It was my fault. I cut your review. Harriet cut me. It'll be something to tell our grandchildren about anyway.'

It took a while for this to sink in.

'Does that mean what I think it means?'

'Well, we are getting married, aren't we?' said Kim, gazing calmly up at the Tower.

251

'Yes, of course we are.'

'So that's all right then. When did Mr Simon say he was arriving?'

'About nine. We've got a couple of hours.'

'Just time to get nicely pissed.' said Kim. 'It's my round.'